Fire FROM Heaven

KEITH J. HARDMAN

OAKTARA

Waterford, Virginia

Fire from Heaven: Ben Franklin and the 1740s Revival

Published in the U.S. by:
OakTara Publishers, P.O. Box 8, Waterford, VA 20197
www.oaktara.com

Cover design by David LaPlaca/debest design co.

Cover images © iStockphoto.com/big ship, Elerium; small ship, gprentice

Author photo © David Morgan

Interior photos: Franklin's print shop with Christ Church in back, © Mary Evans Picture Library/Image Works; Whitefield with arms raised, from Harper's Weekly, Whitefield "Preaching to Soldiers" and Franklin at the printing press, from the author's collection; diagram of the slave ship *African,* © The Art Archive/Musee des Arts Africains et Oceaniens; steel engravings of the Arch Street Ferry and Second Street with Christ Church, © The Free Library of Philadelphia. Used by permission.

Copyright © 2011 by Keith J. Hardman. All rights reserved.

Scripture taken from the Authorized King James Version, 1611.

ISBN: 978-1-60290-140-7

Fire from Heaven is a work of fiction. References to real people, events, establishments, organizations, or locales are intended only to provide a sense of authenticity and are used fictitiously. All other characters, incidents, and dialogue are drawn from the author's imagination.

Printed in the U.S.A.

TO MY PARENTS

Acknowledgments

Many former teachers and friends have given advice on this novel. These include:

> William Jordan, a friend since my youth;
> Warren Wilson, an engineer who is skilled at many things;
> Charles Sharpe, another friend of many years;
> Jim Meals, who did much to improve details in the book;
> Dr. C. Gordon Olson, a wise theologian.

For unusually efficient help in preparing this book, I am very grateful to Ramona Tucker, my editor at OakTara Publishers, who works tirelessly. Seldom does a lapse on my part escape her scrutiny.

In addition, I am grateful to my wife, Jean, for her constant support.

ONE

The Problem of Indenture

July 23, 1736
On board the ship Annabelle, *in mid-Atlantic*

Her death was the most catastrophic thing in Susan's and Tom's young lives.

Other passengers, all from England or Scotland, crowded around on the deck for the ceremony of committal. Many wept.

The sun was sinking toward the horizon, and in half an hour it would be gone. A great wash of color made the sea toward the west iridescent with gold, crimson, violet, and a palette of other brilliant colors that sparkled in the waves. The ship was moving steadily through a calm sea.

Six sailors stood over the body wrapped in the shroud made of canvas sailcloth, holding the wooden plank on which it rested. Captain Higgins lifted his voice so all could hear, and read the well-known words from First Corinthians, chapter 15 in the Bible:

> But now is Christ risen from the dead, and become the first fruits of them that slept. For since by man came death, by man came also the resurrection of the dead. For as in Adam all die, even so in Christ shall all be made alive....So when this corruptible shall have put on incorruption, and this mortal shall have put on immortality, then shall be brought to pass the saying that is written, Death is swallowed up in victory. O death, where is thy sting? O grave, where is thy victory?
>
> But thanks be to God, which giveth us the victory through our Lord Jesus Christ. Therefore, my beloved brethren, be ye steadfast, unmovable, always abounding in the work of the Lord, forasmuch as ye know that your labor is not in vain in the Lord.

Then the sailors, at the captain's signal, tilted the plank toward the sea, and the shroud-wrapped body slid down the plank and fell overboard. An audible gasp came from many of the passengers, although they had buried several other people in the past weeks. Susan was sobbing, and Tom's shoulders heaved as he wept openly, leaning on the ship's rail. They felt utterly desolate and alone.

Captain Jeremiah Higgins was a kindly man and recognized fully how miserable young Susan and Tom Prescott were over the death of their mother. He had lost his own parents when he was only a bit older than Tom's fifteen years. A handsome man in his late fifties, Captain Higgins had a weathered and wrinkled face that testified to years of exposure to wind and weather and the salt spray of the oceans. But he still maintained the erect bearing of a person of authority, and his pleasant smile was belied by a pair of sharp brown eyes. After a time of leaving Tom and Susan to their own grief, he approached the rail where they were standing and put his arm around Susan's shoulder, trying to comfort her.

"Oh sir, what are we going to do without our mother?" Susan cried.

Higgins gazed out over the ocean. "I wish I could do more to help you. Whatever you'd like me to do, just ask. I talked with her several times in the last week, and your mother knew the pox would take her life soon, and then she would be with her Lord. While of course you'll miss her terribly, that should be of great comfort to you." He turned and smiled reassuringly first at Susan, then at Tom.

"We know that," Susan replied. "And we're so grateful that our parents have taught us how to be Christians. But right now, it's hard."

Susan, at thirteen, was petite and, until her mother's illness, usually bubbled with laughter and fun. In time she would be a woman of great beauty, with her wide, medium-blue eyes, light brown hair that tumbled down over her shoulders, and clarity of skin. Her features were so harmoniously balanced that she attracted attention everywhere. She was the talk of the *Annabelle's* crew, and Tom, maintaining his protectiveness, had made sure she stayed away from all of them.

"Thank you for your words," Susan said. "If you don't mind, I'm going below. I need to be alone." With those words, she left them standing at the rail.

Tom gazed at the captain through his tears.

"'Tis a sad loss, son," Higgins said. "Your mother seemed a fine woman. I've been watching you two take care of her; you've been a good son, tending to her."

Tom nodded. "She was a wonderful mother, dedicated and hard-working...."

"Yes, of course she was. Didn't I understand that your father will meet you when we land in Philadelphia?"

"I hope so. Mother wrote him months ago, telling him the ship we were to sail on. I hope he received the letter. I hate to tell him that Mother passed away. They were so in love. And to have buried her at sea, instead of giving her a proper burial in a cemetery—that will upset him more!"

The captain put a hand on Tom's shoulder. "I know, son. But the smallpox is a terrible disease. So contagious that we can't take a chance. Bodies have to be removed as soon as possible, so everyone doesn't get it."

༄༅༅

Although Tom Prescott was in his midteens, he was tall for his age, and beginning to go from the gangly frame of his former years to a sturdy, strong young man. Sandy-haired, he had a few freckles on his nose and cheeks and eyes that might, in shadow, look almost black but were in reality a very clear dark green, almost emerald in bright light. His distress over his mother's death had only grown worse as he contemplated their uncertain future in America.

It had been three days since her body was consigned to the deep. It was a raw, windswept day, and the captain hoped it would not turn into a gale. So far, however, the wind was helpful and not a problem. To take advantage of the wind, most of the ship's sails had been hoisted. They billowed out above the ship, which was cutting through the water at a good speed, casting a wide, foaming wake behind it.

Captain Higgins was pleased at their speed, for, as usual on crossing the Atlantic, it had been a somewhat difficult voyage. It was not easy to be a ship's captain if one was a merciful soul, for the suffering that the landlubbing passengers endured was pitiful. Seldom was the crossing a calm one, even at the best time. During much of the year, on small, frail wooden ships, it was hideous. If a ship was becalmed by lack of wind, going nowhere, everyone, including the sailors, grew nervous and tense.

Many exploded in frustration. Captains had to remain calm.

On the quarterdeck, Higgins was approached by Henry Durham, a passenger who had become a friend during the voyage. Durham's wife had been sick for most of the crossing, and he said, "I know you try to keep this vessel as clean as possible, Captain, but despite that, there's such stench, fumes, fevers, dysentery, scurvy, and much more—some of it I can't bring myself to mention."

"That's true on all ships," Henry," Higgins said thoughtfully. "I could give up sailing these vessels, but then what would I do? It's my trade. And someone has to command them. So I keep on. This voyage has been better than many. Sad to say, children from one to seven years of age often do not survive the voyage. But so far we have not had any children die."

"No criticism at all of you, sir. I know you do your best. It's the cursed sea and the long voyage that makes the water and the food all go bad, and the thirst, the lice, and the dampness of everything on the ship, especially our clothes. We're simply not used to such!"

"I know, I know," Higgins said. "And that recent storm made things much worse, with waves washing across the deck and water going below. Then, in the midst of the storm, Mr. Abernathy fell and broke his leg, and he's been poorly ever since. With no surgeon on board, I've set the leg as best I can, and I can only hope it'll heal proper. On my last voyage, in a great storm I lost two people overboard."

"You did?!" Durham gasped.

"Henry...," the captain started to say, then hesitated. "That's happening often on ships."

"And the constant, everlasting, creaking and groaning of the wooden beams and hull and masts...that's driving many folks belowdeck to distraction, Captain. Seven wretched weeks. So many are cursing the day they decided to leave England, to have to endure all this!"

"All that you say is true, Henry. Still, the immigrants are coming over by the tens of thousands. This ship is full each crossing."

"Why, in heaven's name, do they keep coming?"

"Well, you're coming, aren't you?" Higgins chuckled. "People in the Old World have heard so much of the colonies. Their relatives have gone before and write of the benefits there. And William Penn kept sending notices of religious freedom in his colony, and that's especially what the Germans are desperate for: good land and freedom."

A few lurches of the ship made Henry Durham seasick again, and he ran for the rail, leaving the Captain alone. Higgins was sincerely grateful that this voyage had fewer of the problems he usually encountered. The winds and seas had been generally cooperative, although there had been a few bad days. Some deaths had occurred, but the food and water, poor and repulsive as they were, had held out. All in all, considering what might have happened, there were things to be grateful for.

While walking on the ship's quarterdeck, Higgins saw Tom amidships, staring blankly over the ship's rail at the endless ocean. "Master Prescott, I'm sorry to have to come to you in your grief, but we will need to speak soon."

"I...I'm all right, Captain. I know we must talk. Now is a good time, if it is a proper time for you."

"Thanks, lad. You see, our voyage will be over in a week or so, when we land at Philadelphia. We must speak of the payment for you and your sister. Back in London the arrangement with your blessed mother was that your father and brother would meet the ship when it came into port, and pay for all three of you at that time. Since your mother died before the voyage was completed, I have decided not to charge for her passage. But I need to be assured that your father will be there to pay for you two."

Tom managed a weak smile. "Not to charge for my mother is very kind of you, sir, and my father will be most appreciative, even as he will be devastated when he hears that she has died and been buried at sea."

"No, it's only the proper thing to do, in this case. Although, in similar cases, when passengers have died during the voyage, I have often charged their relatives half-fare for the deceased."

"To the best of my knowledge, sir, my father and brother will be there to greet the ship when they hear of its arrival. And they will pay for us. My father is a most reliable person."

"O, I'm sure of that, son."

"Susan and I would gladly pay our own passage," Tom said with distress, "but while my father is well off in America, back in England we had to pay some large debts before leaving. Since the ship was delayed so long before sailing, we spent most of the money we had for food and lodging at the inn. Finally, when this ship sailed, all we had was a few pounds between us—nowhere near enough for me to pay you. But you can have all my money in partial payment."

"No, you may need that money. I couldn't take your last shilling. We can wait, as first arranged, to see your father. Where is he located in America?"

"The last letter we received said that my father and brother had bought land somewhere near Philadelphia, in Pennsylvania."

"That may be in one of the towns on the Delaware River south of Philadelphia, and the ship may pass it as we come up the river. I was in that area, several years ago. There's good, fertile land in that region."

"Then perhaps my father will see the ship!" Tom visibly brightened at the thought.

The captain laughed. Reaching over, he clapped Tom on the shoulder. He had taken a liking to this young fellow and to his sister, Susan. Tom was much like the son he had lost ten years earlier. Satisfied with their conversation, he went back to his duties on the quarterdeck.

From the shadows of a house directly opposite, a stranger watched Hiram Prescott's shop. His hands were thrust into the pockets of his long coat. His bony wrists tightened as he closed his fingers into fists. He was a short, heavy man with a pointed face like a crafty animal, stunted ears, and a long, sharp nose. Pockmarked and with shifty eyes, he had unkempt black hair, and when he grinned, his dark teeth looked pointed.

He had watched the shop for over an hour, and he could detect no movement within it. Probably Hiram Prescott had gone out with his son, Andrew. He thought that no one else lived in the house. This was the opportunity he had been waiting for. Soon darkness would descend, and he wanted to break in while he still had some daylight. He dared not light a candle inside the shop for fear of someone looking through the large front window and seeing him.

Going to the side door, where he would not be seen so readily, he pushed a long, thin bar into the lock and eventually heard the bolt slide back. Entering, he scanned the shop and listened carefully for a minute. No sound could be heard. Where could the money be kept? It was rumored that Hiram Prescott had a fair amount of currency hidden somewhere, for in addition to his shoemaking, he was also a moneylender.

Partially finished shoes were everywhere. Covering the worktable were leather soles, upper parts, heels, nails, strips of hides waiting to be cut, hammers, awls, and all the tools of the shoemaker's trade. Opening each drawer, he rummaged around, finding, to his increasing annoyance, no money. Then he rummaged through the closets. Again, nothing but tools and leather.

A squeak of the floorboard overhead! And then another. Prescott must have been home all this time. There was a footfall on the stairs. The intruder moved quickly to get behind a door.

Hiram Prescott—late forties, middle height, muscular, long-limbed, broad-shouldered, with a full head of brown hair, and blue eyes—entered the room and called, "Andrew? Is that you?"

From behind him, the intruder bounded upon his victim, striking Hiram over the head with the long iron bar he had used to open the side door. Hiram staggered, hit his temple on a shelf, and tumbled to the floor in a heap.

Then, on the street outside, a rotund man began to knock on the door. The intruder stiffened. Had this man, probably a customer, looked through the window and seen him? He was frozen in place. He stared at Prescott. Was he dead? No. He was breathing. The intruder had to flee, but he had to wait until the customer departed first. Presently the fat man stopped his knocking and left. Then the intruder slipped out the side door and disappeared into the gathering darkness.

※

Within fifteen minutes Andrew, Hiram's twenty-year-old son—muscular and broad-shouldered, with brown hair and hazel eyes just like his father—returned from his errand, put his key into the front door lock, and entered the workshop. Even in the semi-dark room he could see his father crumpled on the floor. Rushing over, Andrew lit a candle and examined his father for injuries. There was a bruise on his temple, but no blood or other injuries. Andrew heaved a sigh of relief, determining that his father had been knocked out but was otherwise not badly injured.

Dashing to the kitchen at the back of the building, Andrew retrieved some rags and a pitcher of water and returned to minister to his father.

7

The wet rags on his brow brought Hiram around in a few minutes, and Andrew helped him into a chair.

"Who did this to you, Father?"

"Son? Is that you?" Hiram shook his head, trying to regain reality. "I don't know what happened. I came down the stairs and suddenly everything turned black."

Andrew allowed his father a few minutes to get his bearings, then helped him up the stairs to his bed. *Well,* he thought, *we were to go to Philadelphia tomorrow to wait for Mother's ship to arrive in port. But with this happening, I guess that will have to wait a day or two.*

✸

As the *Annabelle* cruised up the Delaware Bay on her way to the port of Philadelphia, the ship passed a number of other vessels. Most were merchantmen, like the *Annabelle,* but occasionally a warship of the British navy was sighted. They passed several great ships of the line—the *Intrepid,* 36 guns, and the *Ajax,* 28 guns.

Passengers lined the rails of the *Annabelle*, craning their necks for the first view of their new home. Some who had not appeared on deck for days or even weeks, because of acute seasickness, came up for this excitement. As the bay narrowed somewhat into the Delaware River, towns could be seen along the shore on either side. When they passed New Castle, Wilmington, and Chester—all small towns—and a few ships moored at the docks, excitement grew.

The man standing next to Susan and Tom at the rail pointed to Chester as he said, "That can't be the city of Philadelphia. There's not enough ships in that port."

"No," Tom replied, "I've heard that's the little town of Chester, which lies twenty miles south of Philadelphia."

"Chester, eh? Another town named after our old towns back in the home country."

The *Annabelle* sailed on, and in three hours it came to a place where another river, the Schuylkill, flowed into the Delaware. Then, as they came to the port of Philadelphia, more and more vessels of every size were anchored out in the river or tied up at wharves. There were dozens of masts, the reassuring British flags, other flags from German principalities and Holland, shops along the riverfront catering to the maritime trades, and the docks full of stevedores, warehouses, piles of cargo, and people boarding or leaving ships. Even from the *Annabelle,* in the middle of the river, the thriving activity of this port was obvious.

The sight was almost enough for Susan and Tom to put aside for a time the depression over the loss of their mother. To see their father and brother for the first time in several years raised their spirits, and they surveyed the shoreline with excitement. Philadelphia was the second largest city in the British Empire, second only to London itself, with a population of about 15,000 and growing rapidly.

Captain Higgins was stationed aft by the ship's wheel, calling out orders to the sailors. A number of them were aloft in the rigging, reefing the sails. The ship came almost to a stop several hundred feet from the shore, and after a time a small gig came out from the docks, rowed by two men. In it was an official of the port, and as the gig came alongside the *Annabelle,* this man climbed up a rope ladder thrown over the side for him. The captain met him and offered the ship's documents to him for inspection.

The official took his time looking them over and finally said, "Everything seems to be in order, Captain. It's good to see you in Philadelphia, sir. How was the sailing?"

"I have had much worse. We had a few stormy days, but also some quiet ones with calm seas and good winds. But we did have some deaths aboard from smallpox."

"Yes, that's almost standard. And some ships coming in have had some mighty bad weather in mid-ocean. You were fortunate."

"The last time we were here, we tied up at Clifford's wharf. That's where my cargo is waiting, I think," Captain Higgins said.

The official checked his notes. "Yes! Clifford's. Right you are. That's open too. Waiting for you, I'm sure. All right, I give you leave to pull in."

He directed the captain to Clifford's wharf, and with the main topsail still catching a slight breeze, the vessel picked up enough momentum to come in.

When the *Annabelle* was securely moored next to the wharf, the gangway was put over the side. On the wharf below, men trundled great boxes and barrels into nearby warehouses and onto ships lined up alongside. Horses and oxen pulled carts and wagons filled with merchandise along the roadway, as drivers directed them. Everyone on the ships and on the wharves seemed to be shouting at once. The noise was deafening.

After a time, some of the passengers were allowed to go ashore. Their meager luggage was brought up from belowdeck and given to them, and the unloading of cargo began. Passengers who were to be indentured servants were told to remain aboard until payment for their passage could be worked out.

From the ship's rail, Tom and Susan scanned all the people on the dock. They were eager to see their father and older brother, Andrew, although they regretted having to tell of their mother's death.

A crowd of passengers was gathered around the rail, jostling each other to move along and get off the ship as soon as possible. The first mate was standing alongside the gangway, taking down their names and checking them off the ship's manifest, one by one.

A man who was about to disembark smiled at Tom. "Do you have someone coming to get you and your sister, laddie?" A bundle of belongings was slung over the man's shoulder, and he was dragging a larger pack. Behind him were his wife and three children, looking sickly but almost delirious with excitement after their long confinement.

"Thank you, Mr. Maginnis! Yes, we're hoping to see my father and brother. If they know of the ship's arrival, they will be here."

"Well, let's trust the good Lord that they come. I have enjoyed getting to know you, and I'm so sorry about your dear mother. From what I knew of her early on, she was a blessed saint." He reached out and shook Tom's hand. His wife, eyes filled with tears, said words of sympathy too low for Tom to understand and hugged him.

"Thank you so much," Tom said, choking, emotion almost overcoming him. "You've been a great help and good friends on board. I wish you well in the new country."

"O, won't it be so good to be off this stinking old tub! That alone is cause for rejoicing. Just to move freely and not be surrounded by sickness. I'm sure I've lost twenty or thirty pounds, and I'm so eager to eat some good, fresh food. Then the promise of a new land and a great future! Well, good-bye, and God be with you, my lad!" Then it was their turn to go down the gangway, and the children whooped with joy as they departed, dragging bundles behind them to the dock.

Tom waved a cordial farewell to them. For the next hour, other friends they had made on the crossing came and wished them well, before disembarking.

But where were their father and brother? Even if they were living outside of Philadelphia, in one of the small towns, Tom hoped that somehow word of the ship's arrival would get to them. Though a ship's arrival was a very uncertain thing, due to the problems of ocean travel, Tom wished they had calculated the approximate time of arrival, come to Philadelphia and taken up lodging somewhere, waiting for them. But that did not seem to be the case.

There was nothing to do but wait patiently. Tom and Susan leaned over the rail, anxiously scanning the faces of the hundreds who moved on the docks and adjoining streets. Not one person did they recognize. Tom could see into several of the warehouses that fronted the docks, for their wide doors were swung open to allow wagons to drive in and load or unload merchandise. Inside they could see stacked boxes, wooden chests and barrels stenciled with cryptic symbols of destination and ownership. Hogsheads were tiered five and six high against the walls.

After many of the passengers who had paid for their passage had departed, another group of people came on board, as they did for each arriving vessel. These English, Dutch, and German folk, farmers, or tradesmen were looking for healthy persons unable to pay their passage, such as they deemed suitable for their businesses. On each ship they would bargain with the new arrivals for how long they would serve as indentured servants in exchange for their passage-money. Adults would bind themselves to serve for as few as three and as long as ten or more years.

This indenture system was widespread at all American ports, since many of the immigrants were nearly penniless. In many cases it worked well, and the indentured and their employers were satisfied. But there was also a dark side. Many immigrant parents had to sell or trade away their own children like so many head of cattle when an employer wanted only one or two adults. The parents would not know where their children were going in a new and unknown country. Parents and children would not see each other for many years and frequently never again.

As the employers found immigrants willing to meet the high cost of passage by pledging their future labor in indenture, one after another they left the ship. Remaining on the *Annabelle* were some people with various ailments who could not pay their way. The sick always fared the worst, for the healthy ones were purchased first. And so the sick and wretched stayed on board, sometimes for weeks, and frequently died. On the other hand, a sick person who could pay his fare was allowed to leave the ship immediately, and often recovered.

Susan and Tom watched all this from the deck, saying good-bye to friends, and observing the heartrending situations where families had to be separated. It became increasingly upsetting. To distract themselves from these gloomy scenes, they tried to while away the time by counting the ships in the harbor. There were dozens. Most flew the flag of Great Britain, but a surprising number bore the flags of the German states, or Holland, and occasionally they saw a flag they could not identify. In addition to English, on the docks they could hear the German language used as sailors shouted or passengers talked.

Tom turned his attention to the city itself. What struck him was that, unlike the ancient narrow, winding, and crooked streets of England he was used to, these streets were wide and completely straight. They were laid out in a checkerboard pattern, with streets and avenues at right angles to each other, crossing at spacious intersections. Immediately the advantages of this were apparent.

Jerry, a sailor who had befriended Tom, took a break from his work and came over to the rail. "That's quite a sight, isn't it?"

"Yes! It's completely different from English cities," Tom said. "I'm used to a jumble of roads that wind around like they were never planned. From what I can see, this city seems to have been worked out carefully."

"Oh, you don't know about William Penn? He was given all this land by the king, and it's well known that Penn planned this town first, before it was settled. It's very clever."

"It sure looks like there's real cleverness there. Can you tell me what street that is?" Tom pointed to a wide street that ran away from the ship, at right angles to the river.

"Uhh...let's see. This is Clifford's wharf, and that is...Mulberry Street! Yeah—they also call it Arch Street. I've been ashore here many times. Well, I've got to get back to work." He left.

Then Tom counted the steeples of at least ten churches, and of the church buildings he could see clearly, they seemed to be rather elegant structures. One in particular, a short distance from the ship up a wide boulevard, had a magnificent white steeple that towered over the surrounding buildings, and an impressive Georgian red brick edifice. It bore a great similarity to the fine churches in London designed by Sir Christopher Wren, which Tom knew well. He would learn later that this was Christ Church, the chief Anglican church of the city.

All day long Susan and Tom waited. Their father and brother did not come. Evening was coming on. When Tom next saw the captain, he mentioned that they must stay aboard for another night since no arrangement had been made to pay for their passage.

"I'm sure our father will be here tomorrow, sir," he said.

"Yes, quite likely. No doubt something has held him up. Perhaps he is just hearing that our ship has arrived," the captain said.

And so the two Prescotts spent another night on board. But now, no longer was the lower deck crowded with passengers. Those who were ill, perhaps twelve or thirteen, were still there. The crew bunked nearby.

༄༅༄

The next day dawned humid, overcast, and rainy, amplifying Tom's anxious mood. While the cargo from England was unloaded onto the pier, the captain supervised the loading of some goods meant for Charleston, the next stop. There the ship would pick up bales of cotton to be sent to England, which was buying all the cotton it could get from the Carolinas to supply its clothing mills.

In midafternoon Captain Higgins came to Tom. "Son, you and your sister must go ashore soon. The ship will be leaving. You're two fine young people, but I must have my pay."

"Can't it wait another day? I'm certain my father must be along soon, Captain."

The captain tightened his lips into a fine line. "Lad, here's the situation. You're old enough to understand it and accept it. I'm sure your father is all you say he is. But we don't know where he is. He could be anywhere. America is a huge land. Here are fair cities, substantial villages, decent houses, good roads, orchards, meadows, and bridges, where a hundred years ago all this was wild, uncultivated forest. It's different from England and Europe; here the rich and the poor are not so far removed from each other. England has hardly any other distinction but lords and tenants. There's not much in-between. The rich versus the poor."

Tom was trying to understand what the captain was driving at. "Yes, I believe you. But what does all that have to do with my father and brother coming to get us, and pay our way?"

The captain pulled himself up to his full height, and tried again. "All that adds up to the fact that your relatives may be anywhere here, if you haven't heard from them, or they from you, for some time. They don't know when this ship arrived. They may have moved on to better land somewhere else, and will come here a bit later to find you."

"But my father wouldn't do that!" Tom blurted out.

"Perhaps he had to, lad. You don't know whether your mother's last letters to your father got to him, the way overseas mail is. Perhaps he doesn't even know you came over! If he does know, he couldn't wait here for weeks on end, not knowing when our ship would arrive with you.

Perhaps he has been here already, waited a few days, and had to leave for some reason."

Tom listened patiently to all this. He knew the captain was trying to be kind, even as he had to talk sensibly. Tom also realized that here was the only person with whom he could discuss this. He began to accept the inevitable. But that still didn't answer the question: what were they to do? He was glad this captain was a fair man, trying to work something out, and obviously concerned with their welfare.

Drawing a deep breath, the captain continued. "So here it is, Tom. This ship must depart soon, or I'll be behind schedule. I need your passage money. If it were up to me, I'd just cross it off and let you go free. But we keep records, and if I don't get the money, the ship's owners in London will hold me responsible and make me pay it."

"I don't want that to happen." Tears blurred Tom's eyes.

"No, because the owners may begin to suspect that I'm cheating them. I've already told you I won't charge for your mother's incomplete passage. I must keep good books, and these books are checked. I think I can explain why I didn't charge for your poor mother, but not with you two."

"And we want to pay for our passage," Tom insisted.

"Do you know if your father and brother were able to pay when they journeyed here?"

"Well, in England my family owned property, and I'm quite sure my father had the money to pay their passage—and would have the money to pay for us!"

"I would think so, son. Now, here is what I have come to propose to you. There is a man on the docks I met today, a Mr. Duffy, who is searching for an indentured servant. He is willing to pay your passage, if you will work for him on his farm," the captain said.

Sudden anger overtook Tom. He jumped off the barrel he'd been sitting on. "But why would I do that? I'm not a servant! My father would be very angry if he found that is what happened to me. And what about my sister, Susan? Is she to be indentured too?"

"Calm yourself, lad. I'm only trying to work something out, and you haven't heard my entire thought."

Embarrassed at his outburst, Tom sat down again.

The captain continued, "I am well aware that is *not* what you want to do, but I suggest this to you: first, the other employers who wanted indentured servants have gone; I was lucky to find Mr. Duffy. And he doesn't want a thirteen-year-old girl; he won't take your sister. But I think I can find someone here—a friend—who would take her in and loan the money to pay for her. As for you, if you'll accept Mr. Duffy's offer to take you on, and go with him, I promise to put notices in all the shops of the merchants I know, telling where you have gone. I will even put a notice in the newspaper printed here by a Mr. Franklin, and that goes far afield. Then when your father comes, he will see the notices and get you from Mr. Duffy, pay him what he has paid, and all will be well." Captain Higgins spread out his hands. "I see no other way, Tom. I'm in a bind."

"But how do I know that I will take to Mr. Duffy? What is he like? Are there any other employers still on the docks?"

"I don't know Mr. Duffy. I've only talked with him once, but he *seems* to be a fair man. Yesterday a number of farmers and merchants were looking for help, but today I could find only one—Mr. Duffy. He seems willing to take a boy—I mean, *a young man*—of fifteen years."

Tom put his head down in his hands. He sighed deeply, resigned to this. Finally he said, "All right. I know you have done your best, Captain. I fear it greatly, but I suppose something like this must be done. You're saying that you think someone responsible can take Susan in, and pay for her, until my father arrives? And you will put notices about me, and where I have gone, in those shops, and in that newspaper? But that's asking a great deal of you, Captain!"

"I have promised to do that, have I not? And I am a man of my word."

"I will much appreciate that, sir."

"In all probability, Mr. Duffy is somewhere about on the docks. I'll send a man to look for him now."

Tom said, "And I'll go and explain all this to my sister."

⊰⊱

An hour later, the rain had stopped, at least temporarily, but the sky was overcast and threatening.

Ishmael Duffy came aboard. He was tall, thin, perhaps forty-five years of age, dressed fairly well but threadbare in appearance. His scanty brown hair was tied back from a high and balding brow. Dark brown eyes, bushy eyebrows, a long-beaked nose, and dark clothes made him look somber.

Captain Higgins greeted him, spoke a few words, then took him over to Tom. Duffy managed a vacuous smile, appraised Tom in a critical manner, felt the muscles of his arms and legs, asked him to flex them, and scrutinized his physical characteristics. Tom had never been checked over in this way before and was not pleased with the examination. It was similar to the way one would appraise a horse before purchasing it. Tom wondered if he should show Duffy his teeth.

"Hmm," Duffy muttered, stepping back from Tom. "I wanted a man who was at least twenty years of age, but there don't seem to be any ships in port with men looking for work."

"I think most of those wanting to be indentured were employed yesterday, sir," the captain said.

"I see. Yesterday was impossible for me; I couldn't make it before today. My loss," Duffy said. "This young fellow looks healthy enough. But you say his mother died of smallpox on board the ship? How do I know he hasn't picked up the disease, even though he doesn't show it yet? I could pay his way, take him to my home, and in a few days he could be dead, and I'd lose my money!"

Tom ground his teeth. He wasn't sure he liked this man.

Captain Higgins smiled sardonically. "Sir, the way the pox is getting around, any one of us could have it and be dead soon. You too. The pox was not just on my ship, or in England. It's here in America as well. That's the chance we're all taking. I hear that inoculation against it is becoming more common. You might want to have that."

A dark frown came over Duffy's face. "Small comfort!" he grumbled. "Well, I need a new hand, so I guess I'll take him. I'll pay his way—for four years' work."

Four years! Tom was aghast. With a stranger, in a strange place. He could hardly believe what he had just heard. *My only hope would be for my father to see those notices, and come and rescue me.* He turned to Higgins. "Captain, could I see you for a minute?"

Duffy looked annoyed to be excluded. Tom and the captain walked to the other side of the deck.

Quietly, Tom said, "Sir, I'm not at all sure about this. Four years! My father might never find me. We don't even know where this man's home is. Is there no other way to pay for my passage?"

17

Captain Higgins, sympathetic to the boy's plight, let out a long, slow breath. "Son, I'm racking my brain trying to assist you. But I cannot think of anyone who would loan money to pay your way, other than this indenture arrangement. Don't you see how hard I'm trying to help you? And if your father comes and sees the notices, you could be freed in a short time."

"I suppose you're correct," Tom said slowly. "All right, I'll go with him. Let me explain all this to Susan, and what you want to do for her."

Susan was extremely upset upon hearing the news, but it seemed there was no other choice. Finally they returned to Duffy, who looked peeved, and indicated that Tom was willing to be indentured to him. Almost reluctantly, Duffy counted out the money and gave it the captain, saying, "What is your name, boy, and where do you come from?"

"I'm Thomas Prescott, sir, and I come from Surrey," he said respectfully.

The indenture papers were completed. Typical of indenture documents, they read:

> The said Apprentice, Thomas Prescott, his master shall faithfully serve, his secrets keep, his lawful commands everywhere gladly do, for the term of four years. The goods of his master, Mr. Ishmael Duffy, he shall not waste, nor the same give or lend without license of him. Hurt to his master he shall not do, cause, nor procure to be done. Taverns, alehouses, or inns he shall not visit. He shall not play at cards, dice, tables, or any other unlawful game. He shall not contract matrimony, nor from the service of his said master day or night absent himself; but in all things as an honest or faithful apprentice shall and will demean and behave himself towards his said master and all his during the term of four years.

Tom had never seen such a document, and he read it with some alarm. He took the captain aside again. "But all this demands what *I* must do, for four years. It doesn't say one word about what *he* must do. Shouldn't it say that he has to provide food for me, and house me, and treat me well, and such like? He can't beat me, or mistreat me, can he? It's all on my side—nothing on his. Is that right?"

Captain Higgins stared at the deck for a minute. "Lad," he said ruefully, "I've seen many of those indentures, and they're all alike. That's the way they're laid out. I'm sorry. There's nothing I can do about it.

You're his servant, and the law is almost entirely on his side."

Tom was becoming more unhappy and worried by the minute. But seeing no alternative, he grudgingly signed the document.

His new employer signed, and the captain and the first mate signed also as witnesses. Thus the legal transaction was verified, for a term of four years.

Addressing Tom, Duffy said, "All right, that's signed and done. Do you have much luggage?"

Determined not to allow his anxiety to show, Tom said, "Not much, sir. Clothing and some other things in this bag."

The captain interrupted. "Pardon, Mr. Duffy, but may I ask where your home is located?"

"A few miles west of this city. On the main road." Turning to Tom, he said curtly, "My horse and wagon are on the wharf, and we can begin immediately, before the rains start again."

"I'll remember what we agreed on, son," the captain said to Tom. "Good fortune, and God bless."

Susan came over, eyes red with weeping. "Oh Tom, I don't know what I'll do. I may never see you again!" She threw her arms around his neck and hugged him.

Tom rubbed a hand over his face, trying to summon enough presence of mind to deal with his sister's anxieties as well as his own uncertain future. Susan's eyes were squinted nearly shut, and tears poured down her cheeks. He was holding back his own tears. Tom took her hands in his, and led her to the ship's rail so they could be alone for a minute before he had to leave. He knew this would only irritate Mr. Duffy further, but if this man could not grasp how traumatic it was for a brother and sister to be ripped apart like this, in a strange country, well, too bad for him!

"Look, Susan, I'll be all right," he said. "You heard the captain say that he was going to put notices in shops, telling our father where to find me, and that he will find a good family to take care of you in the meanwhile. Everything will be fine." Tom only wished he could believe that himself.

Susan, sniffling, attempted to speak between the sobs that racked her.

"Until Father comes, you're going to have to be very brave, Susan," Tom said, summoning all the big-brother assuredness he had been practicing on the long ocean voyage, whenever there had been a storm and passengers were getting seasick.

"I know, I know," she stammered between sobs. Susan hunched over the rail, her hands fisted and occasionally hitting the rail in anger and frustration. She shook her head, disconsolate.

Tom glanced over at Mr. Duffy, who was tapping his foot impatiently on the deck and glaring at the pair. Anger boiled up in Tom. *Give us a minute together!*

"Susan, this man is getting annoyed with me," Tom said quietly. "I must leave. Pull yourself together. I'll see you soon; you've got to remember that. Don't fall apart. That only makes it harder for me to leave you."

She lifted her head and gave him a wan smile. "I'll be all right. It's just that this is such a shock, so soon. I thought Father and Andrew would be here waiting for us."

Tom knew he had to be a stand-in for his father at this moment—be the man of the family. So he did something that fifteen-year-old brothers rarely do to kid sisters, and that in ordinary times he would be completely embarrassed to do. But this was not an ordinary time. He put both protective arms around Susan, pulled her off her feet, hugged her, and gave her a hearty kiss on her cheek. Then he said quietly, "I must go."

He went over to Duffy, nodded, and thanked the captain again.

Duffy and Tom walked down the gangway, found his wagon, and climbed aboard. The mare drawing the wagon looked well fed and cared for, so Tom hoped he would be treated the same.

As Duffy prepared to drive the wagon, Tom was told to sit on the floor of the rear, amid the damp straw scattered about. That was *not* very reassuring. Sitting on the floor was uncomfortable and got more so as they traveled. The damp straw was smelly. Tom brushed the straw aside. Why couldn't he sit up on the wide plank seat, next to this man? Was this the first sign that he was to be in subjection and, perhaps, humiliated?

They rattled along the unpaved city streets, throwing up mud, and then over unpaved roads as they left the city behind. Soon night came. There was nothing but darkness, other than a faint light barely illuminating the road, coming from the tin lantern hanging beside the driver.

Then the rains descended, in torrents. In moments Tom, Duffy, and the horse were drenched. Lightning appeared in the distance, and then came closer. Tom had to hold his ears to keep out the crashing of the thunder as the rain pelted them. Whenever a bolt of lightning struck nearby, the entire sky was brilliantly lit for a moment. The horse was terrified by this, and several times whinnied, rearing, its front legs in the air, threatening to overturn the wagon. Duffy had to pull hard on the reins to control the animal. At one point he had to stop the wagon, get down onto the road, and calm the beast. Within minutes, puddles in the road turned into deep water holes and long muddy ruts.

After half an hour in the downpour, Tom saw a roadside inn ahead with a welcoming light in its windows. Duffy guided the horse into the area at the back, drove into the barn, and left the horse and wagon there while he and Tom went into the main room of the inn.

"Do you have a room for the night?" Duffy asked the owner gruffly, shedding his sodden coat and hat.

"Yes, sir. Seven pence. There's not many out on such a night. May I ask where your home is, sir?"

Rather reluctantly, Duffy mumbled "Carlisle."

"Carlisle!" the innkeeper said. "Good gracious! That's over a hundred miles to the west!"

One hundred miles! Tom thought. He drew a slow, deep breath and let it out through his nose. *So my new employer is a liar. How would the captain ever know to put* Carlisle *on the notices he puts in the shops? Duffy told us his home was "a few miles west of the city"!*

Duffy turned and growled at Tom, "You can sleep in the barn. Take care of my horse, too."

Tom thought, *Well, I guess I know where I stand with this liar.*

TWO

The Problem of Indenture

Captain Jeremiah Higgins sat in his cabin on the *Annabelle,* staring at the breakfast the steward had put on the table before him. His mind was filled with so many details that he had lost interest in the plate of fried eggs—the first fresh eggs, brought on board yesterday, that he had seen for many weeks. He took another bite of toast, then drank the last of the coffee, and pushed the pewter plates aside. The *Annabelle* was due to leave Philadelphia on the tide, and he had much to do before then. He had to oversee the last details of loading the ship's cargo for Charleston. But that was rather routine, and his first mate could do much of that. However, there was something that was his responsibility alone.

Captain Higgins took a dozen sheets of stiff paper, and using black ink in a large handwriting, he wrote out THREE POUNDS REWARD and underneath described both Tom and Hiram Prescott, saying, *Anyone who knows their whereabouts should please go to the printing establishment of B. Franklin, on Market Street near Second, for the reward.* Higgins knew his old friend Franklin would be happy to be the contact person, once Higgins had described the situation and left the reward money with him. That part was done; next he would distribute these posters.

A conscientious man, Captain Higgins sat thinking for a minute. Was it right to ask a family to put up the money for Susan's passage—a family who knew nothing of her, even if she did work for them until her father arrived to repay them? No, that was not right. He would pay her passage himself, even if he never got repaid. And so that one matter was settled.

He sent the steward to get Susan, and when she came into his cabin, he was taken aback. This morning she was wearing a dress of soft, pale blue wool, generously embellished with lace and dark indigo ribbons. On her head she wore a white mobcap, a fancy cap made with a high full crown, tied under the chin. The effect was almost electrifying. Certainly these, Susan's best clothes, had been packed away in England, not to be worn until arrival in America. Susan was already a lovely young girl, and it was obvious that in a few years she would blossom into a beautiful woman. Any man who would not be a bit smitten with her beauty would be a dull clod indeed, the captain thought.

Franklin book shop next to Christ Church, Philadelphia: "Keep thy shop & thy shop will keep thee."

"Good morning, Susan." He nodded with approval at her appearance. "That is certainly a lovely dress. I know you will make a good impression. Are you ready to go ashore?"

"I can't wait to arrive in my new country!" she said, almost jumping with anticipation.

He laughed. "Well, let's go."

Leaving his orders with the first mate, he hurried down the gangway with Susan, and they walked over to the shops lining the docks on Water Street and Front Street. There, one after another, he spoke with the proprietors he knew from years of dealing with them, and left a poster that he had made at each shop, asking them to display it.

Then the captain and Susan walked up Market Street and crossed to the print shop of Benjamin Franklin, the owner and editor of *The Pennsylvania Gazette,* the leading paper of the province. Franklin, a rather handsome man with long brown hair that hung to his shoulders, thirty years old and originally from Boston, was a rising star in Philadelphia. He had a broad forehead and a square jaw, and was of average height. His dark brown eyes were bright, suggesting a quick intelligence. He had a good sense of humor, and much self-confidence.

In addition to editing the *Gazette,* Franklin began on December 28, 1732, *Poor Richard: An Almanack containing the Lunations, Eclipses, Planets' Motions and Aspects, Weather, Sun and Moon's Rising and Setting, High Water, &c., besides many pleasant and witty Verses, Jests and Sayings*, and in later editions filled it with his own pearls of wisdom such as "Light purse, heavy heart," "Haste makes waste," "Fish and visitors stink in three days," and "Great talkers, little doers." *Poor Richard's Almanack* was an immediate success.

Higgins had known Franklin for several years, on previous voyages to Philadelphia. Walking into the print shop, they saw the owner sitting at a desk editing material. High off the floor on strings hung sheets of inked paper, drying. Farther back in the shop several young men were busy at the press.

"Jeremiah!" said Franklin, rising to meet him and extending his hand, "I had heard your ship was in port. Good to see you again. How are you?"

"Fine. I am delighted to see you, Ben, and I'm sorry to have been so busy I haven't gotten to see you before this."

Then Franklin, beaming, turned to Susan. "And who is this lovely creature, may I ask?!" His eyes were twinkling.

"May I introduce Miss Susan Prescott, just arrived from England."

"I'm delighted to meet you, Mr. Franklin," Susan said, with a curtsy.

Franklin, well-known for his appreciation of feminine beauty and his flirtatiousness, said, "Welcome to the colonies, Miss Prescott. I hope you will like our country; I'm sure it's very different from England. Please, come and be seated. Jacob!" he called to one of the apprentices, "will you help me move these books off the chairs, so our guests may be seated?"

For several minutes the three exchanged news and pleasantries, and then Higgins got down to business. He explained Tom's situation and how he had promised to put notices around and in the newspaper, and they worked out this statement for the next issue of the *Gazette:*

> Whereabouts Unknown: Thomas Prescott, 15 years of age, from England, tall sized of his Age, who has light coloured Hair, having on when he went away, striped Jacket and Breeches, and a Check'd Shirt. Taken in Indenture by one Ishmael Duffy, Location uncertain. His Father eager to pay his Indenture off and free him. Whoever knows of his location shall have Three Pounds Reward by notifying B. Franklin, Printer of this paper. Also sought, the whereabouts of Hiram Prescott.

"That should do it," Higgins said. "I know the *Gazette* is widely distributed around Pennsylvania, the Jerseys, Maryland, and other places.

With my promise to the young man, I know his father will probably see this, and Duffy too, and I'll give you three pounds now, and pay for the advertisement also. I'm certain Tom's father will reimburse me at some later time."

"Captain," said Franklin, "you are certainly a goodhearted man. And if this lad is as worthy as you say he is, I shall be happy to be the intermediary while you are away."

"Yes, and perhaps, if he is found, someday you shall meet him."

Deborah Franklin descended from the upstairs quarters. "I see we have guests, Ben!"

Everyone rose to meet Mrs. Franklin.

"Captain Higgins, it's so good to see you again," Deborah said. "And your companion is certainly a lovely young lady." She gave Susan a gracious smile and held her hand out to her. Susan took the hand and responded with a curtsy.

"It's always a delight to see you, Deborah," said Higgins. "May I ask how your two sons are?"

"Four-year-old Franky is fine, and so is his half-brother Billy, who is five. They are lively, and at times I have my hands full with them!"

"I'm sure. Two boys at that age are full of life," said Higgins, smiling at father Ben, who beamed back.

"They tie Deborah down," Ben said. "While the boys are our delight, still Deborah has little freedom, and we often have to pay ladies of the neighborhood to come in if we wish to go anywhere."

The penny dropped in Higgins' mind. "Say! I have an idea, friends. How would a full-time attendant for the boys work out? A very charming person, who would be perfect for the job."

"And who might this perfect person be? And would her pay be out of sight?" Ben asked.

"Oh, I don't think so. I think if you could give her room and board, there need not be any pay."

"Wonderful! Do I happen to be looking at her?" Ben asked, with a smirk.

"You do," Higgins said. "What do you think, Susan?"

"I'd love to be with this family. But it's only until my father appears, you understand."

Deborah threw her arms around Susan. "Welcome!"

25

※

Two weeks later, the *Annabelle* sailed into Charleston Harbor, and Captain Higgins prepared his vessel to pick up a load of cotton to be shipped to England. As the cargo was being loaded, he went into an inn and met another sea captain he had known over the years, Joseph Powner, who commanded an older ship, the *Revenge*. Having little to do for a while, they sat and chatted, and Higgins asked how things were going.

"I tell you in confidence, Jeremiah, I'm having great problems. I'm getting desperate," Powner said.

"I thought you were doing well, Joe. You own the *Revenge,* don't you?"

"Ha! That's the problem," Powner said. "When I bought it a year ago, I put every penny I had into buying it on credit, and I'm deeply in debt. It's an old tub, but it's the best I could afford. I've managed to get only one cargo in the last eight months, and the profit from that hardly paid my crew and kept up my payments. So my crew walked off, and I can't get another cargo without a crew, and my ship is sitting at the wharf, rotting! How are you doing?"

"Oh, fair to middlin'. I've got a deal with a London company to bring over immigrants on a regular basis, and take cotton on the return trip."

Powner, being a foul-mouthed fellow, let out a string of curses. "You've got it made, Higgins. Good luck to you!"

※

The ride from Chester in their wagon, over roads still muddy from the recent rains, had taken all morning. As the three rode into Philadelphia, it was a pleasant change for the horse and wagon to leave the dirt, mud, and ruts behind and begin to clatter over roads that were somewhat better, bumpy and noisy as they were.

With Hiram and Andrew Prescott was Sarah Godfrey, who was engaged to be married to Andrew in a few months. Sarah was a fine young lady, and Andrew considered himself extremely fortunate to receive her love. She had wide, dark brown eyes and long chestnut-colored hair that flowed to her waist, and she was wearing a gray dress with a white collar and a pink and white bonnet. Her face showed firmness of character and unusual maturity. Sarah had chosen to wear a gray dress, knowing the condition of the roads and realizing that the mud being tossed around would soon ruin most of her other dresses.

They had bumped their way over the road into the area of the wharves. To their right, towering over the buildings, were the masts of dozens of ships tied to the docks on the waterfront.

"O, I do hope that Mrs. Prescott's and Susan and Tom's ship has not already come into port and perhaps left," Sarah said.

"We will soon know, my dear," said Andrew.

"And what was the name of their ship, according to the letter Mrs. Prescott sent?" Sarah asked.

"The *Annabelle*, out of Portsmouth."

"What I do know is that our trip should have been made days ago, and we would have come, if it hadn't been for my getting hit over the head," said Hiram, lightly touching the bump on his head that was still tender.

"I still wonder why an attacker would break in, strike you, and then leave—probably in a hurry," said Andrew. "Once you were unconscious, he could have stolen anything he wanted. But we found nothing missing. Your money box was untouched, and it was right where you always keep it—just like everything else. So what was he after?"

Hiram, driving the wagon, had steered the horse to the right, and they entered the street that fronted on the wharves. The area was alive with activity. Black slaves and free white men sweated, pushing or lifting large barrels of liquids, heavy bales and boxes, either going on or coming off the fifteen or so ships tied up alongside the waterfront. The barrels and crates being unloaded were trundled or moved by sheer brute strength onto large wagons or deposited in the warehouses along the wharves. The area was a cacophony of shouts, orders, curses, and oaths.

With the frantic activity and confusion of the entire place, it was impossible to take the wagon any farther. Leaving Sarah to mind it, the men walked along the docks, checking each ship to see if it could be the *Annabelle*.

An aged sailor with a wooden leg came along, and Hiram asked, "My good man, do you know of the arrival of the ship *Annabelle*, from Portsmouth? She may be in at any time now."

27

The old fellow sized up Hiram with his one good eye, took the pipe from between his yellow, broken teeth, and said in a loud voice, "The *Annabelle*, eh? Yeah, she were here, to be sure. I talked with her captain and watched her unload. But you're too late. She's left on the tide awhile back. She's gone to Charlestown, and then back to England."

Hiram's mouth flew open. "You're sure? The *Annabelle?* Gone already?"

"Course I'm sure! Do ye think I'm daft?" The old sailor spit on the stones of the wharf.

Hiram whirled and found Andrew. "This fellow says the ship left!"

"B-but—" Andrew stammered. "Where could Mother and Susan and Tom be? Could they be staying at an inn nearby?"

"O my," Hiram said, dejectedly. "Go and tell Sarah. I'm going into some of these merchants' shops to see if they know anything of this."

They separated.

Hiram went first to a chandler's store on the waterfront that sold provisions and equipment for the sailing ships. Once inside, he was confronted with an incredible array of supplies of every kind needed on a ship of that day. Huge rolls of various types of rope, tackle for the ship's rigging, barrels of tar, buckets of paint in a dozen shades, nails, bolts, and hundreds of other items were stacked in orderly rows throughout the store. A man approached and asked if he could help.

"Yes, thanks. This is a strange request, I know, but would you have any information of a woman and her son and daughter that came as passengers on the *Annabelle*, the ship that left for Charleston? We are trying to trace them, and we don't know where they have gone. I am the woman's husband."

The salesman frowned thoughtfully. "I'm afraid I cannot help you, sir. I know of no such folks. The captain of that ship was in here ordering supplies, but he told me nothing of such a group."

Hiram turned to leave. "Thank you very much, my man." As he was exiting the front door, he saw a notice on stiff paper with large, bold lettering nailed to the door frame.

Three Pounds Reward. Whereabouts Unknown. Thomas Prescott, 15 yrs of age, from England, tall, with blond Hair, wearing a strip'd Jacket & Breeches. And Hiram Prescott, shoemaker. Anyone who knows their whereabouts should please go to the printing establishment of B. Franklin, on Market Street near Second, for the Reward.

Hiram had to read it twice to make sure his eyes were not deceiving him. *His* name on this—"whereabouts unknown"! He was even more astonished with this than he had been with the old sailor's information. He tore the notice from the door frame and ran to the salesman, shouting, "Where did you get this?"

Now it was the man's turn to be shaken. "Why...yes, it was left here by the master of the *Annabelle*. Before the ship left, he asked us to post it!"

Hiram dashed from the store to find Sarah and Andrew. Seeing their wagon at the end of the block, he ran the distance like a much younger man. Panting from the exertion and his excitement, he blurted out to them, "Look at this! A notice that Tom was here! And for anyone with any information of him, see a Mr. Franklin, a printer on Market Street!"

"What?" Andrew exclaimed, taking the paper. Sarah and he read it. "What does this mean...'whereabouts unknown'? And it doesn't say anything of Mother or Susan. Where are they?"

Jumping up on the wagon, Hiram took the horse's reins. "Let's go to see this Mr. Franklin, and find what he knows of all this." Urging the horse through the crowded streets, they came to Market, scanned the shops looking for a printer's, and soon found a sign hanging over the front door, B. FRANKLIN, PRINTER. *THE PENNSYLVANIA GAZETTE.*

Entering the print shop, Sarah, Hiram and Andrew asked a journeyman to see the proprietor, and Ben Franklin emerged from the back of the establishment within a minute. Hurriedly, Hiram introduced himself and the others and began to explain his quest.

"You are Hiram Prescott?" Franklin exclaimed. "Then I think I have a magnificent surprise for you!" He called upstairs, "Would you come down, please?"

Within a minute Susan skipped down. When she saw her relatives, a wide smile transformed her face, and she shouted, "Daddy! And Andrew and Sarah!"

Hiram turned in great surprise toward the voice. "Susan!" he shouted back as he ran and embraced her, kissing her a number of times. Andrew and Sarah joined them for a joyful reunion, and for a few minutes there was much chattering and sharing of news.

Eventually things quieted down. Delighted as he was to find his daughter, Hiram had more questions, and he turned to show Franklin the notice, asking what the printer would know of it.

"Why yes, let me first mention that my friend, the captain of the *Annabelle*, Mr. Higgins, was in to see me the other day." Suddenly it occurred to Franklin that this family did not know of Mrs. Prescott's death at sea, and that Susan had not yet told them. This would make him the bearer of dreadful tidings, and it would come as a great shock to them. He stopped and, in consideration for them, suggested they come into the back of the shop and be seated in an anteroom.

"I understand, from the captain, some of the situation," Franklin began. "But I am afraid I have some terrible news for you."

"Yes?" Hiram said, brows drawn down.

"Mr. Prescott, it pains me exceedingly to tell you that your dear wife expired during the voyage."

Hiram swallowed once, hard, then lowered his head into his hands. Both Andrew and his father burst into tears. Sobs wracked Hiram's body. Sarah placed her arms around his shoulders, trying to comfort him.

It took a few minutes for them to control themselves, and during that time Franklin sat quietly.

Through his tears, Hiram asked, "How did she die? And where is her body, sir?"

"From what the captain told me, she was one of a number who died of the smallpox. And, because of the contagious nature of that foul disease, they had to be buried at sea, as soon as possible, to avoid infecting the entire vessel."

Hiram nodded. "I understand. But oh, my poor Julia! And not to have a proper burial, in a churchyard, where I could visit the grave of my beloved." Again he broke into a torrent of tears.

"And what of my brother Tom, Mr. Franklin? Why is his whereabouts 'unknown,' as this notice says, when we have my sister, Susan?" Andrew asked.

"I want you to know, first, that the captain was most concerned about all of this. From what he told me, your son is healthy, and did not contract the pox, nor did Susan, thankfully, as you see her in good health. But the captain needed to get from your children their fare for the journey, and they had very little money left. So Captain Higgins—a kind man, I know—

was at a loss to know what to do. He left Susan here with my family, and I believe he paid her fare out of his own pocket. But he couldn't afford to pay for two fares. The ship was about to depart, and the best solution he could devise for Tom's fare was to let your son be indentured—"

"*INDENTURED!*" both Andrew and Hiram thundered together. And Sarah cried out also.

His voice quiet and calming, Franklin said, "Yes, that's what the captain told me: to a man named Ishmael Duffy. It was, of course, only to be temporary, until you came along and bought your son out of it."

Tom's father beat the air with his fists. "If only I hadn't been attacked in my own shop, we would have been here in time to rescue poor Tom. What cursed luck!"

"Don't blame yourself, Father," Andrew pleaded. All of this bad news coming together was overwhelming, more than they could bear.

Franklin kept quiet for a few minutes, letting them mentally digest the problem. Then he said sympathetically, "Captain Higgins was so concerned that he paid me, out of his pocket, to place this advertisement in the next issue of my newspaper. In addition he gave me an added three pounds to be used as reward money." He got a copy of the ad and showed it to them.

When they had comprehended the entire situation, Hiram said, "First, you may delete my name from the 'unknowns' in the advertisement, since I stand before you. But do you know anything of this fellow Ishmael Duffy, who bought my son's indenture?"

"No, I'm afraid I don't. I've never heard of him."

Another pause to determine what to do. Hiram said, "Well, we have taken enough of your time, Mr. Franklin. I want to thank you sincerely for all this information—sad as it is to us—and I will clear up our accounts now with you and Captain Higgins. You can settle up the amount he paid you, the next time his ship comes here." He took from his pocket enough money to pay for these, then continued, "We live in Chester, and come here only occasionally. Thank you so much for taking care of Susan; she can come home with us now. But until we find Tom, we will be coming here more often. Since the ad asks anyone to notify you, would you be so kind as to continue to be our contact person?"

"I shall be pleased to do that," said Ben Franklin.

31

In 1736 the hamlet of Carlisle was almost at the forefront of the march west. It was a collection of cabins set in a broad, rather flat plain. This was shortly before the Appalachian Mountains began their ascent, which formed an imposing barrier to westward expansion. Here Indians still roamed through the woods, and occasionally a settler would be found with an arrow in his body, and the evidence of scalping all too horrible. Frequently the pioneers in those parts would attempt a peaceful settlement with local Indians for the purchase of their land, and this would be satisfactorily completed. But conflict with the original inhabitants was constant, despite the fact that many frontiersmen wanted to be at peace with them, because there were enough renegade whites who murdered Indians and kept the wars going. And the wars were not declining, but would in the future become even worse.

The dirt roads west from Philadelphia for about forty miles were fairly good, as they were heavily traveled and therefore had to be maintained somewhat. Ishmael Duffy and Tom Prescott had an almost tolerable ride as far as Reading, because the pike through Germantown, Norristown, and Pottstown was used especially by the German immigrants who were piling off the ships from their homeland, thanks to Penn's promise of freedom and land. These hardy folks knew little or no English and wished to congregate together in rich farmland around Lebanon and Lancaster. But west of Reading, the roads were almost nonexistent, becoming little more than rough paths lined with rocks and ruts meandering through cleared fields or woods.

It had taken almost a week since leaving Philadelphia for Tom and Duffy to reach the Susquehanna River, which was the last major obstacle before reaching Carlisle. Each night, Duffy had been able to find indoor shelter and a bed for himself, either in a wayside inn or a friendly farmhouse. But Tom was denied this each evening, and had to sleep in a barn or outside under the wagon. The weather in August was quite warm, so Tom did not mind too much, but he wondered where he would be sleeping in the wintertime. However, Duffy did see that Tom was well fed when they came to an inn, for he had much work for him to do, and didn't want to see him weakening and getting scrawny. Tom's worry deepened. He was being taken to an unknown wilderness. How would he be treated? Would he see his father, sister, and brother soon—or ever again?

After days on dusty and muddy roads, Tom and Duffy were feeling the effects of their difficult trip, and Duffy was getting more irritable and nasty with each day. He rubbed at his face, rasping the bristles on his jaw, having been unable to shave. For a full day they had not found an inn that served meals, and he was hungry. His clothes were grimy and soiled from perspiration after the hot day, and the clammy feel of them made him even more irritable. Since Tom's beard had only recently begun to sprout, he did not mind his light stubble, but his clothes were equally clammy. Occasionally they were able to get rid of some of the grime of the roads by washing and swimming in the little creeks and streams they passed. These were always pristine and pure, the waters sparkling in the sunlight.

In their wagon, Tom and Duffy lumbered along, frequently having to ask directions of farmers, until they came to the broad Susquehanna River. There was a small ferryboat near the village of Highspire, and here they crossed, upon paying the fare, to the western side of the river.

Finally they came to the small settlement of Carlisle. Duffy pulled the wagon up to the front of his log cabin, and they alighted, grateful that the long, bone-jarring, grinding trip was over. Out of the front door came two people, Catherine Duffy, his wife, and also Louisa, his 13-year-old daughter. Running over to Duffy, in turn they threw their arms around his neck and welcomed him. Then they looked with great interest at Tom.

"This is the young fellow who is now indentured to us, Tom Prescott," he announced gravely.

Catherine Duffy said in a kindly tone, "We are pleased to have you, Master Prescott." This was the first pleasant voice Tom had heard in a week, and she seemed sincere. Dressed like most frontier women of the time, in a coarse linen ("linsey") skirt and an upper blouse of kersey cloth, she appeared to be about the same age as her husband. Her dark brown hair was drawn back in a bun. Obviously she was a hard-working woman.

Then Louisa approached, her chin held high in a rather haughty manner. With bright blue eyes, high cheekbones, and the same dark brown hair as her mother, but worn shoulder-length, she was clad in a light-green dress of India cloth with a bodice of delicately applied lace. Her complexion was nearly flawless. Louisa nodded dismissively at him, saying nothing.

But when Ishmael Duffy gave his daughter a warning look, she evidently knew immediately what that meant and backed away, with a slight blush..

Out from the back of the house came another young man. He appeared to be two years older than Tom, slightly taller, with skin darkened a bit by exposure to the sun. He had lively brown eyes, black hair, and a wide smile that showed a set of even, white teeth.

"Prescott, this is my other bondsman, Joshua Morris," Duffy growled. "Morris, this is Tom Prescott."

Joshua put out a large, strong hand obviously used to work and shook Tom's hand with great vigor. He flashed a bright smile at Tom. "I add my welcome to the others. And I wish you'd call me Josh."

"You both must be exhausted from that horribly long trip," Catherine Duffy said. "And I'm sure you are famished, too. We didn't know when to expect you, but I'll get you a good meal right off. Louisa, you can help me." With that the women went inside the house.

"Yes, I'm very tired," Duffy said, "but first, Prescott, I've got to get you dressed as we do on the frontier. Those clothes from England will never do."

Tom knew he was right, and he followed Duffy into the log cabin. This was fairly small, nothing like what a family might expect to have in a city, but what was usual on the edge of civilization. One story, with four rooms: a common room that served as kitchen, dining room, and living room, with a large stone and brick fireplace that heated the entire home; two separate bedrooms, one occupied by Ishmael and Catherine, the other by Louisa; and a small room that was a pantry and storage place. There were several small windows fitted with precious panes of glass. It had been erected by the work of a number of men in the area, as they would combine whenever a house was to be built and thus assist one another in a cooperative manner.

Duffy called Tom into the storage room, and showed him the clothing universally worn by men on the frontier of America. The hunting shirt of linsey was loose, allowing for much movement, with large sleeves. The pair of breeches, or leggings, were made of linsey, or, for cold weather, of Osnaburg or other heavy material. The cap was large and also made of heavy cloth. A belt held up the breeches, always tied behind, and on the left side was suspended a long knife in a leather sheath...some men carried a tomahawk on the right side. It was becoming the fashion among males to give up the breeches or leggins and adopt the dress of the Indians, especially the breech clout. This was a piece of cloth a yard long and a foot broad. This passed under the belt before and behind, leaving the ends hanging over the belt. When this belt passed over the hunting shirt, the upper part of the thighs and part of the hips were exposed. The young white men who adopted this were proud of their Indian-like dress.

Tom looked at this clothing laid out for him. It was totally different from anything he had ever worn. He removed his own clothing and shoes and pulled on the rough breeches and the hunting shirt. They were both too large for him, and he had to roll up the sleeves and the bottoms of the breeches. Then he had trouble with the belt, not knowing how it should be worn.

"Here, let me show you what to do with that," Duffy said, taking the belt and tying it in the back, then hanging from it the leather sheath and its knife.

Rather uncertain of himself, Tom now stood in his bare feet with all these new items on him. He felt strange. But he suddenly realized that Joshua Morris was already wearing similar items, and he had looked fine in them. They certainly conveyed a very masculine, strong appearance. Perhaps he should accept them right off; after all, he was in a wilderness now, far from the city.

"What do I wear on my feet?" he asked.

"The most important piece of all," Duffy said. "In the farm and in the woods, regular shoes are soon worn out and useless. In a few minutes, after we've eaten, I'll change into all this myself. For the feet, we've all learned that the Indians have worked out the best kind of footwear, the moccasin."

Duffy picked up the pair and handed them to Tom. "They are made of dressed deer skin. You'll soon be dressing that yourself, Prescott. They are made of a single piece of hide, with a gathering seam along the top of the foot and another from the bottom of the heel. We make them high on the leg so that no dust, gravel, or snow can get inside them. Now you begin to see why they are far superior to shoes. Flaps are left on each side to reach some distance up the legs, and these can be attached to the breeches to hold them up."

Tom pulled the high moccasins on his feet and up his legs and began to see the advantages that Duffy had spoken of. With the fur inside, they were certainly warm, and that would be necessary in cold weather. And with the stitching as it was, they probably kept out rainwater to some degree. He folded and stowed his other clothes in the bag he had brought.

Just then Catherine Duffy knocked on the door to the store room and said that dinner was ready.

"For this first meal here, you can take it with us, but afterward you can eat in the barn with Morris," Duffy said.

As they went out to the large central room, at first Tom felt foolish in his new outfit. But Catherine and Louisa hardly looked at him.

Ishmael Duffy indicated to Tom and Josh Morris that they should sit at the far end of the rude plank table, away from Louisa and his wife, on a bench made of pine planks cut to size. Unlike many of the pioneer families, the Duffys had brought with them pewter dishes, plates, forks and spoons from the East when they came here, so there were proper settings for the table.

Mrs. Duffy and Louisa brought to the table steaming plates of venison, baked potatoes, squash, and string beans. Milk was served, along with Johnny cake.

Tom ate heartily and had sense enough to keep his eyes down on the food. But Louisa kept darting glances at him.

Evidently Duffy saw this and "harrumphed" several times.

Catherine smiled and stifled a laugh.

Louisa got the point and looked in the other direction.

When dinner was over, Tom thanked Mrs. Duffy for the fine meal. She replied, with her husband out of earshot, that she wished Tom and Joshua could eat with them all the time, but that Duffy would not have it. He considered indentured people little better than slaves, she said, and not worthy to be associating with proper folk. She did not at all agree with this but could do little about it, for she dare not defy her husband, with his fiery temperament.

Tom was rapidly getting the opinion that this man was not only a liar, but also a tyrant in his own home, just as he had dominated Tom since they met.

With Josh Morris working out in the fields, Tom tried to make some sort of sleeping arrangements for himself in the barn. This was a structure about 30 feet wide and 40 feet long, constructed crudely of logs with the bark still on, with a roof made of wooden slats covered with a thatch of straw. In rainstorms the roof leaked badly, and at other times some rodents ran about, making their homes in the thatch. Tom took straw and tried to fashion a bed from it, plus some old blankets that Catherine Duffy gave him. He was thinking all the while that his bed on the *Annabelle* had been constantly damp from sea spray, he had slept in barns since he had met Duffy, and he had not been in a proper bed since he had left England.

From behind Tom came a voice tinged with laughing mockery. "Are you trying to make a bed?"

Tom jumped, startled. He turned to face Louisa, who was standing in the barn's doorway. In the dark barn, his eyes had to accustom themselves to the daylight in which she stood. "Why yes...but I don't have much to work with."

"Well, you're doing a terrible job. Are you slow-witted? I'm so sorry for you. It's terrible to be dull and stupid. You must be if you're indentured."

Unwilling to be sarcastic or disagreeable, Tom responded in a pleasant voice, "Oh, I don't think so. I've had many years of school, and I've done well there. Let me tell you why I had to be indentured—"

"I don't want to hear it. I don't care about that. I suppose you'd tell me that you came from a wonderful family...where was it? England? Scotland? Ireland? A wealthy family?"

"No, not terribly wealthy, but respectable..."

"I suppose you're furious about being here on the frontier, in the wilderness. Do you despise us?"

"No, certainly not," Tom replied, his annoyance and anger rising. "Look, you're getting me all wrong, Miss Duffy. I don't despise anyone, and I'm not furious about anything. It's true I'm not happy about being indentured, but who would be? It's something of an accident and couldn't be helped. I'm hoping my father can find me and buy me out of it." Tom was doing his best to conceal his depressed state. He was not about to let the Duffys know how he really felt....

"Hmm," Louisa mused, sizing Tom up.

Perhaps she should change her tone, she thought, and not be so dismissive—or mean—to him. He had broad shoulders and was good looking. Obviously he was not yet comfortable with the new breeches he was wearing, for he kept pulling them up, as if he feared they might drop down. The breeches were too big for him, and so was the hunting shirt. Louisa had to stifle a laugh at his appearance, seeing that he was a bit embarrassed.

"Really, Tom Prescott, you surprise me with some of your remarks. I didn't mean to hurt your feelings. I'm sorry for what I said." She smiled sweetly. "Let's be friends."

"I'd like that, Miss Duffy. Right now, I need all the friends I can get."

"And call me Louisa. I don't need to be 'Miss Duffy.' And I'll call you Tom, if that's all right."

Louisa came over to where he was standing, knelt down, and began pulling the straw together and stuffing it loosely into a blanket, making a sort of mattress out of it. When she was done, it was a fairly good facsimile of something to lie on with a small degree of comfort, despite the straw poking through here and there, and sticking a person in the back. "I wish I had some goose feathers; they would make it much more comfortable. Perhaps I can get some."

"O, that would be wonderful," Tom said.

༄༅

Now that his daughter, Susan, was living with Andrew and him, Hiram Prescott had changed some rooms around in the home adjoining his shoemaker's shop in Chester, and made a bedroom for her. He had left his apprentice, Ephraim Cooke, to take care of the business. Therefore he had time to devote to searching for his son Tom. He suspected that the search would be a difficult task, but it helped to take his mind off the crushing awareness that his dear wife of many years had passed away of a horrible disease, and had to be buried at sea. How he missed her.

Susan, in preparing to attend the local school when it opened in a week, had asked her grandmother, who lived nearby, to help her with the cutting and sewing of dresses. She was delighted to be in a new home, although she, like her father, sorely missed her mother and Tom.

The last week had been busy for Hiram, as well as for Andrew and

Sarah. They had determined to go to all the surrounding areas around Philadelphia, looking for Tom. Ben Franklin had told them that Captain Higgins recalled some of Ishmael Duffy's statements, and among them had said that his home was a few miles west of the city, on the main road. But there were a number of main roads leading from the city, all of them going in a generally westerly or northerly direction. Which one did he mean? And, more importantly, was the man telling the truth?

Also, they had decided that the best method to search was to split up, with Andrew and Sarah going in one direction using the horse and wagon, and Hiram in another on his horse. And they had been doing this for days.

Andrew and Sarah went in the direction of Doylestown and Gwynedd, stopping at every farm and village along the way, inquiring if anyone knew of an Ishmael Duffy and had seen a young man, newly indentured, with sandy-colored hair, named Tom. No one knew of these two in this entire area.

Hiram went toward the Valley Forge, a small settlement on the Schuylkill River, where there was an iron works. Several blacksmiths were at work in the foundry as Hiram entered. The heat was intense. In the back of the large shop the furnace was roaring, and a young man was off to one side pumping the leather bellows that shot air into it. The small door that was used to put the crucibles in was open, and a brilliant orange glow lit the entire shop. The blacksmiths were pounding red hot iron on the anvils, and the noise was deafening. Sparks flew through the air as the hammers beat the iron. One of the blacksmiths came over to him; to escape the din, the man motioned Hiram to come outside the shop.

Hiram introduced himself, then said, "I'm sorry to interrupt your work...."

Sweating profusely, the blacksmith smiled. "Oh, no, don't apologize. It's so hot and noisy in there that I'm always glad for any break I can take." He laughed.

Hiram described Tom in detail and the circumstances of his indenture to Ishmael Duffy. He asked if the man knew of Duffy, and where he lived.

The blacksmith thought for a minute, then said he knew of no one named Duffy in that area, and had not seen anyone fitting Tom's description.

Hiram went to a number of other villages and towns, always asking the same questions. Nothing. For days Andrew, Sarah, and Hiram continued doing this. It was a fruitless search. Tired and discouraged, and not knowing what to do next, they returned to Chester.

❧☙

Hiram Prescott entered his shop, met his apprentice, Ephraim Cooke, and found that the young man had carried on well in Hiram's nine-day absence. Seven pairs of shoes had been sold to customers, and Ephraim had spent the majority of his time in cutting leather that had been tanned elsewhere, in sewing soles and upper parts together, putting on heels, nailing, polishing and doing the dozens of other tasks that had to be completed before shoes were ready for sale. Hiram picked up a number of shoes that Ephraim was working on and was pleased with the workmanship displayed. In addition, correct amounts of money had been collected for shoes sold, he noted. He had trained Ephraim well. The young man would make a good shoemaker. All seemed in order.

Hiram spoke with his aged mother, who lived nearby, and found that she, too, highly approved of the work Ephraim had done. "I've watched him from a distance while you were gone," she said, "and he worked hard. When customers came in, he was very civil to them, and they seemed pleased. He explained why you had to leave, and they accepted that. He's a good apprentice."

With that recommendation, Hiram and Ephraim shared some sandwiches in the middle of the day.

"I must ask right off, Mr. Prescott: is there any news of your son?" Ephraim said.

"No, I'm sorry to say."

"You have my deepest sympathies over the death of your wife. And may I ask where you looked for your son?"

"Andrew, Sarah, and I searched for miles around, as far away as Doylestown and the Valley Forge. We did find a printer in Philadelphia who has put an advertisement in his paper. But no one has replied to that yet." Changing the subject, Hiram said, "I am pleased with your stewardship during my absence, Ephraim. Now I owe your pay, so let's settle up on that."

Hiram took out his money pouch and counted out the proper amount, then said, "I'm adding a bonus for your very good work. You've earned it."

The young man was delighted. "You may not wish to look at all this right now, sir, but here is the week's mail." He handed a bundle to Hiram.

"Yeah, I'm much too tired from my traveling to look at it now," he said as he gave it a quick shuffle. But one piece, on rough, cheap paper, caught his eye. "What is this?"

The envelope was different from the usual ones. Scrawled on the front in crude letters were the words TO THE SHOEMAKER. Hiram opened it.

On the paper inside, in the same crude lettering, was the message. With amazement, he read, *You have cheated me. You shall pay for it.* There was no signature.

"What in the world does this mean?" Hiram asked. He showed the letter to Ephraim. "I'm an honest man, and I've never cheated anyone. Who could this be?"

<hr />

The man who had broken into Hiram Prescott's shop had been hearing voices for some time. He was sitting in his small log cabin, pondering what to do. Then he heard, softly in the background, *"All your life you have been cheated by many people. You have every right to take vengeance on them."*

He lived alone, and the cabin was in an isolated grove of maple trees near the Delaware River, three miles from the town of Chester. There were two little rooms, and he felt that this was adequate. At forty years of age, he was somewhat shorter than most men of the time, and his tangled black hair was beginning to be streaked with gray.

Softly, *"You are better than they are. Who do they think they are—treating you the way they do?"*

His fiery temperament could partly be explained by the fact that his parents had driven into his mind, as a child, that he was superior to everyone, and need never be subservient. As he grew up, his overbearing attitude made others shun him, and his school life had been difficult, due to no one's fault but his own. Approaching the time to decide on a vocation, he found that when he applied to be an apprentice to various tradesmen, they would take him on for a short while and, when they found what an irascible fellow he was, they would dismiss him.

Louder, *"And all those men who hired you and then fired you. You knew more than they did!"*

Over the years he had grown more and more bitter, blaming everyone but himself for what his life had become. He took on odd jobs to support himself but frequently had little or no money to live on.

He had never married but had a daughter who lived three miles away. As his only living relative, he went to her house as often as he could for some companionship, although she did not encourage his calls. Truthfully, she was a bit frightened of her father, and he frightened her children also. He had beaten her often when she was a child, and this left a psychological scar that had never gone away. In addition, his actions in the last several years were scary.

Softly, *"And that miserable fellow over in Springfield—you should hurt him for what he did to you!"*

He talked constantly of retribution, speaking of people who had wronged him in one way or another, although his daughter had never heard of these people and was tempted to doubt their very existence.

He had been brooding for some time, and a week ago had sent that letter to Hiram Prescott. How he hated that man, he told himself. The previous week he had broken into the shoemaker's shop in Chester, and hit him over the head with a blunt instrument.

The voices came again. Sometimes they were soft and distant; at other times they were loud and insistent. But always they had the same message. He was what he was because of the evil of other people toward him. He was never wrong, but always the innocent victim.

Now he must act again. He had warned that shoemaker. This time he would really deal with him.

THREE

Danger in the Wilderness

In the first weeks that he spent at Ishmael Duffy's farm near the hamlet of Carlisle, Tom found that Joshua Morris was a capable person who knew most of the techniques needed on a frontier farm. But more than that, Tom found that they were forming a real friendship, as Joshua was pleased to show Tom how to master many jobs, and give him much-needed advice. Tom badly needed advice and direction; things were much different here than in his homeland. Certainly Ishmael Duffy was no help—with his beastly treatment of his two indentured workers, he only added to Tom's depression. Tom had been raised in a suburb of London where his father was a shoemaker, and he knew little of rural life, especially life on the American frontier. So he appreciated Joshua, as the best friend he had. But underneath the cheerfulness he tried to show, his depression continued. Were his father and brother trying to find him? And could they? Such nagging thoughts could not be denied.

Joshua had asked Tom to call him "Josh," and they worked together on jobs around the farm that called for more than one person. Josh had been indentured to Ishmael Duffy for half a year, after he had arrived from a farm near Gloucester, England. There, in Gloucester, Josh had been converted to the Christian faith under the ministry of a dynamic preacher, George Whitefield.* This young man was becoming the talk of England and had already caused revivals to break out in major cities.

Josh was especially good with horses, and on the farm there were mares, colts, and a stallion. Ishmael Duffy's farm was about twenty acres, which was about all that Josh could plow, tend to, and harvest by himself, so he was grateful to have Tom as another farmhand.

*pronounced *Wit-field*

Josh had already made a place to sleep and keep his few belongings in the barn. He had gone up into the loft, and found there a wooden partition that separated an area from the rest of the loft. Since it was in the loft, which was little used except to store some hay, it was out of the way and available.

Several cats were kept, to keep down the rats. Josh invited Tom to join him there, and showed the newcomer how to make a minimally acceptable bed like the one he had already constructed for himself. This was made out of some wooden boards, rope, and old canvas that had been tossed aside. Catherine Duffy, regretting they had to sleep in the barn to begin with, had given them several old blankets. These weren't needed in the summer, as the one problem they had was that the loft, with no windows or ventilation except for some cracks in the logs of the outer walls, became stiflingly hot. Josh commented that in the coming winter the reverse would be true, and it would be freezing.

"The one real danger that you must watch for," counseled Josh, "is Indians. While Mr. Duffy tries to be on good terms with all Indians, and most are peaceful, there's always the possibility that one or a few might come to kill or steal." He pounded a nail in the board with his hammer.

"Has anything happened recently?" Tom asked.

"Well, last year over in Middlesex, we hear, some Indians were given plenty of whisky, and they got roaring drunk. Then they killed a settler."

"But most of the Indians are peaceful?"

"Yea, the local tribes are usually inoffensive. As long as the Indians believe that the settlers are treating them fairly, and paying proper amounts for the land they purchase, and don't get whiskey, everyone gets along quite nicely." Josh fitted another board in place and nailed it in.

"Well, that's only right! After all, the Indians owned the land first."

"Yea, but you don't understand, Tom. It's more complicated than that. There's the French to the west, over the Allegheny Mountains, who hate the British and are fighting fiercely to keep them from crossing the mountains. The French have many Indian tribes on their side. And the British have what is called the Iroquois Confederacy, which is an alliance of Indian tribes friendly to England. And there's much more to it, as you'll hear. Grab that rope, will ye, and help me stretch it."

Tom's eyes widened in surprise as he took the rope's end. "Oh, I didn't know that."

"Oh, aye. And we're really only at the beginning of all this, I fear. Battles between the English and the French have been going on for more than fifty years. The French are just beyond those mountains, and control the land from Canada all the way south to Spanish territory, from what I hear."

"Thanks for telling me. I didn't understand all that, but I'm not totally dumb about these things," Tom said. "When I was growing up in England, I heard much about the war with France. That was because the French king was furious over the British getting rid of King James the Second, and bringing in William and Mary."

"That's about it! Now look—you've got a fairly acceptable bed, my friend!"

※

A week later, soon after daybreak, Louisa brought their breakfast out to the barn. Josh and Tom were still in their beds up in the loft, and she called up to them, "Hello up there! Are you still asleep? It's dawn! I was sent out with your breakfast."

The fellows climbed out of bed, shouted that they were up, wiped the sleep out of their eyes, and pulled on their clothes. They climbed down the rickety ladder from the loft and greeted Louisa. Going to the hollowed-out log that served as a horse trough, they splashed water on their faces.

Watching them, Louisa smiled at these ablutions. Clearly, she was lonely, with no one else her age for miles around. "You know, I do wish you two weren't indentured servants," she said with a frown.

Both Tom and Josh hid their reaction, but they were surprised at her statement. In a minute she turned and walked slowly back to the farmhouse.

When Louisa was out of earshot, Josh smiled. "Humph! I guess that means she likes us!"

"Oh, she's just a child. Pay her no attention." Tom grinned. "And I too wish we weren't indentured. Come on, we'd better eat breakfast and get to work, before her father comes to see if we're loafing. And if he ever finds her out here with us, watch out. He won't take it out on Louisa. He'll take it out on us, thinking we lure her out here."

45

They went to work in the fields, tending to the potato, corn, bean, squash, and pumpkin crops, which would soon be ready for the hard work of harvesting. After three hours of that, the sun had increased the heat of the morning, and it had become sultry. Both were hot, and their backs were aching. They were sweating profusely and had doffed the hot deerskin breeches and heavy hunting shirt in favor of the Indian breech clout. Drops of sweat were hanging from their chins and brows. They decided to work with the horses outside the enclosure, welcoming the opportunity to leave the backbreaking farming aside. But there was one benefit: all the work was helping Tom to keep his mind off his troubles.

Tom was learning how to harness, tame, and ride horses, as Josh gave him instructions. Tom was riding a mare, which was rather docile, and Josh was riding the stallion. Josh's horse was well-nourished, large-boned, and sound of wind, and could get quite obstreperous if given free rein, so Josh did not want Tom to ride him yet. The two rode up a nearby ridge, and as they came to the top the horses jumped over a fallen log, waded over a small creek, and fought their way through tangles of persimmon, chinkapin, scrub oak, and poplar. A few swarms of mosquitos had attacked them, looking for blood, and the fellows had spent some time swatting them. Tom's riding ability was improving rapidly; in time he might turn out to be a good horseman.

They stopped at the top of the ridge to admire the view. The Allegheny Mountains, bathed in the full light of the sun, were a spectacular vision of emerald green speckled with yellow and brown. They could see for miles in most directions. The undulating hills and valleys, with little streams frequently running between them, were a fascinating sight to Tom, the English lad who had never imagined such grandeur and seemingly infinite space, off to the distant horizon. The breeze was from the west. He lifted his chin, enjoying the cool touch of the wind on his heated skin. It was a joy to be alive on a day like this.

Tom let the reins go slack across his horse's neck. The horses stood still. They were somewhat lathered and seemed quite willing to rest. The massive withers of Josh's stallion gleamed in the sunlight. This was most peaceful, Tom thought. The two were happy to be away from the farm for a while and glad to have the excuse of exercising the mounts. Their more onerous chores could be left for a time. Tom sensed that his friendship with Josh was deepening, that they understood one another. However distressing and difficult being indentured under Duffy would be in the years ahead, it would be lightened by having a reliable friend who shared his work and trials.

Suddenly, Josh shouted, "Let's see how good a rider you are! I'll race you back!" And he kicked the stallion in its ribs, goading it to plunge down the slope, galloping over the thickets of brush, sending coveys of quail exploding into the air in fright.

Tom knew he couldn't match that display of horsemanship, but he urged his mare down the hill after Josh. Several times the mare brushed Tom's bare leg against a tree, which caused painful bleeding from half a dozen scratches, since he was not wearing the long breeches.

He looked at the cloud of dust up ahead, which was about all that could be seen of Josh's flight.

Still Tom urged the mare to a gallop. But it was no use trying to catch up with Josh. The mare moved down the slope as fast as it could, but Josh's stallion won the race handily. When Tom finally reached the bottom, there was Josh, his horse pawing the ground and snorting from the exertion, and its rider smiling broadly.

"You did well," Josh said. "Let's just take it easy from here to Duffy's."

The two rode slowly for the few miles until they reached the farm. Coming to the horses' enclosure, there, leaning on the fence, was Louisa Duffy. In spite of the day's heat, Louisa looked cool and comfortable, dressed in a frock of light brown with a white bonnet on her head. Josh gave no indication, but his reaction was that Louisa was dressed too well for existence on a rural farm.

Louisa looked Josh and Tom over; there they stood, perspiring profusely, Tom bleeding from a number of small abrasions, hot and dusty, with a minimum of clothing on, not expecting any woman around. And there she stood, relaxed and cool, wanting to chat. This was one time when the fellows were not especially happy to meet her.

Louisa was effusive over this display of manly bravado on the horses. "How gallant! And what happened to you, Tom? You've got cuts; you're bleeding."

Was Louisa being sarcastic? Tom didn't know. Was she mocking him? He hoped not. He had felt Louisa's mockery before. He certainly didn't appreciate it now. So he focused on the ground, then cast a glance at Josh.

"Oh, I really meant it, men," she said softly.

Josh and Tom had never been called "men" before...till now. Duffy had always called them "young fellow," "lad," or worse than that, and usually just "you." So they preened a bit. Perhaps Louisa considered Tom's minor wounds and blood as badges of courage.

"Yes, I was watching for quite a while from here. Oh, how I wish I could ride a horse like you, Josh. Could you teach me?" Her coyness was subtle.

Josh mumbled something, then said, "I guess so, but it would have to be with your father's permission."

"Oh, he wouldn't mind. My father does *everything* I ask him to." She tossed her head back.

I don't think she understands, Josh thought. *If Duffy comes out here now and catches us talking to his daughter, we will be blamed, not Louisa! It won't matter that she came out here; in that varmint's mind, we're not even supposed to be talking to her.*

So Josh said carefully, "But Louisa, your father calls us his indentured servants—little better than slaves. Just farmhands...low people, to him. I think you are a fine girl, and I wouldn't be rude to you, but if I saw your father coming out here just now, and he saw the three of us talking, I'd probably just walk away, before...before..."

"Before what?"

"Before your father exploded, and severely punished Tom and me. Don't you understand?"

Louisa was stunned. "Nonsense! Fiddle-dee-dee! He wouldn't do that," she said angrily.

"I believe you're completely wrong. Don't you think so, Tom?"

"Miss Duffy, I'm afraid I must agree completely with Josh."

"Haven't you thought about it, Louisa?" Josh said kindly. "I don't mean to make your father look bad in your eyes, but think of our situation. He won't let us eat in the house; he makes us sleep anywhere we can, so we sleep in a miserable, filthy old barn, with rats and squirrels and raccoons and who knows what else; he makes us work from dawn till dark; he won't let us talk to you, and on and on it goes."

Louisa was almost weeping after that. She kept her eyes fixed on the ground, then shook her head. "I really hadn't thought about it too much." She hesitated. "Until now. But you're right. I'm going to have a talk with my father. And Tom, I'm going to ask my mother to bandage your wounds."

And off she ran to the farmhouse.

"Well, friend, you really laid it on the line to her," Tom said.

"Look, if her father comes storming out here, furious with us, we'd better not be standing here talking. I'll get these horses unharnessed and cleaned up. You need to tend to those cuts and bruises."

Josh took the horses to the barn, unsaddled them, wiped them down, and turned them out to their feed. Now they might have more problems with Duffy.

                        ℰℭ

To their relief, Louisa had apparently said little of all this to her father. The next day Josh and Tom were working in the barn, and Louisa appeared—but not by herself. A young fellow, who could not have been more than thirteen, was holding her hand. With a toss of her head, Louisa said, "I'd like you to meet my boyfriend, Jeremy Dill. Jeremy, this is Tom and Josh."

Boyfriend! The two could not disguise their astonishment. They looked Jeremy Dill over. He was tall and skinny, freckle-faced and red-haired, with two front teeth that protruded. Bashful, Jeremy nodded to them, uncertain what to say or do.

Josh, not wanting to take advantage of the boy's shyness, extended his hand. "Jeremy, we're glad to meet you…aren't we, Tom?"

"Oh…yes. Very glad. Where do you live, Jeremy?"

"Uhh, we live in the town of Carlisle. But my father tends a farm outside of town."

Louisa turned to go, saying, "Come, Jeremy." Then to them she threw over her shoulder, "I just wanted to introduce my *boyfriend* to you!"

When they were well out of earshot, Tom and Josh exploded with laughter. "I'm delighted!" Josh said. "Now we don't have to tolerate her coyness and flirting any more. Louisa has someone her own age."

"And isn't he *handsome?*" Tom chortled.

"Now, now. Let's be glad for small blessings," Josh said.

A week later, while there had been no change in Ishmael Duffy's attitude toward his two workers, he had allowed Louisa to begin taking riding lessons from Josh Morris. Tom and Josh, ever hopeful, took this as a good sign, thinking it might lead to better things later. Duffy was extremely protective of his only child, which was understandable, and he had lectured Josh before the first lesson on how careful she must be. No jumping of the horses over obstacles; no faster than a canter, and never a gallop; keep the lesson to half an hour, and so on. While almost all women would ride sidesaddle, Duffy was fearful that this would increase the possibility that Louisa might fall off, and therefore he had his wife make a pair of pants for his daughter to wear, so she could straddle the horse. Louisa was delighted.

※

Tom was working outside the barn when Josh came in from the fields. "How are the riding lessons going?" Tom asked.

"Rather well, I think," Josh said. "Louisa is a clever girl and listens carefully to every instruction I give her. She is progressing nicely. Of course, Duffy has set strict limits on everything, and that is bothering her no end. Now that she is doing well, she wants to begin to go faster, but I have strict orders not to allow that. And there is one other thing that is really irritating me."

"Only one?" Tom asked with a smile.

Josh laughed. "Well, maybe there are others too, but Duffy has made it very plain that I'm not to get too friendly with his daughter. Of course, now she has a *boyfriend.* So I'm always to keep my distance. Call her 'Miss Duffy.' Don't allow her to get her hands dirty! Help her mount. Help her dismount. Lead her about. And Louisa hates it! She wants to do everything that any rider of horses does. And she calls me Josh and doesn't treat me like a slave at all, but like an equal."

"What did you expect out of that miserable monster? I've told you how he treated me on the way here from Philadelphia."

Josh nodded. It was a fine October day; the summer heat was leaving, and there were only a few wisps of filmy clouds in the sky. The leaves on the deciduous trees were just beginning to turn to crimson and gold, cardinals flashed among the trees, and two ravens flew past, high above, giving out raucous, urgent cries. An occasional mosquito buzzed about. One of Duffy's cows in the pasture lifted its head and watched them.

Josh went inside the barn for a moment and returned with his Bible. They walked together from the barn to the pasture.

Josh cocked his head toward Tom. "We've become good friends. It's over a month since you came. I think you trust me somewhat, don't you?"

"Of course."

"Then I want to ask you a very important question. We have discussed other problems, like the Indians, but we haven't had much opportunity to talk about important items, such as spiritual things. And that's the most important item of all, by far. I must ask, as your friend, are you a child of God through Jesus Christ?"

Tom stopped walking and looked at Josh. This question surprised him. "Why, yes, I think I am."

"Do you know Christ as your Savior?"

"I-I'm not sure." He bit his lip.

"You see, I wouldn't be much of a friend if I wasn't concerned about your eternal salvation."

Tom was silent in thought. He had often seen Josh reading his Bible in the last month. Tom didn't own a Bible, and was tempted to think that reading the Bible was mainly for women. But since he admired Tom's mastery of so many physical activities, and his masculinity, he had to re-think that. Here was a person he looked up to, and this fellow loved the Bible!

"Tom, I've heard talk that a great revival has begun, where people are coming to God in great numbers. People are already calling it 'the Great Awakening.' I want to be in on this, even out here on the frontier. And I want you to know about this too."

"I've never had much teaching about religion, back in England," Tom admitted. "My family went to church a few times, on holidays, and I was baptized, but I didn't learn much."

There was a huge old oak by the cow pasture's fence, and they sat on some logs under its shade. "Well, Tom," Josh said, "I'm really not talking about religion. Being baptized won't save you. You see, lots of people have 'religion,' but they don't have eternal salvation. Religion alone is not saving faith. What I'm talking about is taking Jesus Christ as your Savior—

51

that's saving faith. And when a person takes Christ as Savior, he or she becomes a child of God immediately."

Tom had never heard salvation explained in this way. Because he had learned to trust Josh, he listened intently. This was fascinating. And he realized how important it was. "Do you mean that if a person has Christ as Savior, they are definitely going to heaven when they die? You can be sure of that?"

"That's exactly what I mean. The Scriptures tell us that, in many places." With that, Josh opened the Bible and began to show Tom what it taught about Jesus, His death and resurrection, and what that means.

Heads together in conversation, they spent an hour studying the Scriptures. Then Josh said, "Well, my friend, there it is. Would you like to know that you're a child of God, and bound for heaven?"

Tom said, "Yes, but...this is all so new to me. Let me think about it for a while. I'm not trying to put it off. I just want to understand it better. May I borrow your Bible?"

"Certainly. I'll be praying for you." Singing one of Isaac Watt's new hymns, Josh went to his chores.

❧❦

Hiram Prescott was a busy man, engaged not only in running his shoemaking business but also in doing a bit of moneylending. He was enormously concerned over his son's disappearance and was spreading word of this everywhere he went, asking for help. But he was getting along in years and not able to travel as much as he did in his younger days.

His son Andrew, however, was physically fit and able to ride his horse over long distances. He was learning to be a chandler, making soap and candles, but when he was not needed there, as now, he was available to continue searching for his brother Tom.

Therefore Andrew began from Chester and determined that he would travel around the eastern portions of Pennsylvania and possibly go into Delaware and Maryland if necessary. On the first few days he went west as far as Lancaster, and then turned north toward Reading. Wherever he found a town with a local newspaper or a print shop with a press, he would pay to have an advertisement placed, such as had already been done in Franklin's *Pennsylvania Gazette,* which he found circulated as far west as he had gone. In each town or hamlet he asked as many people as possible if they had heard of a young man answering Tom's description. While he encountered many indentured people bound to masters, he heard nothing of a young man resembling Tom.

Refusing to get discouraged, Andrew traveled toward Allentown, and then crossed the Delaware River on a ferry into New Jersey, working his way toward Trenton.

He found no trace of Tom.

While Hiram Prescott was away searching for his son, the man who had broken into Hiram's shop continued to hear voices. They always said the same thing—that he had been treated miserably by many people all his life, and that he had every right to exact vengeance on all of them.

Currently he was obsessed with Hiram Prescott. He had gone to Hiram's shop a year ago, bought a pair of shoes from him, and they dickered over the price. The shoes were new and perfect, but Hiram wanted a price for them that was more than this man possessed. Finally, as Hiram noted his shabby appearance and ugly manner, he let the fellow have them for what little money the man had. Grumbling, the man went away angry, convinced that he had still paid too much for them.

Two months later, after constantly wearing the shoes in rain and snow, the soles had warped somewhat, as was natural. This incensed the man, who was convinced that no shoes should ever do this. Shoes should be indestructible! For this he vowed retaliation. This shoemaker was just like all the others who had treated him badly all his life, or cheated him. His voices were right!

He had broken into Hiram's shop and clubbed him over the head and sent the shoemaker a warning note recently. He intended to follow it up with still more punishment. What that was to be, he would determine in time.

A month later, Louisa Duffy's riding lessons were going well, and Ishmael and Catherine Duffy were pleased. Louisa had a talk with her father and persuaded him that he should treat Tom and Josh better. Duffy was uncertain what to do; he still felt they were little better than slaves, but he couldn't contend with his daughter *and* his wife, both of whom were now agitating him about the two. As for *their* welfare, he couldn't care less. But to placate Louisa and Catherine, he knew he had to do something. He couldn't imagine why, but they were accusing him of being *almost brutal.*

So suddenly he reduced the number of hours he required Tom and Josh to work each day and asked if they would like to move their sleeping quarters from the barn loft to a fairly large addition made of logs that was connected to the back of the cabin. While this shed was still not ideal, at least it was better ventilated and warmer than the barn, with winter coming on, there were fewer rats, and a window let in daylight. Also, since there was no hay in the shed, they could light candles. They could not do that in the barn, which was full of combustibles.

The shed was large enough for their quarters and also contained the family's food supply. It was entered by an outside door, which had to be sturdy and well bolted at night to keep out prowling bears attracted by the smells of food. Carefully organized inside the shed were baskets of dried squash, a crock of salted butter, sacks of rice and dried beans, bags of oatmeal and cornmeal, a basket of goat cheeses, bushels of black walnuts, butternuts, and hickory nuts, several jars of honeycomb, a small barrel of salted meat, several smoked hams, and other foods, all of which made the shed so aromatic that Tom was delighted. And they could eat all they wanted!

After this improvement in their living quarters, they were even more pleasantly surprised at Duffy's next offer. Since it was late-October and the harvest of the crops was in, the amount of farm work was lessened. Duffy came to Josh and asked if he and Tom would like to go on a journey to get several horses that he wanted to buy. He declared that some business kept him from going. Some miles to the west, near the Tuscarora Mountain, a friend of his had written saying that the horses were available. Josh jumped at the chance to be away for a week or so, going to some new places, and he quickly told Tom of the opportunity.

Another reason they were pleased was that Duffy entrusted them with the money needed to purchase the horses and a musket, should they run into any trouble. This astonished them. After all, with horses, a gun, and a good sum of money, if they were not honest they could flee into the wilderness. That thought never came to Josh. But momentarily it occurred to Tom that he could run away and try to make it back to Chester. He constantly thought of his father, sister, and brother waiting to hear of him. But then he sobered and knew that if he fled, he would be a runaway, with a large reward out for his capture and return. So, with Duffy's trust offered to them, they would faithfully do what he asked.

<hr />

Early on a marvelous and cool morning, with bright sunlight falling on the meadow, the two started out on their horses—Josh on the stallion and Tom on his favorite mare. After leaving Duffy's farm, they went along cornfields that were now barren and brown, and through dark and tangled wooded paths that only the deer and black bear had penetrated recently.

Although they anticipated no problem in finding his friend, Duffy had provided them with a crude map that showed the way. The roads or paths were only vaguely marked and little traveled, but frequently they came to a wide meadow or field where they could allow the horses to let out their pent-up energies and go for all they were worth, with the stallion always far in the lead.

Tom and Josh were determined to enjoy themselves and make the most of this holiday. When they came to a slow-flowing river, around noon, they tied the horses up and doffed their clothing, plunging into the still warm stream for a bath and some fun. It was a release they needed, after months of endless, backbreaking work on the farm. The little river was deep enough for them to swim, and they splashed about, sending up geysers of spray, and then climbing the bank and diving back into the water.

When the two had enough of swimming, they came out of the river and threw themselves down on the grass to dry off. The air was still cool, but the sun was high and hot on their bare skin. After a time, when they were dry, they dressed and thought about lunch, and got some smoked ham, cheese, and cornmeal bread from the packs on the horses. Leading their mounts to the river to drink, they sought some shade in a grove of oaks that stood near the river, ate, and discussed what they were experiencing.

"You know, Josh, I was thinking as we rode. Duffy has trusted us with money and a gun. We'll need the money for the horses. Do you think we'll need the gun?"

"He probably thought we would, or he wouldn't have lent it to us."

"But I've never shot a gun. Have you?"

"Yes, many times. I'm going to show you how to use it. Let me get the gun from my horse." Josh went to the river, tied the horses to some trees, and brought the gun, some shot, and powder back. "Let's go over to the field there, away from the horses, so the shots won't frighten them."

When they were far from the horses, Josh inspected the weapon, and showed it to Tom, who lifted it. The firearm was long, almost five feet in length.

"Zounds! It must weigh ten or twelve pounds or so!" Tom exclaimed.

"Of course it does. It's a Long Land pattern musket, made for the British soldiers mostly, and they've nicknamed it 'the Brown Bess.' It's the latest type of firearm, just made for a few years over in England. Duffy must have bought it in Philadelphia. It's a great improvement over earlier guns."

Josh got the leather pouch that contained the ammunition, and began to demonstrate getting it ready to fire. "This is a flintlock muzzleloader. Here, Tom, you do it. Send the bullet down and ram it in."

Tom did as instructed. Josh said, "Right. That's fine. This is a good firearm; it's a rugged and simple design. Duffy let me use it a number of times before you came, to shoot wild turkey and other game for food. But I've also shot guns before I was indentured."

"How accurate is it?"

"Oh, pretty accurate up to about 50 to 75 yards. Let me show you. First we choose a target." Josh walked about 30 yards to a large boulder, placed a smaller stone atop it, and walked back to Tom.

He took the firearm, pulling the paper cartridge open with his teeth, priming, loading, ramming, and checking it as he had described to Tom, and swept the stock up to his shoulder in one quick motion. Then he took aim. "Now, there's going to be a kick to it, so be prepared! Then squeeze the trigger...."

Josh did, and the firearm roared.

To Tom's surprise and delight, the smaller stone was struck and shattered.

Then he looked at Josh, and burst out laughing, for Josh's face had black soot over it. "I'm sorry! I didn't mean to laugh – but I didn't think you were going to get smoky powder all over your face."

"Well, we'll see how you do. Go ahead and swab the barrel, and reload."

Tom took the gun, rather clumsily tried to duplicate what Josh had shown him, raised it to his shoulder, took aim at a rag they hung from a tree in the near distance, and pulled the trigger. The firearm boomed. The rag remained untouched.

Tom was unprepared for the recoil from the gun, and was thrown backward, almost landing on the ground. When he recovered a bit from the shock, he got to his feet, looking amazed.

"Why didn't you warn me....?!" Tom said angrily, brushing himself off, his ears ringing from the blast of the firearm.

"I did! Didn't you watch carefully how I braced myself before pulling the trigger?"

"Yes, but I didn't think it would have such a kick! All right, give me the gun, and I'll try again." Annoyed, Tom grabbed the weapon.

Each time Tom fired, he improved somewhat and soon was going through the procedure of cleaning the barrel, loading, and firing, in a fairly smooth manner, under Josh's supervision. He managed to hit the rag occasionally, and after about twenty shots, the rag was looking tattered. Clouds of smoke drifted over the field. Tom was pleased with his own progress, although his shoulder and upper body ached from the pounding it was getting.

"Had enough for this session?" Josh asked. "We can try again tomorrow."

"I think so," Tom said with a deep sigh, obviously relieved. "Thanks for the instruction. Do you think I'll ever get to be a good shot, like you?"

"Certainly. You're doing fine for your first lesson." Josh showed Tom how to carry the gun while walking, and they went toward the horses, untied them, mounted, and rode through a field overgrown with yellowing pawpaw and high grass. There was a stand of rust-colored aspens on their left, and some gold and red maples on their right, vivid against the brilliant blue sky.

That afternoon they made more progress toward Tuscarora Mountain.

All around, the hills were getting higher and higher, and the trees on them had turned into a lavish display of golds and crimsons.

Suddenly, as they were about to emerge from among a clump of black-green hemlock, Josh reached over and touched Tom's arm, motioning him to stop his horse and be quiet. Josh's quick perceptions had alerted him to something up ahead, not yet in sight.

In a minute what had alerted Josh came into sight, going at right angles to them perhaps two hundred yards ahead, across a meadow.

"Indians," Josh whispered. They could see a dozen warriors mounted on steeds, armed with bows. He waited until they had crossed and gotten beyond earshot, then said quietly, "Delawares, I'm certain. They are usually peaceful and make treaties with the whites, but it's better if we don't take a chance on meeting them. All right, they're gone now. We can go on."

Overhead a flock of long-necked geese honked their way through the hills, as free as these two humans were feeling.

⁂

Two days later, the two woke with the dawn of another brilliant fall day.

It was cool, but the humidity of summer was gone, and the coolness was stimulating. They had a distance to cover, but the pleasures of this trip were lightening Tom's worries. He thought about God's goodness and His awesome creation, and what Josh had said to him. There was something about the sheer size and beauty of the wilderness that soothed him. Among the gigantic trees and teeming wildlife, he found a quiet peace. But maybe there was something missing, and it might be what Josh had talked about. Josh had a much deeper peace and more confidence.

As Josh and Tom ate a cold breakfast of cornmeal bread and cheese, they checked the map Ishmael Duffy had given them. They had already located several probable landmarks.

"I'd say we are only about four miles from this place," Josh said, indicating the symbol on the map where the horses were.

In two hours they were at the farm. Glenn Hunter, the farmer, was pleased to see them, for he had sent the letter a month earlier to Ishmael Duffy and had received no reply and did not know if Duffy would want the horses. To send and receive mail on the frontier was, of course, a dubious business.

Josh was in no hurry to begin the return trip, nor was Tom. Glenn Hunter, his wife, and five children (three sons and two daughters) were so happy to have visitors—especially visitors who had money to buy something—that he insisted they stay for dinner and sleep inside overnight, then leave, if they must, the next morning. The invitation to sleep indoors—in a proper bed!—was so intriguing that Tom and Josh accepted immediately. Of course it meant that the older boys had to give up their bed and sleep on the floor, but all agreed that one night wouldn't be a major inconvenience.

"Do you have much trouble from Indians?" Tom asked.

"Yes and no," Hunter replied. "I bought this land ten years ago from the Delawares, fair and square, and the Indians agreed they got a fair price. So I've had no trouble there. But this whole land is almost into the Appalachian Mountains, and the various tribes are fighting to gain control over it. It's very complicated. A number of tribes side with the English—you and me—the Six Nations of the Iroquois Confederacy, and the Delawares, Twightwees, Owandaets, and Shawonees, even though at times they fight among themselves. But just over the mountains are the French, and they are constantly fighting with the English, here and in Europe, and they have a number of savage tribes on their side."

"Yes, I know; Josh told me. So the fighting goes on over the mountains to the west?" Tom asked.

"Mostly, but not entirely. I've been fortunate; the tribes siding with the French haven't come to my farm, to do any damage, but a few miles north, those tribes came and killed some settlers last year. So I'm very nervous. I see some of their warriors prowling around from time to time. And I've warned my children to stay close to the farm. One of my neighbors has a livid tomahawk scar that runs from his hairline to his jaw, bisecting a blinded eye."

Josh and Tom gave a significant glance at each other. Tom swallowed hard.

"When those Indians come, they not only kill the settlers, they set fire to their homes as well, and burn them to the ground. Many a man has gone on a hunting trip and come back to find his place burned and black and his family gone. Or, what's worse, still there."

Tom shuddered.

"So we have to be on guard constantly. I don't leave this farm. Well, let's talk about something more pleasant," Hunter said. "Come with me; I want to show you all that I'm raising."

Hunter took them to his barn and orchards. He showed them the recent harvest of potatoes and many other vegetables, enough to get the family through the coming winter. "Then over in that field I've planted raspberries, strawberries, squashes, and watermelons—all from seeds I brought with me," he said.

"That's amazing," Josh admitted. "You're doing beautifully." They looked over the orchards, walked around, pulled some berries off the bushes and ate them. They were succulent and rich.

"I guess it's time we dickered over the horses. Let's go see 'em." He led the way to the barn, and the heavy, acrid smell of manure hit them before they were near it. There were eight horses in the stables—a two-year-old, two mares, a large stallion, and four powerful, rugged draft horses, tawny brown with long manes and tail, and hoofs that were enormous. These were the ones that Ishmael Duffy wanted, to pull the plows and wagons on his farm.

"What do you think of these draft horses?" Hunter asked.

"They're beautiful," Josh said. "We'll take two, if you will sell them."

"Yup. I'll part with two of them. I need only two here. I'll let Homer and Dace go."

Josh and Tom began to inspect the fine beasts. Ishmael Duffy had trusted Josh's judgment in regard to the quality of draft horses, and Josh didn't want to be responsible if Duffy found anything wrong when the horses were brought back to Carlisle. He checked the teeth, eyes, flanks, withers, joints, nostrils, and everything else that was important, and found both animals sound in wind and body. Josh asked the price and was told.

"May I run them around the farm?" Josh asked.

"Certainly," said Hunter. A profitable sale was in the wind.

Putting a harness on Dace, and not needing a saddle, Josh jumped on the horse's back and took him out to canter around the fields. For a distance he urged the horse to a gallop, although the breed was not meant to race. Satisfied, he brought the horse back to the stables and took Homer out to do the same.

Returning, Josh jumped down from Homer and said, "Fine animals.

We'll take them."

⛤

Early the next morning, Mrs. Hunter gave them a hearty breakfast and some fresh food to take on their trip. Tom and Josh saddled their own mounts, thanked the Hunters for their hospitality, tied long ropes to the draft horses, and set off for Carlisle. The autumn morning was crisp. Some leaves still held to the trees, and flakes of red, brown, and gold floated down on them like a gentle rain as they went through thickets of sweet bay and dogwood. They were dressed in their heavy hunting shirts of homespun and breeches of deer skin, with the moccasins that came up the lower part of the leg, but they knew that when the sun rose high the temperature would rise rapidly and they would divest themselves of their shirts and possibly of the breeches, switching over to cool breech clouts.

They had been on the road for about a quarter of an hour, going under a canopy of old oaks that had lost most of their leaves. The two draft horses followed obediently on their ropes, and Tom was constantly impressed by the strength of these animals. In addition, they were beautiful. He told Josh that he thought they had made a good deal, and that Duffy would be pleased.

"He'd better be!" Josh responded. "If he doesn't like them, or the price, he can go back himself and straighten things out with Mr. Hunter. I don't intend to go this long distance again—do you?"

"Oh, I don't know. You can't argue that it wasn't good to get away for a few days, can you?"

As Josh said the last, with totally unexpected suddenness there came a hideous Indian war cry, as three savages on horses appeared over a rise, a quarter mile behind them.

The war whoop was so chilling that Tom, who had never heard it before, was aghast.

"Go! Go! Ride for all you're worth!" Josh shouted at the top of his voice. "Forget the draft horses! Leave them behind!"

Tom and Josh kicked their horses in the flanks and screamed at them, dropping the ropes to the draft animals. Their mounts seemed to sense that they were in real danger. They broke into wild gallops and raised great clouds of dust in the dry soil as they barreled down the road. If Josh had thought that leaving the draft horses behind would placate the Indians, and that was really what they wanted, he was utterly mistaken. They were after scalps.

For over four miles the race continued. At times Josh thought that they were gaining and leaving the savages behind. But no. After a while the distance between them closed a bit, and the Indians came within a few hundred yards of them. The war cries were harrowing, giving them chills. Josh knew that soon the Indians would be shooting arrows, and their aim could be deadly. Further flight was not wise.

Josh shouted at Tom, "Ride on! I'm going to hold them off, if I can!"

At the same time Josh leaped from his horse, grabbed the Brown Bess from its case as fast as he could, and raced to get behind a tree, from which to fire at the marauders.

Tom was bewildered. His mind raced. Of course he thought of flight from there. But he couldn't leave Josh behind to try to fight off these Indians by himself! That would be the worst kind of cowardice he knew of, even if there was only one gun between them.

Tom leaped down from his mare. Bursts of adrenaline tightened his belly.

The savages were bearing down on them, screaming the war cry as they came, waving bows and tomahawks in the air. Even from a distance, Tom could see the red, blue, and black war paint that covered their faces. He was petrified, never having experienced anything so hideous and scary before, and he took cover behind a tree next to Josh.

Loading the musket as quickly as possible, Josh raised it to his shoulder and seemed to fire in the same motion. He had aimed at the lead Indian, but the motions of the Indians' horses made them difficult targets, and Josh's shot missed.

On they came, readying their bows to fire arrows as they got within range.

Calm and determined, Josh was a model of steadfastness as he rapidly ripped a second cartridge open, primed, loaded, rammed and raised the Bess to his shoulder, aimed and fired a second time. The Indians were somewhat closer and better targets.

This time the bullet found its mark in the chest of the Indian on the right, and his war cry changed to a shriek as he fell to the ground.

Still the other two came on, waving their tomahawks and screaming the war whoop. Since the rate of fire for an experienced handler of the Brown Bess was three or four shots a minute, and six were possible under favorable circumstances, again Josh took the gun, loaded it, and fired. Again his aim was accurate. A second Indian was hit, in the shoulder, but he remained on his warhorse, which skidded to a halt. The savage tottered to the ground, flinging his tomahawk as he fell, dead.

Coming close now, the third Indian took his bow and, from his mount with great accuracy, shot an arrow at Josh. It hit him in his side, and his eyes went wide with surprise. A dark red stain flowered across the side of his shirt. He staggered, screaming with pain, blood spurting from the wound as the arrow stuck out from him. He toppled over. Tom rushed to Josh and, in the clarity of fury and fierce determination, grabbed the musket. He quickly went through the loading procedure he remembered, raised the gun, and fired at the head of the last Indian, who was aiming another arrow.

How he did it he could not tell for years afterward, but the bullet went to the forehead of the savage, and crashed through his skull. He was dead before he hit the ground.

Tom knelt by Josh's side, ripped open his shirt, examined the wound, and was horrified. The arrow had opened a large hole in Josh's side, just below the rib cage. Very carefully, Tom attempted to extract the arrow, and after a minute the arrowhead and the broken shaft came free. Taking their shirts, Tom made bandages and tried to stanch the blood, which was flowing freely. He wrapped one long strip of cloth completely around Josh's torso, to hold the other bandages in place, and pulled it tight. That seemed to work somewhat.

But there was so much lost blood. And the wound gaped so wide. Could Josh survive?

FOUR

In the Middle of the Night

Joshua Morris was losing so much blood from the wound, Tom feared he might be near death. What to do? The nearest place of help would be the Hunter's, for they had gone only a few miles down the road. Tom determined that he must get Josh there, as quickly as possible. He knew that, literally, he held Josh's life in his hands.

Josh was barely conscious, but Tom explained, "This is what I want to do, Josh. We must go back to the Hunters' house. Since they know us, they'll be glad to help. I know you can't sit upright on your horse, even for a few miles. So I think the best thing is for you to bend over your horse, with your belly cradled in the saddle. That won't be comfortable, but honest, Josh, I don't know what else to do!"

In great pain, Josh grunted, "All right. Do what you think best." He groaned and was close to passing out. Tom almost wished he would lose consciousness, for then he would not feel the pain.

But he was not light, and it was all Tom could do to boost him up and over the saddle, since Josh could do little to help. However, the pressure of the saddle helped to stem the flow of blood. The trip back to the Hunters' house took nearly an hour, for Josh's horse could not travel at more than a fast walk, with Tom leading from his horse. Any faster travel would be too painful and dangerous for his friend.

The miles seemed to stretch endlessly. But eventually they came to the clearing where the Hunters lived, and Tom shouted and called from a distance to tell them they were coming. Mrs. Hunter appeared at the door of the house, and Glenn Hunter and his children came running across the field, knowing something must be wrong for Josh and Tom to be returning so soon.

"Indians attacked!" Tom yelled, and the Hunters called out their horror, as they came and crowded around the horses. Glenn Hunter gently lifted Josh down and carried him inside the house.

Amy Hunter said, "Put him on the large table. Children, get some candles for more light." The best one to treat illnesses, she unwound the bandages and examined the gaping wound. When she saw the seriousness of it, she drew back with a gasp, then tried to hide her concern from Josh.

"Quick!" she commanded, taking charge. "Everyone can help here. Glenn, you and Tom stand by me. Put Josh's head on a roll of cloth. Children, fill the kettle with water and put it on the fire to boil."

With dexterity and a certain amount of experience, she cleaned the area, making sure all parts of the arrowhead and shaft had been removed, sterilized the wound with the methods of the day, and applied her medications. Josh lay still as she worked, half conscious, and tried not to cry out from the pain. Then Mrs. Hunter decided to call a conference with her husband and Tom as to how to proceed.

They gathered out of Josh's hearing. Amy Hunter said, "The problem, as I see it, is that this large wound should be stitched up so that it will heal properly and stop the bleeding. A bandage alone won't hold well and close the wound. But I'm not experienced in stitching large injuries in skin, and there's no doctor for miles from here who could do it. What do you think?"

Glenn gave no quick reply. His eyebrows went up, and he made a guttural sound and pursed his lips. "Right. You're not a doctor, but you *have* healed all of your family, and some neighbors, when they were sick. *And* you're a very good seamstress, Amy. You have needles and thread. Is sewing up skin so very different from sewing cloth? What do you think, Tom?"

Tom was as reticent to reply as Glenn, but he said slowly, "If stitching is what's necessary, Mrs. Hunter, and if you can do it, then I don't see any other way. I say go ahead."

"Then it's decided," Mrs. Hunter said. "I'll do my best. You two stand by to help." She gave Josh some liquids to dull the pain, then talked with him for a few minutes, explaining what she was about to do, telling him it would be painful, but no worse than what he had endured already. She gave him a clean rolled-up cloth to bite on when the pain was at its worst, and then she went to work with her needles and suture. When Mrs. Hunter was satisfied she had done all she could, she bandaged and bound up the wound with strips of cloth. Josh was carried to a bed. He was trying not to groan, and after a while he did manage to drift off to a troubled slumber.

Tom sank into a chair, totally exhausted, as he tried to recount what had happened. However, he hardly needed to tell; it was all quite apparent.

<hr />

Those voices were coming to him again, since he had broken into Hiram Prescott's shop and attacked him, and left his threatening note. For the last month he had heard the voices only occasionally, and they were muted. But now they were more insistent. And they were saying the same thing he had heard many times before: since he had been cheated by others all his life, and he had every right to take his retribution on them.

He had tried to talk to his only daughter, who lived three miles from him, but she seemed more and more distant. Was she frightened by him? He hoped not. After all, she and her children were his only living relatives, and he needed some companionship, someone who could try to understand him. He needed to tell her, as he had often, of the voices and what they were saying to him.

Her children were frightened by him also. When he came to their house, he would smile and put his arms out to greet them, and they would run from him, their faces frozen in fright. If he sat for a while in their little shack, he thought that the children might get used to him, realize he wasn't leaving soon, and would eventually lose their fear and come to him. But no. They cowered across the room.

His daughter thought that he badly needed help, knowing his mental condition, but to whom could she go? The doctor who lived in the next town? But any doctor would ask for money if she took her father to him, and she had very little of that. And she knew that a doctor might be good at treating diseases, but could he do anything when a person's *mind* was sick? He, like other professional people, might simply declare that *demons* were tormenting her father. Or the doctor might say her father was insane, and what could he do about that? Should she go to the pastor in the town? She knew pastors did not want to be paid and sometimes worked with people who did strange things like her father did. But she was almost ashamed to go to this godly man, because she never went to his church, or any church. And so she did nothing, merely hoping it would all go away.

But it didn't. And the coming of winter wasn't helping.

It was already dark on this cold, windy night when he left his daughter's house and stumbled three miles to his own little cabin. An early snow was coming down heavily now, almost blinding him. His shoes were tattered, there were holes in the bottoms, and as he stumbled along, his feet were wet and almost frozen. Here and there he collided with tree stumps in the dark or almost fell over tangled vines. Thickets of bamboolike cane rose higher than his head, and he trudged on, pushing his way through them. Occasionally he became confused and lost his way, but then, consulting the stars and locating the Big Dipper or something else in the heavens, he was able to get his bearings.

Finally, after an hour and a half, he arrived at the cabin. The voices were coming on strong now.

Hurt them! They have hurt you, again and again, haven't they? You have every right!

By this time the snow was several inches deep. He was exhausted, and he opened the sagging planks that served as a door, went inside, and closed the door. A sudden blast of freezing wind blew through the single, small window, lifting the loose hide that covered it, and showering the small room with a spray of snow. He went to the window and stuffed more rags against the hide. Then he threw himself down on the pile of straw that was his bed, pulling the tattered blankets over him. Soon he was going to do something, he promised himself.

ഋരു

Josh Morris was making a slow recovery. At first Mrs. Hunter was extremely worried that infection would set in to his wound, but her primitive antiseptics, combined with his youthful vigor, worked. It took several days until the pain diminished sufficiently and he was able to get up off the bed and begin to walk a little, and it was four weeks before Mrs. Hunter felt it was safe to remove all the bandages. Josh was still pale and weak from loss of blood, but he was determined not to be an invalid any longer than he had to be. He felt that he had healed sufficiently to be able to travel.

Josh and Tom were sitting outside the Hunters' home on a cold afternoon. Tom had been helping Glenn Hunter in the fields all morning and was taking a break.

"I'm feeling strong enough to ride my horse," Josh said, "and I'm totally bored sitting around not doing much. We shouldn't impose on these good people any more than we have to. They have been extremely gracious to us, tending to my injury and caring for me all through my healing. I think we should leave."

Tom nodded in agreement. "I agree, if you think you're up to it. They have housed and fed us and put up with crowded conditions in a house that's already too small."

"Yes, and there's something else. It's late November, and a snowstorm could hit at any time. We don't want to be caught in that."

Tom laughed. "Are you eager to get back to our beloved master Duffy?"

"Now don't make me laugh, or my wound will hurt. But you know that he's concerned; he's saying, 'Where are they, and where are my horses?'"

"Right. By now he could be putting out notices that we're runaways and offering a reward to anyone who captures us."

So, determining that Josh would ride as comfortably as possible, they were ready to set off. The two draft horses had been recovered, and Tom insisted that they pay the Hunters something for all the food and care they had given. There was some money left over from what they had originally paid for the draft horses, so Tom gave it to Glenn Hunter, who reluctantly accepted it.

With many thanks to their hosts, at two in the afternoon Josh and Tom set out for Carlisle. They made frequent stops, especially when Josh felt pain or was tired. Knowing the mare was a more docile animal than the stallion that Josh had been riding, they switched horses.

By five o'clock, they had made several stops to allow Josh to rest. It was getting dark and cold, and time to make camp for the night. They had seen plenty of wildlife in the last several hours. Raccoons, foxes, beavers, and several herds of deer had crossed their path and seemed to resent the intrusion of humans in their native domain.

Coming to a small glade surrounded by poplars and aspens that were bare of leaves, with a small river nearby for water and to allow the horses to drink, they decided this was a good spot for camp. In her usual considerate way, Mrs. Hunter had provided them with enough food for their trip back to Duffy's, and Tom cooked some of it for their evening meal.

After tending to the four horses, and making sure the Brown Bess was at hand, loaded and ready to fire, they prepared to retire, spreading out their bedrolls near the fire, and keeping some of their warm clothing on. Tom fed more wood to the fire so it would burn for a time and also keep curious animals away that would be foraging for food. Josh, exhausted, was soon asleep, his soft breathing coming at regular intervals. Tom watched his friend. After the Indian attack and Josh's severe wound, his recovery had been remarkable.

Soon Tom also was asleep.

"Where have you been?" Duffy thundered as they rode into his yard. He swore and raved for three minutes, giving them no chance to explain. "You've been gone well over a month! I gave you up for dead, or runaways!" Then, unable to think of anything more to rant about, he looked at the two draft horses they were leading, went and examined them thoroughly, could find nothing to criticize, seemed satisfied, and calmed down somewhat. Tom quickly took the opportunity and led the four horses into stalls and gave them their feed.

"It's a long story," Josh said simply, when he had the first opportunity. "Everything happened that could have happened. Here is the change from the money you gave us to buy the horses." He gave Duffy some coins.

Duffy looked at the coins, counted them, and his countenance lightened. "You bought them for that amount of money? And they're very good animals!" Uncharacteristically a bit chagrined, Duffy said, "Perhaps I was too hasty in misjudging you both. Why don't you come into the house, and we'll talk about what has happened to you. Have you had dinner?"

Entering the home, Catherine Duffy and Louisa were delighted to see Josh and Tom again. "You haven't eaten for a while, of course," Catherine said. "I'll fix something immediately." She went out to the kitchen and soon returned with steaming plates of mutton, sweet potatoes, carrots, and apple pie.

As they ate, Ishmael, Catherine, and Louisa gathered around to hear the story. When they came to the Indian attack, the women were horrified, and Ishmael Duffy asked Josh to lift his hunting shirt and show them the wound. "It's not that I don't believe you, you understand," he said apologetically.

When Josh pulled up his shirt, the women gasped, wide-eyed. Catherine's hand went to her mouth in horror. Although it had been weeks since the attack, and the wound had largely healed, the four-inch long scar was still an ugly red. The scar tissue was in a ridge that was raised a bit above the surrounding skin, showing the stitches that Amy Hunter had put in.

"Oh, that's terrible," Catherine exclaimed. "Did it bleed much?"

"A great deal," Tom said. "The wound was quite deep. I was afraid Josh might die from loss of blood. He might have, if the Hunters' home had not been fairly close. Mrs. Hunter was excellent. She cared for Josh night and day."

"I'm asking Doctor Carruthers to come over and examine you immediately!" Catherine said. "Louisa, go to the doctor's home and ask him to come, right off."

When Louisa had gone, Duffy said, "And may I ask, how many Indians were there, and what happened to them?"

Tom answered, "There were three of them, and they went to the happy hunting ground."

༺༻

Whenever they had time, both Hiram and Andrew Prescott continued their search for Tom, despite having to run their shop. They were both convinced that Tom must be somewhere not too far away, since Ben Franklin had told them what he knew of the episode.

Andrew had more time than his father and, being younger, more energy to expend on the search. He determined to make still another tour of eastern Pennsylvania, and this time he went as far as Lancaster on his horse. While Lancaster was still a small town, it was on the main route that multitudes, especially Germans, were taking as they forged westward across Penn's Woods, seeking good fertile farmland.

Seeing a church that was newly built, Andrew wondered if the pastor was about, and as he walked to it, leading his horse, a man in a black suit came out the door. Andrew went to him, introduced himself, and the man smiled broadly and said, "I'm the Reverend John Dylander. I am a Swedish Lutheran pastor at Wicacoa, and I come here as often as I can to minister to these people, who don't have a clergyman as yet. Another pastor, Peter Tranberg of Christina, also comes here to serve them."

Andrew was intrigued by this man, because Wicacoa was sixty difficult miles away, and to come here often demanded dedication. "You speak English well, Pastor," he said.

Dylander laughed. "You must be a true linguist to deal with all these people. When I am here, which is not every Sunday, I must preach sermons in three languages: German at eight in the morning, Swedish at ten, and English in the afternoon. And then I baptize in all three languages as well, and also conduct marriage ceremonies—and bury the dead! Among the places where I minister the Word of God, I frequently find myself preaching at least sixteen sermons a week. Now, where is your home?"

"In Chester, near Philadelphia, and I wanted to ask you: have you heard of a man who may live nearby named Ishmael Duffy?"

Dylander thought for a while, pursing his lips. "No, I don't believe I've heard that name. Perhaps the sales people in the general store might be able to help you." He indicated a building down the street.

"I'll try there," Andrew said. "May I ask, what is the state of religion hereabouts, Pastor?"

"In this area, it's very rural, and so the religious life is quite mixed. But back at Wicacoa, where my church is, the Awakening is underway, and people are turning to the Lord in numbers that I haven't seen before. I believe great things are going to happen, and I'm very encouraged by it."

Andrew thought for a minute. He had heard of the revival that was beginning in eastern Pennsylvania and other places, and he knew that his own pastor was preaching for an Awakening. He was very curious, so he asked, "Tell me, Pastor, are you an *enthusiast?*"

Dylander looked somewhat shocked. His eyebrows arched, and he responded, "You should know it is a serious charge to suggest that someone is an enthusiast. Do you know what that means?"

It was Andrew's turn to be unsettled. "Uh, no, I've heard that term used, but I don't know—"

"My friend, don't use that word lightly," said Dylander. "That word is *never* used with a good connotation. Especially in England, they are immersed in a stress on *reason* alone, and any expression of emotion is frowned on as being *enthusiastic*, which to some means about the same as 'fanatic.'"

This was all new to Andrew. He pondered it. "Well, are there many 'enthusiasts' around, since revival is beginning?"

Dylander said, "I haven't met any! Just because a person gets excited or joyful or sad at a game or a funeral, does that make him an enthusiast? Religion also can make us a bit emotional, but I hardly think that makes a person an enthusiast. I suppose every human activity has a few of those who go too far. But simply to slander a person as an enthusiast in religious circles is enough to classify him as a weird character incapable of reason and on the brink of lunacy."

Andrew was a bit startled by all this new information from the pastor. Dylander was obviously a dependable, sensible person, and no fanatic. And he was very much in favor of the Awakening.

"God bless you, son," said Dylander, and they parted.

Tethering his horse outside, Andrew entered the general store. This was much larger than the other buildings around it, and like most of its kind had hides, small barrels, huge hogsheads, and boxes of assorted goods stacked outside the front door. The smells inside the store were rich and pungent, from the variety of goods carried. The air was perfumed with the rich scents of tea, spice, candle wax, soap, oils, tar, coffee, and the odors all mixed together. There were a number of people in different parts of the room, mostly men, talking with salespeople and examining goods for sale. After a few minutes a man came over to Andrew and asked if he might be of service.

"Yes, I'd like half a pound of cheese, a loaf of your best bread, and a small crock of honey."

While the clerk went to get those items, Andrew looked around the store. Against one wall was a large open hearth with firewood blazing, keeping the store moderately warm. In a few minutes the clerk returned bearing the food, and Andrew said, as he paid for them, "May I ask a question? I'm searching for my brother, and I wonder if you might have heard of Tom Prescott, fifteen years of age, light-colored hair, about five feet, eight inches tall. He was indentured by mistake to a man named Ishmael Duffy, but we do not know where this man lives. Have you heard of my brother, or know of this Duffy?"

"No, I don't believe so," the clerk said. "But let me call over Mr. Coyle, our owner. He knows people for miles around." The clerk went to summon the owner.

A short, bald man with a large, bushy gray beard and mustache to match, soon approached. "Good day, sir. I understand you are looking for someone?"

Andrew went through the description again, and Coyle rubbed his bearded chin, searching his memory. "You know, now that you mention it, there was an advertisement in *The Pennsylvania Gazette* sometime back. I didn't recall the lad's name, but when I read the advertisement, I remembered that I had met a man not too long ago by the name of Duffy."

"You did?!" Andrew was startled because he had asked this question so many times, and had never received such an answer. "Do you know anything about him? Do you know where he lives?"

"Let me think...where did I meet him? Ah yes, now I remember. He came in here from somewhere out west, looking for farm equipment. Said there weren't any stores west of Lancaster that stocked what he wanted. We do have a wonderful line of equipment for farmers, you know."

"Yes, I'm sure you have," Andrew interrupted, "but don't you have any more information about him? Did he buy anything?"

"Indeed he did. I think he purchased a plow, and some other items as well. We have a fine line of plows. Can I show you some?"

"Not now, thanks. Would you have a record of the sale?"

"Oh, yes. We keep complete records of all sales." He went over to a high wooden desk that had many books piled upon it, looked them over, and selected one. Then he flipped through it, saying, "Duffy...Duffy...let me see now...ah yes! Here it is. Seems he lives at quite a distance. West of the Susquehanna River, in the village of Carlisle."

"Are you sure? Carlisle?"

"Well, no, I can't guarantee it's the same Duffy you're looking for. 'Duffy' is a fairly common name, you know. But I think this is the only person by that name who has dealt with this store for a while. Took the plow and the other items with him. Good thing. We don't deliver that far out."

Andrew was so delighted he could have taken this man up in his arms and danced a Highland Fling with him. "Thank you, thank you, Mr. Coyle!"

Excited beyond measure, Andrew dashed out of the store, forgetting the cheese, bread, and honey he had purchased. As he was mounting his horse, the sales clerk came running out of the door carrying the items in a burlap bag, calling, "Sir! Sir! You paid for these already!"

"Oh yes. Thank you," he said as he took the package. Now where to go? Should he go directly to Carlisle? Or should he go back to Chester to get his father, and the two of them go to Carlisle together, in the wagon?

Chester won out. He had only the one horse. If he found Tom, they would need a wagon. Oh, his father would be so thrilled at the news!

※

The first signs of spring were slow in arriving. As Hiram and Andrew Prescott drove their wagon across Penn's Woods, the breath from the horse came as clouds of steam being puffed from its lungs into the chill morning air. The sigh of the wind in the trees was mournful, and the day was overcast and dull.

Hiram and Andrew were leaving the town of York and would soon be within a few miles of the town of Carlisle. To their distress, the sky was beginning to darken with rain clouds. The rain had been threatening all day, and its smell was in the air. A strong wind had arisen, riding on the edge of the approaching storm, and gusts of dirt were being whipped up, causing little vortices of dust to swirl along the road. The wind began to lash through the trees, ripping off small branches, and occasionally a larger limb, and throwing them everywhere. Within a few minutes, the entire sky became an ugly violet-black, and the first rumbles of thunder could be heard coming from the distant mountains.

Andrew and Hiram drew their coats up over their necks, and pulled their hats down tighter on their heads, in feeble protection against a downpour. They hunched down on their seat in the wagon and knew that they were going to be drenched. Should they stop, try to throw some cover

over the poor horse, and climb under the wagon for some slight protection? The horse was very restless, stamping and snorting and rolling its eyes, frightened by the oncoming thunder. Hiram decided to continue on for a bit farther, hoping to find some shelter. It would be dangerous to park the wagon under a tree, for that would be an obvious target for a lightning strike. Better to tough it out in the open during the storm, bad as that might be.

The storm moved closer as the wind howled. Then the lightning broke, and the thunder crashed in a loud explosion overhead. Up ahead the two men saw a middle-aged woman bent against the wind, trying to cross the road, holding her long skirts up. She was attempting to get to her house, a log cabin by the side of the road, before the storm hit.

At that moment a man emerged from the front door of the home, as this woman dashed inside. He rushed over to the two in the wagon. "You have no cover. Storm's here. You'll be soaked. You look like good people. Why don't you come inside my home till the storm is over? And run your horse and wagon around to the stable in the back."

"That's a wonderful idea," Hiram said, and the two men jumped down. Heavy drops of water started to pound on them. As the rain began to fall in earnest, jagged forks of lightning sliced across the black heavens above the mountains, thunder grumbling a few seconds later. Andrew quickly took the horse back to the stable, unhitched it from the wagon, tried to calm it as best he could, and tied its halter rope firmly to a rail. Then he and Hiram went inside, behind the owner of the house.

An enormous crash of thunder rent the air, with a brilliant flash of lightning that struck not too far away. The owner slammed the door shut, and said, "Just in time!"

"Your hospitality is much appreciated," said Hiram as he introduced himself and Andrew.

"And my name is Horace Wilcox, and this is my wife, Annie."

"We would be happy to meet you at any time, but especially now!" Hiram said, laughing.

Wilcox was in his fifties, slightly shorter than Hiram, with a barrel-shaped torso. He had lively brown eyes and a mop of wavy brown hair turning gray. He invited them to sit down before a roaring fire in the hearth, and within ten minutes his wife brought cups of tea. After they had discussed the violence of this storm and told them where they lived,

Wilcox said, "That's a distance! And would you tell me the reason why you have come into our part of the country? I know you are not from around here."

Andrew smiled. "May I ask, how did you know that?"

"Very simple. Your clothes. They are the clothes of people who live in cities, not rough clothes like we wear on the frontier. And your boots. They are sturdy enough, but still are not the type of boot worn here."

"Yes. Dead giveaways, I'm sure," said Hiram. "I'm a shoemaker, Horace, and I make all types of shoes and boots. I do admire the sturdy kind of footwear that you have, but in the towns of Chester and Philadelphia they would look a bit out of place, I'm afraid."

"Not fancy enough, I suppose?"

Hiram laughed. "I guess that's right. Not fancy enough for city folks. They like their shiny brass buckles and high polish on the leather. At any rate, to answer your question, we are here looking for my son Tom, who came from England last summer. We were to meet him and my daughter at the ship and pay for their passage, but we were delayed, and they did not have the money to pay. The ship's captain didn't know what to do, from what I can guess about this, and he allowed Tom to be indentured to come up with the money. And we believe that a man from Carlisle was the one who bought Tom, and has taken him here."

Wilcox's brows knit together. "Do you know this man's name?"

"Yes. Ishmael Duffy."

"Ishmael Duffy?" Wilcox exploded, half rising off his chair.

"Well!" said Hiram. "From that I take it you know Duffy?"

"Know him?! The blackguard. Yes indeed, I know him. Not that I want to. Duffy's one of the most miserable men I know of in this region. He cheats, and he lies. He cheated me in a deal a year ago, and I know others hereabouts who have been cheated by him and who hate him."

Hiram and Andrew were astonished and angered to hear this, and there was silence for a minute as they digested it. Then Hiram said, "You know, perhaps that explains about Duffy being here in Carlisle. He apparently told the ship's captain that he lived close to Philadelphia, but we searched everywhere in that area and could not find Tom. Then Andrew was in a store in Lancaster. And by chance this Duffy had purchased some things there, and left his address—Carlisle."

Andrew said, "I was astounded to learn that. Carlisle is hardly close to

Philadelphia. It's a hundred miles away! Certainly the truth is that Duffy didn't want us to locate Tom. It's as simple as that."

"Exactly," said Wilcox. "That's this fellow all over. A trickster. Now, what do you intend to do?"

"To pay Duffy what he paid to indenture Tom, and release him."

"Do you think he'll accept that? Obviously he values your son as a laborer, and it might be difficult for him to find another. He'll not give in easily, I tell you. That's not in him."

"I don't know what else we can do," said Hiram.

Wilcox was mulling this over in his mind. "You know, now that I think about it, I've heard that there are *two* young men working for Duffy on his farm. I suppose one of them is your son. I don't know who the other fellow is."

"May I ask, how far is Duffy's farm from here?" Andrew said.

"Oh, about five miles, I'd say. On the other side of Carlisle."

"Is it easy to find?"

"Oh yes. When you leave here, I'll draw you a map to find it."

Three hours later, the rain finally stopped. But as they surveyed the landscape, everything was totally drenched. The road, bad to begin with, was a quagmire. Enormous pools of rainwater were everywhere, especially along the road.

"It looks as if the rain has moved away. We have enjoyed your hospitality long enough," said Hiram. "We must be going."

"Oh no," said Wilcox. "You and your horse would be bogged down half a mile from here. You can't go anywhere tonight! It's getting dark already. There is no inn in Carlisle, so we invite you to stay for the night. Annie, we have enough dinner for our friends, haven't we?"

"Of course. We will enjoy your company. There's not much news we get out this far, so you can tell us what is happening. You must sleep here tonight, and then you can be on your way tomorrow morning. We have a spare room with a bed. It will be no trouble."

Looking at the travel conditions, Hiram realized that this was a wise course. Andrew went to the stable to feed and take care of the horse.

ℛℭ

The morning dawned clear but cold. Annie Wilcox prepared breakfast for her husband and the two Prescotts, and Horace had more to say about Duffy over the eggs, cornmeal muffins, and tea.

"Hiram, what's your strategy going to be, when Duffy *refuses* to release your son from his indenture?"

"What else can I do but plead with him?"

"You might as well be prepared for the worst. I know him: no matter what you offer to pay, you'll get nowhere."

"Then I suppose I must cross that bridge when I come to it."

Wilcox put his elbows on the kitchen table and assumed a look of determination. "Now listen, Hiram. Take my advice. I have a bit of a personal stake in this myself. And so do a lot of others around here, who've been cheated by Duffy. When he throws you off his property—as he will, I tell you—come back here and make this your headquarters for the time you're here."

What could Hiram say to that? So, after agreeing to Wilcox's offer, they left for Duffy's farm with the map that had been drawn for them.

As they came up to the farm, Andrew and Hiram found a large fence constructed of horizontal boards all around it. They located the gate and went in.

Off in the distance two young men were working in a field. They approached and recognized Tom. His father ran to him, calling out his name. Andrew followed. Tom looked up and dropped his hoe. "Dad!" he shouted. Then he ran toward Hiram and Andrew. Hiram threw his arms around Tom and hugged him. There was a minute where words were inadequate. Then, "It's so good to see you, son. We have looked everywhere for you! Are you all right?"

"Oh yes, Dad. I'm fine. And Andrew!" He grabbed his brother, hugged him, and they shook hands vigorously, slapping each other on the back and laughing hard out of sheer joy.

There was a general catching up of what had happened for some minutes, and Josh came over, smiling. Tom introduced him to his father and brother.

"Dad, I have to tell you, when this man Duffy took me out here, I knew you'd look for me. You must know that I wanted to contact you, and let you know where I was. I knew you were somewhere around Philadelphia, and I wanted to send you a letter—smuggle it to you, if I had to—but I didn't know where you were in Philadelphia, and that's a big city. I couldn't just address it *Mr. Hiram Prescott, Philadelphia.*"

"Of course not, Tom. You did nothing wrong."

"And I want you to know that Josh here is a fine friend. He's indentured too. We've been through a lot together in the last six months."

They turned to Josh, who was standing by, patiently waiting. Hiram said, "Do you have a family near here, son?"

"No, I have parents and a sister back in England, but I indentured myself to come over here."

Tom looked toward the house with some concern. "I think that Duffy will see you and be out here to find out who you are. Before he comes, let me show you where Josh and I sleep. Do you see that addition to the right of the house? That's where we are at night. And there's an outside door to the shed, so we don't have to go through the house."

Hiram knew exactly what Tom meant. He said, "I will offer to pay to redeem you, but I very much doubt he will accept that. So we'll have to leave money to pay him off, to keep us honest, and take you with us tonight. Tom, are there any vicious dogs that roam the ranch at night?"

"Yes, there are two watchdogs, but they will be asleep in the barn." Tom laughed at their plotting. "When we feed them this evening, we'll put something in their food that will make them sleep like babies through the night. How would that be?"

Hiram said, "Is this fellow Duffy as bad as we hear? How have you been treated, son?"

"Bad. When he first got me, he was terrible. He's a tyrant, he lies, and he made Josh and me sleep in that miserable barn, and never let us come inside the house to eat or anything else. He has lightened up a bit recently, and now we sleep in the shed alongside the house. We do all the work here. We must take care of all the animals and work on all the crops. But his attitude toward us still is that we're almost no better than slaves."

"And what does Duffy do around here?"

Josh looked at Tom, and they laughed. "Nothing."

Hiram asked Josh, "You have been here longer than Tom, Josh. Do you agree with what Tom said?"

"Oh, absolutely. And I could tell you much more of his cruelty."

Hiram gritted his teeth. "I'm sure you could. Josh, how much did Duffy pay for your passage over?"

"As I recall, it was seven pounds."

"And Tom, how much for you?"

"It was also seven pounds, which I believe is the standard payment for passage."

"Josh, we want to take you when we come for Tom. If Tom goes and you stay, Duffy will take it out on you. Will you go?"

"Absolutely. That will be wonderful. I'm so grateful."

"You're sleeping in that shed?" He pointed to the house, and they nodded. "All right. We'll be back after midnight. And make sure the watchdogs are having good dreams."

Just then a man came running from the house, carrying a musket. "And who might you people be, disturbing my workers, may I ask?!" He swore at them and raised the musket in their general direction.

Hiram turned and said, calmly, "I take it you are Mr. Duffy?"

"What if I am? This is my farm. What are you doing here? Get out!" he screeched.

Hiram extended his hand, offering to shake hands with Duffy, who sneered at it. "I am Tom's father, Hiram Prescott, and this is my other son, Andrew."

"Oh!" said Duffy, anger building in his face. "And what do you want with him? He's legally indentured to me, you know! For four years. There's three and a half years to go. Indenture papers all signed and sealed legally. I understood from the captain of the *Annabelle* that you didn't come to pay for his passage, and so I paid it. That's your failure. Now he's my farmhand, and you can't do anything about it." He shot them a look of contempt and defiance.

Andrew's fists coiled and uncoiled. He would have liked to strike this miserable jackass.

Hiram tried to keep this talk civil and maintained his composure and a calm voice, though inside he was seething with rage. "Yes, you are correct, Mr. Duffy. I agree it was my failure to get to the ship on time to pay for him. We were detained unavoidably and didn't know exactly when the ship would arrive. So you had a perfect right to pay for him, and I appreciate your doing that. We got there later and found that Tom and the ship had gone."

"So what more is there to say? Now begone!" Duffy uttered some blasphemies and pointed to the gate in the fence, across the fields. Glowering fiercely, his jaw was set in a way that brought his lower teeth to dig into the flesh of his upper lip. Meanwhile he continued to swing the musket in their direction.

"Well, Mr. Duffy, if you will listen to reason, may I pay you what you paid for Tom, and free him? You've gotten seven months of work out of him, but we can just let that go. I'll pay you every penny you paid, so you'll be well compensated—"

"Certainly not!" Duffy shouted, his face purple. "I've paid for him, and I need him on my farm. Now I told you to get out!" He pointed the musket directly at Hiram's chest.

The man was far beyond reasoning. Further words were impossible, and they knew that Duffy might actually fire the gun at them, as trespassers. They gestured good-bye to Tom and Josh and walked across the fields toward the gate.

At one the next morning, the moon was intermittently appearing from behind the clouds, and when it did, it cast a pale luminescence across the fields. But mostly the clouds covered it, and then the night became dark indeed. This was exactly what Hiram Prescott had hoped for. A chill wind blew, and the two furtive figures, hardly more than shadows, drew their coats up around them as they crept toward the log cabin. They had come in their wagon but had left it a quarter-mile away and walked the rest of the distance.

Andrew and Hiram had come prepared. In their afternoon visit, they had noted carefully that from the front gate to the cabin, there was a well-defined pathway that led under some trees, and had hedges on either side. Across this path, a foot above the ground, Hiram now stretched thin wire from a tree on one side to a tree on the other side, and secured it tightly. While he was doing this, Andrew climbed one of the trees whose limbs were directly over the path. On a sturdy limb he placed a small barrel he had brought, balancing it carefully. Then he ran another wire down to the wire below.

That work completed, they approached the door of the shed behind the cabin, as silently as ghosts. Andrew gave it a little shove, and it opened, the hinges squeaking slightly. Inside the room, Tom and Josh were waiting anxiously, their few belongings stuffed in cloth bags.

Whispering, Hiram said, "Let's meet outside...less chance of being heard." They went around to the far side of the cabin, and he asked, "Are the watchdogs asleep?"

"Oh, they're having wonderful dreams, Dad. They won't wake up till dawn—and maybe not till noon." Tom chuckled.

Hiram whispered to Josh, "You're coming too, right? I will leave enough money for Duffy to pay for both of you—fourteen pounds."

Josh was exuberant. "I will repay you later. But I'm only too glad to come with you!"

"But Dad, fourteen pounds!" Josh said very quietly. "That's far more than enough, because Duffy has already gotten a year or more of work out of Josh and half a year out of me."

"Shhhh," Hiram whispered, as he laid the money on a rock where it would be seen, attached to a note to Duffy he had previously written. "Let's get out of here, before we're discovered. But follow us carefully, and we'll show you where to walk."

Silently, all four disappeared into the night.

But they had been detected by Duffy. Suspecting that Hiram and Andrew might return, he was waiting inside the cabin, listening for the door hinges to squeak, which he knew would happen. Taking his musket, he came around the cabin and began to follow them down the path, moving along as silently as they were. He would be within his legal rights to shoot them as trespassers. And he intended to. The trees overhead made it too dark to see the four, but Duffy knew they were ahead on the path, going toward the front gate.

At least, he *thought* they were on the path.

Their eyes accustomed to the dark, Hiram and Andrew carefully guided Tom and Josh *around* the outside of the path, avoiding the stretched wire.

Seventy feet behind the group, but *on* the path, Duffy moved along, ready to fire the musket. Pitch dark, he could see nothing, but he knew the path very well. Suddenly he tripped over something, and as he went sprawling, his trigger-finger, caught in the musket's trigger guard, was pulled backward. The musket went off with an enormous *boom!*, which reverberated over the fields. As Duffy flopped on the ground, he was completely unprepared for the gooey stream of molasses that poured onto him from the bucket on the limb overhead, dumped when the wires were tripped. Then, when the bucket was empty of molasses, it brought the final indignity by dropping and crashing onto Duffy's head.

"It worked!" Andrew chortled as they dashed for the front gate. "It was perfect!"

"Oh, so *that's* why we had to go around the path," Josh said, laughing.

"Come on, let's get out of here! The wagon is over this way," Hiram shouted. They were running.

FIVE

What the Future Holds

After leaving Ishmael Duffy's farm in the middle of the night, the three Prescotts and Joshua Morris stopped briefly at the home of Horace Wilcox, who was waiting to hear the outcome of their meeting with Duffy. When he saw Josh and Tom, he and his wife were elated. Horace promised to spread the word of the payment and Duffy's behavior far and wide, so that Duffy could not charge the Prescotts with being thieves, and not paying for Tom's and Josh's indentures.

Then they traveled in their wagon thirty miles or so to the town of York. Dawn had arrived, and they stopped at a wayside inn to rest the horse and themselves, to have some breakfast and feed the animal. Moving on, they came to the Susquehanna River at Marietta and waited for the arrival of the small ferryboat from the other shore.

In a few minutes the ferry came to the dock on their side of the river. It was little more than a flat raft about thirty feet long with rails along both sides, having a donkey on board for motive power. To keep it from being swept downstream, it was attached to a strong rope that went through pulleys on each end of the boat. The rope was tethered to a tree on either side of the river, and so the boat ran back and forth without having to be turned around. Another rope was attached to trees on both sides of the river. This rope was wound around a windlass that was turned by the donkey that walked on the treadmill.

"It's quite a system, isn't it?" said Josh as he inspected the windlass. "Very clever."

"Yes, and it's well worth the fare," Tom commented. "The river is far too deep and swift to swim across. I wonder what people did before a ferryboat was put here?" Tom asked.

"For the most part, they didn't get across!" Hiram answered. "It was pretty much Indian country, so you see, the frontier has moved west about thirty or forty miles since then."

When the ferry came to the opposite shore, they led the horse and wagon off and jumped aboard, Andrew and Hiram on the seat and Josh and Tom sitting in the rear on the floor.

After a few minutes, Tom asked, "Do you suppose Duffy will try to follow us? He'll be plenty angry!"

"Yes, certainly angry enough," Andrew said, "but he doesn't know exactly where we live. He may look all over Philadelphia, but we'll be in Chester, fifteen miles away."

"And," said Josh, "he can't easily leave the farm. Now that we're gone, if he leaves, that means only his wife and Louisa are there to do all the work. He had a hard enough time when he was the only man there, and we had gone west to get the draft horses. No, he'll stay there."

☙❧

When they arrived in Chester, Susan came running out of the front door of Hiram's shop, throwing her arms around Tom. "Oh, all of us have been so worried about you," she said, fairly dancing for joy. "When you went down the gangway with that Duffy, I thought I might never see you again, Tom!"

"I wasn't so sure I'd ever see you again, Sis." He took her up and twirled her around, then gazed at her. "And look at how you've grown since then." Everyone laughed, and Tom said, "I've got another surprise for you. Susan, meet this handsome young fellow, Josh Morris." Josh blushed and shook hands with Susan, who looked him over, obviously approving what she saw.

In the next hour, Hiram found that again his apprentice, Ephraim Cooke, had done a good job keeping the shoemaking business going during Hiram's nine-day absence. Indeed, he had sold so many shoes and boots that the stock needed to be replenished. Ten pairs of shoes had been sold, and Ephraim had used his time well in cutting leather, sewing parts together, polishing and doing the other tasks necessary. Hiram inspected his work and noted that his helper was learning his craft well.

If Tom and Josh were going to live with him and Susan and Andrew in Chester, as Hiram wished, he had to get busy rearranging his home to make room. Fortunately the house and shop were large enough to allow for that. On the first floor there was a storeroom that could be emptied, its contents consolidated with another half-empty room. When furnished, that would do beautifully for Josh. On the second floor there was an unused room that, again when furnished, would do for Tom. The two newcomers were delighted with the accommodations. Furniture was found, blankets and linens gathered, and the young men moved in.

Now that the episode with Tom's indenture was concluded, Hiram was able to relax, go back to his trade, and help Andrew prepare for his wedding to his beautiful fiancée, Sarah Godfrey. This was scheduled for May, and preparations had been made for months. On an evening a few days later, Hiram was in his favorite chair in the large sitting room, before the hearth. Tom entered the room.

"Is everything satisfactory, Father?"

"Sit down, Son. I'm pleased that you are with me now, and I have my daughter and both of my sons here. You're able to be part of the joy over Andrew's and Sarah's wedding. But oh, I have to tell you, how I wish that your dear mother were here also! My great mistake, I suppose, was in not bringing all of you with me when Andrew and I came over four years ago. Then we would have been together."

"But any of us could have contracted the smallpox then, just as Mother did on this voyage."

"Yes. You're right. There was plenty of the pox on the ship I came on. A number got it, and died then, and had to be buried at sea, just like your dear mother." At that, Hiram broke down and sobbed.

<hr />

It took a few days for Tom and Josh to accustom themselves to freedom in America, since both of them had been indentured as soon as they departed the ships they had arrived on. Freedom was wonderful! Ishmael Duffy had been such a miserable master and had treated them so harshly that it took them some time to try to erase their memories of the man, and the conditions under which they had suffered.

They had no regrets about what they had done. They would miss

Louisa and Catherine Duffy, but life on the frontier, with all its dangers and hardships, was not to be desired. To turn his mind to more positive thoughts, Tom had been wondering about Josh's comments on the Awakening that was beginning. In addition, Tom had seen stories of the Awakening in several newspapers. And Josh had said that he had been converted just before he came from England. Tom was curious about all this, and since he had come to Chester, he'd been attending church with his family, and reading the Bible. But he knew something was missing.

On this clear April day, the fellows were walking on the banks of the Delaware River, near Hiram's home. The day was overcast and cool, with a light breeze coming from the river. The air was damp, and it looked like it might rain before long. Trees and grass had begun to respond to the throb of spring in the ground, but they knew the river water was cold, not far above freezing.

Without any preface, Tom turned to Josh and said, "Can we talk about spiritual things?"

Josh's brows went up. "Of course we can. You mean about faith in Jesus Christ, right?"

"Yes. One day in Carlisle you said you wouldn't be much of a friend if you weren't concerned about my eternal salvation. That really got me thinking. I can confide in you, Josh. I don't know where I'm going to spend eternity. And I do care about that—very much. Back in England, I didn't go to church much. But since we've been here, going to Pastor Caldwell's church on Sundays, I've been faced with my uncertainty about salvation. The rest of my family are Christians, I know, and last Sunday after church the pastor asked if I was a believer...and I couldn't answer yes."

They came to a fallen log by the riverbank, and sat down on it to talk. "Look, my good friend," Josh said, "I'm glad you're concerned about this. So many people just go through life, fiddle-dee-dee and la-de-da, sure I'm going to heaven, they think! Why wouldn't I go to heaven? They say, I'm a good person, aren't I? What's all this Jesus stuff, dying for sinners? I'm not a sinner! I've never killed anybody, they say. And yet they commit sins all the time. And they go to a Christless eternity, because they're blind to scriptural truth. It's so upsetting to see how people take heaven for granted."

"I know. Will you lead me in accepting Christ as my Savior?"

"Tom, you can't know how happy I am to hear you say that. It will be the greatest privilege I can have. Saving faith is so simple. All you have to do is pray to Christ, acknowledging that you are a sinner, like everyone else, and asking Jesus to come into your heart and life, and make you His child."

They prayed, and talked for hours, with Tom accepting Christ as his Savior, to his great joy. "I feel so liberated, Josh. First I've been redeemed from Ishmael Duffy, and now I've been redeemed from Satan! Redeemed from *two* enemies!"

☙❧

George Whitefield was born in Gloucester, England on December 16, 1714. His eyes were dark blue, with a squint in one of them. His hair was brown, over a high forehead, and he was above average height. He graduated from Oxford University, and was ordained in the Church of England by the Bishop of Gloucester, Martin Benson, who was deeply troubled by the immoralities and low tone of the age. He recognized Whitefield as a preacher of extraordinary abilities and insisted on ordaining him at the unheard-of age of twenty-one, on June 20, 1736, waiving his own rule that twenty-three was the minimum age for ordaining clergy.

Whitefield had a power in the pulpit that was attractive to people who came increasingly in large numbers to hear him, in London, Oxford, Gloucester, and Bristol. Wherever he traveled, news of him spread by word of mouth, and crowds came out of nowhere, far too big for any church to hold. They became almost frightening in their intensity and size, making officials fear they might turn into mobs. But Whitefield learned to control his hearers, and they were mesmerized by him, rarely creating trouble.

There was another problem. At that time, most English clergymen thought of Christianity as being confined within church walls. They could not understand, as Whitefield saw clearly, that many people would never enter churches, but they might be reached by going *outside* of the churches to influence them. Too often the clergy were simply unconcerned with common folk, whereas Whitefield was determined to preach the Gospel to everyone. Coupled with his power as a preacher, he used a much-admired dramatic talent to act out his sermons, making them come alive, with suspense, humor, and pathos, in ways that audiences had never heard before. He was a spellbinder, and he knew it.

In addition, numbers of ministers were jealous of his popularity, and were prohibiting him from preaching in their churches. Some bishops especially considered him and his close friend John Wesley as disruptive and troublesome—and possibly as *enthusiasts*...that dreaded term. As his choice of ministry, Whitefield decided to go to Georgia as a missionary, to follow up where John Wesley had previously failed and returned to England. As he grew in experience, Whitefield depended not only on his skill as a speaker but also learned the value of press coverage of his activities, and the wisdom of having his many sermons published far and wide. Before Whitefield left for Georgia in December 1737, he had forty-six of his sermons printed, and they were reprinted both in England and America for years. Newspapers in both places reported on his activities, making him an international celebrity.

Among the most needy of people, Whitefield felt, were the coal miners, who were known as violent and ignorant, horribly grimy, dirty men who were outcasts from decent society. In the coal-mining region of Bristol, England, on February 17, 1739 this twenty-four-year-old minister took the decisive step of preaching in open fields, standing on a wagon. Would the miners listen to him, an unknown to them? He timed it as several hundred miners were at the end of their long workday, coming up out of the mines. As they emerged, their eyes adjusting to the sunlight, a loud voice called them to him.

"I want to tell you a wonderful story, told by Jesus!"

Catcalls came from a few miners; he ignored them.

"There was once a man who had two sons, as some of you have. The sons were growing up, and the younger son said to his father, 'I want to leave—it's too boring around here! Please give me the inheritance you're leaving to me now, so I can go and have some fun somewhere else.'"

Whitefield threw up his hands, asking, "Now, was that a wise thing to do? You know it was very foolish of the father, as the lad would certainly waste the money and soon have none left. But the father was persuaded to give the son his inheritance. The boy immediately went off to a country as far away as he could get. There he made many new friends, because he had *money*. These new friends cared nothing for him, but were always looking for *dupes* like this lad, whom they could suck dry with 'riotous living,' as God's Word says. And he had women and liquor. What do you think happened next?"

Whitefield was watching this tough crowd carefully. Most were intrigued, partly because no other clergyman had ever bothered with them. Several called out, "He spent all his money and went broke!"

"My good friends, you are correct!" Whitefield said in his booming voice. "And *then* where do you suppose were all of those new friends?"

Others shouted, "If he was broke, they left him!"

"Correct again. Well, spendthrift folly became destitution. This prodigal had to get some money. He sold his donkey, just to feed himself, but that money was soon gone also. No more parties! And his fine, expensive clothing was soon falling into rips and tatters. What had happened to his boasted freedom? Gone! He had experienced it all. What was left of his life?"

The crowd of several hundred was with him so far. These rough-and-tumble men were curious; this was a good story—very true to life. Some of them had prodigals who had run away from home. This preacher seemed to care about *them!* Those who were hecklers were quiet now.

"In desperation, our young fellow tried to get a job. He was a Jewish boy, and he found a Gentile farmer who hired him for hard work on the farm. But the farmer sent him to feed his *swine!* Now, you know Jewish folks don't have anything to do with *pigs,* so this was an unspeakable degradation for a Jew, bringing utter shame. Making matters worse, a famine came, and the lad was so hungry that he longed to eat the pigs' food. This was terrible food, garbage! Slop! The pods of the carob tree, used for feeding swine in Mediterranean countries. Soon the lad was starving.

"Then Jesus said, 'When he came to himself...' That is as divine a word as any from the lips of the Lord Christ. Alien from God, we are alien from our true selves. The lad came to his senses. He woke up to reality! He said, 'My father's servants have plenty of food—and I'm starving! Oh, what a perfect fool I have been! I will arise and go to my father, and say, Father, I have sinned against heaven, and before you, and am no more worthy to be called your son. Make me one of your hired servants.'"

Whitefield continued to watch his audience. They were getting the point powerfully.

"Jesus did not make light of sin. He showed its tragic consequences with terrible accuracy. The boy resolved to cast himself on his father's mercy, and ask forgiveness. He ran home, across many miles, constantly rehearsing his speech, 'Father, I have sinned....' But the father was already waiting for his beloved son, knowing that someday he would return. From a distance the father saw him, ran to him, kissed him, and would have none of the speech. He said to his servants, "Bring forth the best robe, and put it on him, and kill the fatted calf...For this my son was dead, and is alive again!"'

This parable had gotten to the tough crowd. No one moved. And no one dared ridicule.

Whitefield continued, "Who is the 'prodigal' in this parable? It is the entire human race—it is I, and it is *you!* Who is the 'father'? He is the picture of God, the most winsome picture ever drawn on earth! This parable is the heart of the Gospel. God is eager to forgive you completely of your sins."

A voice called, "Pastor, God wouldn't want *me.* I've done every sin a man could do."

Whitefield shouted, "Oh yes, God wants you. Christ's blood can cleanse every sin—even yours."

Many were shedding tears, and the tears made white rivulets down their coal-blackened faces. From that point, Whitefield invited these hardbitten men, most of whom had never been in a church, to come to Christ. Grateful that this pastor cared about them, many responded to the invitation. This bold move, preaching in the fields, proved to be the beginning of the revival in England's West Country. Across the south of England, the Awakening was attracting tens of thousands everywhere, with Whitefield drawing vast crowds wherever he spoke.

On June 1, 1739 in London, preaching in Hyde Park, he was able to speak to an estimated 80,000 people. And all this without any amplification—just his natural, incredibly powerful voice. He wrote, *It was, by far, the largest I ever preached to yet.*

As Whitefield came down from the speaker's stand in Hyde Park, exhausted from the ordeal, he was met by a young man elegantly dressed, and about the same age as Whitefield. "Do you remember me, sir? I am William Seward, and we have been together several times in the past."

"Of course I remember you, Mr. Seward! It's so good to see you. How are you? And how are your parents?"

"All of us are well, thank you. May I ask, are you lodging near here? The reason I ask, you see yonder my carriage, and it is yours to command, if I may take you anywhere."

Whitefield saw, two hundred feet away, beyond the departing crowd, a handsome gentleman's carriage, with two liveried footmen on the front box. Seward came from a wealthy family and had taken Whitefield to his preaching engagements several times in the last year. He had declared that he was a Christian and was so impressed with what Whitefield was doing that he wished to place his fortune at the evangelist's disposal.

෨෦෬

In the days that followed his arrival in Chester, Josh thought much about what occupation he wanted to pursue. He was eager to repay Hiram Prescott for the money paid to Duffy, and that came first in his priorities. But he also had to consider his entire life. Josh was beginning to entertain ideas of going to college and getting a degree, and perhaps becoming a schoolteacher, or something similar. Several friends had told him that he was qualified for that, and he showed real interest in it. He considered the three colleges in existence in America—Harvard, Yale, and William and Mary. If he was hoping to enter a college next fall, now was the time to choose the college, make application to it, begin saving money for the expenses, and otherwise prepare by studying various subjects. Josh asked to help in the shoe shop for a time, while he considered his options, and Hiram was glad to take him on, temporarily. And Josh also worked around the town of Chester for any employer he could find. In this way he accumulated some cash to repay Hiram.

Tom also sought work throughout the town. He had determined that he did not wish to become a shoemaker, like his father and brother. While the shop had an extensive clientele of people from miles around, it did not need any more help on a full-time basis. But Tom was frustrated in his search for meaningful work around Chester. There was not any type of employment in this small town that intrigued him or seemed to offer permanent work for him.

Hiram and Andrew were hard at work as Tom came into the shop on a weekday afternoon. For another day he had scoured the town.

"Son, you look discouraged," Hiram said, laying down his thread and awl.

"I am, Father. I can't find anything here that offers me steady employment. There's only a handful of shops in this town to begin with, and they're fully staffed. All the owners know you well, and they say that any son of yours would be dependable, but they don't need any help."

Hiram nodded. "I've been asking around myself, and I know what you are saying."

"And in addition no craft here really interests me. I want to learn a craft that I enjoy!"

"Of course you do, son." Hiram thought for a while, then said, "Why don't you go to Philadelphia and look around? I've been thinking about this. Every business conceivable is there. And I would be sure that the firms there need workers more than we do here."

"You wouldn't mind if I went that far away?"

"Philadelphia is only fifteen miles off. That's not far. You could get a room there, and come home every Saturday, and spend Sunday here. You're sixteen years old, able to strike out for yourself. There is a coach that departs for the city every morning and goes back and forth all day long."

"And there, with a good trade, I could earn enough to repay you soon!"

"Son, save your money. You will need it to rent a room and pay for your food and clothing. As for repaying me, you need never do that. Your love repays me abundantly."

Tom went around the worktable and hugged his father.

Arriving in Philadelphia by coach the next morning, Tom was a bit awed by this city. He had seen it from the deck of the *Annabelle*, but as soon as he stepped on the wharf from the ship, he had been whisked off to the countryside by Ishmael Duffy. Tom knew William Penn had stipulated that his "Green Country Towne" should be well planned, with wide streets, but other than that, Tom knew next to nothing of it.

He stood on the corner of Second and Chestnut Streets, holding a bag with some clothes and belongings, looking north to the large red brick Court House, where the coach had deposited its passengers. He gazed about, trying to get his bearings. Tom had eaten a substantial breakfast before he left home, so that was not a problem. Should he walk around the entire town, attempting to locate as many important spots as he could, so he would know his way about? Perhaps that might be a good start.

Second Street was a residential neighborhood, with substantial brick-front homes, clean and well kept, he saw. There were no sidewalks, and the street was unpaved, as were all the other streets. Tom saw that whenever a horse with rider or a coach came along, since it had not rained recently, a cloud of choking dust was raised, and he imagined that in rainy weather the streets would become quagmires of mud. Occasionally a lady with a gray bonnet, or a man with a flat hat and sober dress would come along, and Tom recognized this clothing as belonging to Quakers, who were very numerous here. He had been told that there were two or three Quaker meeting houses, and these lacked any ornamentation.

Tom reached Market or High Street, the chief commercial thoroughfare, which had a long market shed running along the middle of the street. People were patronizing the numbers of stalls and storefronts along it. He had not seen such congestion since he left London. Despite the width of the street, it was thronged with wagons, horses, and pedestrians.

And there ahead of him, towering over the street, was the magnificent church edifice he had seen from the deck of the ship: Christ Church, the center of Anglican Church activity in this city. While he had seen its architectural splendor from the ship, quite equal to anything in most cities, he had not been close enough before to note the fine Palladian window that fronted on Second Street, the eight banks of beautiful windows on the long red brick sides of the church, and especially the detail on the white steeple that towered above the city. It spoke volumes of the city's prosperity.

SECOND STREET North from Market St. & CHRIST CHURCH, PHILADELPHIA.

He continued on Second Street, noting the types of businesses that were along it. He came to Elfreth's Alley, a street of neat little homes with windowboxes out front that would be spilling flowers in another month. Tom knew he should search for a suitable place to lodge. Down the street he saw a sign hanging out from a building, announcing The Pig and Whistle Tavern. A Quaker approached, appearing pleasant.

Tom stopped him. "Sir, would you tell me, is that a good place to stay?"

"Strangers do indeed stay in that place," the man replied, "but not the sort a decent fellow ought to share a table with."

Well! Tom certainly did not want to risk staying in a hostelry that might be inhabited by thieves and cutthroats! He cringed at the thought.

Did Philadelphia harbor many despicable characters, as London did? He had assumed that this city had respectable people! Tom said, "I thank you for the warning. Do you know of a better inn?"

"If thee will come with me, I will show thee a place that good people approve of. It is called the Crooked Billet, and it is on Dock Street, next to the river."

Following the Quaker to this inn, Tom thanked him, entered, and told the proprietor that he needed a place to stay and would take his meals there also.

The owner looked him over, wondering about the youthful, beardless age of this person. He did not wish to turn a paying customer away, but this lad might be a runaway, he thought, and without funds. There were runaways coming to the big city. They tended to be slick and crafty; he had dealt with some of them previously, and they had tried to steal from him. "Laddie, do you have money?" he asked.

"Certainly!" Tom said, somewhat insulted. He had a mind to say, "Do you think I'm a crook? That I'd want to accept your hospitality, and cheat you?" But he curtailed those thoughts, smiled, and pulled from his pocket some large coins. "You see?" he said, with a large smile. "I'll even pay in advance."

"Oh! Yes, fine," the proprietor said. "I take it that you are new to our city?"

"Yes, sir. I live in Chester, and I'm looking for work here in Philadelphia."

"I see." In all likelihood, this fellow would be a good guest for some weeks. The owner's attitude changed immediately; this lad did not appear to be a thief. He was well dressed and clean, not scruffy with tattered clothing, like the runaways. He may not be a runaway, but he was likely a naïve young fellow and open prey for sharp operators to take his money. The owner decided to have some concern for Tom, and said, "We do have a room on the second floor that you would share with two honest gentlemen. The charge for the room and meals by the day is two shillings and six pence."

"But don't you have a room for one person? I'm sure the gentlemen are fine and honest, but—"

"Hmm. Don't you know, the usual practice in inns is for several men to sleep in the same bed?"

Tom's father had told him about this common practice, but he wished for something better. "Don't you have a room just for one person? I can pay!"

The proprietor scratched his bristly chin. "Yes, I do have one quite small room. One shilling, nine pence a day for room and meals."

So Tom was led to a room on the third floor that was even less than quite small, with a tiny window on one end looking out over the harbor, and one narrow bed and a chest of drawers. "It's perfect for what I need," he told the owner. He deposited his clothes in the room, excused himself, and went downstairs to get a meal. When he had eaten, he went out into the city, looking for a job.

He went first to a candle maker's shop. No, they had all the help they needed. Then to a butcher's. Then to a dry goods store, and a bakery, with the same response. On and on to a dozen shops. Tom was getting a bit discouraged. His father had said that Philadelphia would need workers. Was he wrong?

Coming to a park with some trees just beginning to bud in the early spring, Tom sat upon a bench.

His head down, he contemplated what he should do. He couldn't go back to Chester—that would admit defeat. Besides, he had paid for his room and board for several days in advance.

A wagon went by, its wheels making much noise and raising a cloud of dust. He looked up and saw a new sign, down the street. There, on Market Street among the other bustling businesses, was a sign reading B. FRANKLIN, PRINTER. *THE PENNSYLVANIA GAZETTE.* A printer. Well, that might be interesting work.

Going to the shop, Tom gazed through the front window for a moment before going in. He could see several men busily setting type from a handwritten text, putting the cast-lead letters in rows in a metal holder, in forms that would make the lines of printed text.

At the back of the shop two men were operating the flat-bed press, a machine six or seven feet high, having two heavy vertical pieces of wood uprights supporting a large table between them. Over this table and between the uprights was the press, a metal screw pushing down on a flat metal platen, the screw being turned by a large lever. Underneath the platen and on the table was a flat piece of stone about two feet by two feet. The metal type was locked, image facing upward, in the large rectangular chase, corresponding to the printed pages, and the chase was placed in the coffin, which sat on rails of the horizontal carriage above the flat stone. Ink was applied to the type, and a dampened sheet of paper was placed between the tympan and frisket hinged to the coffin. Then the coffin was slid under the large platen of the press. When the screw was turned by the lever, the platen descended and pressed the paper against the inked type, and the image was transferred from type to paper. Then the platen was raised, the paper withdrawn and hung up to dry, and another sheet inserted for the process to be repeated. When the last impressions were made and the ink had dried, the sheets of paper were cut into their separate pages, which were then collated and bound.

Fascinating, Tom thought. *Most interesting. I might like to run that press.* He entered the shop and asked to see Mr. Franklin.

Tom was taken to an office at the back of the shop. Mr. Franklin was sitting at a desk, cutting a new quill in preparation for writing. His long brown hair hung down over his shoulders, and he was gazing intently at the feather he held that was being shaped, his brows knitted in thought. When Tom was brought in, Franklin looked up, smiled briefly, and sat back, flexing his shoulders. "Yes sir, what can I do for you, young man?"

Tom introduced himself and explained his errand. Franklin studied him and said, "It so happens, this business is growing so rapidly, I could take on another man. Let's discuss this."

They went from the office into the shop, and he explained what setting type was like and asked Tom if he was dexterous with his hands. Tom responded that he thought he was. Then he asked Tom if he was strong enough to swing the bar on the press, and answered this by saying, "That's a foolish question. I can see by your build that you have developed a manly frame."

Then something occurred to the printer. "Just a minute, young man. What did you say your name was?"

Tom repeated it, and Franklin said, "Hmm." Then he went out of the shop and returned a minute later with a nine-month-old copy of the *Pennsylvania Gazette.* Flipping through its pages, finally Franklin located what he wanted and said, "Ah ha, here it is. I thought that name rang a bell! Have you seen this?" He handed Tom the newspaper, pointing to a particular part.

Tom read the advertisement that Captain Higgins had placed in the previous August. "I'm found!" He laughed. "Did anyone ever claim the reward from you?"

"No, but I would ask if the advertisement was of any value in locating you?"

"Yes it was, Mr. Franklin. It was the clue that opened the trail to me. My brother Andrew tells me a storekeeper in Lancaster had read it, and recalled the name Ishmael Duffy as one of his customers. That led him to find me."

"I'm very happy the paper was helpful. Is it only a coincidence that you come here, asking for work? Well, with that history, I guess I can't help but hire you. Also, your sister, Susan, has been minding my sons. Come, let's discuss your pay and the working hours, and I'll introduce you to your new coworkers."

In early May, as the climate warmed, trees and bushes were beginning to bud. In this lovely time of the year, the long-anticipated wedding of Andrew and Sarah took place. It was conducted by Pastor Caldwell of the church in Chester where the Prescotts belonged. The church was crowded with well-wishers, and everyone remarked that Sarah was a radiant bride. Tom had asked for a leave of several days from his work in Ben Franklin's printing shop, and this was quickly granted. He served as his brother's best man, with Susan acting as the maid of honor.

The next day, after all the festivities, Tom took the coach back to his job in Philadelphia. The wedding had been a welcome interlude, and he left Chester somewhat reluctantly.

Tom Prescott had tolerated the Crooked Billet Inn for over a month, with its mediocre food and his tiny room. Then he decided to look for better accommodations, and he found them on Race Street in the home of Mrs. Kirkpatrick, a widow. She took in boarders, and offered Tom a garret just under the building's roof that had a minuscule window looking out onto the street. It was low-raftered, and there was only room for the bed, a chair, and an upright chest with four drawers, whose top held a lamp and a tray with some glasses and a pitcher of water. But Mrs. Kirkpatrick was a kindly older lady, and her price for the room and two meals a day was what he had paid at the Crooked Billet. She grew fond of Tom, and asked if she could bring a small vase with some red roses from her garden to brighten the room. The room was just what Tom was looking for, and he moved in without delay.

Tom was having an enjoyable time working for Ben Franklin in the print shop. He was learning from the other workers how to set type, run the press, and do the hundred other things associated with a printer's shop. In addition Franklin's wife, Deborah, took a liking to Tom, as Mrs. Kirkpatrick had.

He was busily setting type for a printing job when Deborah came down from their upstairs rooms. "I hear, Master Prescott, that you are getting to know our fair city. Do you like it?"

"Oh yes, Mrs. Franklin. In the times that I have off from work, I have been walking around, and I find it to be beautifully laid out, and quite clean…err…except for the dusty streets, that is."

"You know London, I've heard. How does it compare?"

"In many ways, very well, ma'am. Of course London has more shops of various manufactories, since it's such an old city, but I think in time Philadelphia will have them too. And I have to say, London's streets are much dirtier than here."

※

At that moment Ben entered the room from his office. "Ah, my dear! And good morning, Tom. How are things going today?"

"I'm quite happy, Mr. Franklin. I've just moved from the Crooked Billet Inn to a boarding house on Race Street." He gave Franklin a broad smile. Tom appreciated Franklin's concern for his welfare, and he knew it was sincere, as they had taken good care of Susan when she stayed with them.

"Ah yes, the Crooked Billet, on Dock Street. Do you know, Tom, when I was about your age, and had just arrived from my parents' home in Boston, with three large rolls in my hands, that I spent my first night in this city at the Crooked Billet? I recall it well."

Franklin mused for a minute on those memories of his arrival from Boston, and his conflicts with his parents and older brother. They were not his most pleasant memories. But Philadelphia had opened up vistas of promise and opportunity for him, and he had prospered in his new home, found a wife, done well in business, and become an appreciative citizen of his adopted town. He was, at thirty-one, a rising and increasingly important leader in the city.

Then, brushing aside the past, he said, "Say, I've just thought of some new maxims to put in *Poor Richard's Almanack:* 'He that lieth down with dogs shall rise up with fleas.' What do you think? Or, 'He's a fool that makes his doctor his heir.'"

"Hmph," Deborah said. "They're fair, I suppose. I think you've done better!"

A bit chagrined, Ben said, "All right. I'll try harder. And how is our son Billy this afternoon?"

"There's no problems, Ben. Mother is taking care of him, and I thought I'd come down to get a bit of fresh air outside, and also to invite young Tom to supper when you both are done for the day."

"That's a fine idea. Can you take supper with us, Tom?"

"Yes, it would be my privilege. It will be a pleasure to be with you."

Franklin smiled at the young man, so reminiscent of himself at that age.

At supper that evening, as the Franklin family sat around the table, a lively conversation began, as always happened when Franklin was present. Tom was eager to ask Ben some questions about the things he had heard Franklin was doing. And Ben was perfectly happy to talk about them.

"May I ask you, Mr. Franklin, about the Junto? What is that?"

"One of my favorite endeavors, Tom! About ten years ago I organized some of my more inquisitive friends into the Junto, a society that meets weekly and probes into scientific, political, and ethical questions of the day."

"And I've also heard that you began a large library here in the city," Tom said.

"I'm afraid I must take credit for that also. In 1731 I organized the Library Company of Philadelphia. It also is doing well, I'm happy to say."

"And isn't it true that just last December you organized a group of men into the Union Fire Company in this city?"

"Guilty again, my boy!"

"You know, Mr. Franklin, your apprentices talk about you." Tom smiled. "They say you do some amazing things, and sometimes the way you achieve them is to write articles in the *Gazette* using a name you made up, like this one." Tom took a page of the *Gazette* from his pocket and read:

> In the first place, as an ounce of prevention is worth a pound of cure, I would advise them to take care how they suffer living brandsends, or coals in a full shovel...for scraps of fire may fall into chinks and make no appearance till midnight; when your stairs being in flames, you may be forced (as I once was) to leap out of your windows and hazard your necks to avoid being over-roasted. Signed, A. A.

Tom continued, "Mr. Franklin, didn't you write that, to encourage the start of a fire company? And did you ever really have to leap out of a window?"

Ben was convulsed with laughter, and Deborah Franklin was laughing also. "Guilty again of the first charge, and innocent of the second! Yes, Tom, I have to admit that's a trick of mine, to make up letters about something I believe is for the public good, and invent a name to stick to the end of the letters to make it look as if others are urging it. Isn't that an innocent trick?"

"I suppose so," Tom answered. *This man is amazing. He has so many projects, and he's always thinking up more. I wonder what he'll come up with next?*

Ben interrupted to say, "I just concocted this maxim for the *Almanack:* 'Love your neighbor; yet don't pull down your hedge.' Or this one: 'Creditors have better memories than debtors.' Well?"

"A bit better than the last ones. You're improving," Deborah said.

Ben grimaced.

The lively conversation continued over the meal until Ben said, "Debbie, and Mother, and Tom, I have a bit of an announcement to make."

"Oh, Ben, what is it?" Ben's mother-in-law, Sarah Read, asked.

"Today I received by post a most interesting letter from Colonel

Alexander Spottswood, the governor of Virginia. He is also the postmaster-general of the colonies. You recall that my printing competitor here in town, Andrew Bradford, also runs a newspaper, the *American Weekly Mercury.*"

"You've never thought much of that paper, have you?" Debbie asked.

"Certainly not, Deborah. And it's not professional jealousy. But in his jealousy toward me, Bradford has done a miserable thing. Some time back he was appointed postmaster for this area, and that has attracted advertisers to his paper. But, in his capacity as postmaster, he has instructed all of his carriers *not* to deliver my *Pennsylvania Gazette!*"

"Why, that's outrageous, Ben! Bradford has used his postmaster position in a most unfair way!"

"He certainly has, my dear," Ben answered. "But at the same time, so typical of him, he has been keeping the post-office accounts in a slovenly manner. The accounts, I understand, are in a mess."

"In other words, Bradford has been running the post office about the same way he runs the *Mercury,*" his wife said.

"Precisely. Colonel Spottswood, down in Virginia, has learned of the situation and has just demanded Bradford's resignation. And Colonel Spottswood has offered the job of postmaster to me."

"Oh, wonderful, Ben!" Deborah said. And after a moment, "Doesn't this job pay a salary too?"

"Absolutely. It's not a great deal of money, but it will lift my newspaper business and give me the first view of news from England and around the world. I can find out what is happening elsewhere and print it, long before the other papers learn of those matters."

ഇരു

Determined to carry out the revenge he had promised to Hiram Prescott, on this warm night he again went the three miles from his cabin to the town of Chester. His hatred smoldered and drove him on. It was a night where the clouds were covering the moon and stars, a perfect time, he thought, where his deed could be shrouded by darkness.

It was past midnight when he entered Chester. Only in an occasional house was a light still burning, a faint gleam coming through closed shutters. This town was as yet too small to have street lamps. However, with their dim candlepower, lamps did little to alleviate the darkness.

He came up to the front window of Hiram Prescott's shop, and peered through into the workshop beyond. All was dark. He knew that Hiram slept upstairs, but he did not know that Andrew Prescott had recently married Sarah and moved to their own home, Josh had taken a room elsewhere, and that Tom was working and living in Philadelphia. Nor did he know that Ephraim Cooke, the apprentice, lived with his family. Only his daughter Susan was with Hiram.

His voices, angry and vengeful, began speaking to him again. Clenching his fists, he listened intently. *Go on! Do what you came to do! He's only getting what he deserves!*

Going to the side door of the house, he pushed a long, thin bar into the lock, as he had done the first time he had broken in. After working it back and forth for a minute, he heard the bolt slide back. Pushing the door open, he entered and listened carefully. No sound could be heard. The door that led to the upstairs steps was closed, so the chances that he would be detected were small. This time he did not try to look for the money that he thought Hiram kept.

His revenge was to be drastic. He had brought some loose paper with him, along with flints and wood shavings. Kneeling down on the shop floor, he quietly began to strike the flints to create sparks, and with them he set the paper on fire, and then the kindling. Getting dry wood from the stack next to the fireplace, he added it and soon had the blaze going. He put a wooden chair on top of the fire, and it began to burn quickly.

As the wood caught, bitter, acrid smoke billowed up and began to choke him, creeping into his chest and gripping his lungs, burning, keeping him from drawing a full breath. Soon the entire room was full of hot smoke.

He coughed, choked, and gulped as much clean air as he could. His eyeballs felt seared. It was time to get out, and quickly. Shadow and light were beginning to fuse together, and he blinked hard, the rawness of his eyes bringing tears that ran down his cheeks. He left the way he had come in, and went around to the front of the shop, to look through the front window. From across the street, he could see that the fire was covering half of the room. Soon the whole room would be an inferno.

He had his revenge.

SIX

The Curse of Slavery

Soundly asleep, Hiram and Susan Prescott had no sense of the danger on the floor below them. Their bedrooms were near the top of the stairs, and even with curls of acrid smoke drifting up, at first they slept on. Then Hiram half-woke with the smell burning in his throat. The smoke was so irritating that soon he was forced fully awake, gasping for breath, coughing and choking.

His consciousness returning quickly, Hiram jumped from the bed, and pulled on his pants, shirt, and shoes as fast as he could. In moments the smoke became thicker. He had to stop and cough, clutching at his throat. His eyes began to stream tears. He ran to Susan's bedroom, threw open the door, and shook her awake. The smoke was not so bad in her room, and she was not coughing as much as her father. Hiram told her to get dressed quickly, and then he ran to the stairs, telling Susan that he would be back in a minute.

As he got halfway down, it was apparent that the heat and smoke became stronger. There was an acrid and bitter taste at the back of his mouth as he tried to breathe, putting his arm across his nose. He stopped on the stairs, knowing what he would find if he opened the door to his shop. Heat seemed to radiate from the door. Should he open it? He kicked the door, and it opened enough to have flames flash from the shop, singeing the hair on his arms and almost burning his body and face.

Hiram was aghast. Much of his shop was on fire, a hellish orange vortex of flame, heat, and smoke. What to do? Escaping through the shop was obviously impossible. Risking serious burns, he slammed the door shut to contain the fire as long as possible, and dashed back up the stairs to the upper floor. By this time Susan was dressed.

"Darling, the fire downstairs is very bad," he cried. "We've got to get out through the upstairs window. Grab anything that's valuable. Quickly, sweetheart!"

Susan grabbed a number of things, and Hiram gathered some clothes, valuables, and money. These items were dropped out the open window to the ground below. Taking Susan by the hand, they went to the window and began to climb out. There was a tree growing alongside the house, with a sturdy limb that came close to the window. The drop to the ground below was about twelve feet. Hiram reached over to the limb, helped his daughter put her hands around it, and carefully helped her as she swung, unhurt, to the earth below. Then he did the same.

They began shouting to wake up his neighbors. "Fire! Fire!" Hiram ran to a horse trough full of water down the street, filled a bucket hanging there, and ran back to his shop. Looking through the front window, it seemed as if swirling flames had engulfed the entire room. He picked up a nearby rock, smashed the window panes, and threw the water inside. Then he used the empty metal bucket to break the rest of the wooden framework.

By then people from nearby houses were responding. In their nightclothes, men came shouting with buckets, running to the horse troughs in the streets to fill them and coming with water to Hiram's shop to douse the flames. The threat of fire was so real that they had mentally rehearsed many times what they would do if fire broke out.

The men with buckets of water kept coming, and when the troughs were empty, they ran to the nearby Delaware River. The sluicing of water began to contain the fire after a time, and eventually it was extinguished. Exhausted, Hiram went to a nearby home to rest from the ordeal.

As morning came, Hiram looked at the charred ruins of his shop, and his neighbors helped him inspect the damage. They determined that the building was still structurally sound. No major supports had been burned through, although the shop's ceiling had been majorly damaged in addition to the other problems. Everything, however, was repairable. As to his burns, they would heal in time. Hiram's shoe shop would be out of business for a long while, and all his new shoes were ruined, but he determined to rebuild and start again. Susan and he had managed to rescue most of his really valuable things before they tossed them out of the upper window. He had his good credit, and Susan was safe and well. He praised God that they had gotten out alive.

"Listen to this, Deborah!" Ben Franklin exclaimed to his wife. He was reading through the stack of newspapers from England that had just arrived on the ship *Essex*.

Deborah Franklin examined the piece of toast in her hand. "I would guess you found a news item that's of some importance and can be used in the *Gazette?*" She spread some honey on the toast.

"I think this is. My new postmaster position is paying off already. I told you it would! *Ha ha.* I'll get the drop on all the other papers! Soon the word will get around that Franklin's newspaper gets the British news first."

"That should make more people buy it. Well, tell me: what's this item that's so important?"

"The headline reads, 'Bishop of London Rebukes Cleric, and Cleric Rebukes Bishop.'"

Deborah's eyes widened in annoyance and disapproval. The piece of toast slipped from her hand, and the honey spattered on the table. Staring at her husband, she exclaimed, "Oh, Ben, what's so important about that?! I'll bet the old bishop is always rebuking somebody." She took a knife to scoop up the honey, and sniffed her impatience.

"No, no, my dear. You don't understand. This isn't about some local squabble in London. This concerns the young fellow who has been causing such excitement in various cities over there. He's only in his early twenties, but already he has become famous. His name is Whitefield, and he has been publishing sermons. The bishop has chastised him for not submitting them to him, and for going from one city or parish to another, without getting the bishop's permission. But what is causing such a stir is that Whitefield rebuked the bishop in public, and thousands heard it! My dear, that's just not done! The London papers are laughing about this."

"Hmm. I see what you mean. If this young fellow is becoming such a firebrand, maybe that is a good story. Yes, I think you should reprint it." She picked up her toast again.

By the Treaty of Utrecht in 1713 the British won limited trading rights in Spanish America, and the virtual monopoly of the slave trade. At the same time Britain contracted to supply the Spanish West Indies with 144,000 blacks during the next thirty years. But this involved much friction over smuggling. The ill feeling flared up when an English Captain Jenkins, seized by the Spanish revenue authorities, had one of his ears sliced off. The Spanish commander reportedly sneered, "Carry this home to your King, your master, whom, if he were present, I would serve in like fashion." Captain Jenkins wrapped the severed ear in a handkerchief, and when he got back to England, with a tale of woe on his tongue and the shriveled ear in his hand, furious resentment was aroused. However, far greater gruesomeness could be seen on the streets of London any day of the year. But with Jenkins, it was the symbolism and not the actual barbarism of the act that counted.

The War of Jenkins' ear, curiously named, broke out in the late 1730s between the English and the Spaniards. It was confined to the Caribbean Sea and to the buffer colony of Georgia, where the philanthropist-soldier James Oglethorpe fought his Spanish foes to a standstill.

The small-scale scuffle with Spain in America soon merged with the large-scale War of Austrian Succession. This was waged mainly in the Old World, although side-show skirmishes also occurred in the Caribbean and along the English colonial frontier in North America. Spanish warships were constantly sinking English merchant vessels or seizing their cargoes. All of this was a major problem for shipping from East coast ports from Georgia to Maine, and up into Canada.

A career captain with a ship had great difficulty in securing cargo and sailing safely under these conditions. He was at a distinct disadvantage in terms of income, occupation, and keeping a good crew. This was the problem Joseph Powner faced. His ship, the *Revenge,* was older but still sea-worthy. He had put every penny he had into buying the ship on credit, and he was deeply in debt. He had complained bitterly to Captain Higgins of the *Annabelle,* and many others, of his problems. Powner was a foul-mouthed, lecherous man of fifty years, thin and shorter than most men, with a spade chin and dagger beard, and a vulpine, swarthy face sporting a large mustache. His black eyes glittered like jet, and his pigeon chest thrust out like a challenge to all. He kept wives or concubines in six ports he occasionally visited.

But now he felt trapped. He had a crew of twenty-two, his money was running out, and he could not pay them. With nothing to do but sit in port, the crew was getting rebellious and threatening various unpleasant things to get their back pay.

Over his rum in the "Bull and Bear" Inn, on Tradd Street in Charleston, South Carolina, he was complaining to his friend Captain Ridderow of the ship *Nassau.*

"I haven't been able to get a full cargo for three months," Powner said, pounding the table. "I can't keep a crew, because I can't pay them. I'll soon lose my ship. Bertrand, what am I going to do?"

"Hah! Why don't you do what I do, Joe? Does your crew still trust you, and believe what you tell them?"

"Perhaps—to a point, I suppose. But they're ready to do something violent." Both Powner and Ridderow had been drinking for an hour. Their speech was slurring a bit, and their eyes glazing, but their minds were still alert enough to discuss the problem, as they could hold their liquor well.

"Look—here's what you do," said Ridderow. "Call your crew together and explain to them that, if they will trust you one last time, you can get some enormous profits, and all of them will soon be rich."

Powner drew his chair closer and stared intently at Ridderow. "Tell me more," he said, his mind clearing a bit from the alcoholic fog.

"First, load up your ship with any kind of trading goods. It doesn't matter what—cotton, molasses, or corn, or anything that you can sell later. I've been able to get my ship out of Charleston by sailing in the middle of a dark night. The Spaniards haven't caught me yet, and won't catch you if you do it right. Run straight to Africa. And pick up as many slaves as your ship can hold. Bring them to Brazil or Cuba or Barbados and sell them there, where they'll bring high prices. Then load up again with sugar and rum, and go through the routine again. That way, you may meet some Spanish warships in the Atlantic, but if you're smart you can outrun them."

Powner mulled this over for a minute and smiled broadly. "Brazil, eh? Sao Luis, maybe?"

"No reason why not. Slaves will sell there, as well as anywhere. Do you have friends there?"

"I have a wife there! Margarida. I haven't been there for a year. But she always waits for me."

"Then it's perfect for you. Now, when you sail to Africa, go to Walabo, on the west coast."

"Why Walabo? What's there?" He took another swig of rum from his pewter tankard.

"It's a miserable little African town owned by Portugal. Not much there, except slave traders, and plenty of slaves. Muslim Arabs collect slaves in the jungles, and bring them in chains to Walabo for easy shipment."

"You say there's good profits?" His eyebrows arched.

Ridderow leaned back and roared with laughter. "Joe, I'm rich! And all from the slave trade. There's huge profits! My crew wouldn't desert me now, for anything. They're very well paid."

"And the slaves are right there in Walabo? You don't have to go into the jungles to get them?"

"That's what I'm telling you. The Muslims get them out and put them in barracoons in Walabo. The slaves may be in the barracoons for some weeks, and they don't feed them much, so they're docile and weak by the time you get them out and load them on board. And the Arabs don't charge much for the slaves – maybe some shillings for the big strong men, but not much for the women, and almost nothing for the children. But when you get to Brazil or Cuba, or the swamps of Georgia or Carolina, you can get maybe twenty or thirty times that, if the place is in great need of slave labor. You can almost set your own price where they need slaves badly!"

Powner whistled with surprise. He had heard accounts of the slave trade before, but it had never been explained to him this clearly. His eyes widened, and he grinned evilly, greed taking over. He took another big swig of rum, then wiped his mouth with his coat sleeve. Letting out a few expletives, he said, "All right, Bertrand, I'm interested. I've got to get some money, somehow. As long as you think it's not too dangerous, and there's plenty of money in it, I'll round up my crew and explain it to them. Then what do I have to do?"

"You have to refit your ship to hold the slaves. The biggest problem would be a slave revolt, in the middle of the ocean, if some of them get free of their chains. So you have to get carpenters to build pens to keep them imprisoned till you get back to the Caribbean. Why don't you come over and I'll show you my ship? It's all been redone, and already I've made seven runs to Africa."

Powner rose, swaying somewhat from the effects of the rum. Steadying himself, he said, "I know where your ship is moored. Let me go and get my first mate, Jacobson. I want him to see your ship too. I'll meet you at your wharf in half an hour."

༄༅༄

The first mate, Jacobson, was more dissolute than Powner. A cruel man, when he heard this plan from the captain, immediately he envisioned the potential for profit and the power it would give him over the dozens of slaves he would have on board. His eyes danced at the thought of all this, and he uttered several blasphemies.

Coming to the *Nassau,* they found Captain Ridderow waiting for them on the wharf.

"Have either of you ever been on a slaving ship before?" he asked.

They indicated they had not.

"Then you probably will be somewhat surprised at what I'm about to show you."

When they went on board, they were not surprised; they were *shocked.* Whatever alcoholic haze they had immediately disappeared. Powner and Jacobson were men who were completely accustomed to the seamy side of life, with sailors who were rough and tumble, and much worse, and with seaports around the world which drew the dregs of humanity to them. And they were anything but upright themselves, despite the fact that they were men of some authority. So they thought they had seen everything.

But what they found on Ridderow's vessel, the *Nassau,* overwhelmed them. The slaves had been unloaded several days previously, and that was as well, because the sight of these pitiful beings would have accentuated their shock—if that was possible—even beyond what it was. The first thing to assault them was the overpowering stench in the vessel. It was simply indescribable. Powner gagged, and thought he could go no farther. But he forced himself, out of his great curiosity, holding his nose with a handkerchief. Ridderow took them to a ladder down to the lower decks. And there they got their first look at the place where the slaves were kept, crowded together in unbelievably inhumane and filthy, completely unsanitary conditions, with no provision for anything.

After a minute of this, Powner and Jacobson could take no more. Powner gasped to Ridderow, "I can't stand this. I must get up to the deck again, so I can breathe some good air." With that he climbed the ladder, Jacobson right behind him, and Ridderow last.

Because he could hardly talk, from a combination of choking, astonishment, and disbelief, Powner indicated by a wave of his hand that he wanted to get off this death ship. When they were back on the wharf again, he said to Ridderow, "Bertrand, how do you tolerate this? It's the worst thing I've ever seen, and I've seen plenty! How can you live on that ship for weeks at a time? I had no idea."

Ridderow laughed, because he had expected a reaction like this, and had his answers ready. "Oh, you get used to it. I know it's awful, but I just keep reminding myself of three things: first, of the huge profits to be made; second, that slaves have no souls—they're just beasts; and third, in a way, we do 'em a favor to take 'em out of the jungles, where they die early from diseases and warfare with other tribes."

Powner's eyes widened. "Bertrand, do you believe all that? What I've heard from you amazes me. Do you really think slaves are beasts, with no souls? I've heard slaves in Georgia singing and praying to God, and they seem to have souls and be sincere, just like free folks! And why do you think you do them a favor to take them from their homes? They were happy there, and didn't go voluntarily!"

Ridderow frowned. "Joe, do you really believe in the existence of a soul? A stupid, old-fashioned idea. There ain't no such thing as a soul. When you're dead, you're dead. That's all. Don't be so sentimental," Ridderow answered with a snarl. He cursed up and down for a minute. "I ain't never seen you so conscientious, Joe. Yeah, on my first trips to Africa I was upset too, I remember, but when the money began to come in, I soon forgot all that. Now, you want to get into slaving, or not?"

Powner looked hard at Jacobson, and they shook their heads. The memory was too recent. "Well, I dunno, Bertrand. Yeah, the money looks good. We believe what you say. But there's problems, too. It ain't that easy. My ship is old. I'd have to get carpenters to rip out my lower deck, and build pens like you've got on your ship. That'd cost a lot of money, and I ain't got any. Let me think about it."

In a voice that suddenly turned ugly, Ridderow said, "Well, if you want my help in getting started, you've got to be quick. My ship leaves tomorrow. It'll be a dark night, and I can get through without any Spanish warships seeing my vessel." Cursing and muttering, he turned away, furious and disgusted with them.

As Ridderow left, Jacobson said, "Maybe the Spaniards won't be able to *see* that ship in the dark night, but they ought to able to *smell* it from miles away, if the wind is right!"

In fifteen minutes, Powner and Jacobson got back to the *Revenge.* There they found a surprise awaiting them. The entire crew was gathered on the dock, looking angry. Phipps, a burly seaman who might have been the toughest of the lot, stepped forward. "Captain, I've been appointed by this crew to speak. You owe all of us a lot of back pay. You can't pay us. So we're leaving. Good-bye ." And with this, the men began walking away.

Powner looked at Jacobson with desperation. Then he shouted to the crew, "Wait a minute, men. Your first mate and I have a new plan that will give us plenty of money, if you stay with me. I'm going to turn this ship into a slaving ship, going to Africa. If you'll wait a few more minutes, me and Herman will explain the whole plan to you!"

Grumbling among themselves, the sailors came back, doubtful but willing to hear the details.

When the *Revenge's* crew heard the plan to turn the *Revenge* into a slaving ship, and the huge profits of the slave trade, they dropped some of their skepticism and became interested in the possibility of getting their back pay and having jobs again.

Captain Powner turned to First Mate Jacobson and said quietly, "Well, that's a first step. I was excited too, until I saw Ridderow's stinking tub. So were you. Then reality set in. What do you think of taking the crew to go aboard the *Nassau* and see the stink of it?"

"I wouldn't, Captain. On the way over to Africa, our ship will be clean as it is now, so they won't know what it will be like after one trip back. They'll find out soon enough what they will be living through. Let the men stay in their dream world, thinking of the profits they'll make."

"My thinking exactly," Powner said. He turned back to the crew. "Men, we must have our ship refitted to hold the slaves. I have to find carpenters and blacksmiths who can do that job, and when they come aboard, all of you can help. The ship has been idle here for weeks. Go aboard and clean it up. Mr. Jacobson will supervise."

He went directly to the *Nassau* and found Ridderow, who considered him angrily. "Well, have you decided that my idea is a good one after all?"

"Yes, Bertrand, I explained the possibilities to my crew, and they are all for slaving. I'd like to sail for Africa as soon as possible. Do you know how I can get my ship ready for holding slaves?"

Ridderow snickered. "Ha. I thought you'd see it my way sooner or later. Let's talk this over."

They went to the Bull and Bear, and over their liquor Ridderow explained the situation. "You saw the pens I have on my ship. That's what you'll need. And they've got to be strong pens. You need to understand thoroughly that eventually the slaves will break even the strongest bars and pens. If any of the slaves get loose during a voyage, they'll try to free other slaves, without you knowing what's going on belowdeck. When they feel united enough, they'll surge up onto the main deck and kill all of you. That has happened on several ships recently, so don't say I didn't warn you! Slaves must be kept chained at all times. Every slaver captain learns one thing right off—if they do break loose, the only thing you can do is shoot 'em dead."

"Right. I understand, Bertrand."

"As to getting the ship ready, you're lucky. I had the *Nassau* worked over right here in Charleston," Ridderow said. "First, we need to get the foundry in town to make iron bars and chains, and the local blacksmiths to be ready to forge them in place when the carpentry work is done. There's a carpentry shop over on Gillon Street with six or seven men working there, and they know how to do the job. Let's go over there now."

Leaving their tankards of rum half emptied, they went to the owner of the shop, and explained the situation. His shop was not very busy, he said, and his carpenters could take on the job the next day. He went with them to the *Revenge,* looked over the work to be done, and discussed the price of the job. Painful as it was for him, Powner explained to the owner that he had little money. The owner wanted the job, as his own business needed more work, so an arrangement was worked out whereby Powner would make a small downpayment first, and the balance would be paid after the first shipment of slaves came over.

Ridderow sailed the next day, and early that morning, the team of carpenters swarmed into the bowels of the *Revenge*, accompanied by members of the crew, and began tearing out what needed to be changed to make room for the pens. Great amounts of lumber, carried on wagons drawn by oxen, were brought aboard. Using this lumber, the men began installing massive barricades to prevent slaves from escaping. The sound of saws and hammers reverberated throughout the ship. When that was done, the iron bars, locks and chains were delivered, and blacksmiths came aboard to forge them into place.

The work took over a month, and that gave time for Powner to get the money to pay for the slaves when he got to Africa. The risk to a lender, of course, was great. What if, after getting the funds, the slaver and his ship never returned to Charleston? He investigated, and found that there was one moneylender in Charleston, a Mr. Ormsby, who might take a chance on such a risky venture with his money. Phineas Ormsby was a wizened, short man in his seventies, with a pinched face, heavily wrinkled and distinctly looking like a prune. The swept-over curl of greasy gray hair almost met with his bushy eyebrows, which only accented the barbed glint in his small, beady black eyes.

Ormsby stared at the two men standing before his desk for a full minute. "Well, I *may* be willing to advance the funds to you, but what guarantee do I have that you will return to Charleston?" he cackled in a voice reminiscent of a chicken. "You might take my money and head for China!"

"But we have to return here to sell the slaves," Powner argued.

"Do you take me for a fool?!" Ormsby screeched. "You could go to Barbados and sell them!" He thought for a long minute. "All right, here are my terms. You can have the money, if you will sign your ship over to me until you come back to Charleston. That way, I'm sure you *will* return."

"What?!" Powner thundered. "Sign my ship over?"

Powner looked at Jacobson, and the first mate shrugged. "All right, we have to agree to that."

"Don't worry. You'll get your ship back when you return. Here's the rest of my terms: I am to own and be able to sell for myself one-third of the slaves. And I am to have my pick of them."

Powner and the first mate were stunned. There was nothing for Powner to do but agree to this, and the papers were signed, and the funds given to him. As Powner and Jacobson left Ormsby's office, the captain, clutching the cloth bag holding the money, snarled, "We've been robbed, Jacobson! Giving that little toad one-third of our slaves!" He swore.

"And that miserable thief gets the best of them. He'll take the strongest men and leave the women and the old and the children and the weak ones to us!" Jacobson spat on the ground in his anger.

When the work on the vessel was completed, Powner and Jacobson inspected it. They were surprised by the massiveness of the bulwarks, and the very cramped space allotted to the slaves. It was standard on the slaving ships to give each African eighteen inches of room, no matter how big or wide they were. In this appallingly narrow space, the slaves would be chained for the entire voyage. Where the foremast came through the deck to seat itself in the keelson, a solid wall had been erected. Where the mainmast came down, a vertical grating had been built, and twenty feet aft of that, a second massive wall had been built, ending the holding area.

But something else was what astounded the captain and his first mate. "Look at that!" Powner said, pointing down. "They've put in an entire new floor between the bottom of the hold and the deck. And look at the heights of the ceilings. In the lower hold the height is about four feet, and here in the upper hold it's about four feet, nine inches. Now, when our crew comes down here to feed the slaves and check on them, how are they supposed to stand up straight?"

"Obviously they *won't* be able to stand erect," Jacobson said. "We'll just have to get used to it."

The owner of the carpenter shop came to them, and said, "I followed the design we've used on several slaving ships. I've made four compartments, two below, two above. Now you have room for about three hundred slaves altogether."

Jacobson and Powner couldn't believe their ears. "Three hundred?" Powner exclaimed, his jaw dropping.

"Well, I'm just doing a good designing job for you, Captain," the carpenter said. "I made two layers so you could put in more slaves. That's where your profit is."

"Hmm, I suppose so," Powner said. "But three hundred! They will be jammed in like dead fish in a barrel."

"Oh, maybe more, depending how you herd them in," the carpenter said. "Now, you put the strongest ones, the troublemakers, down there in the lower hold. The women and the children, and the older and weaker ones, you put up here."

They came up on deck, grateful that the vessel still smelled fairly clean, and the carpenter went to check on something else.

"It's inhuman," Jacobson said. "Three hundred. I can't believe it. And only twenty-two in the crew."

"Now I begin to see why Captain Ridderow thinks that slaves have no souls—that they're not even human. You can't think they are human beings, and still treat them like that, so you have to put them down," Powner said.

Jacobson looked down, studying his shoes, or the deck. He really didn't want to look the captain in the eye. "Will *we* be like that soon?" His viciousness, his greed, and his madness for power were being shaken somewhat.

"Probably," Powner said. "You remember what Ridderow told us: You get used to it."

"I suppose you can get used to almost anything, no matter how bad," Jacobson said.

❧

Josh Morris had been looking into the three colleges in America since April, and was becoming discouraged. While educational standards then were not high, and most qualified students would be accepted at these schools, there were still the problems of cost and distance. The first problem was easily understandable, and afflicted students constantly. Josh had very little money.

But the second was equally difficult. It was simply that there were no institutions of higher learning in the Middle Colonies. To the north, Yale was in New Haven, Connecticut, over 200 miles from Chester. Farther north, Harvard was in Cambridge, Massachusetts, about 320 miles away. And to the south, in Williamsburg, Virginia, there was William and Mary, about 340 miles away. These were daunting distances, given the fact that Josh had no horse. Because colonial roads were so poor, most travelers going north or south would take a ship, going from a major port such as Philadelphia north to Boston or New Haven, or south to Norfolk. That would be easier than going by land.

Josh had been working around Chester since March, and much of the money he made he gave to Hiram to repay him for what he had given to Ishmael Duffy. But he had not repaid the debt fully, and he was determined to do so, however long it took. How then could he expect to have money for college?

So Josh talked with all those he had come to know, who understood the problem. He chatted with schoolteachers, with clergy, with medical people, and anyone else who could give him advice.

And then he learned something of importance.

There was a man in Neshaminy, Pennsylvania, which was not far north of Philadelphia, who had opened a school that was being called the "Log College." This was the Reverend William Tennent, Senior, and he possessed a Master of Arts degree from the University of Edinburgh in Scotland. It was reputed that, as a scholar and teacher, he was without an equal in the Middle Colonies. Josh learned that early in 1735 Tennent had put up a building to train young men, and the costs of studying there were minimal or next to none. On a number of counts, Josh realized that this might be an ideal situation for him, if he could be admitted. It was close by, and the financial demands were so slight that his slim resources would not be strained.

With these things in mind, Josh went to Hiram Prescott and explained his hopes to further his education. "I know I'm just a humble farm boy with no family in America and no money. But I thought that with more training, I could do something else, such as teaching. I'd like your opinion on the entire matter, sir," he said.

"I'm all for it!" Hiram said. "Wonderful. I have been hoping that my sons—and you—might go on to get more education. Now, what is the next step?"

Josh explained the financial and distance problems of the other colleges, and then he told of the "Log College," and William Tennent.

"That sounds like a real possibility, Josh," Hiram said. He thought for a minute. "You should investigate this school carefully. If you could begin attending there in the fall, you need to look into it right off, to see if Mr. Tennent would accept you as a student. Can you go to see him at

Neshaminy?"

"Yes, if I could impose again on your generosity and borrow a horse."

"Would you like me to go with you, in the wagon?"

"Oh, would you? It would be wonderful to get your opinion, sir!"

❧☙

The ride from Chester to Neshaminy had been easy for Hiram and Josh, for the roads in this section of Pennsylvania were passable, and the day was warm, with the sun high overhead and few clouds in the sky. Recovering from the fire, Hiram came with Josh to the Log College in the wagon. When they arrived at the college, Josh tossed the horse's reins over a nearby low-hanging tree branch.

In a minute Mr. Tennent emerged from the building. "Hello, friends," he said, introducing himself and inquiring as to their identities.

"We have come," said Hiram after the formalities had been covered, "to inquire into your school."

"Ah!" said Tennent. "Then please come inside, out of this hot sun." He escorted them in.

In this building that was only two years old, the room they entered was fairly large and obviously designed especially for teaching. There were four windows, and sunlight streamed in. Two stories high, there were steps to the upper floor, and several young men were seated at desks built to hold books and notepaper. They looked up and greeted the newcomers with smiles and welcoming nods and went back to their studies.

Josh began, "Reverend Tennent, I hear much of your abilities in conducting a college, and I would like to inquire about admission."

"Indeed," Tennent responded with a smile. "Well, there are some things I must be sure you understand before going any further. This is a Christian school, and my students come with a certain amount of spiritual growth behind them already. Tell me, my son, what is your belief?"

"I believe that there are three Persons in the Holy Trinity, that Jesus Christ is the Son of God come in the flesh to die for mankind's sins, and that he is my Lord and Savior," Josh said.

"Wonderful!" exclaimed Tennent. "I am delighted to hear that. How long have you been a Christian, Josh?"

"Perhaps three years, sir."

"And what are your vocational goals?"

"I'm really not sure, sir. I thought I might like to become a teacher, or something like that."

"Well, like both Harvard College and Yale College, this college was founded to train pastors for the Gospel ministry. While we are small, most of the young men here are convinced that God has called them into His service to preach the Gospel. Even though you aren't sure what you want to do, would you be happy studying among such men?"

Josh thought for a minute, then said, "Sir, if you teach Christian truth from God's Word, I don't see how I could be unhappy."

"Hmm. Now there's something else very important that I must explain to you. I don't know how much of this you already know. Are you aware that a spiritual awakening is beginning here in America?"

"Yes. Isn't that magnificent!" Josh said. "Are you in agreement with it, Pastor Tennent?"

There was silence for a moment, and Tennent smiled. Then he said, "Very much so, Josh. There is much activity going on in various places, such as New England. But here in the Middle Colonies, you happen to be at the center of support for revival. This college was begun for the purpose of training fine young men to serve the living God and His Church, in bringing life back into it."

Josh was so astounded he was speechless. When he regained his tongue, he stammered, "Then Jesus must have brought me right here, to this place! There's no other place I'd rather be."

Hiram was also pleased. "Our pastor in Chester is preaching for Awakening. And he tells us of revivals beginning in different places. Isn't there some activity over in New Jersey?"

Tennent responded, "Ha! Yes, there is, and it happens to be where some graduates of this school are ministering. Over in Jersey a young pastor, Theodore Frelinghuysen, began attacking the apathy of his Dutch Reformed people about 1720, and revival broke out. Then my son, Gilbert, began as pastor of the church in New Brunswick in 1726, and saw what things Frelinghuysen was bringing about, with people getting saved. So Gilbert began cooperating with him, with both of them preaching for conversions all over northern New Jersey. Hundreds have been saved."

"That's exciting!" Josh said.

"It's the Lord God at work, son," Tennent said. "It's not what humans are doing. This is an Awakening that is coming straight from God. You can't explain it otherwise."

"Do you teach regular subjects, as in most colleges?" Hiram asked.

"Certainly. The men who come here have varied backgrounds. Some have had much schooling elsewhere, and want more. Others come who haven't had a great deal."

"That's me," Josh admitted. "So you take men who haven't had much background?"

"If I feel that they are qualified in other ways. I wouldn't deny a worthy person the benefit of an education. I teach all that Harvard and Yale colleges are teaching. My curriculum is taken from the University of Edinburgh, in Scotland, my own alma mater. After I have trained them, I would pit any of my students against any that Harvard or Yale might put forth."

"There is a problem, sir. I doubt if I'm a good enough scholar," said Josh.

"Nor am I sure until I know you better," said Tennent. "And I appreciate your honesty. Let me ask you, Josh, what is most important. Would you be comfortable with the spirituality we encourage here, since you are already a Christian?"

"Oh, I would love that!" Josh said. "I would love to have a deeper spiritual life."

"Let me suggest something. Already on several counts you seem to have passed my tests for entrance. So, would it be possible for you to spend two weeks here, while I assess your abilities further?"

"Pastor Tennent, I must be honest with you immediately. There is another problem. I have very little money to pay you."

Tennent laughed. "If that is a problem, forget it. There is little or no cost. I am pastor of the nearby church, which gives me a salary. If a student has nothing but his life and talents to offer to God, I will gladly take that as a most acceptable payment."

"I can hardly believe what I am hearing," Josh said, looking at Hiram. In the last minute his eyebrows rose, and his face was registering delight.

"Nor can I," Hiram said. "Josh, if Pastor Tennent is willing to take you tentatively as a student, I urge you to remain here for two weeks, and accept the good pastor's most generous offer. I will leave for Chester and wait to hear from you by mail."

Thrilled with this, Josh turned to William Tennent. "May I stay?"

"I wish you would."

※※※

Ben Franklin was in his office, surrounded by the piles of books and assorted papers that any editor must deal with. He had no secretary to help him keep some order amid the clutter, although his wife frequently helped him with correspondence when he got too overwhelmed. He was reading newspapers and letters just received from other provinces and England, untying the strings holding parcels together, and culling items of public interest that he might include in *The Pennsylvania Gazette.*

As Deborah came down the stairs, he called to her, "My dear, here's more papers from England just arrived by ship, *The London Chronicle* and *The London Citizen.* And they both have stories about George Whitefield. They are saying that this young man is so energetic, he is not content with taking a parish in England. You recall his name, don't you?"

"Oh yes, didn't you print a story about his feuding with a bishop over there?"

"That's the one," Ben answered. "Well, it seems he wants to become a missionary to America, and he has thoughts of beginning an orphanage in Georgia for the children of settlers who have died."

"Really? Will he come to Pennsylvania also, or just to Georgia?" Deborah asked.

"Oh, just to Georgia. There, Whitefield won't have many people to preach to. I predict that he will soon go back to his crowded congregations in England, where they love him so." He laughed.

"He is still a sensation in England?"

"It seems so. The English papers are carrying stories of his exploits, and his friend's—a fellow named Wesley. Both of them are becoming well-known in America, and people here are interested in the English Awakening that these men have started. Hmm, it's an item of general interest to reprint in our paper, even though it has little to do with Pennsylvania. But perhaps he will come here sometime."

⊱⊰

Two weeks later, Josh was hard at his studies, in the upstairs room of the Log College, when Reverend Tennent came and found him. "Ah, Josh, there you are. I was looking for you."

"Yes sir." Josh knew that sometime soon Tennent would want to speak with him about the future.

"Josh, as you know I have been looking over your work carefully since you came. I have been particularly attentive to your progress in Latin, Mathematics, and Literature."

"Yes sir." Josh's hands curled into fists, thinking he was about to be told he was deficient, and would have to leave the college.

"I am pleased to say that I'm impressed with your work. It is quite satisfactory. And I must also say, Josh, that I'm pleased with your Christian witness. You have given much evidence of sincerity and growth in the faith. Your fellow students have remarked to me that they appreciate you, and find you to be a genuine believer. When I asked you to give a brief devotional the other day, everyone thought you did a fine job. So, I'd like to invite you to remain as a regular student, if you wish."

Josh was so thrilled he choked up and could say nothing for a minute. Then he managed, "Thank you, sir."

⊱⊰

Two months elapsed, during which there was much activity in the Prescott family. The repairs to Hiram's home were completed, and he and Susan were able to move back in. Andrew and Sarah set up housekeeping in their own home, and Andrew began his chosen trade, making candles and soap in his own shop. Tom was doing well in the printing trade, and was pleased with his room in Mrs. Kirkpatrick's boarding house. Things were definitely improving.

Hiram Prescott had gotten a letter from Josh and was planning to go to Neshaminy to see him. When Tom came to Chester for his usual weekend visit, Hiram asked him, "Could you take a day off and go with me? I will be coming through Philadelphia on my way to Neshaminy."

"Of course I want to go! Mr. Franklin will give me a day off, I'm sure," Tom answered. So they planned their visit for the next week.

The day was cold but clear when Tom and his father arrived at the Log College in their wagon.

Josh was delighted to see them and ran out to throw his arms around them.

Josh listened patiently as Hiram and Tom brought him up to date with their activities. But he could hardly wait to tell them of the things that were happening at the Log College. "I'm very pleased with Mr. Tennent's teaching, and I can say that all of our students here love him a great deal. However, since the Awakening is gaining strength, and since our graduates and students are supporting it strongly, there are some who oppose what the Lord is doing. A few people in Mr. Tennent's own congregation are trying to make trouble for this dear man. Last year when the Synod met, these few went and made complaints against him. They want Mr. Tennent to be ousted from his pastorate, so that the Awakening can be hampered. I have the Synod report right here. It condemns the troublemakers."

Josh pulled out a paper he had been waiting to show them. He read:

> Their reasons are utterly insufficient, being founded partly upon ignorance and mistake, and partly upon prejudice; it is therefore ordered that...said people lay aside such groundless dissatisfactions and return to their duty, which they have too long strayed from....

"Well! What do you think of that?!"

"Strong language!" said Hiram. "But these troublemakers probably won't stop making problems in every way they can."

"Yeah, but there are exciting things happening here!" Tom said. "I envy you, Josh."

"I haven't told you the best thing yet! I've saved that for last," Josh said, giving a wide smile that spanned his face. "In the past several months, with all this excitement here, I believe the Lord has been speaking to me. I've been praying about this a great deal. I believe God is calling me into the ministry!"

Surprised over this news, Hiram said, "I'm delighted, Josh. But somehow, for quite a while, I thought this might happen. You are a wonderful candidate for a pastor, with your sincerity, personality, and intelligence."

Tom said, "I totally agree, Josh. That's the best news ever." He shook his friend's hand, then hugged him.

※

The day had dawned cloudless and clear, and a brilliant sun throughout the day had made it unusually warm for that time of year. While work in Franklin's print shop was as heavy as ever, Ben knew that everyone—he and his staff—needs a break occasionally. In midafternoon he appeared in the shop, to his workmen's surprise, clothed only in a loose pair of pants, stockings, and shoes, and bare from the waist up. Then, to their further surprise, he said, "Fellows, it's a fine day. I'm going for a swim. You've been working hard recently, and I appreciate it. Take the rest of the day off!"

The scramble of bodies out the front door was immediate. Only Tom was left, setting type in the middle of a word. Ben laughed. "That's a sight! They stopped cranking the press halfway through. But no harm done. Well, Tom, aren't you going to join them?"

Tom gazed, curiously, at the half-dressed publisher and inventor. "Uh, sir, I didn't want to quit till I'd finished this sentence of type."

"Most conscientious, my boy. Commendable. But it's too grand to stay inside. I'm having a dip in the Schuylkill River. I'd like to have company. You can swim, I suppose. Like to join me?"

"The Schuylkill, sir?" Tom was trying to fathom all of this. "Is the river still warm enough?"

"Yes, quite warm, and it's much better than the Delaware River. The Schuylkill is clean, and the current is much less. Better swimming, and marvelous exercise! I go over there on weekends whenever I can. You could just remove your shirt, and roll up your pants. My wagon is right outside."

Tom was a good swimmer. Taking the opportunity, he joined his employer, and for the next two hours they enjoyed themselves thoroughly, racing each other up and down the river.

SEVEN

God's Remedies for Human Sins

The *Revenge* had been completely changed into a slave ship, and Captain Powner followed Ridderow's advice. He bought some bales of cotton for cargo and sailed for England, leaving Charleston in the middle of the night to elude Spanish warships that might be nearby in the Atlantic. When he reached England, the cotton was sold, and Powner purchased hogsheads of cheap beans that would later be cooked as the food for slaves. Then the *Revenge* headed south toward Africa. Arriving off the coast of Africa, Powner searched for the small village of Walabo. This was not on any map, so when they came close to an English ship, he hailed it, asking if they knew of the settlement. They did, and directed him to it.

At Walabo, two hundred yards offshore, the crew took soundings to see how close the vessel could come in without running aground. A boat was sent out, with First Mate Jacobson in it, and he landed and found a Portuguese official who seemed to have some authority. The man spoke enough English to convince Jacobson that the water at the outer end of a pier was deep enough for the craft to come that far. The pier had been deliberately built out into the Atlantic for a hundred feet, to service slave ships. With this assurance, Jacobson signaled the ship to come up to the pier, lines were thrown to Jacobson's team, and the craft was made fast to the pier.

The village, if such it could be called, was built on the very edge of the jungle. A few thatched huts nestled under gigantic trees of the virgin rainforest. The limbs of the giant specimens stretched in a canopy overhead that shaded the ground, so that it was a struggle for things underneath to grow—delicate wildflowers, small plants, gorgeous, huge blossoms—and the trees' dead leaves rained down in such profusion that they formed a thick, spongy mat. Dense and tangled vines and thickets of bamboolike cane higher than a man's head made going through the jungle difficult, except on a few well-worn paths.

Three insect villains had been largely responsible for keeping Africa a dark, unknown continent for centuries. The anopheles mosquito, breeding in watery areas, carried malaria, Africa's most devastating disease. The tsetse fly, bearer of sleeping sickness, had not only killed thousands of Africans, but in many areas had made it impossible to keep domestic animals. And locusts, attacking every decade or so, consumed entire crops in minutes. The combined onslaught of these three villains, along with other problems, held the unfortunate people of the continent in a vicelike grip.

Powner came down the gangway onto the pier. It was incredibly humid and hot. Having left the breezes and coolness of the ocean, he had taken off his coat and left it on the vessel. He wiped his face with a shirtsleeve, looked about, and, mingling his evaluation with a string of blasphemies, said to Jacobson, "It's just what we heard it would be. A stinking hot, disease-ridden, miserable place!"

The Portuguese official approached the captain, gave a slight bow, and asked if he could assist.

"Yes," Powner said curtly. "We're here to buy slaves. This is my first time. How does this work?"

The official asked if the ship was properly fitted to hold slaves, and asked if he could go on board to see for himself. He explained to Powner and Jacobson that recently, on a vessel that was insufficiently protected, slaves had managed to break loose from their chains when the ship had been out from Walabo only two days. The Africans had stormed the flimsy partitions that had been erected, broken them down, and mutinied onto the deck of the craft, overpowering the officers and crew and killing all of them. While this had not happened in the harbor of Walabo, he said, the Africans had been procured there, and any further mutinies such as that would give the village a bad name.

"Oh, we wouldn't want that, would we? Thunderation!" Powner laughed cynically and turned to Jacobson. "I thought it already had such a bad name, it couldn't get any worse," he muttered.

The official went on board, inspected the entire vessel, and pronounced himself satisfied. "I see everything is clean," he said to Powner. "I'm afraid it won't be for long."

"Yes, I'm well aware of that. What happens next?"

"If you wish to buy slaves, we have a gentleman, Senhor Obidros, who works with the Muslim Arabs to get them from the jungles. He speaks good English. If you follow me, I will take you to him."

Powner and Jacobson ordered some of their crew to busy themselves with filling water casks with fresh water from a nearby stream that flowed into the ocean. The rest of them were sent to buy live sheep, pigs, and other foods from the Arabs, so that fresh meat and vegetables could be had for the crew on the return voyage, while the chained slaves would be fed slops, and not much of that. Then they met Obidros, a short, bald, obese man who constantly wiped his forehead and hairless crown with a sodden handkerchief.

"*Si, Si,*" he said, "I have many slaves ready for purchase. You wish to see them? They are in the barracoons. Please to come this way."

They were led into the jungle a short distance, and to their surprise found a large number of stout pens, or barracoons, made of upright stakes dug into the ground, with their upper ends cut to sharpened points to prevent anyone climbing over. These stockades were perhaps forty by sixty feet, and Powner heard loud noises coming from within them. Voices were crying out, some in agony, others in outrage. Outside these enclosures dozens of guards were posted, carrying spears and knives. These guards were dressed in long, flowing white robes and on their heads were the traditional *keffiyeh* of the Arab Muslims.

Obidros explained, waving his hands in the air, that these guards needed to be on constant alert because the natives they had recently captured from the jungles were riotous, and if they could escape from the pens they would kill with their bare hands if they could, or disappear into the jungle again.

There was a rough platform that had been erected between the pens, with a ladder attached to its side, and Obidros suggested that Jacobson and Powner climb it to see over into the pens for themselves. Standing on the shaky platform, the two men were amazed at the sight that greeted them. Inside each pen were perhaps one hundred natives crowded in—men, women, and children intermixed—all moaning, crying, or venting rage. There was no shelter from the blistering tropical sun, and some of the men were quarreling among themselves, shouting and pushing. Some of the more muscular men had iron manacles around their wrists and ankles, with stout chains connecting them. A few had iron collars around their necks.

"You see," said Obidros, "we must chain some of the more violent ones. They are very dangerous." He shook his head, tight-lipped.

"I've seen a lot of things in my time," Jacobson said, "but I've never seen anything like this before!" His shaggy brows shot up, and he exchanged a glance with Powner.

"Nor have I," said Powner. "So it's these Muslim guards that go into the jungle and capture the natives. They go in and raid some of the native villages?"

"Usually, yes. But sometimes the village chiefs themselves sell their own people to the Arabs for knives or whatever is valuable. And the Arabs bring the natives back here in chains, or else the Arabs might get killed." Obidros's arms never stopped flailing about.

"And then you sell these people to slavers like us?"

"Oh, it's not so horrible as it seems. These people go all over the world, to good owners and bad. You can't afford not to have them. You buy a slave once, and he or she is yours for life. He and his children. It's the best bargain ever offered." His lips were drawn into a puckish point, and he nodded vigorously in absolute conviction.

"All right," said Powner, "I've seen enough from up here. Let's go down and negotiate. I'll take three hundred of them."

Obidros mulled that over. "Hmm. Do you have the money for three hundred? That's a lot of slaves. Will your vessel hold that many?"

"Yes; it was just refurbished to hold that many. And I have the money—*if* your price is right," Powner said, in tones of finality.

They climbed down the ladder, and went into a little thatched hut that Obidros indicated was his office. Inside, they sat on rough chairs, and Obidros had more questions of them.

"You must understand; before we get to the subject of payment, with each captain of a slave ship I must ask some questions, for your own good. Particularly with captains who are new at carrying slaves. One of the main points is how many men in your crew?"

"Twenty-two, plus Jacobson and me."

"Hmph. Twenty-two against three hundred. My, my. Now, do you have sturdy chains in the ship's hold to restrain these people? Because my men are going to remove some of the chains, and you will need new ones.

We will leave the iron collars around the necks of the worst ones, and we'll leave some of the wrist and ankle manacles on them."

"Yes, the blacksmiths in Charleston knew how to do that. There's plenty of chains."

"Good," said Obidros. "Also, if you want to buy a mix of men, women, and children, we must bring first the strongest, most powerful men—the troublemakers—so that they can be chained down in the lower level of the hold. Have you trained your crew to chain them, and feed them?"

"Yes," Powner answered, "We've practiced all that on the voyage over. We chained each other up."

"All right. It seems that you have thought of everything. Now to our price...."

They dickered over costs for each African for an hour. Back and forth the negotiations went, in hard bargaining. Finally they agreed on three pounds, two shillings and six pence for young adult males, three pounds for young adult females, and less for older Africans. Children under eight years of age would be quite cheap. Children over that, the price jumped. Old people, quite cheap.

Finally they arrived at an agreement and an overall price. Powner had deliberately left the bag of money on board in his cabin, and he sent Jacobson to retrieve it. A document of sale was drawn up and signed, and the funds were paid that Ormsby, the moneylender in Charleston, had given. Hands were shaken over the deal. The cruel business was concluded.

ଛଓଓ

With the negotiations over the prices for slaves settled and the money paid, it was time to load them onto the *Revenge.* Captain Powner had asked for three hundred slaves, divided into 100 strong, younger men, 100 younger, child-bearing women, 50 older men and women who could still do some work, and 50 children, 25 under eight years of age and 25 between the ages of eight and sixteen.

Senhor Obidros left Powner and Jacobson to have a conference with the Portuguese officer and the leaders of the Arabs. It was up to them to do the job of taking the ones in each category out of the barracoons, and here was where the dangerous part began for them. Having done this a number of times previously for other slave ships, they knew that as soon as the gate to one of the barracoons was opened to let them in, anything could happen. Even if many Arab guards went in, they were still outnumbered, and violence and a riot could easily occur. Although the slaves were unarmed and chained, and the Arabs had spears, it was a chancy situation. So, the Arabs took every precaution.

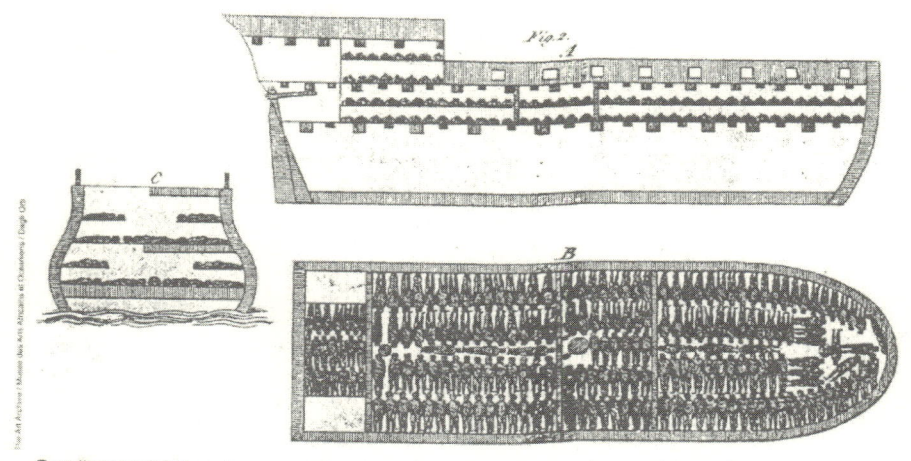

GRIM "LIBRARY." A biographer wrote of Newton's vessel, the *African*: "The space between decks was five feet and eight inches. Shelves divid[ed] this space into two along each side, with a passageway down the middle. The slaves would be packed to cover the whole floor and also the broad shelves; as Newton said, 'close to each other like books upon a shelf.'" (Pictured: a typical slave ship.)

With Obidros and the officer looking over the wall from the platform, Arab guards went to one pen, unlocked the gate just wide enough for one at a time to go through, and motioned the prisoners inside to move back. The Arabs were after the stronger, younger men, who would be loaded into the ship first and chained down in the lower compartment of the hold. In this pen they were able to find twenty-seven powerful, angry men. These were pulled out of the crowd, and goaded through the gate by Arab spears. With the slaves and the Arabs outside, the gate was quickly closed and securely locked. As soon as that happened, there was a loud roar from those who were left inside the pen.

Obidros, atop the platform, indicated which pen they should go to next, repeating the process. In that pen they singled out thirty-one furious slaves. That totaled fifty-eight younger men. They needed forty-two more to make the hundred. These were taken from two more pens, and the entire group was marched single-file down to the pier. It had been dangerous until this point, but the guards knew that now even worse problems could begin. For, when the desperate prisoners saw the slave ship, they knew what was about to happen to them. They were leaving Africa and their families forever. They would never return.

An enormous roar went up from the slaves. Shouts of defiance and fury were hurled at the Arabs, who stepped back but kept their spears pointed at the prisoners. Even chained slaves were dangerous. Obidros wanted to get this over quickly, so he signaled the Arabs to have the slaves move onto the little pier. The ship's crew, having completed their task of re-provisioning the vessel with fresh water, fruits, and live animals, stood ready on the pier, the gangway, and the vessel's deck. Half a dozen of the crew stood around with guns drawn, ready to shoot any slave who resisted. As each prisoner came aboard, he was taken down the ladder to the lower hold by three sailors and securely chained there. Then the next three sailors would come down the ladder with their prisoner, who would be chained next to the other slave, with no room between them. This would be repeated until all one hundred were firmly fastened to the bulwarks, screaming their hatred and fury, and straining at their chains with all their might.

This entire process was repeated in the pens for one hundred younger women, choosing them and bringing them aboard to be put in the upper compartment. Here the Arabs were somewhat more lenient, especially if the women had children with them. In that case, especially if the children were young, they were allowed to stay with their mothers. The women were chained by wrist manacles, tightly grouped together, but they did not have ankle manacles or iron collars put on them, and were allowed to sit up and move about somewhat in the upper compartment.

Then, the process was repeated for the twenty-five older men in one section of the upper compartment, the twenty-five older women in another, and the fifty children. For the last, the incredibly sad nature of the task was most apparent. The children, many mere infants, wailed so pathetically when they thought they were being separated from their mothers, that the Arabs took pity on them and left them together.

All this took several hours. When it was completed, the sailors were exhausted from their labors, and their prisoners belowdeck were sending up infuriated shouts. Powner ordered the lines cast off from the pier and regretfully set sail for Charleston. He would far rather have gone to Brazil.

❧❦❧

As his choice of ministry, George Whitefield decided to go to Georgia as a missionary, to follow up where John Wesley had previously failed and returned to England embittered. The newspapers, even the antagonistic Anglican *Weekly Miscellany,* covered his activities constantly, and most were favorable to him. In the remarkable time of only a few months in Georgia, he did much: he ministered to the needs of the sick, urged the beginnings of churches and schools, gave much-needed food and medicines, and began to plan for a charitable orphanage. With his supplies and money running out, he set sail for home in September, 1738 with two friends who would be of great benefit to him in the future, Joe Husbands and a shipwrecked sea captain, Hosea Gladman.

With that favorable experience behind him, Whitefield landed in England on November 30th. On December 8th he reached London, and the next day he went by appointment to a room at the House of Lords where he met the Archbishop of Canterbury and the Bishop of London. Knowing his reputation, these two dignified clergy handled him a little gingerly, as if he might burst into flames before them. With great dignity the Archbishop said, "I am pleased to greet you, Mr. Whitefield. Please be seated. I hear from Governor Oglethorpe that you performed well in Georgia, and that the colonists liked you very much."

"Thank you, your Lordship. Yes, it was a good experience."

"And I also hear that you took much pity upon the poor orphans there, and wish to begin an orphanage for them. Is that not true?"

"Very true, your Grace. The situation with many of the people there is not good. We have sent over a large number of indigent folk, and many have died of diseases which rage there. That has left orphans to roam about, with scarcely anyone to care for them. My heart bled for these poor children. And with your Grace's permission, I wish to begin taking collections for them, to put the orphanage on a sound footing. I expect that quite a large group of children will be coming there."

"It seems to be a worthy endeavor. If you wish to take collections in our London churches, Mr. Whitefield, I hereby give you permission, and you may tell our clergy that you have my approval and support." After some other discussion, Whitefield thanked the Archbishop and departed.

Shortly thereafter, the man who had ordained Whitefield, Bishop Martin Benson, invited his friend to see him. "George, I keep hearing excellent things about your preaching, and what you are doing with the orphanage in Georgia. You have become famous all over the southern half of England. I read of your activities in all the newspapers."

"I have much appreciated your support, your Grace, and I thank you for those kind words."

"Oh, that we had more young men like you in the clergy! I fear very much for the future of our church, and of England itself, if the people do not reform themselves quickly, stop being a nation of heathens and inebriates—drunks—and return to God who has blessed us so in the past."

"Yes, and when I preach that very thing, it is sad when our own clergy hate me, and keep me from preaching in their churches."

"I hope none of the clergy in my diocese will try to keep you out of their pulpits, George. If they do, please report it to me immediately, and I'll see to it."

And so Whitefield went on preaching in London, Oxford, Gloucester, Bath, and Bristol. People of all churches flocked to hear him, and he began to think he had more in common with them than with many in his own church. His increasing willingness to cooperate with any sincere people was a testimony to the broad ecumenism that he practiced.

Despite the needs of the British Isles and the warm welcome that the vast crowds were giving his preaching, Whitefield was looking farther afield as well, once again to America, and to his planned orphanage in Georgia. With his usual careful planning, he sent William Seward, his advance man, across the ocean to investigate the possibility of his preaching in the Pennsylvania and New Jersey area, with the intention of getting supplies in Philadelphia and eventually heading south to Georgia.

෴

A number of bound volumes, newspapers from a number of cities, piles of paper, bottles of ink, and various paraphernalia cluttered Ben Franklin's desk and an adjoining table in his office at the back of the printing establishment. He pulled several sheets of rough foolscap from the stack before him, and spread them out on the desk before him, preparing to write. Then he called, "Tom, are you free?"

"Yes, Mr. Franklin. I've almost finished this job." He entered Franklin's office.

"Do you remember my mentioning an English preacher named Whitefield?"

"Oh, of course. And you inserted half a dozen articles about this gentleman in the *Gazette,* in the last few months. Wasn't he in Georgia? He has become very famous, hasn't he?"

"Yes," Ben said slowly, pursing his lips. "But I'm not sure of his integrity. I intend to investigate him thoroughly. We shall see. At any rate, he is coming to this area, and—"

"He is?" Tom blurted out.

"Yes. I've had a letter from him, asking if I might be the printer of his sermons here in America."

"Really?! Then perhaps I'll have a chance to meet him!" Tom's eyes lit up with anticipation.

"Hmm. I don't know if I *want* to be his printer, my lad. Don't get your hopes up. I must determine if he's the genuine article. He may be a grand fraud, a charlatan, just out to collect money for this orphanage scheme. We will see about that later. I will announce his coming in our paper, since he is so well known, but I'll be cautious about it. I haven't given him any encouragement about being his printer. Now, to business. Would it be possible for you to deliver this package of pamphlets to Walnut Street?"

"Of course, sir." Tom came and took the package and noted the address. He walked through the shop, saying a few words to Stephen Webb and the other fellows at work on the press, and went south on Second Street, going the two blocks to Walnut Street. The day was hot, with the sun beating down on the paving stones. Tom found the shop where he was to go, delivered the package, and started back to Market Street. He decided to take another street to vary his route, and by this time, like everyone else he passed, he was perspiring.

He came up Water Street, by the wharves, overlooking the Delaware River. How inviting it looked! There was the usual number of ships lined up here. Tom would have loved to take an hour off from work, gone to the

135

boarding house where he lived, got an old pair of breeches, and gone for a swim. Upstream perhaps five hundred feet, by Bickley's wharf, south of the Arch Street ferry, several young people were in the river near the bank, swimming, having fun, and shouting to each other. He came closer to them, and noted that this was a perfect diversion on a hot day. Oh well, he had to get back to his job.

As he turned up the street from the wharves on Water Street, he heard terrible, terrified, pleading screams. He looked about. The shouts were coming from the riverfront. Tom bolted back to the wharf area.

"Help! Help! Someone is drowning!" This was being shouted frantically by the young people, at the top of their lungs. They, all about ten or twelve years old, had come out of the water, and were jumping about with panic, pointing out into the river.

Tom ran to the bank. Looking up and down, as far as he could see, he was the only person who was older. A boy of perhaps ten years old dashed over, screaming, "My sister is in the river! She can't swim very well, and she's being carried out into the fast current!"

About one hundred feet from where they were, and perhaps fifty feet from the shore, Tom saw a girl frantically thrashing about in the water, being swept downstream. The current was taking her farther and farther out into the middle of the broad Delaware River.

Tom ran to the edge of the river and kicked off his shoes. A rush of adrenalin surged through him. He plunged in. Even though it was summertime, the water was cold, but not numbing. The pull of the current wasn't too strong near the shore, but as he swam out, its force increased. It was the time of day for the tide to be going out, and this increased the current. He began to pass ships that were anchored in the middle of the river. Some sailors on these ships saw him swimming, and were leaning over the rails, wondering why anyone would be in the middle of the river.

Soon both he and the girl were far from shore. While he concentrated on swimming, frequently he had to stop for a second, raise his head above the water level, and look ahead to check on her whereabouts. He gulped air. With strong strokes he swam toward the girl, but as fast as he moved, the distance between them did not seem to get smaller. Minutes went by, and still she was perhaps thirty feet from him. The cold water was chilling Tom, and he shuddered. He swam past a very large vessel, whose bulk loomed above. Several sailors at the rails were shouting down at him.

Again he sought to locate the girl. *But where was she?*

To his horror, she had gone under!

He redoubled his efforts. It was difficult to keep his bearings, to see where she was. Of course if she had gone under, he had to dive down to find her. And the problem there was, although the river water was fairly clean, it was murky with mud, and visibility underwater was only a few feet. He looked above the surface, and under. And then, above, he saw her come to the surface...without any movement. She was unconscious. How many times had she gone under? Twice? He did not know. All he could do was to keep swimming as fast as possible toward her, fighting the current.

The current in the middle of the river was pulling both of them downstream rapidly. Tom exerted all of his strength. He felt an almost superhuman burst of energy and managed to swim closer to the girl.

Tom heard faint shouts of encouragement and screams of panic from the shore. They were passing large ships drawn up to the wharves or moored in the middle of the broad river. Sailors had heard the melee and were peering over the rails to see what was happening in the Delaware.

Swimming as fast as he could, somehow he got within five feet of her. By then they were about 200 feet from the shore, and the current was by far the strongest Tom had ever felt.

It took another minute for him to come up to her. He reached out, touching her. The girl was limp in the water, head down, and unconscious. When Tom tried to pull her to him, so that he could begin to swim to shore with her in tow, she seemed to be totally lifeless.

He got behind her body, and put his left arm around her. In this way he had the use of his right arm to take powerful strokes, but he knew that against this swift current, trying to swim with one arm would be very difficult. Could he make it to shore? And was she dead?

Now that Tom had this girl in tow, he felt his strength draining quickly. How much longer could he continue to swim? It had been bad enough trying to catch up to her when she was being swept downstream. Now he knew that he could not swim at a right angle to the current, with its full force against him, but that he had to swim diagonally over to the shore, gradually. And not by himself alone, but with another person being pulled along, making the struggle that much harder.

Desperately, Tom kept swimming. His strength was almost gone.

EIGHT

The Joining of Forces

By this point, a number of people on the wharves and sailors on the ships had heard the commotion, and were calling and cheering Tom on. Exhausted, he doubted that he could make it to the shore.

He was about to go under himself. At the last moment he looked up and saw a small boat approaching quickly. Four sailors were at the oars, and another man was at the bow of the boat, ready to throw Tom a rope when they got close enough. Tom's strength was utterly depleted. Hands reached down to haul Tom and the girl from the river, and in a minute they were in the boat, she completely limp and lying on the bottom, and he sitting on the plank seat, taking huge gulps of air, and shaking all over. He was as cold as he had ever been.

"Thank—you—for coming—to get us," Tom stuttered to the man at the bow, shivering.

"The least we could do," the sailor said. "Son, that was a heroic thing you did."

As the other sailors worked the oars, drawing closer to the shore, one sailor took her wrist, trying to find a pulse, but said he could detect none. Her hand was as cold as ice, and her face a pasty white. "I-I think she may have drowned," he murmured. "The girl wouldn't be the first to drown in this river. And you did everything anyone could have done to save her. Very sad. She looks to be a pretty one, too."

When the small boat came to the dockside, eight or nine sailors came down the steps to grab the prow of the boat, tie it up, and help them out. One man climbed into the boat and lifted the girl out, carried her up the steps, and laid her gently on the wharf. On the dock her brother and the other young people were waiting for them, throwing their arms around one another and weeping.

A crowd had gathered to look at the girl—the skin on her face and arms so white. Tom stood nearby, shaking with exhaustion and disappointment to think that, after all he had done, she was gone. His tangled hair and sodden clothes drained water, and he was terribly cold.

Through the crowd a middle-aged man pushed his way, calling out, "I'm a doctor! I heard all the clamor. Let me through!" Quickly he knelt over the girl, felt for a pulse on the wrist and on the carotid arteries, and examined her. Then he said, "She's alive, but barely! Get some blankets!"

Tom felt limp. He was thrilled with the news, but his emotions and his body were exhausted. He threw himself down on the wharf, his head in his hands. His teeth chattered from the cold.

Dr. Kushner, the physician, knew well the steps to take to resuscitate one who had nearly drowned. He found the girl slightly responsive, breathing irregularly, beginning to moan softly, and moving her fingers. This indicated that the heart was beating, and chest compressions were not needed to help her heart pump blood. But she had swallowed a good amount of river water, which was clogging her airway, so she was turned on her stomach to allow it to drain from her mouth. Blankets were quickly brought out of one of the ships to cover and warm her.

After fifteen minutes of his treatment, the physician, Dr. Kushner, rose from her side and announced, "She's had a bad time of it, but she will recover. Let's get her to her home."

The ten-year old boy who had first pleaded with Tom to dive into the river had been sitting on the wharf next to him, sobbing. He called out through his tears, "She's my sister, Rachel. If someone can carry her, I'll take you to our home."

"Where do you live, son?" the doctor asked in a kindly way.

"In Elfreth's Alley," the boy said. He held out to Tom his shoes that had been thrown aside.

A brawny sailor volunteered to carry the girl, and the doctor, his patient, and a small group followed her brother. As they walked, Tom got his first good look at the girl. She was older than he had thought; probably sixteen or seventeen, he guessed. The girl appeared to be forcing herself toward consciousness. She was wearing a dress of thin black material that came to her ankles—what feminine modesty demanded—but had allowed her enough movement to swim. The dress dripped water and clung to her, and her long hair hung in tangled knots. As they walked, she opened her eyes and gave Tom a weak smile.

"Hey, mister, what you did was great," her brother said. "Thanks so much. Rachel is a fair swimmer, but she didn't realize the current was so strong."

"Neither did I!" Tom answered.

The home was a short distance from Water Street, north of Arch Street. Rachel's mother came to the door as her brother opened it and threw up her hands in shock. "What happened?!" she cried. Then, even before the questions were answered, she urged them to bring her daughter inside. She said to the sailor, "Could you help me take Rachel upstairs, so I can remove these wet clothes and let her lie down? I'll be down in a few minutes to find out what happened." The sailor carried Rachel up the narrow stairway to her bedroom.

The front room of the house was small, and the group filled it entirely. Soon the mother reappeared. Dr. Kushner introduced himself, gave her some medicine to help Rachel relax and sleep, said she should recover nicely now, and that he would be happy to come back tomorrow and check on her. Her mother thanked him profusely, and he left.

The mother turned to her son and said, "Bobby, what happened?"

"All of us were swimming in the river—right near the bank," he emphasized. "But Rachel swam out a little too far, I guess. The next thing, the current grabbed her, and she began to go out into the middle. She was screaming, and so were all of us. This man heard us and jumped in. It took a long while for him to swim to her, but he finally got her back to shore."

"O, thank you!" the mother exclaimed, holding out her hands to Tom. "I'm Mrs. Nicholson. Rachel would have drowned, except for your rescue, I see. I know the Delaware is very dangerous, and I only let the children dip in it because the day is so hot. My husband and I are very indebted to you. How can we ever repay you?"

"He's a hero!" her brother said.

"There's no need to repay anything. My name is Tom Prescott." He was shivering and certainly didn't look much like a hero, he knew, with his clothes dripping water on the living room floor.

"You're terribly cold, I see. Bobby, get Mr. Prescott a blanket—quickly! My husband will want to meet you; can you return?"

"I could come back tomorrow. I'll check on her recovery."

Bobby returned with a woolen blanket, and Tom wrapped it around himself.

"Please do. We'll look for you." Mrs. Nicholson ran up the stairs to tend to Rachel.

ಬಿಲ್

Once outside the Nicholson home, Tom took the blanket from around him. There was no need to get the blanket wet from his sodden shirt, so he removed the shirt, and again wrapped the blanket around his upper body. With the blanket's warmth, his shaking and chill were leaving him. But wearing the blanket posed another slight problem—he knew that he looked like an Indian, with that blanket on. Tom laughed at that thought; well, people passing by could just stare at him! There were still some Indians who came into the city, and they could think he was one of them.

He immediately went to Mrs. Kirkpatrick's boarding house. She was in the front room when he entered and threw up her hands when she saw his condition. She asked him what had happened, and when he told her, she was horrified. After a minute Mrs. Kirkpatrick went to boil some water for him to wash in. By this time he had regained his strength and stopped shivering from the cold of the river, but his trousers were still dripping. He went to his room, dried himself off, and changed to dry underclothes, breeches, and shirt.

Then he returned to Franklin's print shop. He went to the back office to explain his reason for lateness. Ben Franklin might be angry with him until he heard the reason. Franklin looked up as Tom came to the door of his office.

"Mr. Franklin, I've just returned from the errand you sent me on. As I was returning, there was some difficulty. A young lady was being pulled out to the center of the river. There was no one else able to swim out to get her, so I jumped in and brought her back to shore. But then my clothes were soaking wet, and I had to go to my boarding house and change them before returning. I'm sorry for my lateness. You can reduce my pay if you'd like, but I hope you won't fire me!"

Franklin's mouth dropped open with surprise, and his eyes widened. "She could have drowned! You certainly did the right thing—the thing any red-blooded man would have done. I'm proud of you, son! And this shall certainly be printed in the *Gazette,* next issue, naming you and this young lady. What is her name?" Ben was already scratching down the details with his quill pen.

"Let's see...Rachel..."

"And her surname?"

"Oh yes, Nicholson!"

"At any rate, well done, Tom!"

ॐ

Martha Bullard was in the midst of bathing her children. Without warning, the door to her little home opened, and her father ambled in. Immediately the children cringed at their grandfather's appearance. And Martha had to admit that she was not especially pleased when he came, because everything he did was unpredictable, and he always upset her day with his ramblings, hearing of voices, and weird utterances. But she knew that he was a desperately lonely person, usually very hungry, with no other relatives or friends, no money or trade, and with some sort of very serious problem. And, of course, he *was* her father.

Martha greeted him cordially, took him to a chair, and got him settled down, and finished drying her children with a towel. He began to mumble and mutter incoherently, and she bustled the children off to the other room. To try to distract her father from the usual gibberish he babbled, she began to chatter on about anything she could think of.

"Can I get you something to eat, Father?"

He stared at her and then nodded, so she got together some ham and potatoes, put them before him, and he began to eat ravenously.

"I did the washing and ironing for several people in the village, and got paid for it. Here, I want you to have this," Martha said and put several large coins in his tattered coat pocket. "Now don't lose them."

Then, knowing he rarely bathed, she said, "Oh, Father, I've found the best soap for sale in a store in Chester. It's the softest soap I've ever used—not so much lye to be harsh on the skin. Would you like to wash up, and try it?"

He indicated that he would.

"All right, let me put the kettle on the fire to heat some water for you. You'll find this is the best soap, from Prescotts' shop!"

Prescotts'! Startled, he came out of his daze and stared at Martha. How he hated that name! Was this the same family? He asked his daughter to give him the location of this shop in Chester.

Martha noted her father's strange reaction to what for her was harmless small talk. Why would he act that way? While he often acted in odd ways, this was a more animated reaction than usual.

The voice came to him. *We must look into this. Is this a relation of Prescott's?*

ಸಲ

Elfreth's Alley had rather small two- and three-storied houses facing on an unpaved street barely wide enough for a carriage to get through. It was near the river, and only one block long, between Front and Second Streets, north of Arch Street. Of all the streets in William Penn's "Green Countrie Town," the appearance of its houses and the narrow, cramped roadway was more like European or English streets than any other in the city.

The day after Tom had rescued Rachel from the Delaware River, Tom knocked on the door of the Nicholson home on Elfreth's Alley. It was opened almost immediately by a man who greeted him with "You must be

Tom Prescott!" The man, smiling widely, shook Tom's hand and invited him inside, closing the door behind him.

"That's Tom, Dad," Rachel's brother called out, excitedly. "And he's a great swimmer!"

"I'm Rachel's father, and I am so grateful for what you did yesterday. My daughter could have drowned, if it weren't for you. Please be seated." Mr. Nicholson was a tall, thin man, neat in appearance, with dark brown hair that came to his shoulders. His eyes were brown and bright, set in a pleasant face with high cheekbones, having a sharp and somewhat pointed nose; altogether, thought Tom, a rather handsome man. He offered Tom the best chair in the room as Mrs. Nicholson came in from the back of the home, bringing cookies and tea. Now that the excitement was over, Tom noted she was a fine woman, with a lovely face.

For five minutes the family plied Tom with questions: Where do you work? Is your family here? Where do you hail from? And Bob's (the son's) eager question, Where did you learn to swim so well?

Tom answered the torrent of questions as best he could, and then, down the stairs, came Rachel.

He was speechless. This young lady looked totally different from the one he had helped yesterday. Instead of a bedraggled, sopping-wet girl with tangled hair dangling over her face, he saw to his surprise a dignified young lady of exceeding beauty, poised and confident. She had wide, dark brown eyes and light brown hair, carefully combed and falling down over her shoulders. Her face was delicate, elfin, with high cheekbones, and her smile revealed white and perfect teeth. She was wearing a green dress with a white collar. Tom had guessed before that she was sixteen or seventeen, and she looked every bit of that.

Now that Rachel had rested, her face showed maturity and firmness of character. Tom was enchanted. He had not expected anyone like this.

"Mr. Prescott, I am so grateful to you. You saved my life!" Rachel said, with a dazzling smile.

"No, no—it was n-nothing," he stammered, almost swallowing his tongue.

"Nothing?! It was everything. I was close to drowning! I was such a fool, to go out into the river more than a few feet from shore. But I didn't realize that I was drifting out. Dad, there was no one else around to dive in and save me! If it hadn't been for Mr. Prescott, I would be gone."

"Yes, so I've heard. We'll be forever grateful. It was a very courageous act," her father said.

Tom was now as red as a tomato. "Please...please."

They saw his embarrassment and changed the topic. He noted, incidentally, that there was a strong resemblance between Rachel and her mother. As the fierce heat on his face receded, he watched Rachel. Could she really be all that she appeared to be? Was she intelligent, as well as beautiful?

To find out more, Tom asked Rachel about her life. She had spent many years in school, she said, and loved to read books. While she was not the best swimmer, Rachel was somewhat athletic, going in for the games that young ladies liked. And she loved her faith.

Then the talk turned to Mr. and Mrs. Nicholson. He owned a dry-goods store on Third Street and was doing well. The family had lived in Philadelphia for years and liked the city.

The topic turned back to Tom. When they found out he worked for the well-known Ben Franklin in his print shop, they were fascinated. How did the printing press work? How was printing done? How were books bound? Was Mr. Franklin as clever as he seemed to be in the *Pennsylvania Gazette?* And in *Poor Richard's Almanac?* And, now that he was getting into politics and activities like the Junto and the Union Fire Company and the Library Company of Philadelphia and being postmaster, how was he going to have time to continue in the printing trade? Tom answered all these to the best of his ability.

While he was willing to answer their questions, Tom decided that his real mission here must be to know Rachel better. Other girls he had known were nice; Louisa Duffy was pretty, but she was a frontier girl, not cosmopolitan like Rachel, and there were others back in England, but they were dim memories.

Tom could not take his eyes off her. She was the most compelling human being he had ever seen, although in front of the family he had to take darting glances from the corner of his eyes, to conceal his fascination. At least, however, he got Rachel and the other Nicholsons to call him Tom, rather than "Mr. Prescott," which was so distant and formal, and to him, strange.

Now that he saw what Rachel was like, what he had done in the Delaware River to rescue her was as nothing. He would swim the Atlantic

Ocean for her!

He would have liked to stay longer, but that would have been too obvious. It was time to leave. He had received their thanks in abundance. There was little more of that to say. There was no excuse for remaining.

And then, more than what he could have hoped for, did come to pass. As he was getting up to depart, Mrs. Nicholson asked, "Tom, could you come for dinner on Sunday, after church? We'd love to have you."

Could he?! Tom had to control his enthusiasm, and he managed to answer in a calm voice, "Why, yes, I may be able to arrange that. Thank you, Mrs. Nicholson."

Rachel hid her own delight. This was just what she wanted. What a dear mother and father!

※

A week had never moved so slowly, Tom thought. Each day he tried hard to keep his mind on his work. This was especially important when he was working the press. If he was not paying close attention, his hand could get caught in the mechanism if another person was pulling the large lever and he was feeding the paper and inking the type. So, he forced himself to concentrate on business and not to be daydreaming.

But Rachel filled his mind. He thought of her superb figure in the green dress, her long, lustrous hair, her wide, brown eyes. He had never heard a name so totally appropriate, so euphonious as Rachel Nicholson.

Finally, Sunday arrived, bright, clear, and warm. Tom attended morning worship at St. Peter's, which because of the size of the sanctuary was relatively cool. Impatiently he waited for the afternoon.

At the proper time he knocked at the door of the home on Elfreth's Alley. He held a bouquet of flowers. A few neighbors observed him and smiled knowingly as he stood on the front step waiting for the door to be opened.

The door opened, and there was Rachel. She was even more lovely than he remembered! She wore a yellow dress with a large white bow at the front, the wide ribbon extending around the collar.

"Please come in, Tom," she said with an inviting smile.

He entered the home. Passing through the dining room, he noted on the table an array of porcelain bowls, silver and pewter dishes and wooden platters, some of which held foods such as breads and rolls, apples and pears. In the kitchen, he found Mrs. Nicholson and a servant girl busily preparing the dinner. The succulent smells of roast turkey wafted from a large pot hung over the fire in the hearth, and other containers held more aromatic dishes. Rachel's mother greeted him cordially, saying, "I'm so glad you could come, Tom. Dinner should be ready in half an hour or so."

He said how appreciative he was of the invitation and proceeded through the back door to the garden. The flowers were presented to Rachel, and she thanked him, with a bit of a blush. The garden was enclosed by a red brick wall, and in it were several climbing rose bushes with fragrant red flowers.

"I thought you might like to play a game before dinner," she said, pointing to two chairs around a small table that held a checkerboard. "We could play draughts; that shouldn't take too long."

They sat, and Rachel offered to let him move first, which he did. After three moves, she jumped his piece and took it. She had on a perfume with the delicate fragrance of lavender, and it was hard for him to keep his mind on the game. Two more moves by him, and he lost another piece. And so it went.

Soon Rachel had lured pieces from his back row, and crowned four kings. Because she had kept her back row intact, Tom got no kings. Her conquest continued. A few more jumps, and Rachel had won the game.

Tom was a bit miffed at playing so poorly and thought to himself that he had been unable to concentrate. That lavender perfume was too strong! Rachel evidently didn't want to show him up further, so she said, "I know you haven't played draughts for a while. And we play frequently, so we're practiced. Why not another game, to allow you to retaliate?"

That was considerate of his male ego. So they played again. This time Tom concentrated and played more shrewdly, trying to ignore the perfume. He kept his back row intact, but so did Rachel. No kings bounced about the checkerboard. And he was able to take a few of her pieces. Then Rachel did something odd; she broke her own back row, and this allowed Tom to get two kings. With these he began to take her pieces, and within a dozen moves she was defeated.

But Tom got the distinct impression that Rachel had wanted him to win. Hmm. Strategy, beyond the checker game?

"Dinner is ready," Mrs. Nicholson announced, and they gathered at the long table. The parents sat at either end, with Tom and Bob on one side, and Rachel on the other. The family's servant girl, Jolie, brought in the food: the turkey, browned, simmering and steaming in its own juice, roast potatoes, beans, carrots, turnips, onions, asparagus, and for dessert, several fruit pies.

The Nicholsons knew that Tom was alone in town, living in a rented room, and that his meals must be wholesome but occasional and not all that delicious. So they made sure he had plenty to eat. Had they deliberately put Rachel across the table from him, so he could see her plainly? During the lavish meal, Tom tried not to cast his eyes too obviously at her. But he glanced enough to know that this incandescent young lady mesmerized him. Good as the food was, really, that was secondary.

ಸಿಂಧ

The crossing of the Atlantic Ocean from Africa had been a rough one. Hurricane season had brought several monster storms in mid-ocean to the *Revenge,* and the mainsail had split in one of them.

Enormous waves and howling winds tossed and battered the ship, and created chaos aboard. Much of the time it was impossible to keep anything upright, and at mealtimes the plates and cups went sliding across tables, sending liquids and food flying.

The crew was used to gales and heavy seas, and took them in stride. But the condition of the slaves was pathetic during the turbulence, especially the smaller children, who were constantly terrified. Even though the hatches were battened down and the holds sealed to keep out the sea water from going below that was surging over the deck, the crying and wailing from the prisoners came through. Completely unaccustomed to oceangoing travel and violent storms, all of them were seasick, and a number of the older people were ill from other causes, and some died.

The members of the crew soon learned what it meant to serve aboard a slave ship. They had to be not only sailors but also jailers, and every member of the crew was pressed into service for the new duties. Ordinarily, before slaving, on balmy days when the ship's sails were up and the vessel was moving along, there was not a great deal to do beyond regular maintenance. But now with slaving, regardless of good weather or bad, there were always chores for each crewman: cooking the cheap beans brought from England as slaves' food, distributing it among the prisoners, chaining and unchaining those to be exercised, cleaning and washing out their filthy quarters, giving the sick what little attention was possible, and removing the bodies of those who had died, plus tending to the ship itself.

Eventually the vessel reached the coast of America and headed for Charleston. The weather had moderated, but that did not placate Captain Joseph Powner. With each day, he increased his disgust at what was about to happen. First Mate Jacobson shared his fury.

"When I think what we have been through, refitting this old tub to hold slaves, going across the ocean to some miserable hole to get them, and coming back through mountainous seas to give one-third of the slaves we've brought back to that thief in Charleston, it makes me furious!" Powner ended with a string of curses and pounded the ship's rail.

"So Ormsby will come down to the ship to inspect the lot of 'em?"

"Yes, of course. He'll have to...." Powner stopped midway through his sentence, lost in thought. He held a finger up, to indicate to Jacobson that he was pondering the situation and coming up with something new. Eventually he said, slowly, "Wait a minute! That gives me an idea. This plan might just be what that old crook deserves! Jacobson, what do you think of this?"

"You got a good idea, Captain?"

"Oh, I think this is a magnificent idea, Jacobson. We'll have to give Ormsby the hundred slaves we owe him, although I'm going to tell him that we lost a number through disease, and it's only right that he share a proportion of the overall loss. But that's not what I'm suggesting. Now, listen to this...." And with the expression of cunning that two conspirators might assume, Powner beckoned with his forefinger to Jacobson to attend closely to the plot. Powner lowered his voice, although there was no one nearby to overhear and used his hands in an excited fashion to help describe what he wanted to do.

He spoke rapidly, and as he went on, Jacobson's eyes lit up with understanding. His smile broadened. Finally, after ten minutes, Powner concluded his plan, and asked, "What do you think?"

"That's brilliant, Captain. I think it'll work!"

※

Two days later, the *Revenge* pulled into Charleston harbor, and when it was securely moored to a wharf, Powner and Jacobson went to Ormsby's office and confronted the man.

"Well, how did it go?" he asked, his little eyes darting about, his fleshless lips raising in what passed for a smile. He was wringing his hands in anticipation of getting one hundred valuable slaves.

"Oh, fairly well, Mr. Ormsby," Powner lied. "The crossing was rough, and a few of the prisoners died, but overall it went all right."

"Where are the slaves I own?" he cackled in a voice sounding like a chicken. "You remember our agreement—one third are mine, and I am legally able to choose the ones I want. I have the legal document right here!" He waved it at them. His attitude was totally condescending, demanding.

"Yes, of course. All of them are still on board my ship, chained, as they have been for the past seven weeks. We just tied up at the dock two hours ago."

"Hmph. Well, will you have your crew bring them off the vessel, so I can pick the ones I want?"

"Uh, I'm afraid that's impossible, Mr. Ormsby. Do you want us to take them out of the holds, and line them up on the docks, so you can go along and make your selection? The city authorities would never allow three hundred slaves just out of the jungle to be on their streets, even on the public docks. They're chained, of course, but they could break their chains and get loose, and…three hundred totally uncivilized and very dangerous people running all over Charleston??! Even a small army would have trouble rounding up all of them!"

This unexpected turn of events produced several reactions—first, surprise; second, puzzlement; and third, anger. One could read those movements of Ormsby's mental faculties as he went through that sequence. "Huh! Never thought of that! I could get in big trouble with the city authorities, if we don't do this carefully. Maybe you're right. Well then, what can we do? How do I pick my slaves?" Ormsby's prune-like face was turning purple. He'd never been aboard a slave ship before, nor seen the condition. And he'd certainly never faced a situation like this. In previous negotiations with other slaver captains, they had their own money to buy slaves in Africa, and he loaned them nothing, but simply bought a *few* slaves that had been brought ashore.

Powner and Jacobson had carefully rehearsed this. They pretended to mull over the problem, looking at each other quizzically, and shrugging in mock uncertainty. Then Jacobson said meekly, "May I suggest something, sir? The only thing I can think of is if you could come down to the *Revenge* and look over the prisoners for yourself, while they are chained up on board. That way, there's no chance of any escaping, and you would be perfectly safe."

Now it was Ormsby's turn to cogitate on the problem. "Hmm. Yes. Yes. I suppose you're right."

Powner and Jacobson were enjoying every minute of the fellow's predicament. They knew he was thinking, *It's true, now that I think about it; the mayor would have my head if I allowed three hundred naked savages to be out on the streets. Think of the scandal! Our dear ladies would be shocked! Outraged! Mortified! Oh! The city would be up in arms! And I don't want to get in trouble with the city fathers.*

Ormsby thought some more, then finally said, "Wait a minute. If you turn my slaves over to me, what'll I do with them?" His attitude had changed totally from demanding to consternation, bewilderment. The old fool was out of his league, and clearly he knew it.

"You don't expect to keep all hundred of them for yourself, do you?" Powner asked innocently.

"Of course not! What would I do with one hundred slaves?"

"Then I guess you want to sell them at an auction, don't you? I suggest you get your auctioneer all ready, and do it quick!"

Ormsby coughed, then blinked several times. "Yes. I suppose you're right. Which auctioneer should I use? McGonigal? No, he hates me. Selfridge? He might do a good job. All right; I'll come down to the ship. Right now?"

"Right now is fine, sir. No time like the present," Powner said, stifling his mirth. "You'll be welcome aboard."

Ormsby grabbed his coat and some paper to make notes, and off they went.

When they arrived at the wharf near Concord Street, Ormsby had overcome his confusion, and was eager to see his new prizes. He was quivering like a child on his birthday, waiting to get his presents.

They went up the gangway. Powner had rehearsed the crew how to act, not to smirk, and to keep the hatches battened down and the holds sealed, to contain as much as possible the overpowering stink from below. The ghastly aroma was somewhat detectable, for there was no way to conceal it entirely. But the waterfront shops and warehouses were producing other smells, a breeze was blowing to waft it away, and Ormsby was too preoccupied with thoughts of his new prizes, and the profits to be made, to notice anything. He gazed around the ship. All the members of the crew saluted him, some of them greeted him, and he preened at this mark of respect. "Hmm," he decided, "the vessel looks quite prim and tidy, Captain. My compliments!"

"Thank you, Mr. Ormsby. We always try to keep it that way. The prisoners are below, of course. Would you like to begin inspecting them and choosing the ones you want?"

"Oh yes, yes. Let's see them right now."

"Mr. Phipps, would you open the hatch and take Mr. Ormsby below to view the slaves?"

Phipps saluted, said "Yes, sir!" and led Ormsby to the main hatch. He began to open it.

The rest of the crew and the captain had to turn their backs to conceal their merriment.

As the hatch was opened, Ormsby shouted, "Oh!" He stood there for a minute, shocked and uncertain.

Phipps said, "Please follow me, sir," and Ormsby began hesitantly to go down the ladder.

He shouted, "OH!!" and held his nose. "What in the world—?!"

Halfway down the ladder, Ormsby shouted "OOHHH!" and covered his nose with a handkerchief.

At the bottom of the ladder, he screamed "OOOOHHHH!!!" and began to scramble up the ladder as fast as he could. The crew exploded in gales of laughter.

Back on deck, he confronted Powner and Jacobson in a rage. "Why didn't you warn me there would be such an overwhelming stench? How am I supposed to go down in that? I'm not used to such a thing! It's terrible! Do you think I'm a fool?"

"I thought you knew all about slaving ships," Powner said calmly.

"W-well, yes, but..." He sputtered and waved his arms about wildly. In other financial deals, Ormsby was used to being in control. He wasn't accustomed to such dilemmas.

Jacobson spoke, with muted contempt showing through, "Mr. Ormsby, on this ship, as on all slavers, WE must tolerate these smells all the time. What else can we do? We live here. Do you think we like it? No. You live in your nice little house, with the smell of sweet perfumes. BUT, if you're going to indulge in getting profit from slavery, you too, little man, are going to have to endure this sort of thing occasionally! This entire crew thinks you're a jackass. Now, if you want your hundred, get down that hold and pick them out!"

Thoroughly cowed by this attack, Ormsby shrank back. "All right," he mewed, his face white as a sheet. He went back to the hatch and down the ladder, holding his nose and looking very sick.

He descended slowly, led by Phipps and five other seamen They had the keys and would begin to unlock the chains from the bulwarks, so the prisoners who were picked could move to the ladder and climb up to the deck, still with chains to their handcuffs and neck and ankle manacles.

"Ormsby won't be down there long," Powner laughed. The crew applauded. "He'll pick the first ones he sees, just to get out of there quickly—the old folks and the others on the top compartment. He won't suspect that there's the valuable ones below," Jacobson predicted.

Sure enough, in a few minutes Ormsby's head popped out of the hatch, coughing and almost retching. He looked the color of raw rutabaga and seemed about to faint. Stumbling to the deck, he said to everyone in a loud, choking voice, "I can't stand any more of that! Captain, is that the best you have? Wouldn't the Muslim traders sell you some younger ones? There's mostly women and old people. I managed to count out forty-two of them. Then I had to get out of there. It's too horrible. They're coming up now." His eyes were wide, and he grasped the ship's rail for support.

A number of older men and women, and some younger women, were climbing out of the hatch, obviously pleased to be released from that foul dungeon.

Powner looked over the ones coming up. "Why yes, Mr. Ormsby, those are some of the best I have down there!" he lied with a straight face. "Must you take some of the best specimens? You're leaving us with a lot of sick folks and little children. I'll be lucky when I go to another port if we get much money for the rest of them...."

Now up in somewhat cleaner air, able to breathe again, Ormsby was trying to pull himself together, having been humiliated in every way. He had never been treated like this in all his life. And he knew now that he had little control over it. "Now look, Powner," he said in a tone somewhere between supplication and fury, "I don't know what to do. We're rational men. Let's try to work this out as gentlemen. I need one hundred out of the three hundred...."

"But, Ormsby, some have died and had to be buried at sea. We started out with three hundred, but there's only about two hundred eighty left."

"All right! All right! Give me ninety then!" He had the distinct suspicion that he was the butt of an enormous joke—that he was like the poor little nut in the jaws of the nutcracker.

"Fine. That's fair," said Powner. "Let's see—forty-two from ninety. That means we still owe you forty-eight. Wouldn't you like to go down again and choose the best that's left?"

"NO, you idiot!! I wouldn't go down in that cesspool again if you paid me fifty guineas!"

The entire crew was crowded around, laughing and slapping each other on the back, and enjoying this comedy immensely.

"All right, Ormsby, First Mate Jacobson and I will select forty-eight more and deliver them to the wharf in two hours. Will you be there to get them in two hours?"

Now it was Ormsby's turn to swear a blue streak. "I guess so. I've got to go to Selfridge, the auctioneer, and see if he can put them in his stockade until he runs an auction! I'll probably get in plenty of trouble with the city authorities, but frankly, at this point, I don't care!"

With that, he stormed off the vessel.

❧❦❧

There couldn't be two *Prescott families, in a small town like Chester! All of them must be hurt! Find them and punish them all!*

From what his daughter had said, the other Prescott was a candlemaker. This day he trudged the three miles from his shack into

Chester to find out what he could. He approached a woman on the street. She was working hard at ignoring him...a common reaction.

"Uhh, wh-where is the, ah, candlemaker's shop?"

The woman took a step back. Revulsion waved across her face. She appeared to give a quick thought to running away. But she settled for blurting out hasty directions and pointing toward the shop. He didn't bother to thank her.

He stood a hundred feet from Andrew Prescott's chandlery, looking it over, from behind an old oak. He did not dare to approach more closely. A few other people were about, so he was not too conspicuous. Patiently he waited, watching. A half hour later, Andrew came through the front door, talking with a customer. He scrutinized Andrew. *Yes,* he thought. *I've seen him before, several times, at his father's shoe shop, and through the window at the Prescott home during their Christmas party.*

I can wait. I'll go back into town and do a bit of begging. Perhaps someone will give me enough money so I can buy some food. Then I'll stay down by the river until dark.

By six o'clock, the sun was setting behind the trees. He came within two hundred feet of the shop and waited behind a grove of maples. He observed two young men emerge from the shop and go their way, and he assumed that these were Andrew's apprentices, leaving for the day. Ten minutes later, through the windows the shop went dark as candles were extinguished. Andrew came out the door and turned, walking to his home up the hill.

He doesn't even lock the door, the man thought. *How foolish.*

Still he waited. He was in no hurry. What if this Prescott fellow returned? He could not take that chance. With the small amount of money he had collected that afternoon while begging, he had purchased several rolls in a bakery, and he made a meal of those as he waited.

Several hours later, Andrew had not reappeared. The glow of a rising moon was visible above the trees, and the man was pleased with this, for it meant there might be some limited visibility when he went inside the shop. No one was nearby, so he walked rather determinedly to the shop's door, lifted the latch, and entered.

Inside, it was murky, for the moonlight hardly came through the two small windows. He had never been in a chandler's workshop before, so its layout was a mystery. And what he might do here in the way of destruction was also uncertain. He would see.

Groping around in the large room, he found shelves on the walls well stocked with candles of all sizes, and dozens and dozens of bars of soap. Gradually his eyes became slightly more accustomed to the dark, and he walked to the other end of the room. This, he thought, was where the apprentices worked, dipping the candles and doing all the other jobs. Then he came to a wall at the back and found a door that led to another workroom. Here there was total darkness, even darker than in the front room.

Colliding with some obstacles, he stopped to assess where he might be. It seemed somehow different from the previous room; there were smells here that were pungent, acrid. These same smells had been in the front room, but not nearly so strong. Here they were almost overwhelming.

Moving slowly and cautiously, and feeling his way along, he continued to bump into things: wooden boxes, tables, workbenches, and something else. He could not determine what it was, but it seemed to have rounded wooden sides about five feet high. Several iron straps ran horizontally around it. While he could not understand its function, it was one of two giant round wooden vats used to heat rendered tallow fat, ashes, and oils into the right consistency, when it would be poured into large wooden molds. Then it would begin to gel into a soap, or wax for candles. The mix had been simmering all day, ready to be used on the morrow.

Out from the bottom of these huge vats wooden spouts protruded, from which the mixture would be poured when the spouts were opened.

Stumbling around in the dark, the man collided heavily with one of the spouts, knocking it out of the vat. Immediately a vast flow of the hot mix poured out in a stream that shot across the room, knocking the man down and covering him with tallow fat. He groveled on the floor, trying to catch his breath and swinging his arms and legs frantically, attempting to rise and escape the relentless stream. The tallow was so slippery it was almost impossible. After a few minutes of gasping and choking, he got to his knees and managed to crawl away from the flood that now covered most of the floor in the room to a depth of several inches. And still the flow of hot mix continued to pour from the vat.

Shaken and bewildered, he crawled on hands and knees toward the doorway to the outer room. Once through it, he managed to get to his feet. He wiped the tallow fat from his face and could vaguely detect the faint light from the windows at the front of the shop. Slowly and painfully, he staggered toward the windows and the nearby door, went through it, and slammed it behind him. In the chill night, the wax cooled and began to harden on him. He walked with exhausted steps toward the confines of the woods beyond, there to collapse and go into a fitful sleep.

❧

The next morning, when Andrew opened the front door of the shop and beheld the ruin, he exclaimed, "Oh my stars! Look at this! Somehow one of the vats must be leaking! The tallow is everywhere."

Andrew assumed that the vat's spout had dislodged on its own. It took him and his apprentices two days to clean up the mess.

❧

The news got around Philadelphia quickly. From one person to the next, the word was passed: "The English preacher George Whitefield has arrived in town!" It was Saturday, November 3rd, 1739, and people who had been alerted to his coming across the Atlantic by the newspapers had waited anxiously for this news. There were only a few in this city who did not know something of his reputation in England, since it had been reported for almost two years.

Whitefield had arrived in America on October 30th, landing at Lewes, Delaware, and immediately set out for Philadelphia. He got there late at night on Friday, November 2nd, but he was expected and taken immediately to the home of a friend of William Seward, who had arrived earlier in the city.

The next morning, visitors began to come to greet him. Shortly after dawn, Whitefield was awakened by voices in the street and was astounded to find about thirty people already gathered there, hoping for a glimpse of him. He dressed hurriedly, went outside to meet them, and was delighted with their warm felicitations. Then the arrival of notable people began.

Whitefield took a quick breakfast, and finished just as the Proprietor of Pennsylvania, Thomas Penn, the son of William Penn, came to the house. He was eager to establish a relationship with this internationally famous preacher. After him came the Reverend Archibald Cummings, the Church of England Commissary and rector of Christ Church. Whitefield did not know what kind of reception he would get from Anglican Church officials in America; would it be like the rebuffs he had gotten in England? To his surprise and delight, Cummings welcomed him cordially, and after getting to know each other the rector invited Whitefield to preach daily in Christ Church's magnificent sanctuary for as long as he was in the city. The Englishman was astounded and accepted the offer.

As the morning wore on, the pastor of the Presbyterian church, Jedediah Andrews, arrived to welcome Whitefield to the city, and later the Baptist pastor, Horatio Gale, also came. Both offered their pulpits to Whitefield, who graciously replied that he appreciated the offers, but probably would be preaching either at Christ Church, which was larger than theirs, or outdoors.

On Monday, Whitefield came to Ben Franklin's print shop, and they had an hour's discussion. Tom was away on errands and missed meeting him, which would disappoint him greatly when he returned. During this time Franklin was able to frame an opinion of the preacher. He was amazed at the amount of experience Whitefield had behind him, despite his youth. Overall, Franklin's impression dispelled his earlier skepticism about the preacher's integrity. Whitefield seemed so transparent and sincere, and at the same time so visionary and driven to achieve.

The next morning, Franklin was eating breakfast with his wife Deborah and mother-in-law, Sarah Read, on the second floor of their home. The day had dawned cool and bright. Deborah was curious about Ben's activities on the previous evening. "You told me that after dinner you were going to hear the new preacher from England, Whitefield. Well, did he live up to your expectations?"

Ben took another spoonful of oatmeal porridge into his mouth before answering and swallowed it. "Oh yes, dear; he's most exceptional. An amazing speaker. He has a loud, clear voice and articulates his words and sentences so perfectly that he might be heard and understood at a great distance. He preached from the top of the Court House steps, in the middle of Market Street, on the west side of Second Street. Both streets were filled with his hearers to a considerable distance." He reached for his cup of coffee and drank from it.

Sarah Read said, "I've heard the crowds coming to hear him are getting larger and larger. Christ Church is crowded out each time he preaches, and I think he's held three services there. I heard him preach on Sunday afternoon, and the church was absolutely packed, with hundreds waiting outside. So it's no wonder Whitefield is going outside to preach."

"Yes, Mother, and the people don't mind at all. I've heard there were about six thousand there outside the Court House last evening. I got there a bit late, and being among the hindmost in Market Street, I had the curiosity to learn how far he could be heard, by retiring backwards down the street towards the river. And I heard his voice distinctly till I came to Front Street, when some noise in that street obscured it. Imagining then a semi-circle, of which my distance should be the radius, and that it were filled with listeners, to each of whom I allowed two square feet, I computed that he might well be heard by more than thirty thousand."

"Thirty thousand! Oh, that's incredible, Ben. I can't believe that," Deborah said.

"I too doubted this previously, but now I accept the possibility. And last evening I saw it!"

"My goodness, Ben," Deborah said, "you're always the inquisitive one. You had to do the mathematics on that, didn't you?" The two ladies laughed, and Ben smiled at them.

"And what's wrong with that?" he said, taking another long drink of coffee. "I may well want to use that statistic in my newspaper reporting. And yesterday, Whitefield was downstairs in my shop...."

"He was?!" the ladies said, startled and a bit indignant. "Why didn't you call us to meet him?"

"Oh, ahem—I thought you might have gone out.... Anyway, first he told me that he has decided to remain preaching in this area for a while, instead of going immediately to Georgia. *And* he has a number of sermons that he needs printed here in the colonies, and he likes what he has seen of my printing, so he has asked me to be his printer. Isn't that interesting?"

"Ben, that's marvelous," Sarah exclaimed.

WHITEFIELD PREACHING TO SOLDIERS.

"As many as were in debt came to David, and he became a captain over them."

On the next afternoon, a visitor came to the house Whitefield had rented, and he soon realized that this was not the average clergyman. It was the Reverend William Tennent, Sr., and he had come as soon as he could from the Log College. That evening Whitefield wrote in his Journal, he:

> was much comforted by the coming of Mr. Tennent, an old grey-headed disciple and soldier of Jesus Christ....He is a great friend of Mr. Erskine, of Scotland, and, as far as I can find, both he and his sons are secretly despised by the generality of the Synod, as Mr. Erskine and his brethren are hated by the judicatories of Edinburgh, and, as the Methodist preachers are by their brethren in England.

When Tennent was invited in, Whitefield asked him to be seated on a comfortable chair, seated himself opposite, and had the maid bring them tea. The old teacher immediately told why he had come.

"We have heard much of the amazing success of your preaching in England," Tennent said. "The Lord is surely at work, and is using you."

"Thank you. I am trying to be His devoted servant, sir."

"Mr. Whitefield, are you aware of what is happening here?"

Whitefield thought a minute. "I have heard that a number of pastors are preaching for revival, and that stirrings are beginning. I do see, from my crowds, that people are hungry for spiritual truth."

"I am pleased to tell you that the Lord has been at work here in our provinces, and in New England. There are Awakenings in progress in Pennsylvania and New Jersey, and people are coming to our Lord Jesus in numbers, and have been for some years."

Whitefield's brows shot up. "That's more than I had heard! Praise God! Tell me about it."

"There are a number of us who are trying to raise up Christ Jesus, and draw others to him, but we are being resisted by others in the ministry. Our opponents are calling us *New Lights*, and we suspect that some of those who oppose us are unconverted men who hate the preaching of salvation through divine grace."

"*New Lights* is a mild term, compared to what I am called—an *enthusiast*," Whitefield said.

"Yes, we know. The London newspaper accounts about you have given us the details. Our enemies are saying the same things about us. Now, there are several reasons I have come to meet you. We hear that you preach to all indiscriminately, without regard to what church the people belong to, or no church at all. And yet you are a priest of the Church of England. I like that. We are trying to do the same here, delivering the Gospel to the entire populace, believing that God is not so interested in denominational titles as He is in sincere, heartfelt faith."

"Mr. Tennent, more and more I feel you are a man after my own heart."

"And that's why I came to see you. Mr. Whitefield, I would be very plain. *We need you.* Our burdens are enormous, if we are to touch this entire region with the Gospel. Your name and reputation are already well known, though you just arrived in Pennsylvania, as is shown by the huge crowds you are drawing. If you joined forces with the New Light preachers in this area, our cause and impact, *and yours,* would be greatly advanced."

"O my. I had no idea," Whitefield said, shaking his head slightly.

"I don't mean to suggest that we aren't hard at work already, teaching the Gospel. My own sons, and a number of other men, are devoted to this cause, and some of them are very effective evangelists. But they do not have the reputation that you have, or your effectiveness in drawing great crowds."

"I must say, Mr. Tennent, that to this point I have been most favorably impressed by the openness of your people."

"Yes, I believe our people are wide open to whatever the Lord is doing in our midst," said Tennent. "I heard that you had an audience of six thousand people on one evening, and eight thousand on the next. Those may be standard audiences for you in a city as large as London, with tens of thousands of people, Mr. Whitefield. But here in Philadelphia the entire populace is only about twelve thousand. So, last evening you had *two-thirds of all our populace* before you, listening to your words!"

"Mr. Tennent, I am most humbled. And the behavior last evening! Even in London, I never observed so profound a silence. The people did not seem weary of standing, nor was I weary of speaking. I thought I could have continued my discourse all night."

"The people here are prepared, Mr. Whitefield!" Tennent said. "If you join with us and help in furthering the Awakening, I can promise that you'll be supported by Moravians, Congregationalists, Baptists, Presbyterians, Quakers, Church of England people, and others. We are on the brink of a tremendous movement of the Holy Spirit, and you can be a major part of this."

"You stagger me. I had no idea of all this. How can I say no? Of course I must go where the Holy Spirit leads me. What would you have me do?"

Tennent told him and gave a deep sigh. He had achieved the purpose of his trip from Neshaminy. The most famous preacher in all Christendom would join with them. God was blessing.

The work in Philadelphia had begun on a very high note, with no difficulties. George Whitefield would return to the fine harvest field of Philadelphia, but first he was eager to view for himself the Awakening as it was spreading through the Middle Colonies by the Log College "New Lights," and they were happy to show it to him.

On November 13th, 1739 Whitefield, William Seward, Joe Husbands, John Syms, and Captain Hosea Gladman set out for New Jersey on horses that were lent to them, and they went to Trenton and then on to New Brunswick. At the church there the oldest son of William Tennent Sr., Gilbert Tennent, was the pastor. Gilbert, at 36, was scholarly like his father, and theologically they thought alike.

Whitefield preached at Gilbert Tennent's church on November 13th, and on the 14th the two, with others, went on to Elizabethtown and then, by boat, reached New York City. Whitefield had been urged to visit this thriving city by a wealthy merchant, Thomas Noble. He became another of the friends assisting in the establishment of the orphan house, and agreed to work with William Seward in the growing promotional efforts to expand the ministry by extensive letter-writing, the printing of Whitefield's sermons, the use of newspapers, and other methods. In New York, Gilbert Tennent was asked to preach in the Presbyterian church. Later, Whitefield said to a friend, "Never before have I heard such a searching sermon....He is a son of thunder, and does not fear the faces of men."

When he came to a new area, Whitefield tried to win the Anglican authorities to his side, hoping he would have their blessing as fellow Church of England clergy, and allowing him to preach in their churches. This had just happened in Philadelphia. In New York City he called on the Reverend William Vessey, the Commissary, or deputy of the Bishop of London. Accompanied by Thomas Noble and William Seward, Whitefield came to Vessey's home and knocked on the door, which was opened by the Commissary. He was short, in his fifth decade, with black hair that came to his shoulders. His eyes were gray and cold. He had a hard face that suggested he had seen everything and that there was nothing left in this world to surprise him.

"Mr. Vessey? I am George Whitefield. May we speak with you?" He introduced his friends.

"Yes, come in. I know why you are here. Before you ask, you may not have the use of my pulpit or my church." Vessey did not invite them to be seated but sat himself in a large chair. They stood.

"Well, I was hoping..."

"Sir, may I see your Letters of Orders, to confirm your authority?"

"I am sorry, Mr. Vessey, but I just came from Philadelphia, and I left them there."

"Well then, do you have a license to preach from the Bishop of London?"

Whitefield responded, "I never heard that the Bishop of London gave a license to any clergyman who went to preach the Gospel in the colony of Georgia. I was given the parish of Savannah by the trustees of Georgia, and I had letters to that end from the Bishop of London, which I thought was sufficient authority to preach anywhere throughout his diocese."

Drawing back in horror, Vessey said, "Why no; that is by no means satisfactory to me. You have broken your oath, and broken the Canon which enjoins ministers and churchwardens not to admit persons into their pulpit without a license."

Whitefield said quietly, "But how could I have broken that, when I am neither a churchwarden, nor have any church to admit anyone to? But sir, speaking of breaking canons, I know that you are a frequenter of bars and taprooms for the sale of liquor, and I would remind you of that Canon which forbids the clergy of the Anglican church to go into any such places."

Vessey jerked bolt upright and went into a rage. He shouted, "How dare you! I know that you made a disturbance in Philadelphia and have been sowing and causing divisions in other places! But you think, in your arrogance, that you have a necessity laid upon you to preach!" His face had taken the color of a beet.

William Seward wanted to jump into this, and tell Vessey there had been no "disturbance" in Philadelphia—just the opposite—but he knew Whitefield wanted to handle this himself, so he held his peace, growing furious with this man, as was Thomas Noble.

Whitefield wished to remain calm and not answer him in like manner. "Yes, that is true, because the Lord Jesus has commanded me to preach. But the clergy and laity of our church seem to be settled on their tails. My end in preaching is not to sow divisions, but to propagate the pure Gospel of Jesus Christ."

"Well, we don't want your assistance here."

"If you preach the Gospel truly, I wish you good luck in the Name of the Lord. But as you have denied me your church even before I asked for it, I will preach in the fields. For all places are alike to me."

In a sarcastic way, Vessey said, "Yes, I find you have been doing that. And another thing; I know you have been censuring those who are older than you. How old are you, anyway?"

"I am twenty-four, and a graduate of Pembroke College, Oxford University, and an ordained priest of the Church of England. I am no respecter of persons; if a bishop commits a fault, I will tell him of it. If a regular clergyman doesn't act properly, I will be free with him also, as well as with a layman."

Seeing he was getting nowhere, Vessey, full of resentment, rose from his chair saying, "I have business to do, and can't give any more time to you. Mr. Noble, as it was you who sent for this man to come to New York, I guess you will find him a pulpit." He escorted them to the door and closed it behind them.

The pastor of the Dutch Reformed church, Henricus Boel, also closed that church to him. The pastor of the Presbyterian church in New York, Ebenezer Pemberton, gladly opened his church to Whitefield, and he preached to packed congregations seven times. But the opposition of a few clergy only inflamed the curiosity of the people.

With Whitefield's rejection by those in authority in some sects, it is little wonder that he reacted and broadened his loyalties. He told his hearers that a Christian was a member of any sect who had experienced regeneration. The Church of England preacher set no exclusive bounds: Quaker, Baptist, Lutheran, Dutch Reformed, Presbyterian, Church of England, Moravian, and others—all could claim no special merit because of their church membership, but all through the New Birth could be God's children. One of his most famous illustrations before great crowds had him throwing back his head and raising his arms to heaven, crying to Father Abraham, asking, "Are there any Baptists up there?" The answer came back, "No!" to the crowd's surprise. Then, "Are there any Presbyterians there?" "No!" "Moravians?" "Quakers?" "Anglicans?" and through the list. Each time the answer came down, "No!" "Why," cried Whitefield, "who have you then?" Answered Father Abraham, "We don't know those names here. All that are here are Christians!"

***

Gilbert Tennent was observing all of these events, and he knew increasingly that Whitefield was the very answer to the New Lights' problems. Growing divisions among the Presbyterian clergy of the Middle Colonies in recent years had resulted in the formation of three separate groups: the New Lights, or those supporting the Awakening; the Old Lights, or those against it; and the New England party, who had kept some distance from the debate as it swirled in Synod meetings for year after year. The New England group was larger and included such prominent men as Ebenezer Pemberton, pastor of the New York church where Whitefield had just preached, John Pierson of the Woodbridge church, Aaron Burr of the Newark church, and Jonathan Dickinson, pastor of the Elizabethtown church, as well as others.

So, if they were to advance the Awakening, the New Lights needed new recruits to their cause. And the New Englanders were the obvious candidates, because theologically they were in agreement, as against the Old Lights, who opposed the Awakening and differed on major issues. Gilbert Tennent was delighted that a prominent member of the New England party, Pemberton, had been quite receptive to Whitefield and his evangelism, and he realized that Whitefield might be used to bring all of the New Englanders to the side of the Awakening.

With the Awakening underway, turbulent feelings were being stirred up everywhere by the heated controversy. A crisis in the life of the Christian church had come. But, Gilbert Tennent realized, the entire scene had been changed by the sudden arrival of George Whitefield.

The evangelist said to Tennent, "You know, Gilbert, I am full of amazement and appreciation of the long-standing efforts of many people to bring about a general Awakening. Suddenly I have become conscious that what Jonathan Edwards has achieved in Massachusetts is not unique, but that here in the Middle Colonies is a company of fellow evangelists who are working hard to bring about revival in the churches and among the people."

"Yes, and beyond that, George, we are welcoming you and begging for your help."

"Not to cast my lot with you, I feel, would be a great mistake," Whitefield replied.

NINE

Whitefield Turns the Tide

Captain Joseph Powner on the ship *Revenge* had been making regular runs to Walabo in Africa to pick up slaves. He had not returned to Charleston but had made stops in Havana, Brazil, Haiti, and Barbados. In each of these places he had a wife, although none of them knew that the others existed.

The place he preferred above the rest was Sao Luis in Brazil, where his wife Margarida lived, and he took the *Revenge* there as often as he could, loaded with slaves to be sold. Then, when the slave auction was held, and the ship was being provisioned, he spent a week or two with Margarida.

On this trip the vessel arrived in Sao Luis on a morning when a storm was brewing. The clouds were scudding across the sky, driven by a rising wind. As the *Revenge* was coming into the port, the crew could see on shore the wind lashing through the trees, blowing up great puffs of dust. Powner ordered most of the sails taken in. The whole sky was becoming an angry dark blue-black, and the sun that was visible a few minutes before had been covered by the clouds. Rumbles of thunder came across the land, and then the first large drops of rain spattered on the deck.

Rain was as nothing to a ship such as this, which had come through hurricanes and fierce gales.

Powner stood at the helm, guiding the sailor at the wheel to the dock he wished to use. With only two small sails still aloft, the momentum of the ship carried her forward slowly. When they came up to the dock, half a dozen sailors jumped over to the land and took the hawsers thrown to them, tying the ship to large boulders placed at dockside for this purpose. This port was so small that the Brazilian authorities paid little attention to tax collecting there, and that was another reason Powner came. Few ships visited Sao Luis, and it was the perfect place to sell slaves, once word had been sent to surrounding towns and plantations.

The downpour continued for an hour. This was common in the tropics, where the rain forest brought forth lush growth everywhere. Powner used the time to go to his cabin and drink rum with his first mate, Herman Jacobson. When the last drops fell and the sun began peeping through breaking clouds, Powner conferred with Jacobson about getting the news out that slaves would soon be available to the locals.

"With only twenty-two in our crew, we'll need all of 'em to spread the word that we have a shipful, and the auction will be on Tuesday, here in town."

"Right, Cap'n. I'll get them ready and send them out. Too bad that so few of the crew speak any Portuguese."

"Yeah, Jacobson; and most of the natives speak no English at all, except for a few of the plantation owners. Well, the people around here have seen us before, and they know what we're here for. Teach the crew a few words in the lingo before they go: slaves, and auction, and Tuesday. That'll get the message across. And then the word will spread."

"Do you want us to do anything with the slaves down in the hold before we go ashore?"

"Yeah, there's a lot of sickness down there. Maybe ten or twelve have died in the last couple of days. If we pull all of them out of the hold and put them in the stockade, it would probably stop some of the sickness."

"You're right. I'll send three men to make sure the stockade is still in good shape. When they return, if the stockade's all right, then we'll unload the slaves and put all of them in there until the auction."

The compound was used as a holding pen each time the *Revenge* came to Sao Luis, and the sailors found it in the usual secure condition.

The gangplank was put down to the dock, and Jacobson and a number of the crew opened the hatches and went down to the compartments where the slaves were quartered. As soon as they descended the ladders, a great cry erupted from the slaves, who sensed that the ship had docked and that they were about to be taken ashore for an unknown future.

On the deck, the crew had formed a line, with each man about twenty feet apart from the next man, to convey the prisoners down the gangplank, onto the dock, and over to the compound. They carried long rawhide whips. After the upper compartment had been emptied, the crew was rotated. The men who had been on the deck or ashore were sent down into the hold, and the men down there were brought up, as no crew member would stay in that ghastly fetid sewer for long. Trouble was expected in the lower compartment where the most powerful, younger men—the troublemakers—had been chained, with iron collars around their necks. The sailors carried pistols, ready to shoot any of the violent slaves who had not been pacified by the long sea voyage, the poor food, and the brutal coercion of being chained up. They too had their chains unlocked from the bulwarks, and they went up the ladder last, and into the compound.

Word was sent to the entire area that a large auction of three hundred slaves would be conducted the next Tuesday. Until then, the slaves in the compound, while they were finally in clean air and had fresh water, were treated almost as badly as they had been in the horrible compartments below deck. However, they were fed somewhat better than they had been, subsisting on a "hog and hominy" diet, which consisted of some corn, fatty salted meat, and a few vegetables.

On Monday the ship's crew, well armed, moved into the compound and brought out about two dozen slaves each time, took them to the nearby shallow river, and made them jump in and wash off the filth that still clung to them. Whereas till then they had been naked, now as they emerged from the river they were given some clothes—the women smocklike gowns, the men shirts, loincloths, or pants, all made from shabby homespun or cheap fabrics known as "Negro cloth." Children of both sexes received only shirts, and went barefoot. Since Sao Luis was tropical, these minimal clothes served year-round. Now the slaves were freshly washed and dressed in clean clothes for the inspection of potential buyers.

Then Tuesday came, with the auction. Plantation owners and managers arrived from miles around. It was held just outside the compound, so that a few slaves could be brought out at a time. This was a wide area, with a raised platform, on which the auctioneer would stand and bring a slave up to stand next to him. Most of the slave auctions in the Western hemisphere were conducted much the same: the young males would be auctioned first, as they were considered the prime properties. Being strong, they brought the highest prices, because supposedly they could work for many years for their new owners. Then the women of childbearing age, often with children clinging to them, then the older men and women, and finally any children without a parent. Slaves approached the auction block in dreadful uncertainty, fearing the worst. Customers would frequently feel their bodies and make slaves show their teeth. Nothing in their dreary lives was quite so frightening, or so degrading.

If somehow an entire family had been brought over from Africa, a slave family sent to auction was seldom sold to a single buyer. Then followed one of the most tragic episodes, the breakup every slave expected: a child taken from its mother, or a couple separated. The brutal men of the *Revenge* could not care less. It was no wonder that every slave thought of trying to escape the demonic slavers and their uncertain future. But where could they escape to, in a strange new land? And recapture would certainly bring fierce retribution. Wherever there were slaves, they frequently wished for death, that they might be delivered from their endless agonies.

The auction took all day Tuesday, and when the sun set, all the slaves had been sold. The wagons pulled by oxen trundled up to the compound, one after the other, and the purchased slaves were loaded aboard. Usually three to six were bought by their new owners, sometimes even more.

Senhor Delgado was a manager at a large plantation ten miles inland. He said to a neighbor, as his new hands were loaded on his wagon by previously gotten slaves, "Good batch from Powner on this trip, eh? I've got three strong men, and two women of childbearing age. They've had those chains and collars on for ages, and their skin is raw. Should I take them off?"

His neighbor looked the slaves over, noting the fierce stares of the men and the way the women held themselves proudly. "If I were you, Otelo, I'd leave the chains and collars on for a while. No telling what those young bucks might do. Safer to keep 'em bound till they're at your place. Then, when they're among other slaves, maybe they'll settle down and figure they'd better behave themselves."

Delgado said, "You're right, Francisco. That's what I'll do. Did you buy many?"

"Four—two men and two women. All prime. My secret is, buy them cheap, and work 'em to the bone. Best bargain you can find. If they die, it don't matter. They ain't got any souls, or anything. Just bury 'em and forget 'em, and go and get another one." He smiled cruelly.

On the seacoast of Brazil, as elsewhere, labor on the farms and plantations was specialized. The managers and owners relied on their previous slaves, who spoke some Portuguese and could communicate with the new Africans, to train them in various skills. Slaves who seemed less capable were put into the fields for the never-ending work on the crops, and in the tropical climate, it could be brutal. This was the majority of them. If born on a plantation, slaves normally began to work in the fields by the age of eleven or twelve. From that point on, for the rest of their working lives, overwork was their daily portion. The hands were required to be in the fields of sugar cane, rice, cotton, sweet sorghum or whatever crops were being grown, as soon as it was light in the morning.

Since the chief exports of Sao Luis were sugar and molasses, the backbreaking work of cutting the cane, stripping the leaves, piling the cane in rows along the ground, tying it in bundles, and transporting it to the toothed rollers of the shredding and grinding machines, was all done by slaves. With the exception of half an hour at noon, they were not permitted to be idle a moment until it was too dark to see, and when the moon was full, they often labored till the middle of the night.

Powner had kept a careful record of the amounts paid for each of those auctioned and totaled the prices on sheets of paper. After the auction was over and the auctioneer had departed, Powner and First Mate Jacobson retired to a tavern in town, the Diabolo, and lubricated themselves with rum. Outside the tavern stood an eight-foot-tall devil in ebony with a leering smile carved across its hideous face, as if to suggest it was an omen of what awaited slavers in the afterlife. Each time he entered the tavern, Powner tried to ignore the statue.

"We did right well with this load, Herman," he declared to Jacobson, showing him the computations.

"Ah! Yes we did, I see. The crew's share will be substantial, and they'll be happy."

"I hope so. They've worked hard. Well, we're done in Sao Luis. In a few days we can pull out, and go back to Walabo for more. Do you think they need more slaves here in Sao Luis, or should we go somewhere else?"

Glancing around the crowded tavern, Jacobson spotted the mayor of the town across the room, talking with some other men. "Why don't you ask Carmona over there? He knows everything that's going on in town and around this whole area."

"Ha! You're right. And he's got his fingers in every pie, too. Plenty of graft in this province! Glad you saw him. I've got to slip him his commission. So, I'll ask him." Powner strolled over to the mayor's table.

The mayor recognized him immediately and rose to greet him. "Senhor Powner! How are you? Do you know all these gentlemen?"

The captain nodded to each of them and recognized them as managers of plantations. "Your honor, greetings! And gentlemen, hello. I don't mean to interrupt...."

"No no," the mayor said. "We were discussing your auction. It went well, did it not?"

"Quite well, thanks." Smiling at the managers, Powner said, "I know you gentlemen bought slaves at the auction. Are you satisfied with your purchases?"

The managers agreed that they were, and Powner continued, "Well, my ship is leaving for Africa in a few days, for another load of slaves. We can come back to several ports. Do you need still more, and should I come back here, or go to Havana or Charleston or somewhere else?"

Each manager began to mumble his thoughts, and the mayor said, "Oh no, Captain. They are all in agreement. They need more! Some slaves die, so they need *many more*. Please return."

"All right, I will, someday soon. Senhor Mayor, may I speak with you a moment, outside?"

Excusing himself, the mayor followed Powner out the front door, where he was given an envelope with a large amount of money inside. The mayor said, "Thank you, Captain. I'll do what I can to help your business." Exchanging a few sly winks, they agreed on the deal with a handshake.

In a few days, the *Revenge* set sail for Africa.

ಸಿಂಬ

Sarah and Andrew Prescott had wished to begin a family, and in the spring of 1739 she announced she was pregnant. The baby was born on

November 16th, and the proud parents decided to name her Miriam, after Sarah's grandmother. On Sunday, November 25th, during the church service of the morning in the Dissenter church, her parents presented Miriam to the Rev. James Caldwell for baptism. The baby was sleeping soundly in her mother's arms. Tom had come from Philadelphia for the occasion, and he and his father stood behind the parents as the pastor performed the baptism.

When the worship service was over, and the congregation had largely departed, Pastor Caldwell came over to the Prescott family to congratulate them on the baby's birth. They chatted, and the pastor turned to Tom, whom he had not seen for a while, and asked how he was getting along in Philadelphia.

"I'm working with the printer, Benjamin Franklin, learning the printing trade, sir," Tom said.

"Oh yes, I've heard a good deal about Mr. Franklin. Frequently I get a copy of *The Pennsylvania Gazette*. I take it that it's very interesting work."

"It certainly is. And right now, all of Philadelphia is talking about the Reverend Mr. Whitefield. He has the entire city excited. Thousands go out to hear him."

"Yes, I came to Philadelphia on the 9th to hear him preach. He spoke from the Court House steps, and I could not believe the numbers who came to hear him."

Tom said, "Mr. Whitefield has been in New Jersey and New York for the last week, but I believe he is coming back."

"Indeed! That's all the Synod is talking about! Mr. Whitefield came through Chester when he first landed from England, but he was in haste to get to your city. It was late at night, so he did not stop. And I did not know he was coming through, so I didn't go to greet him. But I hope he will be coming back this way, and will be favoring all of us with a message."

Hiram Prescott came over to them, and said that they would be going home to dinner in a minute. He thanked the pastor for the baptism, and he and Tom left the church.

"Dad, I have something to tell you," Tom said.

"Yes, Tom?"

"I met the most wonderful girl in August, and I think I'm falling in love with her!"

Hiram reached for Tom's hand, shook it, and said, "That's wonderful, son. What is her name?"

"Rachel Nicholson. She lives in Philadelphia, and her father keeps a dry-goods store. Her mother is a fine lady, and Rachel has a younger brother, Bob."

"Tell me more about Rachel, please."

"Well, she is not quite my age, and she has long, light brown hair and brown eyes, and she's beautiful, Dad!"

"Oh, I'm sure of that."

※※※

Josh Morris had reached his twentieth year and had been a student at the Log College for two years. Academically, he was progressing well, and Reverend William Tennent was pleased with his abilities. He had learned Greek, was reading the New Testament in the original language, and was mastering Hebrew. Other studies offered by Tennent included Philosophy, Logic, Literature, Mathematics, Church History, and Homiletics—in other words, all the courses offered at Yale and Harvard Colleges. Spiritually, he had grown much. He had come to agree with what the New Lights were doing, was beginning to do some preaching himself in nearby churches, and enjoying it immensely.

On this day the students at the Log College were talking excitedly. Sorting through the mass of hearsay and rumor, the only fact of which they could be certain was that George Whitefield had been at Maidenhead and Trenton the day before, and might be coming to Neshaminy and the Log College, on his way back to Philadelphia. But exactly when was uncertain. So rumors spread.

The students gathered outside, and waited expectantly, despite the coolness of the day. Suddenly whispers spread through the group, "He's here!" On horseback came a party, including Whitefield, his secretary John Syms, William Seward, and Gilbert Tennent. The group dismounted from their horses, and William Tennent immediately approached Whitefield. "Thank you so much for coming, George."

"Mr. Tennent, I have heard so much about your college. I would love to see it, and talk with as many of the students as are not otherwise engaged."

"It will be my pleasure to show you around. As you see, it is not large...."

Whitefield looked at the building for a minute, and then said, "Oh, but that is *today! Tomorrow* will be entirely different, I know. The word is around, and I am sure you will be attracting numbers of fine young men who know the Lord, to study with you. Then you will need to erect large buildings. I know that already you have sent out more than half a dozen worthy ministers of Jesus. I believe you are now laying a foundation for the instruction of many others."

"Yes, George, but I'm getting to be an old man! I am sixty-six years old, and not as vigorous as I once was. And how old are you?"

"Twenty-four."

"And already you have an international reputation!"

"But you are still quite active, and your mind is sharp, teaching in all those fields of learning. And soon, with more students coming, you can bring on young tutors who are expert in their disciplines, who can take over some of the teaching load."

"Yes; that's a great vision. Well, let me show you around. Shall we go inside the house? I want you to meet my students."

They entered the building. The students hoped to chat with Whitefield, who was hardly older than they were. Tennent introduced them, and for the next fifteen minutes an animated discussion ensued, with the students expressing their admiration for the evangelist, asking questions, discussing plans for the future, and describing life at the college, and Whitefield responding to all this.

"We pray for your work constantly," Samuel Blair said. "Tell us, is there anything more we can do to help spread the Awakening?"

"From everything I see, you are doing much already, Mr. Blair," Whitefield answered.

"In addition to these men coming along, there have been two other helpful events in recent days," Tennent said. "First, our New Lights have been much oppressed by some in the Synod of our Dissenter church, as you know. But just recently the Synod has allowed the formation of a new group, the Presbytery of New Brunswick, in which our men can be separate from those who oppose the Awakening and hate us."

"Most encouraging, Mr. Tennent! There are times when I find myself wishing that I might be separated from those who hinder me in my own church. But then I remind myself that I'm trying to bring my church back to where it was, years ago, on the truths of the Reformation, under the great Archbishop Thomas Cranmer."

"Indeed yes. Up till now it has been very difficult to have any of our graduates ordained by the Synod. No matter how well qualified our men were, most have been refused ordination. Our opponents have sneered at our college, and done much to undermine it and oppose my teaching. If they could close the college down, they would in a minute. But the great benefit to us is that now, this new presbytery can license and ordain godly and well-qualified men for the ministry, who are very much working for the awakening. The Synod cannot stop their ordination, and also it will be much more difficult for them to oppose the awakening from now on."

"That's magnificent. And you said there were two helpful events; what was the other one?"

"That the Awakening is being promoted so well by the press. Newspapers everywhere have carried favorable accounts of your preaching and its excellent results. Also, sixteen different publications by our Log College men are being sold by booksellers from Boston to Philadelphia. So, multitudes are being reached by the press."

"Wonderful. There's much to thank God for," said Whitefield. They left the students, and walked to the other end of the building. "Mr. Tennent, let me discuss something with you. You see what a great help William Seward is to me. He has been in England with me, and has put his health and his wealth at the disposal of the Gospel. He has many contacts, and promotes the awakening in England and here in America in many ways. But William is not terribly strong. And my secretary, John Syms, is kept completely busy by all the correspondence and getting materials ready for the printers. I am in need of a godly man, strong spiritually and physically, to assist. Your son Gilbert has been of much assistance in recent days, but he has a church to care for. I need a man who is experienced in dealing with people, and has a broad background. Do you know of such a person?"

Tennent thought for a minute, then said, "I understand the need, and I don't wonder, with all the burdens on you. You know, I may have the best possible person for your requirements."

"You do? Excellent. And who would that be?"

"You just met him. It's Josh Morris. He's a strong young man, comes from England, loves Jesus, has been a farmhand, is used to hard work, handles horses well, has traveled, even onto the frontier, has battled Indians, has been seriously wounded and recovered, and now wishes with all his heart to serve the Lord. And he is a good student."

"Let me speak with him again!"

Tennent called Josh over to them. "Josh, Mr. Whitefield would like to talk with you."

Whitefield spoke with Josh for quite a long time, explaining what was needed. Then they prayed together. When the interview was completed, he asked Josh if there was a possibility he could volunteer for this, for perhaps a few weeks.

"With all my heart!" Josh said, with great excitement. "Mr. Whitefield, you don't remember me, I'm sure. But it was under your early ministry in Gloucester that I was converted!"

The evangelist's mouth flew open in surprise. "Well, praise God! I am absolutely amazed. And from Gloucester, here you are now, in America. And you will be my assistant. Astounding."

Josh said, "Do you need me immediately?"

"That's asking a lot, I know. But if it's possible.... "

"I can get my clothes and a few books, and be ready in twenty minutes!" Josh dashed off, knowing that as soon as the word got out, he would be the envy of every other student.

Whitefield turned to Tennent. "Dear brother, I stand amazed at what the Lord is doing. Before I came to Philadelphia and met you, only two weeks ago, I had no idea of what was happening in the colonies. You and your sons have opened my eyes."

§)(¢

"What do you mean—you won't print my pamphlets and sermons against this blackguard Whitefield!" Commissary Vessey thundered at the printer. He was used to getting his way, and defiance like this, and frustrations, were rare to him.

The printer was adamant and stood his ground. "I'm very sorry, sir, but I will not. I have read over the material you left with me the other day, and I absolutely do not approve of what you say."

Commissary Vessey bristled with pugnacity like a porcupine. "Do you know who I am, man? I hold the very important post of the deputy of the Bishop of London here in New York City! We have given you printing business previously! But if you refuse my business this time, you shall not see any printing jobs from my church again!"

"Yes sir, I know very well who you are, and I respect that. But that is partly why I will not print your material!"

"What do you mean?" Vessey raged.

"I mean, sir, that I believe what you write in these sermons and pamphlets is disgraceful for a clergyman to say!"

"Disgraceful?!!" Vessey had not been called that to his face recently.

"Yes sir. I heard Mr. Whitefield preach several times while he was here in New York, and I thought he was a fine Christian doing a necessary work, and what you say about him is not true at all. But even if I didn't think that way, I still wouldn't print this stuff you write, because it's full of hate and malice. Imagine, to say the things you do against *another* clergyman! And to boot, if I'm not wrong, Mr. Whitefield is of your own sect, the Church of England, is he not?" the printer said.

"Whitefield is a disgrace to that superb church!"

"I can't see why that is true. I hear nothing but good things about him. And I didn't hear him say a thing against *you*. So why do you hate the man so?"

"OHH! What do you know of these things??!" Vessey said, trembling with fury. Then he made a great effort to calm down, taking a minute to do so. Finally he calmly said, "Listen, my man, I can't get my materials printed here in this city. The other printer, Forsythe, won't do it either."

The printer, rather annoyed to find that he was not the first choice for the print job, said, "Do you know why not? What did he tell you?"

Vessey was also not used to being questioned, but he was now desperate. There were no other printers for many miles; this was his last chance. His shoulders sagged, and he exhaled. "Well, he said pretty much what you say—that he thought my sermons were not very dignified."

The printer looked Vessey over critically, not liking what he saw. "Yes, I think he said much more than that. Sir, if this is the kind of stuff that your church wants printed, I do not want your business. I have more than enough business already, and I don't need yours. Good day."

His face again blotched red with fury, Vessey stood glaring at the man for a minute, then turned and slammed the door behind him.

ಸಾಡ

Ben Franklin was chatting with several of his friends outside his shop. It got animated.

Titus Jones, a wealthy man who owned a brickyard in the city, always dressed immaculately to demonstrate his wealth. On this day he wore green brocade and a powered wig, and the buttons were gilt. His highly polished shoes had silvered buckles that flashed in the sunlight. He was a confirmed atheist and was astounded that a person of some skepticism like Franklin would be interested in George Whitefield. His high-pitched voice rang out and could be heard up and down the street. Heads turned. Franklin was amused that Jones could get so worked up over things. Jones was shrilling, "But Ben, with your principles, why would you go to attend on a fanatic like this Whitefield fellow? I hear he stirs up the common rabble, and they go into hysterics! We are liable to have riots if this continues. And now he is in Philadelphia again! How long will this nonsense continue?" He was red-faced and thunder-browed.

"Now, now, Titus," Franklin said calmly. "Nothing of the sort. First I must remind you that I'm a newspaperman, and I must keep up on the news. Whitefield is all the news these days, so I must know what he is doing. I have now heard him preach a number of times, and I've consulted with others who have heard him as well. What you have said is totally untrue. He is no fanatic. I know what is happening. You have been listening to wild rumors, and you're too sensible a fellow for that."

Jones blustered some more, and with a shake of his head, said, "Hmph! But you're not a religious man, Ben. Why would you waste your time listening to him?"

"First of all, Titus, I am religious. While I may not hold all the doctrines of the Dissenters, I firmly believe in the Deity, and hold that the good works that religion teaches we must do are basic to any good government. I hold that virtue is the most important thing, and I advocate the building of churches for the education and moral improvement of the masses. While I trust in the goodness and wisdom of the Creator God, as to the divinity of Jesus, I am not sure of that, but I respect Him as the wisest of men."

George Hook, a cabinetmaker, had been enjoying the argument, and said, "Well, I'm an Anglican, and to me Jesus is the Son of God and the divine Savior. Mr. Cummings, the rector of Christ Church, has lent Whitefield the use of his pulpit for Whitefield's entire stay, so I would imagine if my pastor approves of him, he is all right."

Franklin nodded. "I can tell you, the multitudes of all sects and denominations that are attending his sermons are enormous. And you are wrong, Titus, about the crowd's behavior. I have observed the extraordinary influence of his oratory on his hearers, and how much they admire and respect him. For the people to act badly, or go into emotional behavior, other than a few tears here and there, would go against that, and furthermore, Mr. Whitefield would not tolerate misbehavior."

Jones said, "No hysterics?" He gave Ben a look of jaundiced doubt.

"Well, I haven't seen any," Ben answered. "Yes, the people are moved, but that's all."

"Hmph," said Jones, unwilling to concede.

"But no matter how much against Whitefield you are, Titus," Ben said, "haven't you noticed how wonderful it is to see the change made in the manners of our inhabitants? From being thoughtless or indifferent about religion, it seems as if all the world is growing religious, so that one cannot walk through the town in an evening without hearing psalms and hymns sung in different homes on every street."

"Yes, I can't help but notice such nonsense," said Jones sourly.

"Well, they aren't fanatics," said Ben. "And also, Titus, there is the benevolent side of George Whitefield. He is most concerned about orphans in Georgia. This new colony has unfortunately not been settled by hardy, industrious people accustomed to labor, but instead with insolvent debtors, many of idle habits, taken out of jails. This kind, unable to endure the hardships of a new settlement, has perished in numbers, leaving many helpless children unprovided for. The sight of their miserable situation inspired the benevolent heart of Mr. Whitefield with the idea of building an orphan house there, in which they might be supported and educated."

"How is he going to build this orphanage? Is he wealthy?" Jones asked.

"No, he has little money himself," Ben said. "He has been preaching about this charity, and making large collections, for his eloquence has a wonderful power over the hearts and purses of his hearers."

Hezekiah Guthrie, the owner of a foundry in the city, said, "Well, that's a charitable idea! But if Georgia was a hard place for the parents to live, and many died, why doesn't Whitefield have the orphans brought to Philadelphia, and the orphanage built here?"

"Precisely my thought, Hezekiah," Ben responded. "This I advised. But he was resolute in his first project, rejected my counsel, and therefore I refused to contribute. I happened the other day to attend one of his sermons, in the course of which I perceived he intended to finish with a collection, and I silently resolved he should get nothing from me."

"Good for you, Ben," Jones said. "Finally standing up for your principles!" Muscles were twitching at the corners of his mouth.

"Well, perhaps, Titus. I had in my pocket a handful of copper money, three or four silver dollars, and five pistoles in gold. As he proceeded I began to soften and concluded to give the coppers. Another stroke of his oratory made me ashamed of that, and I determined to give the silver. And he finished so admirably that I emptied my pocket wholly into the collector's dish, gold and all."

"Outrageous, Franklin! This man is a humbug, don't you see?!" Jones said. "How could he have pulled the wool over your eyes so easily, and you consider yourself such a clever man!"

"Well, I don't think so, Titus. You see, he has already come to me to be the publisher of his sermons, which are to be distributed widely. Some of his enemies are supposing that he would apply these collections to his own private emolument; but he showed me all his accounts, knowing that some would suspect this. I, who am intimately acquainted with his finances, do not have the least suspicion of his integrity, but am decidedly of opinion that he is in all his conduct a perfectly honest man. And my testimony in his favor ought to have the more weight, as we have no religious connection. He has asked me to be his publisher in America, and it's strictly a business arrangement. Ours is a civil friendship, sincere on both sides."

George Hook said, "Well, that settles it. Ben, you are a perceptive man—one of the shrewdest I've ever met. So if Whitefield passes all your tests, I have no further suspicions of him."

"Nor do I," said Hezekiah Guthrie. "Ben, thanks for your appraisal."

"Bah!" Titus Jones fixed them with a stare and narrowed one eye as though daring them to disprove his assessment. He kept interjecting more opinions, pressing his arguments with such enthusiasm that drops of spittle flew from the corners of his mouth. He sputtered some more; then, unable to come up with any more arguments, he strode off. Furiously, he hurled back over his shoulder, "You're all a pack of fools, taken in by a religious pitchman! You too, Franklin!"

❧❦❧

Commissary Vessey had traveled from New York to Philadelphia to confer with some of the Dissenter clergy who were Old Lights, violently opposed to the Awakening. He met with Hosea Dickson, John Thomson, Richard Burbridge, and half a dozen other men who were defiantly against what was happening, and who wished, if possible, to cripple the work of Whitefield and all those associated with revival.

"We're not alone, I can tell you," Vessey said, pounding the table. Since he was a high-placed functionary of the Church of England, the others were impressed and eager to hear what he had to say. "There are any number of clergy who are losing members from their churches and are furious over this man who claims to be an Anglican priest and is leading people astray! Do you know, I can't even get my sermons printed in New York, because of him!"

"That's the situation here also, and in New Jersey, Delaware, and Maryland," Burbridge said. "My church in Bristol has lost about a hundred members, and most of them have gone to a New Light church. I'm almost destitute."

He was answered by a chorus of angry agreements around the table. "Something has to be done—and soon," declared James Anderson, a man who tended almost to be violent at times.

"But what?" Dickson asked, askance. "In the synod, we've done everything we could to frustrate this bunch. We've tried to shut down their so-called 'college,' and still it's attracting more students all the time, I hear."

"Yes, and we've forbidden ordination to their graduates in our presbytery, and now the New Lights have *their own* presbytery in New Brunswick, and they can ordain anyone who agrees with them!" Anderson said with vehemence.

"It sounds as if things are as bad in your sect as in mine," Vessey observed.

"What can we *do,* before it gets any worse?" Dickson asked.

There was silence for a minute. Then Burbridge asked, "Is this a completely confidential meeting? Can you all be trusted?"

Around the table there was a murmur of acquiescence. "Are you asking us to swear a vow of secrecy?" Dickson asked.

"Yes," Burbridge said in a low voice. "I think someone should do something to this Whitefield fellow."

"Do something to—" said Vessey, suddenly nervous. "Oh, I don't know...."

There was silence for another minute.

Dickson spoke up. "Hmm. When he goes to Georgia or somewhere rural and remote, he could get into much danger and easily die. But not in these more civilized areas. So we don't want any harm to come to him. Too obvious. It might point right back to us." More silence.

Burbridge said, "Well, what about bringing scandal on one of his chief supporters, someone less prominent than Whitefield? That might hinder the Awakening."

"Right," said Dickson. "What about his money man—that Seward fellow?"

"The perfect one," said Thomson.

෧෩

While Commissary Vessey of the Church of England in New York City had flatly refused to let Whitefield preach from his pulpit, in Philadelphia the situation was different. Here the Anglican Commissary, Archibald Cummings, invited Whitefield to preach in the magnificent Christ Church twelve times altogether, on and off from Sunday, November 4th to Wednesday, November 28th. All went smoothly there, with the evangelist dining with Cummings and the churchwardens frequently.

Whitefield preached on the morning of Monday, November 26th, 1739 to a crowded congregation at Christ Church. After the service, there were many people outside who couldn't get in, and Whitefield, as always, did not want to disappoint them. The day was cool but without a breeze, and a bright sun shone down. He told the church wardens to announce that he would speak outside to the crowd. Hearing this, they thronged into the adjoining cemetery, some sitting on flat tombstones, and others standing everywhere among the graves.

Whitefield came out, to applause, and chose a high, flat monument on which to stand. He began to preach, and as he did so, he noticed that there were perhaps forty or fifty blacks among the audience gathered together. Some of these had heard him before, and he knew that some were free blacks, and others were slaves. He also knew that they were timid, feeling inferior and perhaps unwanted where white folks gathered. Whitefield wished to dispel this quickly and make them feel very welcome.

He chose to continue preaching on the topic, "The Lord Our Righteousness." As he got into the subject, he saw the blacks giving complete attention to everything he said, as much as any of the whites. When opportunity presented itself, he turned to them, gave a wide smile, and said, "Did you ever hear of the eunuch belonging to Queen Candace, a Negro like yourselves? He had an immortal, eternal soul, just as you do. The eunuch believed in the Lord Jesus Christ, as you must. The Lord was his righteousness, as He must be yours also. If you believe in Him, you too shall be saved."

From the blacks came a loud "Amen!"

                                ಲಿಂ

On the next day, November 27th, Whitefield, William Seward and Josh went to Ben Franklin's print shop. The purpose was for the evangelist to ask Franklin to print and distribute more of his sermons, and as they came to the front of the shop, Tom spotted Josh. He dashed through the door.

"Josh! Oh, how good it is to see you," Tom said, giving Josh a huge hug.

When they had finished greeting each other, Josh said, "Tom, I want you to meet Mr. Whitefield and Mr. Seward."

"I am humbled and gratified to shake your hands, sirs," Tom said. "Mr. Whitefield, I have heard you speak several times, but from afar."

Josh said, "That's the reason I haven't found you before, Tom, I looked all over, but the congregations were so huge, it was impossible. And I knew you were working at Mr. Franklin's shop, but I have been so busy, this is the first I've had opportunity to come here."

"Are you working with Mr. Whitefield and Mr. Seward, Josh?"

"Yes! Isn't it unbelievable?"

Whitefield cut in, saying, "You see, Tom, I need some help, and I met Josh at the Log College. Mr. Tennent recommended him highly, and I find Josh has many abilities."

Ben Franklin saw them through the front window, came outside, greeted everyone, and Whitefield introduced him to Josh. "Mr. Franklin, I understand Josh has known Tom Prescott well for some time."

"Is that so?" Franklin asked. "Well, Tom is a good worker. Are you staying many more days?"

"No, I'm leaving tomorrow for Georgia, to begin building the orphanage. While I have barely enough money collected to begin construction, I am hoping that more may arrive. My good friend William Seward here, whom you know well by now, has purchased a sloop, *Savannah*. The group of friends we brought from England is sailing to Georgia on it, while Josh, John Syms, Joe Husbands, several others, and I will take the more adventurous land route. And this afternoon I give my farewell message in Christ Church. Mr. Seward will be staying in the city for a while, to tend to some business."

"It's always a pleasure to see my friend William," Ben said, giving him a pat on the back.

"Yes, I'll be coming here frequently, I'm sure," Seward said, smiling.

"While you have been in our city, Mr. Whitefield, I must tell you that you have had a salutary effect upon the morals of the people, and I personally am grateful for that."

Whitefield smiled broadly. "Thank you, sir. I happened to buy the most recent issue of your *Gazette*. I appreciate this." He read:

> The alteration in the face of religion here is altogether surprising. Never did the people show so great a willingness to attend sermons, nor the preachers greater zeal and diligence in performing the duties of their function. Religion is become the subject of most conversations. All which, under God, is owing to the successful labours of the Reverend Mr. Whitefield.

"This is wonderful. Thanks, Mr. Franklin," Josh exclaimed.

"It's only the truth," Ben said. "That's all we ever print!" Everyone laughed.

"Why, your testimony amazes me," Whitefield said, "I didn't know you felt so strongly about what I was doing. You realize that coming in a popular paper, this will only infuriate my enemies the more."

Franklin threw his head back and laughed heartily. "George—may I call you that?—you don't have a chance to read my newspaper very often, I'm sure, but if you did, then you would know that I have criticized some of the clergy before—not all, but some of them. I'm well aware that several of the sects are being torn apart, between those who support the Awakening, and those who are against it."

"And I, unfortunately, am in the middle of the struggle," said Whitefield. "I'll return the compliment and call you Ben. This battle was going on long before I arrived, with Mr. Tennent and his sons. And the same battle is going on in England."

Franklin said, "You make excellent copy, George! Please keep supplying me with material!" He laughed again.

"That is the reason Josh and I have come, to deliver the sermons I promised to you." He handed Franklin the manuscripts, and after some further discussion, they parted.

That afternoon, Whitefield went to Commissary Cummings' church to preach there for the twelfth time and found that the congregation that had gathered, an estimated ten thousand, was far beyond what the sanctuary could hold. He led the people to a nearby field, and asked for permission to preach from the balcony of a house that overlooked the field. Permission being given, he spoke for an hour to an attentive audience, who were sincerely sorry to know he was about to leave them.

TEN

New Lights and Old Lights

With George Whitefield traveling to the South, that did not mean that the Awakening would fade. His month-long visit to the Middle Colonies spurred the New Lights on to greater efforts than they had made before. By the spring of 1740 the revival had spread over a very wide area. Many Baptist congregations were involved, as were a number of Lutheran, Congregational, Moravian, and several Dutch Reformed churches, along with a few Anglican parishes. But those most heavily involved were the New Light Presbyterian congregations.

Gilbert Tennent came to speak at the Nottingham, Pennsylvania church on March 8th, 1740. His sermon was entitled *The Danger of an Unconverted Ministry, Considered in a Sermon on Mark VI.34.* Tennent began by pointing out that a godly ministry was a great blessing to those who sat under it, and he described the true nature of the Christian ministry. By doing this, Tennent caught the antirevival group at their weakest point and also allowed him to state fully what the New Light people said was the real issue in the battle. Unsaved men, he declared, cannot have a call of God to the Christian ministry. He spread out his argument that the antirevival forces had deliberately ordained to the clergy some immoral, unsaved men. The antirevival forces intended, obviously, that these unsaved men would vigorously oppose the awakening. Tennent went on to give evidence for all this.

> "As a faithful ministry is a great ornament, blessing and comfort to the Church of God, the feet of such messengers are beautiful; on the contrary, an ungodly ministry is a great curse and judgment....
>
> "But what was the cause of this great and compassionate commotion in the heart of Christ?.... Why, had the people then no

teachers? O yes! They had heaps of Pharisee-Teachers....But notwithstanding the great crowds of these orthodox, letter-learned and regular Pharisees, our Lord laments the unhappy case of that great number of people, who, in the days of His flesh, had no better guides, because they were as good as none (in many respects) in our Savior's judgment. For all them, the people were as sheep without a shepherd....

"From what has been said, we may learn, that such who are contented under a dead Ministry, have not in them the temper of that Savior they profess. It's an awful sign, that they are as blind as moles, and as dead as stones, without any spiritual life or sense. And alas! Isn't this the case of multitudes? If they can get one, that has the name of a minister, with a band, and a black coat or gown to carry on Sabbath-days among them, although ever so coldly, and unsuccessfully; if he is free of gross crimes in practice, and takes good care to keep at a distance from their consciences.... O! think the poor fools, that is a fine man indeed; our minister is a prudent, charitable man. He is not always harping upon Terror, and sounding damnation in our ears, like some rash-headed preachers, who by their uncharitable methods, are ready to put poor people out of their wits, or to run them into despair....

"I beseech you, my dear brethren, to consider, that there is no probability of your getting good, by the ministry of Pharisees....When the life of Piety comes near their quarters, they rise up in arms against it, consult, contrive and combine in their conclaves against it, as a common enemy, that discovers and condemns their craft and hypocrisy...."

After the service, Gilbert Tennent stood at the door of the church, dignified and rather tall, vested in his black robe and Geneva tabs, greeting and talking with the people. Because these parishioners were deeply involved in the Awakening, they agreed with what he had said. On an average Sunday, they were a smiling and happy people, chatting amiably with each other. But this Sunday, after Tennent's stunning message, most were quiet, deep in thought. However, one elderly lady came to Tennent and, shaking her finger under his nose, said to him, "Don't you think you went a little too far, Pastor?"

Behind her stood Elder Abram Myerson, who interrupted immediately. "Mrs. Flint, you must not be aware of what is going on today! Everything that Pastor Tennent said was absolutely on target, and he put it beautifully. Congratulations, Pastor! And thank you, on behalf of the session of the church." He put out his hand and shook Tennent's.

Deacon Gordon Whitson overheard the talk, and boomed out, "Quite right, Abram! That message should be printed and spread abroad widely. I agree with everything that was stated."

"Yes, it will be printed," Tennent said. "In Philadelphia I let it be known what I was going to say, and already Ben Franklin has asked for the manuscript, to publish it." By now a crowd had clustered around, listening to every excited word that was being exchanged.

"I want two dozen copies," Esther Murdoch called out. "I want all my friends to have a copy."

"What was said was the truth," said Tom Finletter. "But I'm afraid it will tear the church apart!"

"If I may say, sir," Tennent said, "the church has already been torn apart. Only the Lord knows what will happen, and only He will be able to heal it."

ℰℭ

Once Gilbert Tennent's Nottingham sermon had been published, and distributed widely, the war was out in the open. Everyone, no matter what their position, could see the issues clearly. Previously, the battles had been in closed ecclesiastical meetings, or in church periodicals. But no longer.

The anti-Awakening group in the Synod was predictably infuriated. With the sermon being distributed in such quantities, it was difficult for them to answer its charges. However, Tennent's use of stinging terms for his opponents, such as Letter-learned Pharisees, Wolves, Blind Guides, Hypocrites, Foolish Builders, Enemies to God, Hirelings, Formalists, and dead Drones, gave them an issue for retaliation. For Tennent to use such terms was a measure of the intensity of the opponents' feelings.

Among those who were furious was John Thomson, a member of the Synod who had often moved from church to church because, he complained, his parishioners invariably refused to pay his salary. His complaints in a printed brochure against Tennent's sermon began:

> How can he [Tennent] know how successful or unsuccessful his brethren are in their work?

If conviction of sin, reformation from it, and fleeing to Christ for mercy, may be accounted success, I hope there is something of that follows upon our ministry. If instruction, edification, and confirmation in the ways of faith and holiness, be reckoned success, I hope there is something of this also; altho' we have all reason to lament that there is so little: But if crying out in our public assemblies, to the disturbance of the worship of God, and if falling down and working like persons in convulsions, I say, if those things only be reckoned signs of success, I must own I do not understand it. I think converting grace works rather on the soul and rational parts than on the body....

Mr. Tennent says that they (viz. the unconverted ministers) seem to imagine that there is a great difference between the old Pharisees and the dry formalists of this generation; and I say that Mr. Tennent seems to me to imagine that every imagination of his crazy brain heated and excited by uncharitable prejudice against his brethren, altho' never so groundless, is infallibly true....

***

John Thomson had been the one delegated to find someone in Philadelphia who could bring scandal to William Seward. So he set out to speak with some of the denizens of the underworld who could recommend the right person to do this. As a clergyman, he had little contact with such people, but he assumed something of a disguise—a wig and a false mustache—and ventured into several taverns in the worst parts of the city, mingling with the types who frequented them. He learned of Gershom Stigler, a sinister fellow who had had many brushes with the law. Thomson located Stigler, and on finding that he was available, Thomson explained what was needed. Stigler listened carefully.

"But why not go after Whitefield himself, Mr. Thomson?"

"Look, Gershom, we must be very careful. We want to discredit Whitefield, but we cannot take a chance that the blame could be traced back to me and my friends. We must remain out of this. Do you understand? If Whitefield is attacked directly, it looks too suspicious. William Seward is the best target. He's Whitefield's money man. Have one of your...uh...men go after him. Bring down some scandal on him. I'm sure you can think of some scandalous thing he could be involved with—perhaps a woman, perhaps something to do with his fortune, perhaps you can find someone who will say he cheated them, or something like that. But just keep us totally out of it. It can't be found out that I, or any of my friends, had anything to do with this. Now here's the money you ask to do the job." Thomson handed Stigler a small sack.

But Stigler did *not* understand.

<hr />

The carefully orchestrated scheme had been planned for a week. The two thugs were to find where William Seward was working on that day, follow him from a distance, and when he arrived at some isolated place, kill him.

The first thug, Ahab Cragg, had imagined that he would simply steal up behind Seward and stab him to death. But the second, Reuben Sobleski, wanted no bloodshed. Instead, he wanted to surprise Seward, to come from behind him and throw a rag over his face, covering his nose and mouth and suffocating him. Reuben argued that then they could place the dead body in their wagon, cover it with blankets, and take it where they wished. They could deposit the body in the most incriminating place, for the greatest effect.

In a room at the Black Swan Inn, Reuben and Ahab were conferring with the couple who were paying them. Gershom Stigler was swarthy, with small black eyes, straight black hair that was pulled into a pigtail at the back, and a beak-like nose. His wife, Lucretia, was slim, with blue-green eyes, and dark, long, straight hair that fell to her shoulders when she had not pulled it up in a mobcap. Both Stiglers had a sinister appearance, and both were known in the city for associations with the criminal element. Of the two, Lucretia was the more dangerous one. She had been known to order a murder in the most casual way, with a wave of her hand and a laugh.

Their hired hands had just explained the plan each had for the murder of their victim. Gershom listened patiently, smoking his long clay pipe, and sending puffs of smoke toward the ceiling. Lucretia sat silently, her lips drawn in a tight line.

"Ahab, we cannot have the possibility of blood left behind, from the stab wounds that you would make on Seward," said Lucretia. "Even if you tried to clean up the blood, you could not eradicate it entirely, and it might be traced later. Then people would know that someone had come to foul play there, and they might connect it to Seward's body. No, that won't work."

Reuben spoke up. "So what do you think of *my* idea?"

"Yes," Gershom said, "that's more what we had in mind. No blood, no trace of where he was killed. Just haul him off when you're done."

"And what do we do with the body?" Ahab asked.

"You wait till dark, most likely after midnight. There's that little street called Black Horse Alley. It's narrow and runs between Front Street and Water Street, south of High. Do you know the alley?"

"Yeah," Reuben said. "It's an area that 'nice' people stay away from. They call it a 'bad' place. Has a lot of gin shops, and a couple of brothels, for the sailors. Yeah." He looked at Ahab, and they laughed. "We know it, don't we, Ahab?"

"All right, you know that alley. That's where you're going to dump the body. Late at night. Then you get outta there, quick. Do you have the plan?" Gershom asked.

"When do we do it?" Reuben asked.

"Seward is staying at an inn on Mulberry Street. A very nice place. He's got plenty of money. So you go there and watch from down the street for when he comes out. Then you follow him, till he goes to a good spot to do him in."

"If he's got plenty of money on him, can we take it?" said Ahab.

"Yeah, that'll be all right. But we split it later—got that?" Gershom looked fierce, and they nodded.

ಸಾಡಚ

William Seward had met with several pastors that day, had written ten or twelve letters to friends in England, Boston, New Haven, and Northampton, and had conferred for over an hour with John Syms, George Whitefield's secretary. It had been a long day, and he was somewhat tired, for he was not well. He went to dinner at his inn, but he picked at his meal and ate little. There was still more he had to attend to, and his mind was on that.

Seward had an appointment with the governor of Pennsylvania,

George Thomas, at 9:00 p.m. They were to discuss the possibility of starting a school for Indians north of Philadelphia, possibly at a settlement called Bethlehem. George Whitefield had suggested the idea, and Seward was to provide much of the money to buy land and erect a building, hoping that the Pennsylvania Assembly would approve the plan and supply more funds.

He rose from his table in the dining room, nodded to the waiter and the manager, and claimed his coat from the hall rack. He donned the coat, for it was March, and a cool evening with a fairly stiff breeze. Going down the front steps of the inn, he turned left and walked a short distance down Mulberry Street.

William Seward did not notice the two men in dark clothes who had been waiting and were watching him from a distance.

The governor would meet him at the Court House on High Street. There was a small, dark lane that ran from Mulberry to High, a shortcut that saved Seward from walking down to Second Street, so he took it. He walked at a leisurely pace, as he was early for the appointment. The heavy clouds in the sky covered the moon and stars, providing no light. The lane, back of warehouses fronting on Third Street, was full of rocks and debris that were almost invisible in the blackness, and several cats ran screeching in front of him as he approached. He felt sorry for these homeless animals that were forced to rely on their wits to catch vermin for their food. A wayward dog was barking continuously nearby, possibly a watchdog protecting the back of a warehouse. Seward came within one hundred feet of High Street, and he wondered if he had been wise in taking this shortcut, with all of its refuse and squalor.

With no warning, from behind him a rag was clapped over his face by some unseen attacker. Seward had heard nothing. The thugs had crept up stealthily, any slight noise they made covered up by the noises of the cats and the dog. The man holding the rag was strong; his hand kept a viselike grip over Seward's face. His other hand grabbed the Englishman around his shoulders, and held him tightly. Seward struggled all he could, but the rag covered his mouth and nose, preventing his breathing. The rag seemed to have some kind of liquid in it. He felt himself losing consciousness. In two minutes he was on the ground, lifeless.

༄༅།

The two thugs took the body and put it in the back of the wagon they had brought twenty feet into the alleyway, out of the eyes of any chance passersby. An old rug was then thrown over the body to cover it.

Climbing onto the wagon's bench, Reuben took the reins and flicked them, bidding the horse to move out of the alley. "That went all right. Now, what's the best way to go?" he asked Ahab.

"It's too early to dump the body. We gotta wait till after midnight. Let's go to the Black Swan. Probably Lucretia and Gershom will be there, and we can report that the job is finished."

Reuben pulled on the reins to order the horse to go in the direction of the Black Swan Inn. "Did you go through his pockets?"

"Yeah—seventeen pound notes and some coins."

"You take five pounds and I'll take five, and we'll tell Lucretia that all he had on him was seven pound notes." They divided up the money.

༄༅།

The next morning, the report was spread rapidly by word of mouth around the entire city. William Seward, wealthy patron and friend of the evangelist George Whitefield, was found dead last night outside the doorway of a brothel on Black Horse Alley. There were very suspicious circumstances.

Realizing that Ben Franklin would want to know this immediately, a friend rushed to the print shop and pounded on the door at 7:00 a.m. An upstairs window was thrown open, and a sleepy and irritated Franklin appeared in his nightshirt, rubbing his eyes. "Oh, it's you, Henry. Yes, what do you want at this hour?"

"Ben, I knew you'd want to hear this right off," Henry Blodgett said breathlessly, in a loud voice. "You know that rich fellow who gives a lot of money to Reverend Whitefield's work—Seward—well, he was found dead this morning in the doorway of a bordello!!" Blodgett was panting from running.

"*WHAT?* I'll be right down!" The window slammed shut.

In twenty seconds the front door of the shop was opened hurriedly.

"Come in, come in, Henry. Now, what's this about William Seward?" Franklin was waking quickly.

"Yes; he must have been in that hell-hole last night, Ben! Visiting some of their prostitutes! Maybe he was killed for his money...who knows? Anyway, they threw him out of the bordello onto the sidewalk, and the night watch found him about 3:00 a.m., as he was going down Black Horse Alley – you know, that notorious lane with all those gin shops and bawdy houses, where all the sailors go."

Ben was staggered...slack-jawed in disbelief. Seward had been through that very door the day before yesterday, and they had become good friends in recent months. Finally Ben said, "Yes, I know Black Horse Alley. But how does anyone know that Mr. Seward was *in* the brothel? He wasn't that kind of person, Henry! William Seward was a good and most decent man, and *very* generous."

"Ho ho! Ben, don't be naïve! How do you know he *wasn't* in there? Whitefield's gone to Georgia, I see from your paper; and 'when the cat's away, the mice will play!'"

Franklin was having about enough of this scandal-mongering. "Oh, nonsense. Henry, I will need more proof than I've heard so far that Seward would go to a bordello. I'll believe it only if it's *proven*. Not from gossip and rumors. Until then, I *don't* believe it. There must be another explanation."

༄༅༈

By 8:00 a.m. of the day when William Seward was found murdered, Ben Franklin had become very distressed. He was rarely upset, for he controlled his emotions well, but the death of this good friend caused Franklin great grief. Not only because of their friendship, but also because he knew how much Whitefield was relying on Seward for support. Ben understood well how this would affect the plans for the orphanage and a number of other beneficial endeavors. Whitefield would be devastated.

There was no quick way for Franklin to contact Whitefield, who was currently in Savannah, Georgia. It might take as long as two or three weeks, at the least, for a letter to reach him. But then, Franklin thought, perhaps it was as well that Whitefield did not know the terrible news. It would only trouble him greatly, and there was nothing he could do. The Englishman might rush back to Philadelphia, but Seward would be buried by then, and what would his coming accomplish?

At breakfast with his wife and mother-in-law, they discussed the problem. Deborah and Mrs. Read had also come to like Seward, and the mood at the table was depressed. Ben trifled with his food.

"As George Whitefield's printer and overseer of the money collected for the orphanage in the Middle Colonies," Ben said, "I feel an obligation to arrange for William's funeral and burial and to help John Syms in other ways, until George's return from the South."

"Oh yes, I think you should, Ben," said Deborah. "George would certainly expect either you or John Syms to do these things."

"Well, John is very capable, but he doesn't know much about our city, and I have many more contacts than he has. I'll discuss it with him. Martin Hepplewhite has been making coffins and taking care of funerals, and it's almost a profession with him. I'll ask him to get the body and do the rest."

"I'm sure John Syms will agree with that, Ben," said Mrs. Read.

"But the question remains, who did this to William Seward? How did he get outside of a brothel? And why did they murder him? Was this a random killing, or had they targeted Seward? I know Seward would never have gone there by himself. He was murdered someplace else, and left there! Oh, this has to be an article in the *Gazette,* but how can I write it so as not to hurt George? Should the headline read, 'Benefactor Murdered,' and never mention the brothel? The more I think about it, I've got to get to the bottom of this! I'm afraid it's up to me."

ΩϾΧ

In the midst of the excitement over the Awakening and William Seward's murder, the Junto sponsored a banquet for a number of guests in the Tailors Hall of Philadelphia. Ben Franklin, as usual, was one of the organizers, and he invited Tom Prescott, knowing that Tom was alone in the city and would appreciate the company. Tom ran to his boarding house as soon as work was over, bathed, and changed into his best clothes. When he came to the Tailors Hall, most of the guests had already arrived.

Tom entered the large red brick building and went into the lavish hall from which the sounds of many voices, and occasional peals of laughter, were coming. It was an intricately plastered large room, doubtless the finest in the city, and most impressive. Several smaller rooms were off to the sides. In constructing this hall, the city had tried to copy the best that London could offer. The walls were painted a pastel green, and from the ceiling hung three large chandeliers carrying dozens of candles and hundreds of cut crystal drops that reflected the light in every color of the rainbow. Mirrors fixed within ornate stucco panels multiplied the blazing spermaceti candles in shimmers of light. The effect was dazzling. Musicians wearing powdered wigs were filling the room with lilting music. At first, Tom was a bit overwhelmed. He knew that everyone of importance in the city would be here, and he felt out of place.

He stood on the top of three steps that led down into the hall, surveying the two hundred or more guests. Many were important in the life of the city, and it was a privilege to be among them. It was kind of Ben Franklin to invite him to this festive occasion. The ladies were resplendent in gowns of every color, bedecked with pearls and jewelry, and the gentlemen, some with powdered wigs, wore velvet coats of bright reds, purples, and blues. A dozen servants passed among them, carrying trays of hors d'oeuvres and the oysters for which Philadelphia was famous. A great fire, banked within the marble fireplace, warmed the room so well that the glazed doors to the garden had been opened, and some of the guests had drifted on to the lantern-lit terraces.

Tom surveyed the hall, looking for anyone he might be acquainted with. He spotted several of Mr. Franklin's printing customers, but he did not want to be presumptuous, feeling that they were above his social level.

After a minute Tom spotted Mr. and Mrs. Nicholson, and, happy to see friends, he went to them.

They interrupted their conversation with others and greeted him cordially. "Oh Tom," Mr. Nicholson said, "I'm pleased to find you here." They chatted for a few minutes, and Mrs. Nicholson said, "I'm sure you'll find conversation with us older folks boring. Rachel is here; I believe she is at the far end of the hall or possibly in one of the side rooms."

Tom thanked them, pleased to hear that Rachel was in attendance. He moved away, to try to locate her. First he went to the far end of the room where there was a magnificent set of double doors, but he did not see her in that area. Then he tried a terrace, where a number of guests had congregated. Beyond all the light chatter from these people who were having an enjoyable time, a number of fireflies glittered and danced against the dark shrubbery. Tom did not see Rachel here, so he left and went to another large portal that led to a second terrace. This one was better lit than the first, and several romantic couples were talking quietly, leaning against a stone balustrade beneath lanterns around which dozens of moths were fluttering. Again he did not find Rachel.

Tom went back to the main hall, and finally he spotted her. When he first saw her, standing with others, candlelight was shining on the waves of her light brown hair, and she wore a dress of green with a white lace collar. Rachel was as enchanting as always and, Tom believed, she was certainly the most beautiful young lady here.

She was surrounded by five or six men, and she was laughing at what was being said. From his distance, Tom could see that the men were delighted at her presence, and she was enjoying their company. Tom looked around the entire hall. He saw that there were five young ladies, gathered together at the end of the room, all lovely but receiving no attention from the opposite sex, and they appeared to be peeved. Rachel was receiving all the attention.

Seeing Rachel being entertained by other men, Tom felt a momentary pang of jealousy. Didn't she know he might be here, and he would like to have her to himself? No, he realized, that's silly. How could Rachel have known that? So he rebuked himself. Rachel being so attractive, what did he expect? Of course other young men would want to talk with her, and there was nothing wrong with that!

It had been a week since he had been able to visit her, because of the demands of work. On the previous Sunday, he had gone with the Nicholson family to their Dissenter church, and after the service Tom had walked with Rachel along the riverfront. They had chatted about a number of things. She mentioned being swept out into the river and his rescuing her. Tom changed the subject abruptly; he did not want to dwell on that. Then they discussed his work, and the clothing she was making, and her family, and his.

Tom moved slowly through the crowd of guests, all of whom were conversing rather noisily with each other. Most of them were older, and all were holding glasses of punch. He wanted to approach Rachel so she would know he was there, but he did not want to appear forward or absurd. Tom got within twenty feet of Rachel. Unfortunately, her back was toward him. He could not be a boor and crash into their company. What to do to get her attention?

Indecisive, he stood there, sipping his own glass of punch. A servant passed by, holding a tray of hors d'oeuvres, and Tom selected a shrimp and nibbled on it, waiting for an opportunity. He did not have long to wait. Rachel happened to turn, saw Tom, and exclaimed, "Oh Tom! How good to see you here. I didn't know you were coming!" He took her wide smile to indicate sincere delight at finding him there.

Was she tired of the company of the other young men? Perhaps. She brushed by them, coming over to Tom, and the look on their faces was unitedly one of disappointment. One fellow in particular glared at Tom, apparently resenting his intrusion.

Tom was delighted. He quickly put down his glass of punch and held out his hands. "Hello, Rachel. Oh, you look beautiful tonight. I haven't seen that dress before. It's stunning."

She laughed. "Thank you. I just finished making it for tonight's banquet. I'm glad you like it. Are you alone?"

"Yes, I am," he said, thinking, Does she think I might have another girlfriend? But he said, "Rachel, you are quite a seamstress. I didn't realize that."

"Well, Mother has taught me everything I know about dressmaking and sewing."

He noticed that her glass was nearly empty, and said, "May I fill it?"

"Yes, please." She lowered her lashes in a coquettish way. He got his confidence back and began to think that perhaps Rachel didn't have other suitors here that she cared for, after all. Maybe he was the only one. He went to the punch bowl, quickly filled the glass, and returned to her. Just then a bell was rung announcing that the banquet was about to be served.

"Where are you sitting, Tom?" she asked. "Do you have a place already arranged?"

"No, I don't."

"Well then, why don't you sit with us? I think there's an empty chair at our table, and I know my parents would love to have you."

Hmm. Things were working out just fine.

The dinner was excellent in every way. Mr. and Mrs. Nicholson were pleased to have him join their table, and chatted in a cordial fashion. The appetizers were delicious, the beef was done to a turn, there were a number of succulent vegetable dishes, and the desserts were numerous and elegant.

After the banquet had concluded and a speaker had addressed the guests on the topic of safety in the city, and the need for lamps to light the streets at night, the event ended. Gradually the people departed into the darkened streets. Some commented that the speaker was absolutely correct, and something must be done about getting street lamps immediately. After all, they had heard that London had recently gotten street lanterns, at least on some major thoroughfares. And as for safety, well! What about the recent murder of William Seward?!

For Tom, the dark was fine. He thought that this was a perfect opportunity to walk Rachel home, and to talk about his intentions toward her. He had been thinking of this for the last few months. Tom had begun to court Rachel four months ago, and, as he told his father, he believed that Rachel liked him, as did her family. He knew that other young men had their eyes on this beauty, and if he stalled and did not make his affection known to her soon, some other fellow might claim her. His sensibilities told him that now was the time to act.

"Rachel, may I walk you home?"

She looked somewhat startled, and hesitated for a minute, looking at the ground. "Tom, someone else is taking me home. I've been meaning to talk with you. David Talcott is here this evening, but he had to sit at his parents' table. He has asked me to become engaged to him. I've been seeing him for some time, and I believe I'll accept his proposal."

Tom was so shaken at this utterly unexpected turn of events he could think of no reply. He stood there for a minute, stunned, but trying not to betray his emotion. Then he turned and walked away.

୧୬୯୧

When Ben Franklin heard of William Seward's murder, he told his workers in the print shop to carry on without him, as he expected to be away the entire day. First he went to Martin Hepplewhite's carpenter's shop, to arrange for him to get William Seward's body immediately and bring it to his shop. Then, one of the caskets that Hepplewhite made was to be reserved for the body. After that, Franklin went to see his own physician, Dr. John Abernathy, a tall, dignified man much respected by Franklin for his professional abilities. He had brown hair going to gray, wide-set light blue eyes, and an aquiline nose. The doctor had heard of Seward's murder and was curious about the entire matter.

"Well, so am I most curious, John, but as one who is somewhat involved, I must be more than merely curious. And I need you to help me," Ben said.

"That's unusual," the doctor said. "You have helped me a number of times in the past, when I was baffled by something. So of course I'm ready to do what I can."

"John, I want to get to the bottom of this. I'm certain there is skullduggery going on. William Seward and I became good friends, and I am convinced that he would never go to a brothel."

"I trust your judgment, Ben."

"Now here's the main question I want to answer: did Seward just have the bad fortune to be the one to get killed somewhere? In other words, was it a random killing by some murderer? Or was Seward deliberately singled out, for some reason?"

The doctor's brows knitted, and he thought for a minute. "How are we to determine that?"

"I don't know, at this point. But we have just started. Are you with me?"

"Certainly. What is our first step?"

"That's why I need you to examine Seward's body, to see if there are any clues to the mystery. I sent Martin Hepplewhite to get the body an hour ago. It should be in his carpentry shop by now."

"All right. The shop is a short distance. Lead the way," said the physician.

When they came to the shop, Hepplewhite greeted them and took them into a back room where he had placed the body on a long table. At their request, he removed the clothing from the body. Dr. Abernathy approached the table and for the next ten minutes examined Seward's body thoroughly. Turning to Franklin he said, "I don't find a single mark that might indicate violence, on any part of this body. Perhaps he died from a heart attack, or a massive stroke. That would be difficult to tell. There are no wounds here."

Ben came to the table and also examined the body carefully. Rigor mortis had set in, and the limbs were stiff. But Ben noticed that the mouth was open slightly. He asked the doctor if the mouth could be opened wider, to look inside. The answer was, "I doubt it, without actually breaking the jaw, since rigor is here. Let me see if I can open it a bit further, without doing damage." He put his fingers on the jaw, and it opened a bit wider. Stooping down to look in the mouth, Franklin saw something white inside.

"John!" Ben said, "Look here. See if you can extract that white thing inside the mouth."

Abernathy took his fleam and used it to pull out a short piece of rag and gave it to Franklin.

"Look at that, would you!" Ben said. "Now, how do you suppose that got in his mouth?"

The two men examined the remnant carefully. "Obviously this came from a larger piece of cotton cloth, since the edges here are so ragged and ripped," the physician said. "The only possibility I can think of is that Seward bit it off just before he died, and it stayed in his mouth."

"Bit it off from a larger piece of cloth?" Ben asked. "Now, what could such a cloth be doing...Oh, of course! A gag over his mouth! Could it be, doctor, that he was smothered to death with such a cloth, and that's why there are no marks of violence on the body?"

"That seems to be the logical conclusion. I can't think of any other explanation as to how a ragged piece of cloth could get in his mouth. Mr. Seward bit it off immediately before he died."

Ben said, "This looks less and less like a random killing. Thanks, John."

Next Franklin went to Black Horse Alley, and asked one of the proprietors of a gin shop where the body was found. The man knew of the episode, took him outside his shop, and pointed to a bordello down the narrow street. Franklin knocked on that door, and it was opened almost immediately by an older, fat woman who wore cheap jewelry everywhere she could put a bracelet, necklace, ring, or pin.

"Yes, dearie? Oh, aren't you a handsome young gentleman! And would you like a nice young girl to entertain you for a while? I've got a good selection for a gentleman like you. There's Matilda, or there's Flossie, or Kate...all very cute."

"No thanks. I just need a bit of information." Franklin held out a one-pound note, which was quickly grabbed. "About the man who was found dead outside your door this morning—"

A thundercloud immediately came over the woman's face, her jaw jutted out, and her voice changed from cooing to a hiss. "Are you from the judge? Will I be taken to jail?" she snapped.

"No, no. Nothing of the sort. The man who died was a friend of mine. And I very much need to know—was he inside here at all last night?"

"That'll cost you two pounds!" she snarled.

Franklin dug in his pocket and handed it over.

"The answer is, I never saw him in my life! And I was at this door all last night!"

Ben said, "Madam, would you swear to that in a court of law, if need be?"

"Absolutely! He wasn't in here. I run a clean house, and I don't want no trouble with the law! Now, is that all? If so, get out!" She slammed the door in his face.

Franklin left. It was as he thought.

That afternoon, after going to the sheriff of Philadelphia and reporting his findings, Franklin had his men print large posters to put around town:

REWARD! TEN POUNDS FOR ANY INFORMATION ABOUT THE MURDER OF WILLIAM SEWARD, ESQUIRE, LAST TUESDAY. THE BODY WAS FOUND IN BLACK HORSE ALLEY. TO COLLECT REWARD, NOTIFY B. FRANKLIN, PRINTER, ON MARKET STREET NEAR SECOND.

Tom Prescott and Noah Williams, an apprentice in Ben Franklin's shop, were taking a break from work, sitting outside the building on a bench. They had been at the printing press for what seemed like several hours and were hot and somewhat tired. Inside the shop, the temperature was much higher. The breeze played about Tom, lifting the damp hairs on his neck with a breath of welcome coolness. He had sweated through his shirt, and the stain of perspiration was over most of it. Noah was the same.

In addition, Tom was depressed since Rachel Nicholson had decided to marry someone else. It had been difficult to concentrate on his work all morning; he could think of little else than her rejection the previous evening. As he sat on the bench, his reverie was suddenly interrupted.

Franklin came outside the shop to them and said, "Men, are you doing anything that is urgent?"

Noah answered, "No sir, nothing that can't wait."

"Well then, would you be willing to take the reward posters that were just printed, and post them on trees all over town? I'd like to get them to the public's notice as soon as possible. Especially I'd like you to cover the waterfront with them, and the parts of town where the lower classes live, as I'm after information from those who may know something about the killers of William Seward."

"Certainly, sir. Tom and I would be happy to post them about the town."

ಸಿಂಃ

By January 11, 1740 Whitefield, Josh Morris, and other friends had traveled to Georgia and found the plans for the orphan house underway. James Habersham, the schoolmaster, had been left in charge of the work, and had chosen a five-hundred-acre tract of land about ten miles from the town of Savannah. "I want to have it so far off the town," Whitefield told Habersham, "because the children will be freer from bad examples. It is my desire to have each of the children taught a trade, so as to be qualified to earn their own living."

Whitefield named the place *Bethesda*, meaning "House of Mercy." Since the invitations went out, eligible orphans were beginning to arrive. He reported in his Journal for January 29, 1740:

> Took in three German orphans, the most pitiful objects, I think, I ever saw. No new Negroes could look more despicable, or require more pains to instruct them. They had been used to exceedingly hard labor.

But, he wrote, it was worth all his efforts.

> Were all the money I have collected, to be spent in freeing these three children from slavery, it would be well laid out....This day I began the

cotton manufacture, and agreed with a woman to teach the little ones to spin and card.

The ground was chosen where the house itself was to be built, and the land cleared. The two-story house was to be sixty feet long and forty feet wide, with a substantial brick foundation. There would be twenty rooms for the youth, with two small houses to the side, one for the infirmary, and the other for a workhouse. With the need so great, Whitefield could hardly wait for the house to be built.

※

Workmen were arriving at Bethesda each day—carpenters, surveyors, bricklayers, and unskilled laborers—and Josh Morris wanted to get to know them. They were ready to be shown what was required of them, and he found them eager to begin the work. Among them were three slaves, and Josh was especially interested in their welfare. He found that they had learned enough English, in the two years since they had arrived from Africa, to be able to converse somewhat.

"I am happy to welcome you to work here," Josh said, bolstering his English with a great deal of sign language.

The slaves smiled broadly, seeming to understand his intent, and pleased that they were given attention and being treated so well.

"Do you have enough food to eat?" He put his hands to his mouth and then patted his stomach.

"Yes, we get plenty good food," one of them responded, and the others nodded vigorously.

The conversation continued for some minutes, with Josh trying to explain to them the purpose of the orphanage. They warmed to him, understanding they would get no beatings or harsh treatment at Bethesda. Curious as to their origins, he asked how they had gotten to Savannah.

"Slave boat. From Africa. Very bad, very bad. All slaves very sick all time. Slaves beaten..."

After that, Josh had no need to ask how they had been treated on the slave ship. He had seen several slavers in port when Whitefield's party had come through Charleston a week before, had seen slaves brought ashore to be auctioned, and had heard of the brutal reputation of the captains and crews. The whole situation made him shudder with revulsion.

Then Josh asked, "Do you know the name of the captain on your slave ship?" More gestures.

The slaves did not understand for a minute, looking quizzically at each other. Then one of them lightened. "Captain Powner!" he said, proud of his ability to converse.

"And do you remember the name of the slave boat?"

Again, concentration. Then, *"Revenge!"*

                                              ಬಿಂ

In Charleston and Savannah, Whitefield learned all he could about conditions in those towns. He reported "they have many ministers, both of our own and other persuasions; but I hear of no stirring among the dry bones." There was little hope that an Awakening could begin such as was becoming so fruitful to the north. He found a few clergymen who appreciated his work, but when he preached in their churches, they were generally filled but not overflowing, and the people did not seem to understand the need for revival. They were curious but seemed content with the current situation.

The needs among the blacks, however, were as great as ever. Both Charleston and Savannah were major ports for the importation of slaves from Africa, and when Whitefield went to Charleston, he saw how hard they were being worked, and how brutally they were treated, in the many plantations of the area. Then, to his surprise, he saw in a local newspaper a large advertisement for an auction to be held that day:

> Auction of 300 Slaves Just Brought from Africa. On Tuesday, By the City Wharf. At 10 in the Morning, to continue All Day until All are Sold. Choice Males and Females, Ready for Work Outside or Inside. Brought over on the fine Slave Ship *Revenge*, Joseph Powner, Master. Herman Jacobson, First Mate. Ebenezer Aiken, Auctioneer.

Whitefield knew of these auctions but had never attended one. He was scheduled to leave for Port Royal but deferred that until he could ride his horse down East Bay Street in Charleston to the large park by the City

Wharf. He was dressed in ordinary street clothes, not in his clerical gown, so he was indistinguishable from the regular citizen. When he arrived, what met his eyes astonished him. The auction had already begun, and a crude stage had been erected at the base of the wharf. To the side was an enclosure of wooden stakes, ten feet high, and from it he could hear loud outcries. Standing before the stage was a crowd of several hundred people, and perhaps thirty or forty wagons and carts were drawn up, pulled by horses and oxen, off to the side. Great activity, and much noise, were everywhere.

On the stage, the auctioneer was at work, shouting and gesticulating with his hands. "All right, boys, bring up another one!" he shouted to his assistants, who were standing alongside the gate to the enclosure. The gate was opened, and a young black male was pulled out and propelled up the steps to the stage.

"Now here's a choice one!" he called out, "not more than twenty years old—ready for a lifetime of hard work for a lucky owner. Turn him around," he ordered his assistants, who duly rotated the man so all could see him. "Pull up his shirt." They did so. "You see, there's no marks on him. He's never been whipped," the auctioneer proclaimed. "Well fed." He poked the slave in the stomach with his stick. The man winced. "Any price you pay, you'll get a bargain! What am I bid for this prime property?"

One by one, Whitefield saw slaves were being taken from the enclosure and brought up to stand beside the auctioneer, as he described the age and physical condition of each one. The slaves had been washed and dressed in new, cheap clothing to make them more presentable. The auctioneer went through the most desirable ones first, the young males. Most of them were chained with cuffs on their wrists and ankles and iron collars around their necks. One after another, bids were taken on them, and they were sold to different bidders. Whitefield watched all this for half an hour, and saw the new owners take the slaves into oxcarts and drive off with them.

When all the young males had been sold, the auctioneer called for young females to be brought up. They came, heads held high, refusing to be ridiculed, and dressed in white smocks. But this soon became more difficult than selling the males, as a number of females had small children with them, clinging desperately to their mothers' legs or arms. Knowing they may well be separated from their children permanently, these mothers were weeping or hysterical, as were the children.

"This is disgusting!" Whitefield said to those around him, full of rage. His hands were balled into fists, and his knuckles were white. "How can this be tolerated?"

"Oh, be quiet, you," one man said, his teeth gnashing. "What's wrong with it? We need workers, don't we? How else can we buy them?"

"But to separate those little children from their mothers! They may never see each other again," he cried. "Are we civilized people, or not? Where are our feelings, our sympathy?!"

"If you don't shut up, we'll have you dragged out of here," another buyer raged at Whitefield.

For the moment there was nothing he could do but watch.

One mother, screaming, held her child tightly and refused to let him go. Three burly keepers took her, ripped the smock off her back, and proceeded to lash her with a whip. Blood flowed from her back.

Whitefield could stand no more. He had worked himself to the front of the crowd and ran to the woman, shouting to the keepers to stop. "She has done nothing to deserve your wrath. Stop this outrage! Let her be!"

The keepers, startled by what had never happened before, were uncertain what to do. They looked at the auctioneer for directions.

A number of people in the crowd began to shout defiance at Whitefield, hurling curses and vilifying him. A few reacted with agreement to Whitefield, calling out their support. Everyone was screaming, and the auctioneer was afraid that fights, or a general riot, might begin. That would be the end of his auction, and his profits!

One plantation owner was also struck by the injustice and barbarism of the beating and shouted to the auctioneer, "I'll buy both the mother and her child! Keep them together."

That solved the immediate problem, and the auctioneer signaled the keepers to let the woman go. Eventually the crowd quieted.

Infuriated at the entire scene, Whitefield determined to find the captain of the ship that brought the slaves to America. He had torn the advertisement from the newspaper, and he read the name: *Joseph Powner, Master, Slave Ship,* Revenge. Leaving the auction in disgust, he went to the wharf and asked a sailor, "Do you know of this ship, the *Revenge?*"

The sailor answered, "Oh yes, matey. That's her, right over there."

Whitefield thanked the man and walked toward the slaver. Seeing a man dressed as an officer, leaning against some hogsheads counting money, Whitefield asked, "Do you know Captain Joseph Powner?"

"That's me. What do you want?" was the gruff answer.

"Then *you* are the one who brings these poor creatures from Africa, to be sold to a life of hopelessness and misery?"

"Ha!" said Powner, following this with a round of curses and blasphemy and sticking his chin out, defiantly. "What's it to you? They ain't got no souls—they're just animals! Who do you think you are?!"

"I am George Whitefield, a priest of the Church of England! And they are immortal souls. They are certainly *not* animals."

Powner spat on the wharf. "I don't care if you're the Pope! Get out of here, you lily-livered pest! None of this is your filthy rotten business!" His face was red with rage. He was not often subjected to questions like this.

With equal fury, and his fist waving at the man, Whitefield responded, "It is my business, and it is the business of the Almighty! You and your filthy lucre are an agent of Satan, and you are destined to an eternity in Hell! And I believe your destruction is not far off."

Mockingly, Powner laughed. "Hell? I don't believe in your fairy tales, Parson! Get away from me."

It was not only his friend Ben Franklin who eagerly printed news of Whitefield's activities. Every paper in the colonies, friendly or antagonistic to him, printed or reprinted accounts of what he was doing and where he was going next. He was, without exaggeration, front page news throughout America, and many of these accounts were picked up and reprinted in England, even as his earlier English exploits had been reported in American papers. In February 1740 he published a series of letters in the newspapers of Charleston, South Carolina. In them, having witnessed the cruelty practiced on many slaves, he wrote and published *A Letter to the Inhabitants of Maryland, Virginia, and North and South Carolina Concerning Their Negroes.* It read, in part:

> Your dogs are caressed and fondled at your tables, but your slaves, who are frequently styled dogs or beasts, have not an equal privilege. They

are scarce permitted to pick up the crumbs that fall from their masters' tables. Nay, some...have been, upon the most trifling provocation, cut with knives, and have had forks thrown into their flesh; not to mention what numbers have been given up to the inhuman usage of cruel taskmasters, who, by their unrelenting scourges, have ploughed upon their backs, and made long furrows, and at length brought them even to death itself. I hope there are few such monsters of barbarity suffered to subsist among you.

Is it not the highest ingratitude as well as cruelty, not to let your poor slaves enjoy some fruits of their labour? Whilst I have viewed your plantations cleared and cultivated, and have seen many spacious houses, and the owners of them faring sumptuously every day, my blood has almost run cold within me, when I have considered how many of your slaves have neither convenient food to eat, nor proper raiment to put on, notwithstanding most of the comforts you enjoy were solely owing to their indefatigable labours.... "Go to, ye rich men, weep and howl, for your miseries shall come upon you!" Behold the provision of the poor Negroes, which have reaped your fields, which is by you denied them, crieth, and the cries of them which have reaped have come upon the ears of the Lord of Sabaoth!

☙❧

Tom's depression had deepened since Rachel Nicholson had decided to become engaged to someone else. The possibility of such an obstacle had never occurred to him since he began seeing Rachel. He had come to believe that she loved him, that she had no other serious commitments, and that she would be a perfect mate for him. Since her rejection, he had thought about little else. His lack of concentration showed in his work, and Franklin had to speak to him about this, with a gentle rebuke. This shook him further; until this point Franklin had been unceasingly kind to Tom, and even a gentle chastising was hard to take.

As his mind wandered over these matters, Tom considered the entire situation. Should he try to forget Rachel? But he found he could not; she was almost indelibly imprinted on his memory. Perhaps if he left Philadelphia, and got a job elsewhere...he could meet new people? Should he give up the printing trade, and try something else? Or what?

ELEVEN

The Wavering of Destiny

The posters advertising a reward for information about William Seward's murder had been put up around Philadelphia for several days. There had been no response. Then a man came to the front door of the print shop and asked Tom Prescott to see Mr. Franklin, saying that he had information about the crime. Tom wondered about this fellow; he looked disreputable and probably indigent. But, Tom reflected, Mr. Franklin asked specifically that the posters be put in the lower-class areas of town, so what kind of characters did he expect to respond?

Hearing the man's errand, Franklin came and took him to his office at the back, carefully leaving the door ajar. "Yes?" said Ben, "what do you know of Mr. Seward's death?"

"Before I tells you, I wants to see the money," the fellow grunted.

Ben put a ten-pound note on the desk before him. "There it is. You shall have it if your information is of any value and completely truthful."

"O' course it is, guv'nor. I wouldn't lie to you, would I?"

"We'll see. Before you take the reward, since this is a murder investigation, I must call the sheriff of Philadelphia to hear this. Will you agree to that?" Ben asked.

"I ain't goin' to be arrested, am I?" The man reared back, startled.

"No, if you aren't actually involved in the murder but are here simply to give information. You needn't be afraid. You can be a great help to us in solving this terrible crime," Ben said.

"Oh," the fellow said, relaxing. "Then I guess it's all right if I won't get in any trouble."

Ben called Noah Williams from the shop and said, "Noah, would you please run over to the Court House and fetch Jasper Eby, the sheriff? Tell him we have a man with information about William Seward's murder, and would he come immediately?" Noah nodded, and dashed off.

Within ten minutes the sheriff appeared, and Franklin greeted him, explaining about this claimant to the reward money. Jasper Eby nodded. He was stout and short, older and with a touch of gout, bald with a bushy black beard. Franklin called Noah and Tom into his office to act as added witnesses, and Tom was asked to take notes. Everyone found a chair and was seated.

"Jasper, as sheriff, would you take over and conduct the interview?" Ben asked.

"Thank you, Ben. Now, first, what's your name?" he asked the fellow.

"Brandon Hicksom." He was asked to spell that and could barely do it.

"Where do you live?"

"Uh, well, here and there."

The sheriff scratched meditatively at his full black beard. "All right, Hicksom; tell us what you know about who murdered William Seward."

"'Twas about a week ago, and I was at the Black Swan Inn on Water Street. I had a bit o' money, and I went to a table behind a big—sort of—pillar, down in the lower part of the inn. Hardly any customers that night. And I was mindin' my own business with my rum, see, when I hear some people come in to a table on the other side of this big pillar. Now, me eyes ain't so good no more, but my ears is still sharp, see? And them on the other side of the pillar couldn't see me and musta thought no one else was around, so they was talkin' low, but I could hear what they said."

"Yes, yes, what were they talking about?" the sheriff asked impatiently.

"I hears one saying he'd stab Seward to kill him. When I heard *kill*, I listened as hard as I could."

The sheriff interrupted, "Was the name *Seward* actually used? That's most important, Hicksom!"

"Oh yeah, yeah, they said *Seward* many times," Hicksom said. "And then a dame's voice comes over, and she says no, no, we can't have any blood. Then another voice comes and says he wants to surprise Seward and come up behind him and put a rag over his face and—uhh, what's the word?"

"Smother? Suffocate?" the sheriff volunteered.

"Right. That's it. Suffocate Seward. In some back alley somewhere, whenever these men could catch him. And then *another* man says, after you kill him, you two wait till the middle of the night, and you take the body to Black Horse Alley and dump it there somewhere. And then you get outta there quick, before anybody sees you."

Franklin and the sheriff eyed each other meaningfully. Jasper Eby scratched his beard again.

"Then this man says, Seward is stayin' at an inn on Mulberry Street, and he's got plenty of money. And one of the guys who talked first asks, can we take it? The man says, no, all of us will split it. And that's about all. I hear the noise of their chairs movin', and they ups and leaves. I made sure they didn't see *me,* but when they was almost outta the room, I looked around the pillar and saw *them,*" Hicksom concluded and sat back with a smug air of confident mastery of his subject.

There was silence for a minute. Tom finished scribbling all of this down, and Noah uttered a low "Wow!"

Franklin said to Eby, "What Hicksom tells us about smothering Seward does confirm the piece of cloth that Dr. Abernathy and I found in his mouth. With his teeth, Seward managed to rip the little piece off the cloth that suffocated him just before he died."

"Precisely," Eby said, and then began again with Hicksom. "Now, what you say is all well and good, but the main question is, can you *identify* any of these people? Without that, we still don't know very much. As you were speaking, I counted four people. Did you recognize any of them?"

"Oh yeah! The first two—Ahab Cragg and Reuben Sobleski. I know these guys a little bit. They're real lowlifes. Do anything for a shilling. They'd kill for ten shillings."

"How well do they know you?" Franklin asked.

"Naah. Not well. I stay pretty well out of sight, away from the docks. Too dangerous," said Hicksom.

"I believe I know Cragg and Sobleski," Sheriff Eby said. "My constables or I will pick them up. Do you know who the other man and the woman might be?"

Hicksom raised a hand and scratched at his chin. He wagged his head and slowly said, "No, I don't think so, from what I could see of them as they left."

"We'll keep your identity quiet, Hicksom," Franklin said, handing him the reward money. "You've earned this. We may need you again, and if we do, there will be more. All right?"

Hicksom exited quickly with the money.

ഗാര

The Sheriff of Philadelphia and his constables were able to apprehend Ahab Cragg and Reuben Sobleski with little difficulty. These two thugs hung around the docks constantly, having no regular occupation but frequently getting into criminal activities. They were brought into the Court House on Market Street and put into two separate jail cells, at a distance from one another, and Ben Franklin was called to be present when the two were interrogated. Jasper Eby questioned Ahab Cragg first.

Eby began by saying angrily, "We know you and Sobleski murdered Mr. William Seward."

"You don't know nothin'," Cragg sneered.

"We have witnesses and can prove it." Eby was exaggerating, hoping for an incriminating response.

"You ain't got any witnesses!"

"You'll hang for this, Cragg. It's probably not the first murder you've committed. However, let me offer you an alternative. First, we know that it was Sobleski who actually put the rag around Mr. Seward's mouth and did the killing; you were the accomplice. But we also know that *you* wanted to stab Mr. Seward to death, and you were prevented from doing so. If you become a witness against Sobleski, while he will hang, perhaps the judge will spare your life. But notice, I say 'perhaps.'"

Cragg was surprised that the sheriff knew he wanted to stab Seward. How did he know that? He said nothing but stared at Sheriff Eby. Maybe turning against Sobleski was worth considering.

"Also," Eby continued, "we know that a man and a woman are behind this and hired you two to do the murder. We're very eager to know who these two are, and why they wanted Mr. Seward killed. If you tell us their names, that also could spare you from hanging, Cragg. Well, I have no more time for you; think about what I said."

The sheriff and Franklin left the cell and went to Sobleski's cell and repeated much the same conversation. Sobleski's reaction was similar. Both were crafty thugs, and they were going to tough it out. Did the sheriff really have witnesses, and who could they be? Maybe he had, and maybe not.

<hr />

Two days before the date set for the trial of Cragg and Sobleski, Cragg sent for the sheriff, wanting to talk. While Sheriff Eby was anxious to get information, he put on an attitude of impatience, as if he wouldn't believe anything Cragg would say. He stood rather than sitting, to convey his impatience.

"I been thinkin' about what you said, about maybe not being sentenced to hang if I told you more about what happened."

"Yes," responded Eby, "but as I said, there's no guarantee of that. The toughest judge of our courts, Judge Hallowell, has been assigned to conduct the trial. And he's well known for hanging criminals, often for less than murder!"

Cragg was silent. That hit home. The blood drained from his face. He knew about Judge Hallowell.

"What do you have to tell me, Cragg?" said Eby. "I'm very busy. Do you have anything to say?"

"Yeah. If it's said at the trial that I cooperated—I think you call it—and gave you the names of the two who paid us to kill Seward, can I be sure I won't be hung?"

Eby laughed. He paused for effect. "I'll present it; it *may* do some good. It's worth a try."

"All right. I'll give you those names...."

"Hold on, Cragg. This is important, and I want Mr. Franklin and some others to hear it. I'll send for Franklin right off. If he's in his shop, he should be here in five minutes." Eby turned to leave.

Ben Franklin dropped everything when he was summoned, and he and two constables went to a room where Cragg had been taken from his cell. One of the constables took notes.

Cragg started off by saying, "I want this man taking notes to put down that I gave this information so that the judge might show some—uh, uh..."

"Leniency?" Franklin suggested.

"Yeah—right, and mercy!"

"Right," said Eby. "Just like you and Sobleski showed Mr. Seward."

Cragg tried to ignore that. "And—and not sentence me to hanging." He was quivering. His voice sounded thick, and he had to clear his throat.

"All right, let's get on with it! Give us those names."

"They're married, I think. Gershom and Lucretia Stigler. He's got a nose like a beak, but *she's* the one who's really scary! Me and Sobleski met them two about a year ago, and they paid us to do a couple small jobs. But honest, sheriff, I never killed nobody before!"

The sheriff turned to his assistants. "Gershom and Lucretia Stigler. Do you know them?"

One constable said, "Yes, I ran into Lucretia last year. She's very slippery. A really bad one."

Eby ordered, "I want those two immediately. Comb the city! And I'm going to Judge Hallowell, and ask him to delay the trial till we arrest the Stiglers, to charge them also."

※

Judge Hallowell of the Superior Court had earned his reputation. The essence of dignity, he was tall and thin, with a high brow and a mane of white hair covered with the standard, powdered white wig. He rarely smiled and projected the full power of the King's law. When he entered the courtroom in Philadelphia's Court House, the visitors' gallery was packed, for this was the most sensational trial of the year. Until that moment the large courtroom had buzzed with conversation. Suddenly it was silent.

The judge sat himself behind the high bench and instructed the bailiff to bring in the prospective jurors, more than would be needed for a trial. Most impressed with their function and the dignity of the judge, they filed in to the jury box with a self-important mien. Hallowell and the attorneys quizzed each of them in turn, excused several for cause, and swore in the remaining acceptable ones.

All four defendants—Gershom and Lucretia Stigler, Reuben Sobleski, and Ahab Cragg—stood in the dock, the fenced-in area reserved for those charged with crimes. Their hands and feet were chained, and they were not allowed to sit. They appeared very grim.

Garbed in a black robe with braided cuffs and powdered wig, the prosecuting attorney gave his opening statement, spending some time giving introductory details and arguments, citing the circumstances of William Seward's death. Then the defense attorney, dressed in the same manner as the prosecutor, gave what opening defense he could. He had interviewed the four defendants extensively, and declared that three were entering not guilty pleas, and Cragg was turning state's evidence.

After these introductory matters, the prosecuting attorney called Brandon Hicksom to the witness stand. Hicksom, most conscious of his importance as a vital witness, came out of the large audience with head held high. When he was seated, the prosecutor asked him to tell all that he heard and saw in the Black Swan Inn on Water Street in the night in question. Hicksom related everything that he had previously declared to Franklin and the sheriff, giving a particularly vivid account of the conversations of the four defendants.

"Mr. Hicksom, you have testified that you were seated behind a large pillar, with the defendants on the other side, out of your sight for the moment. Since you heard but did not actually *see* the defendants when they were speaking, how can you be sure it was they who spoke those statements?"

"Oh, that's easy. The inn was almost empty of customers that night. When I went down to the lower part of the inn, the room was empty. Then these four came down later and took the table on the other side of the big pillar. I'm sure they didn't know I was there – otherwise they wouldna talked so freely. They thought they was alone. So there was no one else who could have said what I heard."

"And then you *did* see them, you say, when they got up to leave?"

"Yeah. I heard their chairs squeak back as they got up. I waited a minute, till I figured they was almost outta the room, and I looked around the pillar. They had their backs almost to me, but when they went up the stairs, I got a very good look at their faces. *That's them!*" He pointed to the dock.

After more testimony, Hicksom was cross-examined by the defense attorney, who tried to rattle him by arguing that he had *not* had a good look at the defendants, but Hicksom stuck to his story. He was excused, and the prosecutor called Ben Franklin to the witness stand to tell all that he knew, and Dr. John Abernathy to give medical evidence.

The prosecutor then called Ahab Cragg to the witness stand, and asked him to describe the entire situation. Cragg did, and then said he was turning state's evidence, admitting he was involved as an accomplice, but denying that he did the actual murder. As he said this, there were audible groans from the others in the dock. Again he was cross-examined by the defense attorney.

Judge Hallowell then asked the other three if they, in turn, wished to speak. Each of them refused the opportunity. The prosecutor then made his closing argument to the jury, calling for the death penalty for all four of them. Ashen-faced, the defendants listened, a cold sweat on their foreheads. There was not a sound in the courtroom.

Judge Hallowell had not made many comments to this point, only occasionally clarifying something that was said. Now he spoke, fixing the defendants with a steely scrutiny. "You are all indicted for the capital crime of murder. If the jury finds you guilty, severally or together, I can sentence you to death.

"But there is one more thing I wish to determine before I dismiss the jury for their deliberations on verdict. It seems obvious that you four did not originate this plan to murder William Seward, although you carried it out. Someone else has done that, and possibly, if we find out who that person or persons is, I shall move to indict him for further judicial proceedings. Your testimony at this point will be decisive. If the jury finds you guilty, and one or more of you identifies the originator of this murder plot, this will influence my sentencing. Will you tell me who that is?"

The Stiglers shuffled for a minute, looking at one another. Then Gershom said, "We were paid by a man who hates this revival that's going on all around us. He said that Whitefield fellow had a generous friend, Seward, who was vulnerable. If Seward was put out of the way, and made to look like a hypocrite by going to brothels and hanging around with prostitutes, the revival might stop. We hate this religious clap-trap too, and we wanted to stop the revival. So we got rid of Seward."

"And the identity of this man who paid you? His name?" Judge Hallowell asked, with ferocity.

Gershom and Lucretia looked at each other, bewildered. They were facing execution. Gershom's brow contorted in desperation. "I-I can't reveal that, Judge. You may sentence me to death, and I may reveal it before I die, but right now I can't," he said.

"Well, you didn't stop the Awakening," said the judge. "And in Mr. Franklin's paper, he has made it clear that Mr. Seward never went to a brothel or consorted with prostitutes. So you didn't ruin his reputation either. Therefore, I now send the jury to deliberate your fate." He brought the gavel down to end the session.

☙❧

The jury took only one hour to reach its verdict. Notifying Judge Hallowell that they were ready, they filed back into the courtroom and to their seats. Hallowell looked at the jury foreman and asked, in a sonorous voice, "Have you reached a unanimous verdict?"

All eyes were on the foreman as he rose. "We have, your honor."

"And what is that?"

"Our jury deliberations decided that all four defendants are guilty of murder, and that Ahab Cragg should be spared the death sentence because of his turning state's evidence."

There was a cry of relief from Cragg.

The foreman continued reading from his sheet, "Lucretia Stigler, Gershom Stigler, and Reuben Sobleski are guilty as charged." He sat down.

"I thank you, mister foreman, and I thank the members of the jury for their work in this case." Turning to the defendants, Judge Hallowell pronounced sentence. "Ahab Cragg, taking into consideration your turning state's evidence, and cooperating in the indictment, I hereby sentence you to ten years in prison. Lucretia Stigler and Gershom Stigler, inasmuch as you orchestrated the murder but did not actually take part in it, I hereby sentence you both to twenty years in prison. Reuben Sobleski, inasmuch as you are the actual murderer, I hereby sentence you to be hung by the neck until you are dead. Court dismissed." There were cries from the spectators, some in agreement, some against.

The judge brought the gavel down.

Cragg and the Stiglers were taken to prison immediately. The sentence on Sobleski was to be carried out within a week.

☙❧

Because George Whitefield was now so well known throughout the colonies, and William Seward was his friend and coworker, Seward's murder created enormous notoriety everywhere. Taking advantage of his investigation of the crime, Ben Franklin had carefully omitted any mention of his own involvement, and had covered the story in *The Pennsylvania Gazette* from the beginning. It was not only *The Gazette* that carried the story on its front page for several issues, but every other paper from Boston to Charleston did the same, often simply picking up *The Gazette's* copy. Even the newspaper editors who were not friendly to Whitefield or the revival understood the gravity of the situation, and could not resist playing up the sensational story. Obviously this redounded to Whitefield's benefit, showing how far the enemies of the revival would go.

Word of Reuben Sobleski's fate had spread widely, and the crowds at the execution were huge. Gallows, which were used occasionally, were set up on the grounds of the State House, at Fifth and Chestnut Streets. The condemned man had not requested that a chaplain be present, but three of Philadelphia's pastors were with him in his cell during the week, and walked with him to the gallows, reading Scripture and praying for him. As the sentence was carried out, a complete silence pervaded the crowds.

Walking back to his shop with Dr. Abernathy, Franklin mused over the events of the past weeks. "You have closely followed all that has happened, John. You know, I'm quite disturbed over one thing."

"I can imagine what it is, Ben."

"Yes, of course you can. We know that an unknown person paid the Stiglers to murder William Seward. Gershom Stigler testified to that, and said the man was careful to conceal his identity. But who was that?"

"Unless Stigler decides to talk, I suppose we will never know for certain," Dr. Abernathy replied.

"No, but I have my strong suspicions! And I may hint at them in the *Gazette*," Franklin said.

❧❦

When her father had stumbled into her home a few weeks ago, covered with tallow fat and incoherently mumbling about what had happened to him, his daughter, Martha, had been horrified. She had tried to decipher his gibberish, to find out the facts, but it had been almost impossible. He kept saying, "Prescotts are bad people. I'll get even with them—all of them." This had frightened her greatly. Who were the Prescotts? And what had they done? Had one of them deliberately poured this gummy fat all over her father? Why would anyone do such a terrible thing to a sick man?

Martha's husband had deserted her, leaving her with the children, and it was all her slender resources could do to raise them. For years it was apparent that her father needed medical help, but she knew that doctors demanded payment for their services, and she had no money for that. She had considered going to a clergyman for his help, and now she realized it was what she *must* do—and soon. Martha had heard of the Reverend James Caldwell of the Dissenter church in nearby Chester, and that people in the area liked him very much. So, leaving her children with a neighbor, she went into Chester and found Caldwell's home.

When Mrs. Caldwell opened the door to her, she greeted Martha warmly and invited her inside. The pastor's wife called her husband. After greeting Martha, Caldwell spoke first to his wife. "Dear, I think you could be useful if you remained with us." Then he turned to Martha. "I'm so glad you came to us. Now, how can we be of assistance to you?"

Martha poured out her heart to the pastor and his wife, telling them the entire story of her father's attacks on the Prescott family. It was hard for her to keep back the tears, and they were much moved. Gently, making sure not to upset her more, Caldwell asked, "Wouldn't it be helpful if we gave you some money? We would like to do that."

"Oh, I couldn't take it, Pastor," she answered. "I'm not a member of your church, or any church. It would be wrong for me to take it."

Since they were dealing with a woman, Mrs. Caldwell thought she might take the initiative, and her husband nodded to her. "No, no, Martha, it wouldn't be wrong at all. It doesn't matter that you're not a member. We're not concerned about that. The church stands here to help people—all people. First, we are going to give you five pounds from our Deacon's fund. That fund is used to help people."

"May I pay it back some day?" Martha asked.

Pastor Caldwell said, "No, no. It's entirely unnecessary, my good woman. The second thing is, I want to meet your father. Perhaps I can help him. At least I want to try. I know it would be almost impossible for you to bring him here, so I'll come to him. Would that be all right?"

"It would be wonderful!"

※

Ben Franklin walked briskly to the Court House on this Spring day. He pulled open the heavy wooden door and was met with the sound of many voices. The Reverend Horatio Gale, the city's Baptist minister, immediately came over and welcomed him. Then Gale turned to the gathering and asked them to find seats. When they did, he announced, "Friends, some people among you have asked that we gather to discuss the needs of George Whitefield. We would like to hear your views on this."

Elizabeth Rowntree, a well-known Quaker leader, rose to her feet and said, "Thank you, Pastor. In the short time Mr. Whitefield has been in Philadelphia, he has accomplished much. The churches and meeting houses are now full to bursting with folks under spiritual concern. When Mr. Whitefield is among us, he is drawing crowds such as we have never seen before, nor even imagined could be gotten together in our city. People are coming miles to hear him. When he speaks outdoors, we have even seen as many as ten thousand people! Amazing congregations for this area!"

Phineas Jameson, a Lutheran layperson, rose. "Yes, it is apparent that Mr. Whitefield is making Philadelphia something of a home base. However, there is a problem, and that is the unpredictable weather. Therefore, some of us have been thinking of building a large tabernacle that would seat many hundreds, for use in any weather. There are far too many people coming to fit into any of our churches, even the largest ones. Instead of people having to stand, we want a building large enough so people can be seated while he speaks. We are suggesting it be approximately one hundred feet long and seventy broad—about the size of Westminster Hall in London. It would not be a church, owned by one denomination. It would be an auditorium, with a lectern on a platform. It would be open to all. There would be no pew rents, or people owning one seat or another. If this meets with your approval, we want to begin receiving contributions to procure the ground and erect the building."

As the meeting was concluded, contributions and pledges of funds began to come in.

Ben Franklin smiled as he departed. He knew Whitefield would be very pleased.

❦

Others could be depended on to build a tabernacle for the evangelist, Ben thought. He had many projects already underway, but his first priority was to try to hunt down the person—or persons—behind William Seward's murder. Ben took it very seriously as his own responsibility for several reasons. First, he had the ability and means, through his newspaper, to focus the public's awareness on this, and keep a certain amount of pressure on the authorities to press ahead with the investigation. Second, he owed this to Whitefield, and also to Seward, as his friends. Thirdly, through *The Pennsylvania Gazette,* he had the means to educate the reading public on the facts of the case, which could hardly be done by any other method than a newspaper.

He sat in his office composing the copy of a front-page article, "Who Is behind Seward's Murder?" for his next issue.

> It has definitely been established that the killing of William Seward was not a random act of violence. There was planning behind it. Seward was the target. As already reported in this journal, the testimony at the trial of his murderers proved this. The foul deed of taking the life of a most generous and innocent man has to some extent been paid for by the execution of Sobleski and the imprisonment of Cragg and the Stiglers. But they were paid to murder Seward by a person or persons still unknown! Who is this?
>
> The killing of anyone is outrageous, brutal, and very sad. It breaks the Sixth Commandment, 'Thou shalt not kill.' But when the one murdered is a fine person who has never done harm to anyone, and when the murderers have done it for a most malicious purpose, that makes the killing all the more despicable. This newspaper is convinced that there must be public outcry and pressure kept upon the authorities to find the killer or killers. When something such as Mr. Seward's murder happens, the public becomes agitated for a time, and then loses interest when the next problem comes along.
>
> This must not be allowed to end here. The public must recognize

the gravity of this event, and press for the final solving of this crime, not just the punishment of four people. There is a faction with a sinister motive behind the murder. The only reason Cragg, Sobleski, and the Stiglers killed Mr. Seward was for money. But where did the monetary payment come from? Whose design was behind the murder originally?

THERE IS MORE TO THIS CRIME THAN HAS YET COME TO LIGHT!

After reading over the copy and making some corrections, Franklin took it to Noah Williams, who was setting type. He handed the paper to him and said, "Noah, this is for the front page center of our next issue. Look it over and see if you have any questions before setting it up."

Noah did so. "Strong stuff, Mr. Franklin. I'll get on it immediately."

ಬಿಐ

After work in Franklin's print shop that day, Tom had gone to his small room in Mrs. Kirkpatrick's boarding house. It had been a long day, and he was tired, but after a dinner of roast chicken and baked potatoes from his kind landlady, Tom regained his vitality. He was eager to send a letter to Josh Morris, which would be posted the next morning. He wrote:

Dear Josh:
How are you? I know you had a long and difficult journey to Georgia with Mr. Whitefield. I read his letter to Mr. Franklin to find out the news.

Everyone here is heartbroken over the murder of Mr. Seward. This may be the first letter you and Mr. Whitefield have gotten since it happened, but the papers there may have reported it already. I am sure Mr. W. will be especially troubled by it. I enclose clippings in this letter of what Mr. Franklin has written in *The Gazette* about the entire matter. He is terribly upset over it.

You will remember when I saw you in November, I told you about Rachel Nicholson, a beautiful girl. She fell into the Delaware River, remember? Anyway, Rachel has a fine family, and I was hoping to ask her to be engaged to be married. I am sorry to tell you that she will be married to someone else.

I am having a good time working for Mr. Franklin. We have been printing a lot of Mr. W's sermons and selling them. People are grabbing them up almost as fast as we can print them.

Everything there sounds exciting! I really envy you. When Mr. Whitefield says that the groups of people he is preaching to are much smaller than what he found in Pennsylvania and the Jerseys, I can imagine that. As soon as you pass Wilmington going south, I hear that the population is much less and it becomes open country. But you and he are bringing the Gospel to folks who are very disadvantaged in having few or no regular pastors. When Mr. W. writes that he baptized a number of babies, or married some couples, I understand that. Because there are so few pastors, there are hundreds of babies unbaptized, and few churches. It's too bad. So you and he are doing a great work.

Pray for me, as I'm praying for you. Please let me hear your news, as soon as you can.

Your friend, Tom

☙❧

Whitefield had met the Bishop of London's Commissary, Alexander Garden, on his first trip to Charleston, South Carolina, in 1738. At that time, Garden assumed that Whitefield was a dutiful Anglican priest who agreed with all the programs, usages, and characteristics of that denomination. At that meeting, Whitefield told him that he had met with the Archbishop of Canterbury and the Bishop of London, who approved of his becoming chaplain to Savannah, Georgia with General James Oglethorpe. Garden was impressed by that.

But all that was changed by 1740. Since their first meeting in 1738, it had been widely reported in the newspapers that Whitefield was preaching in non-Anglican ways, out in fields, to people of other denominations, and to any and all who would come to hear him. In addition he was refusing to conform to the Anglican parish system. His *Letter to the Inhabitants of Maryland...Concerning Their Negroes,* widely published, upset Garden because so many Anglicans were slave holders and were infuriated by this publication.

Whitefield was not alone in using the press. Garden, making himself spokesman for all who were offended, published *Six Letters to the Rev. George Whitefield.* As to Whitefield's charges that slaves were brutally treated, Garden denied it and said that owners of slaves should sue him for slander. Then, trying to make a mockery of Whitefield's statements, he said, "I have heard the report of your cruelty to the poor orphans under your care, not only in pinching their bellies, but in giving them up to taskmasters and mistresses who plow upon their backs and make long furrows in a very inhuman manner."

Whitefield made no reply to Garden's charges in the press, counting on the public's awareness that they were patently ridiculous. But there was another, more subtle reason for Whitefield's not getting down in the dirt and wrestling with Garden. This was a reason that the commissary, along with a number of other Anglican authorities, in America and England, could not seem to grasp. To get sympathy and support from the general public, it was wise for Whitefield to play David to Garden's Goliath, to be the underdog or martyr, always to be "persecuted," as the Journals state. Thus, Garden played perfectly into Whitefield's hand. And Garden never suspected a thing.

It took three days for Whitefield and his group to go from Savannah, Georgia to Charleston, South Carolina in early March 1740, traveling over little more than beaten tracks through forests of pine. It was slow going because the land along the coast was so indented with swamps, tidal marshes, ponds, small rivers and creeks, tributaries, and other barriers to rapid passage. The back country was beautiful land, but almost virgin territory, with only an occasional plantation here and there where the thick stands of trees had been cleared. There were no bridges over the waterways, and few ferries, and they were constantly forced to swim their horses across the waters. Consequently their horses were more tired than usual from the extra exertions, and Whitefield and the others were often soaked from being immersed in the waters. Being young, a good swimmer, and a fine horseman, Josh did not mind the uncertainties of guiding his mount into a river yawning before them. But the others in the group were not always so adventurous and willing to emerge on the other shore with sodden clothes.

Finally, on the afternoon of March 13, they approached Charleston. Here they found roads, or beaten tracks, branching out in various directions. They traveled by a number of large plantations, thousands of acres planted in rice and indigo, and saw multitudes of slaves laboring in the fields.

By 1740 Charleston was already a city of more than a thousand people, prosperous, well laid out, and growing rapidly. As the chief seaport for South Carolina, it was perfectly situated for the export of rice and indigo to Europe, and that trade was thriving, bringing in large profits to the city and its merchants. As they rode into the city, on all sides the prosperity was evident.

Whitefield, Josh Morris, James Habersham, and John Syms rode down Meeting Street on Friday, March 14, looking for St. Philip's Anglican Church. The evangelist wished to make a call on Commissary Garden to report that he was in the area again. Sensing that their meeting would be acrimonious, Whitefield had wisely brought along his friends to witness what might happen. A servant answered the front door, and led them inside to meet the Commissary. Garden was a tall, thin man, fifty-seven years old, bald but now, as often, wearing a large white powdered wig. As expected, Garden was distant and cold. His dark brown eyes, peering over spectacles, were under bushy brows. They met Whitefield's in a direct, challenging manner that foretokened verbal combat.

"I was informed that you have some questions for me, Commissary," Whitefield said with a smile, not wishing to be the one to begin an argument.

"Indeed I have, sir."

"I have now come to give you all the satisfaction I can in answering them."

"Yes, sir, I have several questions to put to you. But you have got above us in your heights, and perhaps you think that I have no right to question you."

"Not at all, Commissary. I have just stated that I will give you all the satisfaction I can."

"We will see. I have learned much about you since our first meeting. Much of what I learn is not to my liking. Savannah, to which you have been sent, is in the diocese of the Bishop of London, and I am his commissary. Savannah, and Georgia, is your assigned parish. You have no authority or commission to preach elsewhere, such as here in South Carolina. And yet you are preaching everywhere, to anyone! I see the papers are full of your activities. And I have read some of your sermons in print, and I have studied what you have written about our dear former Archbishop Tillotson. It is scandalous, sir! I charge you with enthusiasm and pride!"

Garden had begun by being haughty and disdainful regarding the much younger man. But as he got more and more angry, the blood surged in his carotids. Face flushed with fury, he left behind all decorum and dignity, jabbing his finger at Whitefield, who remained calm and unmoved. Garden had his large white wig on, but it had been tilting under the onslaught, and it was now sitting crookedly astride one ear.

"May I ask, sir, how I have had pride, and what you mean by 'enthusiasm'?"

"Your dastardly pride is shown in your speaking against the generality of the Anglican clergy!"

"Sir, when I see wrong, I must speak out about it. When I see Anglican clergy, who have sworn by the Thirty-Nine Articles as their doctrinal statement and directory of behavior, doing such things as gambling and getting disgracefully drunk in taverns, and doing worse than that, I must protest against it. And so should you, sir!"

"Don't you dare tell me what *I* should be doing," he shouted, pushing his wig up, more or less to where it should have been.

"It's the Holy Scriptures that tell you, sir—a far higher authority than I would dare to be."

"And what else would you charge against our good, faithful clergy, who stay and preach in their own parishes?"

"So many of them do not preach the chief doctrine of the Reformation—Justification by Faith alone. Luther's main teaching, based solidly on Holy Scripture. It's what the Apostle Paul taught so clearly in the New Testament books of Romans, Galatians, and others."

"And what," said Garden, "do you think they *do* preach?"

"A great number of Church of England priests, in England and America I find, are teaching their people that Justification by Works is what saves them."

Garden reared back. "And what is wrong with that?"

At that, Whitefield wondered if it was worth any further talk with this man, if he did not understand the basics of Christian faith. Should he just walk out? He saw that his friends, standing around him, were as disgusted as he was and eager not to waste any more time there.

But Garden plowed on. "You are breaking the Canons and your Ordination Vow."

"Nonsense. I was ordained by Letters Dismissory from the Bishop of London, which understood that I would be preaching at my discretion in America."

In a great rage, Garden exploded. "If you preach in any public church in South Carolina, I will suspend you!!"

Calmly Whitefield replied, "I should regard that as much as I would a pope's bull."

The veins in his temples throbbing, Garden clenched his fists and shook them. He did not know what to say, he was so furious. He stammered and stuttered. Whitefield turned to Josh, Habersham, and Syms, concerned that Garden might have a stroke. He did not want to be blamed for that too, if it happened.

After a minute, Garden seemed to have regained some control over himself. He pushed the wig back up and wiped his brow of sweat.

Whitefield waited patiently. Then he said, "But sir, why should you be offended at my speaking against some of the clergy, if they are guilty of drunkenness, lewdness, gambling, and such like? I always spoke well of you." Whitefield thought to himself, *Which is more than you have done of me!* "Sir, you did not behave thus, when I was with you last."

"No, but you did not speak against the clergy then."

"Be pleased to let me ask you one question," Whitefield said. "Have you delivered your soul by condemning the indecent gatherings and immoral dancing here?"

"What?! Must you come to catechize me? To answer your impertinent question, no, I have not spoken against them. I think there is no harm in them."

"Then I shall think it my duty to criticize you."

At that, rage overcame Garden again, and he totally lost control. "Then, sir, get you out of my house!" The wig responded, moving forward almost to cover his eyes. He grabbed the wig and threw it on the floor. They left quickly, with Garden sputtering in rage behind them.

Josh, Habersham, Syms and Whitefield gathered on the street outside to discuss what had happened.

"Whew!" James Habersham said. "What a temper! He's a grown man. He acts like a child having a tantrum. He ought to be able to contain his anger."

"I pity the man. I expected he would be more noble than to give such treatment," said Josh.

"You aren't going to attend services at his church, are you, George? If you do, you know what to expect," John Syms asked.

"Oh yes, I'll go. I bear the man no ill will. I believe he is completely wrong on every point, but I certainly do not hate him. Our Lord Jesus tells us to love our enemies."

༺༻

On this Saturday morning in Chester, the coach from Philadelphia clattered into the square, raising dust, for the spring rains had not yet begun. The two horses came to a halt, breathing hard from the long journey, jerking at the reins, eyes rolling back. One of them raised its head, tossed its long mane, and snorted.

Not waiting for the coachman to climb down from his perch to open the door, Tom opened it and jumped to the ground. His bag was placed on the ground, the driver climbed back to his seat, signaled the horses to drive on, and the coach left.

Tom walked across the square toward Hiram Prescott's shop. Since the fire and its restoration the shop had a new look, with fresh paint and a small front window instead of the large older one that had been torn out. Tom simply opened the front door, not bothering to knock, and found his father at the workbench, nailing a heel on a shoe.

"Tom!" Hiram exclaimed, dropping his tools and jumping up. He came around the table, arms extended, and embraced his son, asking about his health. Then he said, "And how is Rachel?"

Tom's eyes dropped. "I'm sorry to tell you, Dad, that Rachel is going to marry someone else."

"What?! How could that be? From everything that you've said, I thought that she was going only with you."

"It was a complete shock to me too, Dad. I guess I just assumed that she was seeing only me—but I was wrong."

"Has the wedding already taken place, son?"

"No, I checked into that. It won't be for another several months."

"How do you know that everything is going smoothly in that direction?"

231

"Uh, well, I don't."

"Sit down, son." As they faced each other, Hiram said, "I'm going to give you some advice. If they aren't married yet, I think you should go to Rachel and plead your case to her. She may well be having second thoughts about the current engagement. Son, do you remember the true saying, 'Faint heart never won fair lady'?"

෨෬

Tom caught the next coach back to Philadelphia. His talk with Hiram had gotten to him. "Dad is right," he said to himself. "Here I am, sitting around and feeling sorry for myself. How stupid! Maybe Rachel won't want to marry this other fellow. How do I know, unless I investigate?"

The next morning, Sunday, Tom did not attend the Dissenter church he had joined. Instead, he went to the church that the Nicholsons attended. He hoped to see Rachel, if only from a distance. Tom sat at the back of the sanctuary and enjoyed the sermon based on Isaiah chapter 53. Not wanting to appear too conspicuous, after the service he greeted the pastor at the church door and went out into Arch Street. Deliberately, he did not hasten away, and what he hoped to happen, did.

"Tom!" a voice called after him.

He turned around to see who called. It was Mr. Nicholson, who walked to him through the congregation emerging from the church, smiling. "Tom, I'm glad to see you. But where have you been of late?"

"It's good to see you, sir. Well, since your daughter got engaged, I knew I wouldn't be so welcome at your home any longer."

"Not welcome! Tom, after saving my daughter's life, you will always be welcome in my home. And as to Rachel's engagement..." He said the last slowly.

Tom's expression registered uncertainty. "I don't understand. Isn't Rachel engaged to be married?"

"Well, yes, but..."

"Sir, what is it?"

"Tom, I think you should go to Rachel and talk with her. She's coming out of the church now."

"But if she is with her fiancé, I don't want to intrude."

"Rachel is with her mother and me. He's not here. Please, go and speak with her."

Tom nodded and made his way through the crowd. "Rachel! Hello! How are you?"

Rachel beamed. "I'm fine, Tom. It's so good to see you."

"Can we talk for a minute? Let's get out of this group of people." She nodded her willingness, and they went down Mulberry Street a short distance. "How is it going with you?" Tom asked, smiling.

"Oh, so so," she said. But her tone conveyed no excitement or delight.

"I don't mean to intrude, but isn't your fiancé with you?"

"No, he doesn't attend this church." She hesitated. "Or any church."

"Well, is your wedding coming soon?"

"We haven't set a date for it yet, Tom."

"But you're still engaged to this man, aren't you?"

Again hesitation. "I suppose you could say so."

"Rachel, please don't be angry with me, but you must know that I think so much of you. Aren't you happy about your marriage to this man?"

Rachel turned away, and Tom caught a glimpse of a tear in her eye. She said nothing.

"This is none of my business, unless you want to tell me something. But all of this disturbs me. I want you to be happy, but you don't seem to be happy."

She turned back to him. "Oh Tom, David Talcott is a nice fellow, but...I just don't know!"

Tom blurted out, "Well, if you aren't sure, then you shouldn't marry him until you are."

"I know. That's what my parents keep telling me."

"May I walk you home, Rachel? And if you want to, I'd like to talk about this."

Perhaps things weren't so bad for him. Hope sprang eternal.

※

In the week since Ben Franklin's last front-page article in *The Pennsylvania Gazette,* there had been few developments in the search for those behind William Seward's murder. Ben was becoming frustrated.

While his articles did keep public interest high, and he was approached by a number of citizens who were seriously concerned, Ben wanted more action. The city's sheriff, Jasper Eby, was probing everywhere he could, trying to dig up more clues, but nothing of value had appeared.

This week's *Gazette* would go to press in a few hours. Ben wanted to keep up his drumbeat of front-page articles, hoping they might stimulate someone to come forward who might know more about the murder. He sat in his office, pen in hand, writing the next piece:

WHO BENEFITS FROM WILLIAM SEWARD'S MURDER?

Reuben Sobleski has paid with his life for his part in the crime. Ahab Cragg and the Stiglers are in prison. Testimony at the trial proved that these dastardly criminals were inspired and paid for by some vile person or persons to kill William Seward. Whoever that was, their object was to impute disgrace to that which Mr. Seward stood for, namely the Awakening that is thriving among us. All of this comes from sworn testimony before Judge Hallowell.

So, who could be behind this outrageous murder? Who could these culprits be?

It is not difficult to imagine who they are, and what they stand for. Who could possibly benefit from getting rid of a fine and generous soul like William Seward? Surely, for almost everyone, considering the good he has so willingly done, his death is a great loss. Only a few could be helped by this, and they are a reprehensible and vile sort indeed. Their identity may yet be found out.

Ben's wife entered his office. He looked up and grinned. "Deborah, you know, my eyes are not as good as they were a few years ago. All the reading I must do is taking its toll."

"Well, you are thirty-four years old, after all! Do you expect to be young forever?"

"No, my dear. I've gotten a pair of spectacles from Mr. Haskins, the apothecary, hoping they will help my eyesight. But the blamed things are giving me headaches!" he snapped. "So I've been experimenting with a different kind of eyeglasses. See here." He removed the glasses from his face.

"I took Haskins' lenses, cut them in half, and glued them to half of other lenses of a different thickness. With this invention, I can look through the lower halves and read things close up, and when I raise my eyes to look through the upper halves, I can see things clearly at a distance. It works quite well. I'm calling this my 'double spectacles', or 'bifocals.' What do you think of this, dear?"

"Another invention!" Deborah sniffed. "Oh, that will never amount to anything, Ben."

"I'm not so sure, my dear." Ben gave his wife a friendly pat on the posterior and then handed her the copy he had just composed. "Here, Deborah. Please check this, and tell me what you think."

Eyebrows knit, she read it. Shaking her head slightly, she said, "As a short article, I'm sure it's all right. But I'm concerned, Ben. You are doing more than anyone else, including the sheriff, to try to get to the bottom of this. Have you considered that, by keeping this up, you are exposing yourself to danger? Certainly the guilty party is furious with you and the paper."

"But this is simply the duty of a good newspaper, Deborah. Besides, I'm always in trouble over something I've printed, about the Penn family or someone else. No, danger or no, I owe this to George Whitefield. And think of this: if this person comes after me, perhaps he will expose himself, and then we'll know who the culprit is!"

☙❧

Alexander Garden, Commissary of the Bishop of London and pastor of St. Philip's Church, Charleston, was so infuriated by George Whitefield's refusal to accede to his wishes that he did everything he could to silence the itinerant.

After their confrontation on March 14, his sermons from his pulpit centered on one topic only: a condemnation of his enemy. For some reason, Whitefield thought it his duty to attend the service at St. Philip's Church on March 16, and he suffered through a tirade from Garden likening him to a Pharisee who prayed, "God, I thank Thee that I am not as other men are." But that was only a beginning.

Garden's pen flew. Soon he produced a sermon that went into print, in which he wrote that Whitefield was an enthusiast, and he and others:

...conceive and insist upon Regeneration, to be an immediate, instantaneous Work of the Holy Spirit, wrought inwardly on the Hearts or Souls of Men, critically at some certain Time.... But, my Brethren, the Work of Regeneration is not the Work of a Moment, a sudden instantaneous Work, like the miraculous Conversion of St. Paul, or the Thief on the Cross; but a gradual and co-operative Work of the Holy Spirit, joining in with our Understandings, and leading us on by Reason and Persuasion, from one Degree to another, of Faith, good Dispositions, Acts, and Habits of Piety....

You have been amused with the miraculous Conversions of St. Paul, Zaccheus, the Jailor, and the Penitent Thief; but what are they to the Purpose? Can any good Inference be drawn from the miraculous Cases, to what must be the ordinary and common Case of all Christians? No, my Brethren, such Inference would be idle and absurd....

When they read all this, Josh and others shook their heads at the perversions and twistings of logic that Garden was so good at. Josh immediately sat down and penned a letter to the Rev. William Tennent, to inform him of events in the South, and he included copies of Garden's sermon.

Savannah, March 16, 1740

Dear Pastor Tennent:
I hope you are well, as we are. I have not written to you for several weeks, because we have been so busy here, but I wanted you and all of the New Light friends to know what is happening with Mr. Whitefield. Enclosed is a sermon just published by our chief adversary in the South, Alexander Garden, the Bishop of London's Commissary. Mr. W. and our group met with this man on the 14th, and never has Mr. W. been treated so badly. He stood his ground calmly, while Garden raged and ranted like a madman, threatening everything he could think of. I was shocked that such a person could be the supposed leader of other Christians. These "sermons" of Garden's are only bitter tirades, and a disgrace, I think you will agree. But Satan is raging, because his kingdom is being attacked.

Since Mr. Whitefield, like other evangelists, has merely been presenting the Gospel and asking for a response from his hearers, when has he ever been guilty of teaching 'immediate revelations'? And the usual charge of "enthusiasm" is thrown at him—and when has he ever been an enthusiast? In his preaching, he remains as calm as possible, and so do almost all of his hearers. Everyone comments on this—except those who have never bothered to hear him.

But Garden is probably at his weakest and silliest in claiming that the immediate conversions of people in the Bible were any different from conversions in other times and places. I'm sure you will agree that there is always something "miraculous," to use Garden's term, in any conversion, because the Holy Spirit does a supernatural work in the person.

Since Mr. W's group is traveling constantly, it will be difficult for you to write to us, but I hope to be home soon, and will be very pleased to see you then. I trust all goes well at the College. Please say hello to all my friends. I pray for you all constantly.

Josh Morris

🙰

Commissary William Vessey of New York wrote to the Old Light clergy in Philadelphia, asking to meet them on an urgent matter. They knew what he meant and were expecting to hear from him. John Thomson wrote back immediately, asking if he could come the next week.

🙰

When Vessey arrived outside Thomson's home on Fourth Street, he looked furtively up and down the street, although he was aware that few would know him in Philadelphia. He noticed that the window's curtains were drawn, and at his knock someone opened them far enough to observe who was at the door before he was admitted. Inside, he found John Thomson, Richard Burbridge, Hosea Dickson, and half a dozen other Old Lights gathered.

"Thank you for coming, Mr. Vessey," Burbridge said. "How was the travel from New York?"

"Terrible! Terrible! The coach ride from Hoboken to Trent Town was absolutely horrid. I was forced to ride with the most disreputable people.

Two of them were disgustingly drunk, and their behavior—with ladies aboard, mind you—was intolerable."

"Sorry to hear that," said Dickson.

"Well, this is so important that I left all my work in New York to see you. Mr. Thomson, weren't *you* the one we asked to get someone to bring scandal on William Seward? That is my recollection."

Thomson shifted uncomfortably on his chair. "Yes, that's right."

"Well then, by all the poxed polecats, what went wrong, man? This fellow Stigler you secured was supposed to sully William Seward's character—not get him killed! Didn't you make it plain to those thugs what we wanted?"

"Yes, I did, but apparently they misunderstood."

"Apparently? I should say! Seward is dead, one thug has been hung, and three more are in jail."

Hosea Dickson came to Thomson's defense. "From what I gather, the fellow John secured—Stigler—went much beyond what John asked of him. I'm sure John never suggested killing Seward."

"No, of course not," Thomson said weakly. "I told Stigler to get Seward involved in some sort of scandal. That's all I said."

Vessey, trembling with anger, exclaimed, "Confound it, you certainly didn't emphasize it enough! Whatever you told him, with Seward and one killer dead and the others in jail, this has gone far beyond what we ever intended. And instead of bringing disgrace on Seward and Whitefield, it's helping the revival, with much publicity."

Thomson literally wilted. "I'm sorry, very sorry."

"At least no one knows who we are," said Vessey, attempting a faint smile.

With that, Thomson had to clear his throat; his voice sounded thick. "Umm...no, I'm afraid Gershom Stigler knows who I am."

"What?!" said Burbridge. A stunned silence followed.

"What if he decides to reveal who you are—that it was you who paid him?" Dickson asked.

"That trail could lead to all of us," said Burbridge.

"Oh no," said Thomson, wiping the cold sweat from his forehead. "It never occurred to me."

"Now listen, men," Vessey said, "we can't panic. Thomson has done an abominable job with what we asked him to do, but we can't make any more mistakes. Let's think this through. So it's Stigler who knows Thomson's identity, and he is in jail now. If Stigler talks..."

"But perhaps something serious should happen to him before he can talk," Dickson said.

There was silence in the room for a full minute. Then Thomson said, "Look, men. I'm the one who made a mistake in getting someone I knew. Let me try to rectify all of this by seeing that Stigler does not talk and reveal who we are."

Vessey said, "That's only proper. We'll leave it up to you. Don't tell us what you want to do. Just do it. Now, I came here because this is in all the newspapers everywhere, and that must be stopped.

"Listen to this, in *The New York Sentinel:* 'The Reverend Whitefield's Co-Worker Murdered. Most suspicious circumstances attend the tragic murder of William Seward, wealthy English benefactor, in an alley in Philadelphia.' Or this, from *The New York Messenger:* 'Strangest Crime. Rev. George Whitefield's assistant, William Seward, was killed by four criminals found guilty in a Philadelphia court. These killers have pointed to some unknown person as the one behind the ghastly crime, probably with the intent of bringing disrepute on Mr. Whitefield.' Or this, from *The Newark Postboy:* 'Unknown Instigator Behind Seward Murder. The killer hung on Thursday for the murder said that it was committed to bring disgrace on the Reverend George Whitefield's Revival Ministry, and that they were paid to commit the hideous crime.' Well, what do you think of *that?*"

"Yes," said Burbridge, "we've been getting the same thing in our newspapers."

"Ugh!" Vessey choked. "Confound it! This is terrible. In New York, people are coming up to me and asking, Do I know what wretch could have done this? I can't even answer them."

"Oh, it's much worse for us here in Philadelphia," said Dickson. "People in my church are saying to me, 'You know, Parson, since you've been preaching so hard against this Awakening, I'll wager you might have had something to do with Mr. Seward's killing.' Imagine—said to my face!"

"At least they're telling you to your face," said Thomson. "It's what people are saying behind our backs that's much worse."

TWELVE

The Future in God's Hands

When Tom heard from Rachel that she was uncertain about marrying David Talcott, he was much encouraged in his desire to court her. He began to send her notes in the mail, expressing his love for her. He took a large bunch of roses to her home in Elfreth's Alley, doing this deliberately when he knew she would be away for a time. His last note asked if she would see him again. Rachel replied:

Dear Tom:
Thank you again for the gifts and letters you have been sending. I appreciate them. Yes, I would be pleased to meet with you, perhaps after your work some evening soon. How would Tuesday be?
Sincerely, Rachel

When Tuesday evening came, Tom arrived at the Nicholson home with some sweets he had purchased from a baker on Third Street. Rachel answered his knock on the front door, bestowed on Tom a radiant smile, and invited him in, thanking him for the sweets. Knowing he was coming, the rest of the family had decided to vacate the house for a time, so Tom and Rachel would have the place to themselves.

"Rachel," Tom began, "I don't want to pry into your private affairs, so I will not say anything about any subject you don't want to talk about."

"Tom, I'm not going to be very private. I'll talk about anything. You are here because I told you I wasn't sure about marrying David Talcott. And I appreciate your concern."

Tom thought it wise to be quiet. Let Rachel say what she wished.

After some hesitation, she said, "I've been praying a great deal about this. As I told you, David doesn't belong to any church, and I'm not sure he is a Christian. I've talked with him about this, and he says he believes in God, but he's not sure about Jesus Christ."

Another pause. Tom listened patiently.

"So, I've decided I can't marry a person who doesn't share my faith. You know what St. Paul says in Second Corinthians 6:14."

Tom blurted out, "So you've decided not to marry David Talcott?"

Rachel looked at the floor, unwilling to return his gaze. "Yes, I think so. I haven't told him yet, and I know he will be furious, but—"

"That doesn't matter! It's your life, and you must do what honors the Lord and be convinced that you are doing what is best for yourself!"

"I know, I know, Tom," Rachel said quietly.

Tom's mind was in a whirl. He realized how traumatic all of this was for a young woman, making a decision that would affect her entire life. And he saw that if he did not proceed with care, he could distress her and injure his own case to begin courting her again.

So he sat silent for a minute, and finally said, "Rachel, you know what I think of you. I love you. And I believe your decision here is a sensible one, in accord with Scripture. I want to say that if there's anything I can do to help, please let me know."

Rachel reached over and put her hand on Tom's knee. "Oh Tom, thank you. You're a fine person."

Tom knew it was time to leave.

※※

Ben Franklin was in his office when the afternoon mail arrived. Hastily he thumbed through it: seven letters, one from England, all needing answers; five notices regarding runaways and other matters; and half a dozen newspapers, including two from London. He would respond to the letters in his leisure time. But he always made a quick survey of newspapers a priority, because he needed to know of any important news items that had previously escaped him, although few did.

In these papers, there were notices of Indian uprisings on the frontiers, and a major robbery in Edinburgh. But other than those stories, Ben noted with pleasure that he had already included in *The Pennsylvania Gazette* every item that he found in the other newspapers. Even more gratifying, he saw that papers in other cities had picked up his own accounts of the Seward killing and the trial of the murderers.

Deborah came down the stairs and into his office. "Look at these, my dear," he said. "*The Hartford Weekly Journal* and *The New York Evening Post* and *The Baltimore Packet* have all copied almost verbatim my stories on Seward's murder and the trial. And none of them, I note, have had sufficient honesty to credit *The Gazette* as the source!"

Deborah scanned each of the papers, expressing disapproval by clucking. "Dear me, Ben. Isn't that called plagiarism?"

"Hah. I'm afraid, Deborah, that it's done much of the time. If I steal material in writing a book, that's plagiarism, but if I pilfer copy for a newspaper, that's journalism. Not much I can do about it. But I shall write to each of the editors and complain. Oh my." He yawned and changed the subject. "Did you get much sleep last night, with the storm howling outside, my dear? I thought you were rather restless. That rain may have flooded some cellars."

"The wind and the rain were bad enough, Dear, and I managed to sleep through some of that. But it was the thunder and lightning that woke me frequently. And Matilda Burch tells me that a church steeple was hit by lightning during the storm, and some damage was done."

"Yes, I heard that." Ben's face took on a faraway, dreamy look that came on him when he was pondering some problem, scientific, philosophical, political, or otherwise. "I've been considering the problem of lightning, you know...fascinating..."

"Lightning?" She paused. "Ben, be careful. You recall that man over on Fourth Street was killed when struck by lightning in a storm last year."

"Do you realize that we know almost nothing about lightning? I have been trying to find some scientific writing on the subject, and I have found almost nothing. And I'm also most interested in electricity, Deborah. I've heard that the French and the English have done a bit of experimenting with electrical sparks. I suspect that lightning may be nothing more than a very strong concentration of electrical sparks sent to earth from the clouds. Hmm. Very interesting. I must give this much more attention. And maybe I ought to begin some experimenting. Perhaps the next time there's a storm with thunder and lightning—"

"BEN!" his wife burst out suddenly. "Please leave that alone! Lightning is very dangerous!"

Rachel sent a note to Tom at Franklin's printing establishment, saying that she had met with David Talcott and broken off their engagement. She asked Tom to get in touch.

Tom could hardly wait until the working day was over, to go to Elfreth's Alley. He knocked on the Nicholsons' door, and Rachel opened it, looking as radiant as ever. She invited him in.

"I got your news, Rachel! How did Talcott take it?"

"Not well. He cursed a bit and called me a name or two...." She was not smiling now.

Tom curled his fingers into fists. "The louse! Where does he live? I'll teach him—"

"No no, Tom. It's better forgotten. He's not worth getting angry over. He showed what kind of a person he really is. I never saw that before in him, but I'm glad I finally saw it."

Mrs. Nicholson came into the room at that point. "Tom! I heard your voice. You have been a stranger here, and it's so good to see you again. Can you stay for our evening meal?"

Tom, somewhat embarrassed, said, "Oh thank you, Mrs. Nicholson. I'd love to, but I just came from work, and I haven't been to my room to bathe or change from my working clothes. I've got printing ink all over my arms, and...."

Both Rachel and her mother laughed. "Nonsense. You could scrub up here. You look fine. My husband won't be home from his work for half an hour, so if it would make you feel better, there's time to go to your boarding house if you'd prefer."

"I'd much rather. Printing is hard work, and I've been sweating all day!" All three laughed. "I'll be back in half an hour!" Tom said as he dashed out the door.

After the meal, Rachel and Tom took a long walk along the waterfront. They chatted for several hours, but Tom felt it was too soon to propose marriage, after Rachel had just broken off with Talcott.

There was time for that.

✂︎

Pastor Caldwell had promised Martha, the daughter of the man who attacked Hiram Prescott, that he would visit him. Caldwell walked the distance to the man's shack three times and met Martha there. She did her best to convince her father that the pastor was there to help him. The first visit did not go well. To maintain as much quiet as possible, Martha had taken her children to a neighbor. The man, named Collin Bullard, was withdrawn and very suspicious. He eyed Caldwell as a potential enemy and hardly muttered at all. After half an hour of trying to befriend the man, and praying over him, the pastor felt there was nothing more to be gained on this visit. But he vowed not to give up.

The second visit a week later went a bit better, with Martha there again and the children gone. Bullard seemed somewhat less suspicious, but he still mumbled incoherently. This time Caldwell and Martha both spoke to him about his need for healing. Twice Caldwell offered prayer for Bullard's healing, and he seemed to understand that this man was there to help him, and posed no threat. At one point it seemed he almost smiled at his daughter and the pastor.

Through his mumbling, several times Caldwell caught another voice in the background coming through, quietly but with a definite threatening tone. Bullard's normal pitch was higher, more like a tenor voice, even when he was muttering. But this other voice that occasionally broke through was far deeper, more guttural, much more sinister. After the second visit, Caldwell went to his home and prayed for guidance on this, and he was convinced the Lord gave it to him.

On his third visit, a few days later, the pastor was persuaded he had the answer; he understood Bullard's condition well enough. His voices were caused by demon possession. As with all inhabitation by demonic powers, there was an enormous struggle going on inside the man, as the demon fought desperately to maintain control and remain there. In the last few days Caldwell had examined all the accounts of demon possession in the Bible, especially those where Jesus had exerted His mighty power to draw a demon out of some poor tormented, violent person. So many of the characteristics of the demons in the Bible matched what was happening to

Bullard, that the pastor was convinced this was the only explanation that was possible.

Therefore, if this man were to be healed, Caldwell would have to perform an exorcism. He showed Martha the accounts in Matthew, chapters 8, 12, and 17, Mark chapter 1 and elsewhere. He explained all of this to Martha, and she understood and agreed to it. Anything, after all, that would bring healing and sanity back to her parent. It made sense to her that the explanation for her father's trouble was that he was inhabited by a demon.

Pastor Caldwell said to Martha that exorcisms are done only occasionally. Over the centuries the Church had designed the rite of exorcism, performed only by the clergy. Because of the nature of the rite, he suggested that she wait outside the shack, while he worked inside, and she left.

Fortunately, Bullard was quiet, subdued, and seemed almost ready for help. The pastor began by reading from the ordinal the prescribed order for removal of demons. This took several minutes, during which Bullard sat quietly, head bowed.

"May I speak to the voice that inhabits you?" Caldwell asked Bullard, gently.

"Yes.... I am here.... You are disturbing me. What do you want?"

This was frightening. It was a cold, chilling voice that seemed, and indeed was, supernatural. It was hollow, preternatural, otherworldly. Caldwell had been through an exorcism only once before, and that was conducted by an older, more experienced clergyman. At that time, he had heard such an occult voice. Now he heard the same sepulchral sound again. Here was the demon talking.

The pastor put his hands on Bullard's head. He did not resist, knowing that somehow he was, indeed, tormented. He did not understand why or how, but he wanted to be freed. Caldwell prayed a prayer that lasted several minutes. Then he read a number of passages from the New Testament, such as Mark 5, and, following the scriptural formula, he pronounced, "In the great and glorious Name of the Lord Jesus Christ, I *command* that you come out of him!"

There was a great screech—a scream of agony, enough to send chills up the spine of the heartiest individual, as the demon was forced to obey and exit its victim.

Then, just as chillingly, there was a complete, empty silence.

Bullard was freed of torment.

For the first time in years, Bullard smiled, his eyes aglow. He was in his right mind, as he had not been in years. Caldwell went to the door and called Martha in and told what had happened.

Bullard exclaimed, "Martha, I feel that a great weight has been lifted off me! I think God has done it!"

His daughter threw her arms around him, and they both shed tears of joy.

On Pastor Caldwell's next visit, with Collin Bullard a happy man who was being employed part-time by Hiram Prescott at the shoemaking shop, the pastor led Bullard to the Lord.

☙❧

George Whitefield, Josh Morris, Joe Husbands, John Syms, and the rest of the group had returned to the Middle Colonies from Georgia, pleased that the first bricks of the main house at Bethesda had been laid, twenty acres of land had been cleared, and the work was continuing. Whitefield's welcome from the pro-revival people in Philadelphia on April 15 was as great as ever, and one of their first visits was to Ben Franklin's print shop.

On that warm spring day, as Whitefield and Josh tied their horses outside, Tom saw them through the front window and came rushing out, followed closely by Ben Franklin. There were handshakes and questions about each others' health all around.

Josh and Tom sat on the bench outside the shop to exchange news, and Franklin asked Whitefield if he would come to his office at the back, for the onerous task that was now his. When they were seated, Ben said solemnly, "I have awful news for you, my friend. Your faithful supporter and companion William Seward is dead. Did you hear of it before this?"

Whitefield responded, "Yes, Ben. One of the newspapers down South carried the story. It may have been copied from your good journal. But it was a very brief account, and gave no details. May the dear Lord help us! What happened?"

"I'm afraid the details are very bad. He was murdered."

Whitefield repeated the word. It took another minute for the sad news to register fully. "Who would do such a ghastly thing? Has the killer been found?"

Ben said, "Oh yes. It happened several weeks ago. He was killed as he came from his inn. The sheriff was skillful in tracking down the two killers, along with two others who paid them to do it. The matter has already gone to a speedy trial before Judge Hallowell, who sentenced one of them to hang, and the others to serve many years in prison."

Whitefield dropped his head into his hands. Tears came to his eyes. "Poor William. He was only a young man. But he was a magnificent Christian, generous and loving, and now he certainly is with his Lord. Ben, do you know *why* such a terrible thing was done to a fine person?"

"It all came out in the trial, George. Again I am sorry to have to tell you this, but the killers said they did it to stop the Awakening. Since William was such a generous supporter of the revival, they hoped that his death would hinder you and all those who are promoting the Awakening. While we are all so regretful of William's death, I wrote up the entire story in the *Gazette,* and the many who are in favor of the Awakening have read it and see how evil is working. Because of the public awareness of how despicable are your enemies, the revival is flourishing more than before."

༄༅

Later that day, when Whitefield had recovered somewhat from the shock, and had visited Seward's gravesite, Franklin said, "Well, my good friend, how did it go in Georgia?"

"Oh, very well, Ben. The orphan home is under construction, and we have almost forty orphans under James Habersham's care. He is an excellent man, and I can leave Bethesda knowing that all will be taken care of in my absence. How are things here?"

"From my vantage point, George, I would say good. We have printed all of the sermon manuscripts you left with us, and they are selling well. I sent thirty dozen to New York, and I understand they are all sold. I will send more. Do you have more manuscripts to give us?"

"Yes. Here are three more. You're a great help, Ben, and I appreciate it very much. I especially appreciate your managing much of the income here in the Middle Colonies for the orphan house. Now, for the next week,

I must find a place to stay."

"George, I have told you before, you know my house. If you can make shift with its scanty accommodations, you will be most heartily welcome."

"Most generous, Ben. I don't want to inconvenience you and your family, however. But if you made that kind offer for Christ's sake, you will not miss of a reward."

The deist Franklin could not go that far. While he appreciated the fervor and utter sincerity of Whitefield's faith, he was still the doubter. He answered, "Don't let me be mistaken. It was not for Christ's sake...but for yours."

Whitefield smiled at that. He knew Franklin well enough to expect a similar answer. And so he stayed at Franklin's home whenever he was in Philadelphia and was grateful for his friend's hospitality.

On the next day, another meeting was called at the Court House for interested citizens, to discuss the building of a large meeting place for Whitefield's preaching. He had not been at the first meeting and was not fully aware of what had been projected. A contingent of clergy and laypeople were milling around, and at the sight of Whitefield entering the building, the Reverend Arthur Jenkins called the meeting to order.

The room became quiet, and everyone found a seat. Mister Jenkins said, "Mr. Whitefield, we feel this is an important project. The problem is the unpredictable weather. We are in the midst of the rainy season. The crowds have been most patient with the weather, being willing to stand outside in cold, rain and snow. But is this fair to them, if they are so faithful?"

Whitefield arose. "I thoroughly agree, and I am most grateful for my wonderful and patient audiences. But there is more to it than that. There is a major problem. Building a church would, I fear, lead the people into bigotry, and make them think of the Church, Christ's Body, as they have done for a long time, as being merely a building—*that* building. Rather, I want them to realize that the corporate body of believers, wherever it is, is the Church. That's the advantage of being outdoors for worship—there *is* no church building!"

Silence settled over the people. In a few words, Whitefield had said a great deal. With his struggle against entrenched bureaucratic officialdom closing pulpits to him and John Wesley in England and America, and opposing him at every turn, they saw his argument. It was in all the papers. Whitefield simply feared that, even if he warned against it, his followers could become a new sect, perhaps after he had left. He balked at the petty institutional rivalries of denominations, and their infighting.

How to answer Whitefield's concern? Should they drop the project?

Ben Franklin arose after a few minutes of silence. "I can understand Mr. Whitefield's concern that if we put up a building, eventually this may lead to another sect being formed. Let me make a suggestion. I propose that we have a board of trustees that would include members of all of our denominations, so that no one group, new or old, would have total control. And, while this building is particularly for Mr. Whitefield's use, since he is not always in town, that it might also be for the use of any preacher of any religious persuasion who might desire to say something to the people." Ben Franklin sat down.

The Reverend Arthur Jenkins arose and said, 'Mr. Whitefield, what do you think of this concept?"

Whitefield, lost in thought, said, "I suppose having speakers from various groups would keep the building from becoming the center of a new sect, since no one group could claim it. If you don't mind, when the weather is fine, I'd still like to do field preaching in this area. Then, in winter or rain, certainly I'd like to use the new building, to keep my listeners warm and dry."

Jenkins said, "Fair enough. Shall we vote on Mr. Franklin's idea?"

It was unanimous.

∞)C∞

Tom had urged Josh Morris to ride his horse to Elfreth's Alley, to call on Rachel Nicholson. Tethering his horse at a convenient post, Josh knocked on the door, and it was opened by her mother.

"Mrs. Nicholson? My name is Josh Morris, and I'm a good friend of Tom Prescott…"

"Josh?! Oh my, we've heard so much about you! Come in, come in, please. Let me call my daughter. Rachel! There's someone here you'll want to meet!"

In half a minute, down the stairs came one of the loveliest young ladies Josh had ever seen. To Josh she seemed the essence of perfection.

Her light brown hair was tumbling down over her shoulders, and she was wearing a dress of azure blue, liberally embellished with lace and trimmed with lavender ribbons, having short sleeves that left most of her arms bare.

"Hello," said Josh, dazzled, his eyes wide with admiration. "I'm, uh—oh yes, I'm Josh Morris, Tom's friend. So glad to meet you, Rachel..."

"I'm delighted to meet you, Josh! Oh, Tom has told me so much about you!" Rachel's voice seemed to Josh like the musical tinkling of tiny bells.

For an hour they talked. Because they were so eager to hear about the trip South with George Whitefield, Mrs. Nicholson joined them, and they heard all the details. Eventually Josh got to what he thought was the most interesting part.

"Well, I must tell you about our meeting with Commissary Garden in Charleston. He's an unbelievable person. No Christian love in Garden at all. Just a lot of hatred for those he doesn't agree with. From what I could gather, large numbers of his people have deserted his church. It's no wonder. I don't know why we did it, but Mr. Whitefield insisted we attend Garden's church, and we found it quite empty. And then we had to sit through the most disgusting attacks I've ever heard. On the other hand, Mr. Whitefield is a wonderful man, but he's not very healthy. When he gets up to preach, suddenly it seems as if the Holy Spirit's power enters into him, and he can speak with that incredible voice for an hour. But as soon as he's done, he comes down from the stone or wagon he's standing on, and he's ready to collapse. Many times I've had to stand by and almost catch him to keep him from falling off the stone. Usually he has to retire to bed soon after he's preached, he is so fatigued and weak. And I always have to help him on and off his horse. That's constant."

Rachel and her mother listened with rapt attention. Reluctantly, after a time, Josh decided he must leave and excused himself.

As he untied his horse and mounted, he thought, *Wow! What a marvelous and charming young lady.*

ΣΟΩ

Gershom Stigler had been imprisoned for over a month, in solitary confinement. The prison was in the basement of the Court House and was little more than a dungeon, modeled on the jails of England. The prison was designed for punishment, not rehabilitation. Smelly, rat-infested, damp, with bare stone and brick walls and only a few slits of windows high up for light, the cells were small and completely unheated. In winter, they were brutal. In each cell there was only a small cot with a few ragged blankets, and a chamber pot.

The regulations for the prisoners were extremely rigid: two meals a day of poor food and one hour of supervised release from their cells for exercise each day. Prisoners considered violent or unmanageable were kept chained and never allowed out of their cells. No real recreation. The area set aside for the inmates' exercise was simply the hallway outside of their cells. Such conditions were common. With conditions such as these, and little opportunity for prisoners to have contact with other humans, it was no wonder that many inmates in such jails eventually went insane.

During his hour of exercise on this day, Stigler was parading up and down the hall, dragging the chain attached to manacles around his ankles. A guard, bearing a club, watched from a distance. With his back to the guard, Stigler did not see another man's stealthy approach. The awful pain of the knife entering the small of his back caused Stigler to scream before he fell.

The scream brought Sheriff Jasper Eby running from his office at the far end of the basement. He saw Stigler sprawled on the floor, face down, a pool of blood spreading from his body, and a long-bladed knife protruding from his back. There was no one else to be seen.

"Where is the guard? *Guard! Guard!*" Eby shouted. He knelt by Stigler and saw that the wound was deep and probably fatal. There was little he could do; removing the knife might widen the wound and make the bleeding worse. Let a physician do that.

"Carringer! Grady!" the sheriff called at the top of his voice to his constables, who might be anywhere in the building. In a minute Timothy Grady can running down the stairs, shouting "Yes? What is it, Sheriff?"

"Prisoner stabbed, Grady! Run and get Dr. Abernathy. His office is up the street!"

Michael Carringer also came running down the stairs. He dashed over to see if he could assist the sheriff.

"It looks bad for him, Mike," Eby declared. "Let's see if he can tell us anything, before he's gone."

Gently he turned Stigler on his side, being careful not to allow the knife to be pushed in farther.

"Stigler...can you hear me? It's the sheriff. Who did this to you?"

A gurgle of blood oozed from his mouth, then a grunt.

"Stigler, listen to me. You don't have much time left. Before you die, tell us who hired you to kill William Seward. Quick, man!"

Stigler's eyes blinked open and fixed Eby with a sightless stare. He said nothing.

"Stigler, listen. Don't die without telling who paid you to kill Seward. Tell me."

Stigler's vision cleared somewhat. He stared at the two lawmen for a minute. "I don't wanna die," he gasped.

"Well, I think you're going to. Sorry. But tell us who wanted Seward dead!"

A moment's concentration. "Yeah. It was a Dissenter minister."

"His name? Quick, Stigler. What is his name?"

"John...Thomson." Stigler moaned.

"Did you get that, Mike? John Thomson."

"Right. I think I hear Grady coming back with the doctor."

Down the basement stairs Dr. Abernathy came as fast as he could, followed by Timothy Grady. The physician knelt by Stigler, felt his pulse, examined the wound, and said quietly, "Mr. Stigler, I'm Doctor Abernathy. I'll see if I can help you. May I turn you over on your stomach, and remove the knife from your back?"

Stigler only groaned again, then nodded weakly. Abernathy did as he had asked, gently ripped open the man's shirt, gripped the long knife, and needed much strength to pull it out of the great slash.

He examined the torn and ragged laceration, blood bubbling from it. Stigler's face was blanched and mottled as his lifeblood drained away, eyes panicky, mouth moving but saying nothing coherent.

While the physician tried to stanch the flow of blood, the three lawmen had their eyes locked on the dying man's lips, trying to read that last message. Dr. Abernathy knew it was hopeless; the knife had penetrated too many vital organs. He looked at Sheriff Eby, shook his head slightly, and rolled the prisoner back over, that he might die lying on his back. With one last long groan, Stigler expired.

Abernathy and Eby stood up. All of them had seen death too many times.

Eby swung into action. "All right, it must have been that new guard I hired last week. I thought he was all right. I was wrong about him. He was just waiting for an opportunity to get to Stigler. His name is Ducker. Locate him if you can, and arrest him!" The two constables ran to do his bidding.

Sheriff Eby turned to Dr. Abernathy. "I hate to see one of my inmates die in jail, but at least Stigler revealed who the man was that paid to get rid of William Seward. I'll see Mr. Hepplewhite and ask him to come and remove the body. Then why don't we go and pay a quick visit to Ben Franklin? I know Ben will be most interested in all of this!"

The doctor agreed.

Franklin was surprised at what Sheriff Eby and Dr. Abernathy told him. They were seated in his office, mulling over what to do next.

"I don't know if I should arrest this John Thomson immediately," Eby said. "All I have is the confession of a dying man. It might be hard to convict Thomson on the strength of that."

"I agree with you," Ben said, "but more than that, I'm convinced that there are others beside Thomson in on this. Why don't we set a trap? We'll use the newspaper to do it. If we do this correctly, perhaps this will prod the conspirators into some foolish action, and they'll reveal themselves."

Dr. Abernathy smiled. "Ben, you know, you always have something up your sleeve!"

John Thomson, Dissenting preacher who had trouble in each church he came to, picked up the issue of *The Pennsylvania Gazette* that had just been published. He was so started that he almost dropped the newspaper. Across the top of the front page, under the paper's name, was the headline:

SEWARD'S DYING KILLER GIVES STARTLING TESTIMONY!

He had to sit down before reading any farther, trying to compose himself. He was shaking. Then he read on:

> Finally the entire truth is coming to light. Readers of this journal will know that Gershom Stigler was one of the murderers of the fine and gracious gentleman William Seward. Stigler, along with his wife and Ahab Cragg, were sentenced to prison for extended sentences recently in Superior Court, and another man, Reuben Sobleski, was hung for the crime.
>
> The latest episode in this bizarre affair is the killing of Gershom Stigler in the Court House prison yesterday. He was stabbed to death by a guard. Before he died, Stigler confessed that there were several conspirators who paid him to kill Mr. Seward. Sheriff Eby of Philadelphia refuses to give any details of Stigler's confession, or whether it could be used to locate or prosecute these people.
>
> It is all to the good that the public is aware of the motives and operations of those that are opposing the Reverend George Whitefield and the religious movement that is all around us. Mr. Seward was a leading supporter, financially and otherwise, of this movement. It now remains to be seen who might be involved in this sordid mess. This journal will keep the public informed.

Keeping this on the front pages, from issue to issue, is that printer Franklin's doing, Thomson thought. *He's the one who discovered that Seward had been smothered with a cloth. He's the same one who found that fellow who overheard Stigler talking! He's been behind the investigation all along. And he's kept this up with headline articles in his miserable paper for weeks now. He won't let it die!*

Thomson sat, trying to determine what to do next. Did Stigler name him? Should he flee, perhaps to New England, or the South, or even to Britain? Would the authorities come to arrest him? Would he spend many years in prison, with the dangerous conditions that brought about Stigler's death? He shuddered, as his mind conjured up numerous fantasies, all bad for him.

His thinking was interrupted by an insistent banging on his front door. Going to the window and pulling the curtain aside, he saw that it was his friend Hosea Dickson. He opened the door for him.

"Have you seen the *Gazette?*" Dickson asked frantically.

"Yes, yes, I've seen it. There's nothing I can do about it."

"But maybe Stigler named us before he died." Dickson fixed Thomson with a cold stare. "Tell me, John, did you pay someone to put Stigler out of the way, hoping he wouldn't talk before he died? Did you arrange for another murder?"

"Oh, don't be absurd, Hosea. Of course not! Now you're getting ridiculously worried."

"Well, aren't you worried? Our entire group could have been named by Stigler before he died."

"Hmm. That's true, come to think of it. Stigler did know I worked together with a group of friends, and he may have known who you were. I think we need another meeting of all of us, to decide what to do next. I know one thing: this printer Franklin has got to go!"

※

Since his arrival in Philadelphia from the South on April 15, Whitefield found that he was as popular as before, if not even more so. He decided, after conferring with the Tennents and other Log College pastors, to align himself more openly with them. Things were changing rapidly after Gilbert Tennent had preached his blistering sermon on March 8, "The Danger of an Unconverted Ministry."

After that, Whitefield determined to cover much of the territory he had previously visited, going north to New York City. Whitefield's journey through a number of New Jersey towns, continuing up to New York City, went very well, from April 25th through May 7th. The constant problem of huge crowds made him take them into the fields often: 5,000, 7,000 and 8,000 in New York, 7,000 in New Brunswick, and attendances of two and three thousand in Woodbridge, Elizabethtown, Amboy, Freehold, and Newark. At most of these places the awakening was in full flower or had recently begun.

When Whitefield arrived back in Philadelphia with Josh Morris and his other friends, he called first at Ben Franklin's shop. This was to accomplish a number of things: not only to renew friendships, but also to drop off new manuscripts of sermons that were to be printed and sold, and to accept again Franklin's kind offer of hospitality whenever the itinerant was in town.

As they came through the front door of the shop, Josh was delighted to see Tom Prescott setting type.

"Hello, Josh and Mr. Whitefield. It's great to see you again." Tom put down his work, and walked toward them to shake their hands.

George Whitefield said, "I'm pleased to see you here, Tom. I've heard all about your work, and your beautiful young lady." Tom colored at that and smiled sheepishly.

Josh picked up a dipper and drank deeply from a bucket of water that was placed on a stool. "It's been a long and dusty ride," he said with a huge smile, wiping his hand across his wet lips.

In the background the sounds of the shop continued: the press clanking and crunching away as two of the apprentices worked, one pulling at the big lever that lowered the heavy iron platen onto the paper, and another one inking the type with a leather device. But the work gradually slowed down, because at the same time the apprentices were trying to catch as much as they could of the conversation between the famous visitor and Tom. Careless of the danger to their fingers should they get caught in the mechanisms of the press, the young men were peering at Whitefield, twenty feet from them. The apprentices kept winking at each other and exchanging whispered comments, and trying to get all the information they could for later gossiping.

Ben Franklin heard the voices and came through from the back office. He greeted Whitefield and Josh, and said, "George, I hope you are planning to stay with us while you're in the city. Your room is always kept ready for you, you know." He looked over his "double spectacles," or bifocals, at his apprentices. "Lads, I know you are interested in Mr. Whitefield, but watch your fingers before you lose one or more in the machinery!"

The young men were horrified at being caught eavesdropping and ignoring the rules of safety. They dropped their gaze, embarrassed, and began working much more quickly—and safely.

"Ben, your hospitality and Deborah's is much appreciated," Whitefield said. "There is nowhere in this city where I would rather stay. I will get my traveling bags from my horse." He went out the door.

Franklin turned to Josh. "I am sorry, son, that we have only the one spare bedroom with its one bed. Can you find accommodation elsewhere, and accept my apologies?"

"Please don't apologize, Mr. Franklin. It's excellent that you keep the room for Mr. Whitefield. His health is anything but good, and he is so exhausted with all his labors, he desperately needs rest. You and Mrs. Franklin treat him so well."

Tom spoke up. "Josh, I have room at my boarding house! You'll stay with me. My room is small, but we'll make do. Mrs. Kirkpatrick is a kind lady, and she'll be happy to give you meals, also. Then that's settled."

Whitefield returned, with traveling bags in hand, and he was told that Josh would stay with Tom.

"How long do you think we will have the privilege of your company, George?" Franklin asked.

"I think about a week. I'm anxious to get back to Savannah, to see how the Orphans' House is going up."

"Of course you are. But you'll also want to hear what is happening with what is being called 'the new building.' Contributions are coming in very quickly. I'm not sure of the current amount; Philip Armentrout is the treasurer. And our committee is searching for an appropriate location, close to the heart of the city, and convenient to everyone."

"Ben, all of that sounds superb! Are the committees working well?"

"Very well. To this point, I am pleased with the entire endeavor."

"I am as well. I wish I had such diligent and clever people for my orphan home in Savannah."

༄༅

The word had spread quickly around Philadelphia that George Whitefield had returned, and as always, the crowds came to hear him. He spoke from the steps of the Court House in the morning to six thousand people, and at five in the evening to seven thousand. The remainder of the day was taken up with counseling those who wished to speak with him, and Josh and half a dozen pastors of local congregations came to help with this. It had been a long and tiring day.

That evening, after Tom had completed work at Ben Franklin's shop, he met Josh as arranged at Mrs. Kirkpatrick's boarding house on Race Street. She was an older lady, short and heavy-set, with white hair above a round, cherubic face. Tom asked her if Josh could stay in his garret room for a week or so, and take meals there, and she readily agreed, setting the cost at a very small amount.

Already she regarded Tom almost as a son, and she bestowed on Josh the same friendliness. In her common room, with two other boarders across the room, she set before them the evening meal of fried ham, boiled potatoes, cheese, buttered bannocks, coffee, and apple pie.

"This is great!" Josh said, with a third cup of coffee in his hand. "You don't know what it's like to eat when you're traveling in strange country, as we're doing constantly. Unless folks are aware you're coming and send out an invitation to come to their home for dinner, you're at the mercy of little, dirty inns where the meals are awful." The recent memory of this made him shudder. "And then, if you're forced to sleep in those smelly places for the night, you don't know if you're going to be in there with a bunch of highwaymen and thieves—and if you'll be robbed or stabbed in the middle of the night."

"Wow, is it that awful?" Tom asked, a forkful of Mrs. Kirkpatrick's pie in midair. He began to recall what he had tried hard to forget—some of the grubby, miserable places Ishmael Duffy had taken him to on their way from Philadelphia to Carlisle, almost four years previously. Then Tom remembered that Duffy may have had to sleep with highwaymen and thieves, but Duffy consigned him to sleeping in the barn!

"Yes, it is, and worse. I can't describe in words some of the places where Mr. Whitefield and all of us in his group have had to spend the night."

Tom took another forkful of apple pie. "If there's no home or inn available, do you have to sleep out under the stars often?"

"Yes, and sometimes that's better than the inns. That is, if the bears and wolves don't come snooping around, to see what food they can steal. Many a time I've been awakened at 3:00 a.m., with our horses nearby in a panic, whinnying and stamping the ground and trying to break loose. And then in the dark, you see those gleaming eyes of a wolf!"

Now it was Tom's turn to shudder. "I remember some of the things that happened when Duffy sent us for the horses. What did you do—the same as we did then?"

"Oh yes. You remember that well, eh? You keep your rifle or pistol nearby, in case they attack you or the horses. But usually when they see you're awake, if you make a lot of noise to scare them, and keep the campfire blazing, they slink off into the woods, knowing they're not going to get any food. But then, with the horses in commotion, it's hard to get back to sleep. And you keep thinking, the wolf or the bear may return and try again."

Mrs. Kirkpatrick came from her kitchen and attended to the other boarders. Then she came to Tom and Josh. "I understand you've been doing a lot of traveling in backwoods areas," she said to Josh.

"Mr. Whitefield and our group were down South, in the Carolinas and Georgia, where it's milder in December through March. And in the cities, it's very pleasant."

"Still, I'm sure you've had some bad experiences," Mrs. Kirkpatrick said as she cleared away the plates. "You probably didn't eat very well. I can tell that because you're rather skinny. Hmph. I see you both like my apple pie. You've eaten the whole pie!" She put her hands on her hips in mock indignation. "Well, don't worry, young man. While you're here in *my* home, I'll feed you, and get you up to your proper weight!"

Tom and Josh laughed at that, and Tom leaned over the table and gave Josh a sharp poke in the belly. "Just seeing if you're really so skinny, fellow! Oh, I don't think so, Mrs. Kirkpatrick!"

"That hurt!" cried Josh. "I can't take care of you the way I would if we weren't in a respectable establishment, run by a very dignified lady." He smashed one fist into the other, demonstrating.

"Now, no roughhousing in here! None of that here, I'll have you know. Oh, boys will be boys! The two of you are a pair." She uttered a few Irish phrases describing unruly people and walked away shaking her head.

"Dear Mrs. Kirkpatrick; she really loves me, you know," Tom said, with a smile that went almost ear to ear. "Look, why don't we go to my garret room and determine how both of us are going to sleep there?"

"Right," said Josh, getting his bag of belongings.

They climbed the stairs, unlocked Tom's door, and went inside.

"I told you it was small," Tom apologized. "But it's comfortable."

"After what I've just told you, this is wonderful. Quiet, and safe." He put his bag on the floor.

"Now, you take the bed, and I'll sleep on the floor. I'll get a couple of quilts from Mrs. Kirkpatrick, spread them out, and I'll be fine."

"I don't want to take your bed!" Josh protested. "I'm used to sleeping on floors—and without quilts under me."

"Josh, you are my guest. *You* are taking the bed, and *I* will sleep on the floor. That's decided. Just don't step on me if you get up in the middle of the night. I may be dreaming of wolves." They laughed at that.

"All right, I'll be careful." Josh sat on the bed, and Tom on the chair by the window that looked out onto Race Street. He could see some stars that had appeared. It was a beautiful night, calm and fairly warm. After a minute, Tom said, "Josh, let's talk about spiritual things."

They talked for hours, to their great joy.

※

George Whitefield closed his triumphant campaign in the Middle Colonies on May 16, 1740, heading for Georgia, in the company of Josh and his other friends. In Philadelphia the architect was busily working on plans for the "new building." This definitely connected the entire New Light program with the whole Whitefield campaign for an intercolonial awakening. The evangelist was planning, when he left for the South, to respond to the many pleas for a tour of New England in the early autumn of 1740. When that ambitious plan was completed, Whitefield would have covered the entire Eastern seaboard from Maine to Georgia with his evangelistic outreach.

The spring campaign of 1740 by Whitefield and the Tennents had been intense. The opposition had also grown in determination and virulence. The tide, however, had been turned. The laypeople of the Middle Colonies were increasingly supporting the New Light cause, bolstered by Whitefield's vibrant preaching in many different communities, with astonishing attendances. In addition, the New England group of pastors had become their close friends and coworkers in the revival.

When the Synod gathered for its annual meeting on May 28, its sessions were as stormy as those of the previous year. With both sides refusing to concede anything, the situation was becoming desperate. The Old Lights were reeling from the effects of Whitefield's tours and the expanding revival all around them. Gilbert Tennent's recent sermon had heightened the climate of the Synod meetings to one of mutual fury. Seven of the New England group were present, and the Old Lights, who held only a slim majority in the Synod, tried several maneuvers to exclude the Log College preachers. Heady with the successes of the previous year, Tennent and the New Lights were in no mood for connivance or compromise. Within a year the entire Presbyterian Church had split into two parts.

THIRTEEN

The Triumph of Righteousness

Heat. Boiling humidity, and high temperatures day after day. That is Georgia in the summer. When Whitefield arrived in Savannah in July, he found what he called "extreme heat." He was used to the milder weather of England, an island surrounded by water, and had never before experienced a Southern summer. When it was not fiercely hot, it was rainy, with thunder and lightning.

Arriving in Savannah, Whitefield went immediately to the orphan house. He found everything to his satisfaction, and he wrote:

> Our affairs are now carried on with decency and order, and I believe, Savannah will yet become the joy of the earth....The children are industrious. We have now in the house near one hundred yards of cloth spun and woven. We have several tradesmen and teachers belonging to the House, much cattle on our plantation, and, I hope, before long we shall live amongst ourselves.

In addition to overseeing the work on the orphan house, Whitefield paid bills, counseled with a number of inquirers, preached in churches and in fields, and spoke with pastors and citizens. Then he set off for Charleston. On Sunday, July 6th he attended services at St. Philip's Anglican church, hearing Commissary Garden "preach as virulent, unorthodox, and inconsistent a discourse as ever I heard in my life. His heart seemed full of choler and resentment."

With Whitefield getting large numbers as he preached in the fields of South Carolina and Georgia, Garden's fury and jealousy were still not spent. His fulminations from his pulpit were doing little, other than making him look like a fool. And still Whitefield was drawing vast crowds—far more than he was! What could he do, in his desperation, to shut up the itinerant, to expel him from the Church of England clergy, to get rid of this infernal nuisance, to stop the Awakening that was beginning in the colony, and to get his own parishioners back under his control?

So he tried one last tactic, trying to silence Whitefield once and for all. As commissary of the Bishop of London, Garden assumed he had the full power and authority in the bishop's place and could do anything the bishop could.

Although no ecclesiastical court had ever been convened outside of England, and without the presence of a bishop, Garden took it upon himself to hold such a court, with no right to do so. He issued an order for Whitefield to appear before it on a set date. Whereas such courts would have at least one bishop to preside, and often several, with numerous Church of England clergymen in attendance, Garden presided alone, with no bishop. He called several Anglican ministers to sit alongside him to make this travesty look authentic. Wisely, Whitefield wanted to give the appearance of cooperation, so he came, not to leave himself open to the charge of insubordination.

At the court's beginning, the day dawned still and clear, with the temperature in the 70s. While it was fairly cool for the moment, there was already much mugginess in the air, and everyone knew that by noon it would be intense. Windows might be opened, but they would only let in more hot air.

Garden had prepared St. Philip's Church well, with all the trappings of a major and exceedingly important event. Whitefield and some of his friends waited patiently, uncertain of what might happen. Then Garden came into the church, his heavy powdered white wig on his head, clothed in all the ecclesiastical splendor he could muster. The problem was, with wig and heavy robes on, in the heat of the day he would soon be bathed in perspiration, which would increase his irritation. Massive books in hand, he climbed three steps in the chancel to a small platform. On this was placed a large chair with a high back, which had the distinct resemblance to a throne. From there he could gaze down on what he hoped would be an intimidated—perhaps frightened—Whitefield, ready for judgment.

Garden began the proceedings with much pomp and ceremony. At first, he tried to have the defendant stand before him. But Whitefield knew the proceedings would doubtless be drawn out, and the day would get hot, so he requested a chair. Reluctantly, Garden had to agree to this. His clergy minions on either side stared at the defendant as if he were already condemned.

The charges against Whitefield? With great gravity, Garden intoned: Fanaticism. Enthusiasm. Failure to provide properly for the orphans under his care. Forcing the orphans to work in cruel conditions. Dealing fraudulently with money given for the orphan house. Defiance of the Bishop of London's letter. Defiance and disobedience of Church Canons. Refusal to work within his assigned parish. Preaching in non-Anglican churches. Working with Dissenter clergy and laity. Membership among the despised "Methodists." Using new methods not sanctioned by the Church of England. Defying all authority. Causing riots. Writing and speaking against slaveholders who are Anglicans. And many more charges.

As each of these was read by Garden, he asked, "How do you plead to this charge against you?"

In each case, Whitefield responded, "Not guilty."

With each citation, the two scribes at the side of the room scribbled in large notebooks to get down all that was said. Garden read rather rapidly, hardly giving Whitefield time to answer the charges, as if his answers were deceitful, wrong, or inconsequential. Since the quill pens of the scribes held only limited amounts of ink, they had to keep dipping the pens into their inkwells. Soon the pages of their books were filled with ink blots and splashes. Eventually the writing would be completely illegible.

Halfway through the list of charges, Whitefield became astonished and looked over at his friends seated against the wall. They shrugged to indicate their anger and disbelief. Another few charges, and Whitefield became a bit bored with it all. A hint of mockery crept into his expression. Garden saw this and became even more exasperated. His heavy wig was slipping, and frequently it sat crookedly astride one ear. Furthermore, the room was getting hot, he was sweating profusely, and he knew his face was becoming the color of a tomato. The heavy robes he had tried to impress with were hanging on him.

He kept directing questions at Whitefield, and to each the defendant answered factually, citing specific instances and facts that discredited whatever Garden alleged. Whitefield asserted what everyone knew to be true: that the Church of England clergy had done many of the same things that he was being accused of, and he gave examples of that, to the clergy's great discomfort.

By 10:00 a.m., the Anglican clergy alongside Garden were looking at the commissary, wondering if anything of consequence *could* be proven. By noon, the room was a hothouse. Garden, sweat dripping from his eyebrows, nose, and chin, decided to end the session. All of his resplendent robes, once so impressive, were sodden, drooping, and sweat-stained. The wig was a wet sponge.

He declared the court would reconvene the next morning at 8:00 a.m., hoping for a cooler day.

It wasn't. But the court proceedings were much the same. The secretaries had resigned and left.

Whitefield's friends were openly amused at much of it, and Garden was about to eject them from the room. The defendant remained cool and collected, against Garden's anger. By 11:00 a.m., Garden adjourned the court for the day, declaring it would reconvene the third day at 7:00 a.m.

It was still stifling on the third day. Garden appeared in his shirtsleeves, what everyone else had worn all along. By 8:00 a.m., Whitefield had had enough of the charade. The Anglican clergy knew the only things they could prove against him were speaking against Archbishop Tillotson and working outside his assigned parish. All the other charges were either frivolous or wrong. And of the two provable items, not one of them was serious enough to unfrock him. Certainly the *last* thing Whitefield could be accused of was heresy, although that could not be said of some Anglican clergy.

Standing to his feet, and using the powerful voice he had not used before in this trial, Whitefield exclaimed to Garden, "You do not have the authority to try me! This court and this entire silly scene are a mockery of everything—of Christ's faith, of truth, of decency, and of righteousness!!"

Eyes wide in astonishment, the Anglican clergy reared back. They stared at him in bewilderment.

Through clenched teeth, Whitefield said, in a voice that dripped with contempt and fury, "You are nothing but a petty tyrant, Garden. I do not fear you, or your ridiculous so-called 'court'! But I will pray for you, that someday, perhaps, the Almighty's Holy Spirit may convert you. I want you to know that I *will* appeal this to the High Court of Chancery in London!"

Garden was stunned by that. "Appeal this—?!" he said weakly.

"Oh yes," thundered Whitefield. "You'll not get away with this charade. You think that *you* are somehow empowered to judge things. But when I think of you standing before the bar of God's infinite and perfect justice, I shudder for your benefit, sir! You and your kind are ripping God's Church apart—in the midst of an Awakening sent by the Holy Spirit. And what happens next in this great Awakening, only God knows!"

With that, Whitefield turned on his heel and stormed out of the room, followed by his friends.

❧☙

With Rachel only recently breaking off her engagement to David Talcott, Tom did not think it wise to urge her into another engagement too soon. So he bided his time. It would be intelligent to let Rachel be absolutely sure—if and when—about her next engagement.

So Tom called at the Nicholson home once or twice a week, where he knew he was welcome, but he did not want to overdo it. It was obvious Mr. and Mrs. Nicholson liked him very much, for they treated him almost as a son. And their own son, Bobby, looked up to Tom as an older brother, and had begun to play the same sports and games that were Tom's favorites.

Then there was Rachel. Several times she mentioned to Tom why she was glad to be in his company. She was very pleased that, unlike Talcott, Tom was a Christian, growing in the Lord, and one who loved to study the Scriptures and be in the fellowship of other Christians. Rachel was also happy that Tom was doing well in Ben Franklin's printing firm, understood the business well, and apparently had a trade for life. In addition Rachel said that she liked his sense of humor and approved of his friends.

It hardly needed to be said that there was nothing about Rachel that Tom did not approve of, or love. When he was not with her, he counted the hours until he *would* be in her company again.

❧☙

Summer had arrived rather quickly in Philadelphia. There was not much heat as yet, but the buds on the trees had been forced into full leaves weeks ago, the many lilac bushes had borne sweet scents that floated on the air; and roses were blooming in every yard. Outside of the city, in the farms, the cornstalks were growing high and green in the fields, shedding golden pollen on the wind. This summer would live forever in Rachel's memory, a summer heavy with fruit and flowers, a summer for love.

On one Saturday, Tom had invited Rachel to go on a picnic, and she accepted with excitement. She and her mother prepared a lunch basket, and Tom came along two hours before noon. They took the Arch Street ferry over the Delaware River to New Jersey, where there were farms and fields in all directions. Insects hummed in the still air. It was a day of perfect beauty.

When the ferry reached the Jersey side of the river, they left it and began to walk along a well-used roadway, until there was a fork in the path that branched off in several directions. They chose one that seemed to go to a pleasant area, parallel to the river. There were some marshy water-meadows along its banks, and a band of tilled fields with a wooded ridge farther off, of dark green, that hid the scattered farmhouses at a distance. In the fields crops were growing, and here and there orchards flowered. Carrying their lunch basket, they came to a lush meadow that looked down on the water. Brush that was above the knees concealed animal life, and a few raccoons and beavers scampered as they came near. A wood-duck burst forth from a thicket, startling them with the loud drumming of its wings as it took flight. They laughed. Several large pin oaks and a growth of sweet gum cast shade over a patch of grass, and they decided this was the perfect spot for their picnic.

They opened the picnic basket and ate, sharing bread and cold meat and drinking wine. Afterward Rachel lay on her back, while Tom lay on his stomach a few feet away. They spoke of many things, and finally Tom decided this was a fine time to ask her to be engaged, and to marry him.

Rachel said yes.

ಸಿಂಚಿ

Undeterred by Commissary Garden's attacks, George Whitefield stated that he would be speaking in Charleston at the Independent Congregational Church, at the invitation of its pastor, Josiah Smith.

Announcements were made throughout the city, on posted notices and in the local newspaper. When the time arrived, the people gathering were far more than the church could hold, as was expected. So the large field beside the church was prepared, a wagon was borrowed for Whitefield to stand on, and the crowd was told to convene there.

The notices had been put up on trees, in shops, and wherever people might see them. And among those who saw the notices were members of the crew of the *Revenge.* Powner's ship had made a stop at Jamaica and returned to Charleston, sold a few slaves there, and prepared to return to Africa to get more slaves.

"Look at this, men!" Henry Jones called out to the other sailors emerging from the Pig and Whistle tavern. "It's that fellow Whitefield who was annoying Captain Powner during the auction."

"What about him?" Edward Kelsey asked.

"He's going to speak at a meeting this afternoon at four," Jones said. "Whitefield is a preacher, and the meeting is about religion."

At that moment Herman Jacobson, the first mate, came out of the tavern, and Jones called him over to show him the poster. "Well, I'll be," Jacobson cried. "I've heard of this fellow. Hey, Kelsey, fetch Cap'n Powner—he's about to come out of the tavern."

Powner appeared, and Jacobson said, "Look at this notice, Cap'n. It's that man who was telling you off at the auction. Why don't some of us go to this meeting? We're not doing anything important this afternoon—just waiting for a good dark night to sail out and run before Spanish warships can catch us."

Powner exploded with curses that lasted a full minute. "Listen, Herman, you oughta know that I wouldn't go to listen to that miserable polecat if it was the last thing I ever did!" He stalked off, spewing more expletives.

Feeling somewhat rebuked, Jacobson turned to Kelsey, Jones, and the other sailors. "Hmph. Maybe he's right. I don't want to hear a lot of stupid religious stuff."

Jones frowned. "But there's nothing much to do in this town."

"Yeah. I'm bored. Unless the captain forbids us, I'm goin'!" said Ralph Jeffries.

Jacobson was grudging but understanding. "Oh, he didn't forbid us. He just said *he* wasn't going. You can go if you'd like."

Jones and Kelsey began speaking to the rest of the crew, and nearly every one said they were bored and needed something entertaining to do. There was a chorus of "Yeah, let's go." Some were shouting, "C'mon, Jacobson, you go too."

"All right...all right, I'll go. But listen—if you go, take some rotten eggs and tomatoes in your pockets to throw."

This was met with laughter and agreement.

"This meeting begins at four. Let's meet here at half past three, and go over together."

That afternoon, eighteen sailors showed up in the field beside the church, bent on mischief and ridicule. They scattered throughout the crowd that was gathering, laughing and not altogether sober. Jeffries, McGonigal, Kelsey, and Jones had found eggs and tomatoes to throw at Whitefield, and were holding them in their pockets or in bags. For the next quarter-hour they watched as the people flowed around them, a vast gathering of humanity.

"Hmph," Jacobson said with some astonishment. "I had no idea this fellow could draw so many! Oh look; I think that's him coming now, up to that platform. He has the black robe on."

Whitefield and three other pastors ascended the wagon that had been brought in. After one of them spoke briefly, a hymn was sung by the assemblage, and Whitefield stepped forward. He knelt and began to pray in an authoritative voice that carried to the farthest corner of the field. He begged the Almighty to look down from Heaven and bless this gathering, and what he was about to say. Then he arose and looked over the crowd, thanked them for coming, and began his message.

Jeffries laughed and poked Jacobson in the ribs, asking, "When do we start hooting?"

"Uh, let's wait a few minutes. I want to hear some of what this fellow has to say."

"Oh, come on, Herman, we came to have some fun!"

"Shut up, will you?" Jacobson hissed at Jeffries, who looked very disappointed at being squelched.

Whitefield was speaking on "The Kingdom of God," based on Romans 14:17, "For the kingdom of God is not meat and drink, but righteousness, and peace, and joy in the Holy Spirit." He explained that by "meat and drink," the passage meant external, superficial things. Then he went on to declare that externals were such as church membership, or baptism, or orthodox doctrine, or piety, or morality. He said, "The kingdom of God, or true and undefiled religion, does not consist in being of this or that particular sect or communion. Were many of you asked what hope there is in you, perhaps you could say no more than that you belong to such a church. But if you place your hope for the kingdom of God merely in a sect, you place it in what it does not consist. So, neither does the kingdom consist in being baptized when you were young. Do not make a Christ out of your baptism, for there have been many baptized with water, who have never been savingly baptized with the Holy Spirit.

"Nor does true religion consist in being orthodox in our doctrine, or being able to talk fluently of the Gospel. Remember the verse in James 2:19: 'The devils believe, and tremble.'"

Jacobson, who had been listening carefully, whispered to Jeffries, standing next to him, "Does the Bible really say *that?*—that the *devils* believe?"

"Yeah," Jeffries responded, "I remember that from my days as a boy when I went to church. It does say that."

"*You* went to church?!" Jacobson said in a normal voice. Several people nearby looked at him disapprovingly, as if to say "be quiet."

"Yeah, my parents made me go with them. That was before I ran away from home."

Whitefield was continuing. "You may have an orthodox head, but you may have the devil in your heart. You may be able to speak the doctrines of the Gospel, and yet you have never felt them upon your own soul. And if you have never felt the power of them upon your heart, your talk of Christ and free justification, will but increase your condemnation, and you will only go to hell with so much more solemnity.

"Also, the kingdom of God does not consist in a dry, lifeless morality. If you think you are a Christian because you are not vicious, because now and then you do some good action, you are terribly mistaken. If you depend on morality, or any of these things, if you make a Christ of it, and try to make a righteousness of your own, and think your good behavior will commend you to God, you are building upon a rotten foundation, you will find yourself simply adding to your own damnation.

"I speak from my own experience. I know how much I was deceived with a form of godliness. I fasted twice a week, I prayed nine times a day, and received Communion every Sunday. And yet I knew nothing of inward salvation in my own heart, till God was pleased to dart a ray of light into my soul, and show me I must be a new creation, or be damned forevermore."

By this point, an intensity had built up in the audience. Whitefield was striking fear in many hearts.

The people had been silent since he had begun, but from various parts of the throng muffled noises were heard, as some people were weeping quietly.

Whitefield continued: "If a person may go thus far and still not be a true Christian, you may cry out, 'Who then can be saved?' Oh that I could hear you asking this question in earnest!

"I have told you what the kingdom of God is *not*. I shall now proceed to show you what it *is*. It is 'righteousness, and peace, and joy in the Holy Spirit.' First, the kingdom of God is Righteousness. This is the complete, perfect, and all-sufficient righteousness of our Lord Jesus Christ. My friends, we have no righteousness of our own. Our best goodness, altogether, is but so many filthy rags. The righteousness of Christ must be imputed and made over to us, and applied to our hearts, and until we get this righteousness, we are in a state of death and damnation—the wrath of God abides on us."

A tall, muscular man in front of Jacobson suddenly cried out, "Lord, help me!" Behind him, a young woman had tears running down her face, and she was sobbing, "Jesus, save my soul!"

Henry Jones snarled, "Oh, these idiots. I got a whole lot of old eggs in my pockets, Herman, and they're good and rotten. Can I throw them at the preacher now? He's close enough; I can hit him!"

"No, hold off, Henry. There's plenty of time for that. Now keep quiet, all of you."

Whitefield was continuing, "I exhort you to let your conscience speak out; do not bribe it any longer. Did you ever see yourself as a condemned sinner? And after you saw your total need of Christ, did you lay hold of Christ by faith? If not, unfortunately you are in a damnable state, and I implore you to accept Him before it is too late...."

Just then a big, burly man next to Henry Jones began to sway and threatened to topple over. Without warning he crashed heavily into Jones, smashing all the eggs in his pockets. Yellow, runny yolk streamed from his coat, emitting a terrible stink. The ooze permeated Jones' pants and coat, and the smell of the rotten eggs was hideous. His fellow sailors and others nearby all moved away, regarding him as a pariah. Soon he stood alone. The nearest people were fifteen feet away, and they glared severely at Jones.

Seeing what happened to Henry Jones, the other sailors who had brought rotten eggs—Kelsey, Jeffries, and McGonigal—carefully placed them on the ground, shells unbroken, before they endured something similar.

Whitefield continued speaking for another ten minutes, explaining that God's kingdom was not only righteousness, but also peace, "not false peace, or carnal security, into which so many have fallen. It is a peace of God's making, resulting from a sense of having Christ's righteousness brought home to the soul. And there is also joy, the joy of the Holy Spirit." He tore down people's excuses, speaking with authority and conviction, and told them they must be born again, from above.

The power of God was sweeping over this vast throng. Many were weeping quietly, and a number were praying. Jacobson, trying to maintain his criticism, looked for any who were going into convulsions or fanaticisms of any kind. He saw none, to his great disappointment. Instead, he began to sense that something was stirring within him.

"Let's get out of here!" Sam McGonigal growled. "I can't take no more."

"Go ahead—and take Jones and all of his stink with you," Jacobson retorted. "I'm staying." So much of what the preacher said was having a direct impact on his heart and mind. A powerful vision of the evil of his existence suddenly dawned on him. He was vile!

He looked at the rest of the *Revenge's* crew: Kelsey, Jeffries, Thomas, Houlihan, Tindle, Bertcil, and the others. All of them seemed rooted to the ground. They were being moved by Whitefield and had to remain to hear more.

The evangelist was concluding. "There are a great many who think the Christian faith is a poor melancholy thing, and they are afraid to be Christians. But, my dear friends, there is no true joy without Christ. Wicked people and people of pleasure will get a little laughter; but what is that? It is like the crackling of a few thorns burning under a pot. It makes a blaze and soon goes out."

Jacobson saw the hand of Whitefield moving around the throng, and then he imagined it coming straight at him. He was greatly convicted of his sins, of his awful cruelty to thousands of slaves, of the waste of his life. He felt his heart pounding. Against his conscious will Jacobson cried out, "O God, how I have sinned!" and he fell to the ground with groans and tears.

Peter Houlihan stood over him, his hands out in supplication, feeling the finger of God on him also. Homer Thomas could not move; he felt convicted and in the grip of some strange, supernatural power.

Around the entire assemblage of thousands, people were kneeling and praying. Finally Jacobson said in a soft voice, "Jesus, I want you as my Savior. I repent of all the years of evil I have done. Please accept me as Your own."

McGonigal and Jones had gone. But the remainder of the crew echoed Jacobson's sentiment. They now felt guilty that the wealth they had gotten was blood money, gotten at the price of their great human cruelty. It was a wonder that God had not struck them dead. They wanted Jesus as their Savior, and they wanted to be out of making innocent people into slaves. Anything that was totally incompatible with their new faith must go.

꽁꿍

George Whitefield invited those who wished to become Christians to meet with him when the crowd had dispersed. Two to three hundred men and women came up, and he led them in prayer and gave them instructions and suggestions for living the Christian life.

Tears running down his face, Jacobson went forward, along with sixteen of the crew.

Later, coming back to the *Revenge,* they sought out Powner.

He saw this large group of his crew coming toward him. He laughed cunningly. "Well, did you throw your rotten eggs? Did you hear what that money-grubbing blackguard had to say?"

Jacobson, acting as spokesman for most of the crew, confronted Powner resolutely. "Cap'n, I'm quitting this ship, and I'm giving up selling slaves. You'll have to find another first mate."

"WHAT?!" Powner thundered. "Why? I need you!"

A number of voices said, "We're quitting too," and there was a loud chorus of agreement from the rest.

"You're most of my crew! I'll have to get a new crew!" Powner howled in disbelief.

"We accepted Christ as Savior," Jacobson said quietly. He knew the ridicule and hatred they were about to receive. He led the men as they went belowdeck, collected their gear, and left the ship.

Powner was so thunderstruck that he was almost speechless. As Jacobson passed him going to the gangway, Powner plucked at his sleeve, trying to ask if this was only a big joke. Jacobson pulled away, leading his friends off the ship for the last time.

Then Powner began screaming his usual curses and blasphemies.

ഓര

Commissary William Vessey of New York knocked quietly on the front door of Richard Burbridge's home on Vine Street, Philadelphia, after looking furtively up and down the street. After a minute the door was opened slightly, his identity established, and he was admitted. Inside, Vessey found Burbridge, Hosea Dickson, Samuel Black, Hamilton Bell, James Lyon, Samuel Caven, Adam Boyd, and Henry Hook, the leaders of the Old Lights in the Dissenter church.

Vessey greeted each of them in a dismal fashion, and said, "Oh, I hated to come down here again. But I suppose it's necessary for us to meet, given the situation. Where is John Thomson?"

"He's in hiding. He's concerned that he may be arrested. You read in the papers that Stigler named several conspirators in Seward's murder before he died, and Thomson is afraid he may have been named," said Dickson.

"But where is he? You can tell me!" Vessey insisted.

Hesitation. "In the cellar. He will come up in a minute. That's why we are meeting here in Richard's home. It's at the edge of the city. We don't think the sheriff and his men will come here, looking for us."

"Yes. I'm glad you all came for a meeting. We need to put our heads together, and do some thinking," said Vessey.

A trapdoor to the cellar opened, Thomson's head appeared, and he said "I heard that. For me, the thinking is done." He climbed out of the trapdoor, and brushed the dust and cobwebs off his clothes. "That fellow Franklin has got to be taken care of. He has been behind this since the beginning, him and his newspaper articles."

"What do you mean, 'taken care of'?" Vessey asked.

"I mean, before Franklin publishes the names of everyone here, including yours, for the entire world to read!"

Vessey was shocked. "Do you think he could?"

"Before he died, Stigler talked about conspirators, didn't he?! How do you know he didn't name all of us? Stigler knew me, and he knew who some of my friends are!"

Vessey had not considered this possibility. "Oh no, I could never have that. In New York, I have an extremely important position. If *I* was revealed as involved in a murder plot, there would be an explosion. The church would suffer greatly; *I* would suffer greatly! And don't forget. I was never for killing anyone, to begin with."

"Neither were we," Hamilton Bell protested. "That mistake was entirely yours, John."

"Let's not quibble," said Vessey. "Back to my question: what do you mean, take care of Franklin?"

"I mean attack him—put him out of business, maybe kill him! Before he does any more damage."

"Oh no," said James Lyon. "Here we go again with killing. Count me out. I want no part of that."

Thomson was beyond any arguing. "I'll attack him myself. I don't need any of you. But I'm doing this to save your hides…everyone here."

There was silence for a minute.

Then Dickson spoke. "John, I don't want Franklin killed, but if you mean just scouting him out, and perhaps wrecking his press or something like that, so he can't print his newspaper any more, I can agree with that. You shouldn't try to do that alone. I'll get some people to help you there."

"Oh my," Vessey sighed, deeply disturbed. "I suppose you would do that to protect the identities of all of us, myself included. I'd thank you for that."

Ben Franklin was busy writing his next front-page story for the coming edition. The headline read: CONSPIRATORS BEHIND SEWARD'S MURDER BEING SEARCHED FOR.

Ben sat in his office, pen in hand, writing the copy:

> In the last issue of this newspaper, we reported that Gershom Stigler, as he was dying, revealed to Sheriff Jasper Eby that there were plotters behind William Seward's tragic murder. They did not actually commit the murder, but paid for it to happen. Judge Hallowell of the Superior Court has issued a warrant for their arrest. If anyone has any information as to their whereabouts....

Franklin dropped his pen when he heard a scuffle in the press room outside of his office. It was more than the usual clatter and clamor of the print shop. It sounded like a fight going on. Ben jumped up from his desk, tossed his spectacles aside, and dashed to the press room to see what was going on. He was startled at what confronted him. Three men dressed in dark clothing, with their faces hid behind black neckerchiefs, had entered the front door and were attacking Tom Prescott and Noah Williams, the only two printers in Ben's shop that day. The intruders had brought with them knives, axes, and large sledgehammers, and it was apparent what they intended to do. They had pulled over a huge cabinet full of heavy lead type that crashed to the floor with a great noise, spewing type everywhere. What angered Ben was that Noah and Tom were outnumbered, three to two. Those odds must be evened up.

Hearing the crashes and loud voices downstairs, Deborah Franklin came running down the stairs, realized what was happening, and shouted, "I'll go for Sheriff Eby, Ben!" She ran out the front door.

Who were these attackers? Off to the side of the shop, Tom was battling with one man who carried an ax. Tom had been knocked down by the man's sudden rush, but he was able to spring from the floor and grab at the ax handle with his left hand. In his right hand Tom held an iron bar, and was using that as a weapon and as a defense when the man tried to slash at him. He was successful in striking the attacker in the jaw with the iron bar and drawing blood that dripped below the neckerchief. The man screamed and struggled to maintain his footing, and Tom brought the heavy bar up sharply, jamming it against the man's chin. The man spit out several loosened teeth, and more blood ran from his mouth. As the intruder tried to swing the ax at him, Tom used the bar again, bringing it down on the ax handle and almost knocking it out of the man's hand. Ben saw that Tom was holding his own.

Noah was having a more difficult time. This second intruder was intent on wrecking the press and had managed to swing a large sledgehammer at it, damaging some of the wood on the side of the press. He had also knocked over a table with heavy iron chases on it. Stacks of paper waiting to be printed had been scattered, and three large pewter cans of black ink were tossed to the floor, sending the thick ink all over, making the floor slippery. This man was obviously more than a match for Noah. But the sledgehammer was so heavy, it was hard for the attacker to heft it quickly, and Noah had landed a few blows on him. His left hand tried to pull the neckerchief off, while his right punched the man in the midsection several times. Both had struck the other in the face, and Noah's nose was bloody and may have been broken.

Dropping the heavy sledgehammer, the attacker launched himself with a roar, knocking Noah flat. The two of them rolled on the floor, fists flying, and the man let out a howl of outrage and punched Noah in the kidney. Noah doubled in pain and gasped for breath. With Noah lying on the floor doubled up, the intruder got to his feet and took the sledge to batter the press some more.

Ben charged at the third intruder, letting out a shriek of fury. The intruder was startled; he had not realized a third person was in the back office. Franklin was strong. He was glad for his years as an apprentice working presses, which built up his muscles, and for his frequent swimming that kept him in excellent physical shape.

But the attacker was strong also. A long knife glinted in the man's hand, and a surge of determination rose in him. Ben had to be careful. He managed to grab a wooden club that was used to tamp the lead type, and he intended to fend off the knife's slashes with that, if he could. Ben saw the intruder's eyes gleaming hatefully above the neckerchief, and he realized the man intended to do him all the harm he could, maybe even murder him. He backed Ben toward the wall, aiming for a killing thrust, with a short hard lunge toward Ben's chest. First he feinted with the long knife, slashing at Ben, and managed to cut Ben's left hand so that the blood ran freely. The long cut burned like fire.

Then Ben attacked. A second before the knife was plunged downward, Ben twisted and leaped away from where the blade would land. The blade smashed into the wall. Like a coiled snake, Ben sprang forward and clawed for the man's eyes, hoping to rip the neckerchief off his face and reveal his identity. Then he lowered his head and rammed the attacker in the chest, and brought up his knee to strike his jaw. The man recovered from Ben's attack, fists flailing on Ben's face. Some blood oozed from Ben's nose, and he ignored that. To retaliate, Ben drove his left fist into the man's nose. He felt the bone break, and blood spurted from the attacker's nose, spraying over Ben.

The attacker then unleashed a series of hard, stinging blows at Ben. The blood was pumping through Ben's veins, and his skin prickled and tingled with it. He was panting, but so was the intruder. With the knife jammed into the wall, the man had no weapon, and Ben was able to take his wooden club and bring it with brutal force against the man's midsection. The assailant let out a scream, collapsed, and lay curled into a ball on the floor, twitching like a dying centipede. He was making the strange expressions of a person whose last meal has just been slammed up into his lungs. Taking the opportunity, Ben reached over and pulled the neckerchief off with a violent tug, to see the man's face.

With the man down and unable to move for a time, Ben ran over to help Noah. The intruder had smashed the printing press several times with the sledgehammer, doing major damage. This infuriated Ben all the more. The attacker stared at Ben with eyes as hard as a violent animal's. He was taking huge breaths, as if trying to get the strength for one massive attack. The heavy sledge was a disadvantage for the man to swing, so he was slow in his actions. Ben raised the wooden club he had been battling with and brought it down on the man's head, knocking him unconscious. With the fellow flattened on the floor, Ben grabbed the neckerchief and pulled it off. Noah rose from the floor, stood over the intruder, and thanked Ben for his timely assistance.

By this time Tom had subdued his opponent also. He held the man against the wall, having grappled with him to get the ax, and the intruder, an older man, did not have the endurance to outdo Tom. Franklin first tried to stanch the blood flowing from his hand, took a clean rag, and wrapped it around the wound. Then he walked over, seized the man by his shoulders roughly, pulled the neckerchief off the man's face, and demanded to know who he was.

At first he refused to answer. Then, in a whimper the answer came: "John Thomson."

"I might have known," Ben responded in a disgusted, contemptuous tone.

<hr />

Sheriff Jasper Eby and his constables arrived in a few minutes, followed by Deborah. She was aghast at the destruction, went to the three intruders, and slapped each one across the face. "So you're the miserable fellows who have made such trouble!"

"Well!" Eby gasped as he looked at the condition of the shop. "This must have been a battle royal, Ben! There's a lot of damage here. And I see you were wounded. Shall we call Dr. Abernathy to tend to that hand, and the bruises on all of you?"

"No, I think we'll all survive. The doctor can check these scoundrels over later, if you wish. My hand will heal. But look at all the harm done, Jasper!" Ben looked morosely at his beloved printing press with its damage. He plucked at a few wooden splinters, and dabbed at the blood coming from his nose. "Oh, I suppose the press can be repaired. And the next issue of the paper will be a bit late. But I must say, you men put up a marvelous fight! There will be raises in your pay for both of you!"

Tom and Noah, nursing their bruises, let out whoops of joy. "That will help with my wedding," Tom said.

The sheriff grabbed Thomson by the shirt, saying, "You'll give us the names of all your associates, my dear fellow. It looks like we have two of them here with you. And all of you will be facing time in our fine prison, at hard labor, for your part in William Seward's murder. Judge Hallowell will see to that."

Franklin, Tom, and Noah laughed.

Author's Notes

Spiritual awakenings and revivals have played a large part in American history, as have revivals in places as diverse as Korea and Wales. But many Christians know little or nothing about them, and this is unfortunate because an awareness of their past successes and multitudes of converts to Christ can be a great encouragement for other people and times. In America, the Great Awakening of the 1740s had a major impact on colonial history, and historians have frequently noted that it was very influential in making the separate colonies first aware of their essential unity as a geographical entity, thirty years before they came together as a nation. In making this possible, no figure was as important as the English evangelist George Whitefield (1714-1770, pronounced "Wit-field"), who made a number of voyages across the Atlantic, became a close friend of his printer Ben Franklin, and preached from Maine to Georgia, converting thousands and continuing the tradition of Awakening already begun by Jonathan Edwards in New England.

I first became interested in Awakenings during graduate work at Princeton Seminary, Columbia University, and the University of Pennsylvania. One of my mentors in this interest was a foremost authority on revivals, J. Edwin Orr, whose seminars at Oxford University I attended with much profit. Several books have been written by me on the subject, and what follows is the first novel I have penned on the Great Awakening.

There has been much research behind this account, and some of the plots were almost ready-made, only waiting to have the details worked out. Whitefield, Franklin, and his wife, Debbie, William Seward, Gilbert Tennent, his father and brothers, the Log College, the Anglican commissaries Garden, Cummings, and Vessey, the ministers and others are historical figures, and I have tried to present their characters as history has recorded them. I have followed the actual dates when things happened and incorporated them into the narrative. Some subplots and characters have been invented: Tom Prescott, Josh Morris, Ishmael Duffy, Collin Bullard and their families, Captain Powner and his crew are fictional. But the accounts of slave trading and colonial cities such as Philadelphia,

Charleston, and Savannah are presented as accurately as possible, based on extensive research.

In 1736, thirty-year old Benjamin Franklin was becoming famous with his newspaper, *The Pennsylvania Gazette*. In Philadelphia he had already formed the Junto, the first subscription library, and the Union Fire Company, and would soon invent much more. Also in 1736 the Great Awakening was beginning, with Jonathan Edwards in Massachusetts. In England, George Whitefield, a young Anglican clergyman, was pioneering in speaking out of doors to huge crowds, igniting revival. The Evangelical Awakening, which touched much of the English-speaking world for the next century, had begun.

When Whitefield came to America in 1739, he was already front-page copy in every newspaper. Ben Franklin began printing Whitefield's very popular sermons, striking up a firm friendship that lasted until the Englishman's death in 1770. Over his ministry, Whitefield was not only concerned with evangelism, but also with the horrors of the slave trade, and the need to care for the many orphans. What happened is well-documented history, and a fine setting for a novel.

Great Biographies of George Whitefield

George Whitefield's Journals (The Banner of Truth Trust, 1960).

George Whitefield and the Great Awakening, by John Pollock (Hert., England, 1972).

George Whitefield: The Life and Times of the Great Evangelist of the Eighteenth-Century Revival, by Arnold A. Dallimore (The Banner of Truth Trust, 1970).

The Great Awakening: A History of the Revival of Religion in the Time of Edwards and Whitefield, by Joseph Tracy (The Banner of Truth Trust, 1989).

About the Author

DR. KEITH HARDMAN, who earned a Ph.D. from the University of Pennsylvania, served for thirty-five years as Professor of Religion and Philosophy at Ursinus College in Pennsylvania, and chair of the department. With his retirement, he gained additional time to pursue his life-long interest in spiritual awakenings and revivals.

"Spiritual awakenings and revivals have played a large part in American history," says Dr. Hardman, "but many Christians know little or nothing about them...and thus miss the great encouragement of these significant events. I'm passionate about revealing what went on behind the scenes during these time periods."

Other previous titles of Hardman's include: *Seasons of Refreshing: Evangelism and Revivals in America,* which has also been translated into Korean; *Charles G. Finney: Revivalist and Reformer* (considered the definitive biography of this important evangelist); *The Spiritual Awakeners* (Moody Press), *Issues in American Christianity* (Baker Book House), *Ingredients of the Christian Faith* (Tyndale House). He has written a number of articles in *Religious Revivals in America* (Greenwood Press), and in *The New International Dictionary of the Christian Church* (Zondervan, 1985), and in *Church History,* the journal of the American Society of Church History.

For years, Dr. Hardman's chief hobby has been the collection and restoration of antique cars. He has owned four Stanley Steamers, a 1910 White Steamer, a 1912 Oldsmobile Autocrat, a 1929 Packard, a 1929 Ford Model A roadster, and a 1935 Auburn speedster.

He is married and has three grown children.

You may write the author at **drkeithhardman@verizon.net**.

www.oaktara.com